FUTURE LOVECRAFT

OTHER BOOKS BY SILVIA MORENO-GARCIA

𐤊𐤀𐤄𐤀𐤍

Candle in the Attic Window (with Paula R. Stiles)
Fungi (with Orrin Grey)
Historical Lovecraft (with Paula R. Stiles)
Shedding Her Own Skin

FUTURE LOVECRAFT

SILVIA MORENO-GARCIA & PAULA R. STILES

SF

○
PRIME BOOKS

FUTURE LOVECRAFT

ᚤᚼᚻᚤᚼ

Prime Books
www.prime-books.com

For more information, contact Prime Books:
prime@prime-books.com

ISBN: 978-1-60701-353-2

I had a dream, which was not all a dream.
The bright sun was extinguish'd, and the stars
Did wander darkling in the eternal space,
Rayless, and pathless, and the icy earth
Swung blind and blackening in the moonless air;
—"Darkness" by Lord Byron

CONTENTS

CONTENTS

INTRODUCTION: THE FUTURE IS LOVECRAFT

H.P. Lovecraft is not generally considered a writer of science fiction, even though he had a personal interest in the sciences (astronomy, of course) and wrote stories that were rooted in science, even if they frequently had a horror bent ("The Colour Out of Space" is a memorable example). In his stories, Lovecraft explored scientific concepts like evolution, alien invasion and genetic engineering. His aliens were truly alien, not funny-looking people, and had no interest in humans—except, perhaps, to eat us. For that reason, his realistic view of the tiny human position in the cosmos, and his espousal of a very long view of human history, he has had as large an influence on science fiction as on horror. Thus, it seemed to us an excellent idea to develop a whole science fiction/horror anthology, and set all the stories and poems in the future.

The entries included here vary quite a bit. We do have Mythos-inspired fiction—including guest appearances by Nyarlathotep, Azathoth and others. However, our concern is not merely Mythos fiction but Lovecraftian fiction in general. We could go on for pages and pages about what 'Lovecraftian' means to us, but in the end, we think the stories can answer that best.

Thus, there are tales questioning reality, undermining protagonists' sanity, or dwelling on the hopelessness of the characters. There are post-apocalyptic fables and stories in the near future. Space opera and tales set on Earth. Poems and epics told by aliens. Stories where sinister entities slip into our world. Stories where humans slip into other worlds. Tales of chaos and destruction.

Welcome to the future: It is Lovecraft.

—Silvia Moreno-Garcia and Paula R. Stiles

IN THIS BRIEF INTERVAL

Ann K. Schwader

Ann K. Schwader is the author of six poetry collections: *Twisted in Dream* (Hippocampus Press, 2011), *Wild Hunt of the Stars* (Sam's Dot Publishing, 2010), *In the Yaddith Time* (Mythos Books, 2007), *Architectures of Night* (Dark Regions Press, 2003), *The Worms Remember* (Hive Press, 2001), and *Werewoman* (Nocturnal Publications, 1990). Ann was a Bram Stoker Award nominee (for *Wild Hunt of the Stars*) in 2011, and received a Rhysling Award from the Science Fiction Poetry Association in 2010. She is an active member of HWA, SFWA and SFPA. A Wyoming native, she now lives and writes in Colorado, USA.

Before our sun first sparked, the stars turned right
Beyond some liminal apocalypse
To herald the return of elder night.

Sunk deep in ignorance we name 'delight,'
Such cosmic truth will never stain our lips:
Before our sun first sparked, the stars turned right.

One Arab mystic dared describe that sight
Before he suffered sanity's eclipse
To herald the return of elder night.

What matter all the rockets we ignite
To launch sleek probes or long-range sleeper ships?
Before our sun first sparked, the stars turned right.

Mundane events monopolize our fright,
Obscuring time's frail fabric as it rips
To herald the return of elder night.

Dizzied by ascension to this height,
We never feel it when the balance tips.
Before our sun first sparked, the stars turned right
To herald the return of elder night.

IN THE HALL OF THE YELLOW KING

Peter Rawlik

Peter Rawlik is a contributor to the *New York Review of Science Fiction* and has had fiction published in *Crypt of Cthulhu*, *Talebones*, and *Dead But Dreaming 2* (Miskatonic River Press). He has stories forthcoming in *Horror for the Holidays* (Miskatonic River Press), *HPL Mythos 2: Urban Cthulhu* (H. Harksen productions), and *Tales of the Shadowmen 8* (Black Coat Press).

> From Carcosa, the Yellow King reigns,
> Unbroken, unmade, the royal remains
> Eternal, the Regent from death refrains,
> Lest the dynasty of Uoht regains
> The Jejune Throne.
> —*The Prophecy of Cassilda*

As the doors to the throne room opened, the human Erbert Ouest cast a last look upwards at the great, towering spindle that rose through the sky and into space beyond. At the pinnacle, a scintillating light marked the location of *The Armitage*, the Tillinghast transport that had brought him and the rest of the delegation from Earth to dim Carcosa. Six weeks they had spent aboard *The Armitage* with the Tillinghasts, whose skill at traversing the Between Space had made them something more, and something less, than men. Ouest was no stranger to the metamorphic, but even he was disturbed by the dead, black eyes of the Tillinghasts and was grateful that there had been on board one of the few remaining Nug-Soth to serve as steward.

Once the doors had opened completely, an impatient Tcho-Tcho waved Ouest and his companion forward. With a gesture, the twsha master Sthast placed the shoggoth in motion. It slid forward, its hideous, protoplasmic bulk carrying its great load in silence and ease. The lozenge-shaped sepulchre was carved from the finest black coral and massed more than five full-grown carcharadons. As they proceeded, the court tittered. Ouest, though tempted, resisted the desire to cast a foul glance at the school of Hydran Sisters that swam amongst the courtiers whispering and hissing in their strange, lungless voices. Now was not the time for petty acts of reprisal, he thought. Later, when the formalities were complete, then the traitorous sorority would know the skill and wrath with which he could wield a scalpel. Only then would the flaying of Father Dagon be avenged.

Never had Ouest seen such a diversity of creatures in a single place. He supposed that any such court must have its parasites. By far, the most represented were the sycophantic Mi-Go, but there were contingents of Shan swarms, Xiclotl, and Nagaae, as well. There were a dozen Yith, identifiable not by their conformity to a single species but by the mandatory wearing of the Voorish sign. A small cluster of Martian Aihais fretted and tried to remain unnoticed behind a column. Ouest noted their presence and that of a rogue Xothian that he could not identify by name. Yet, despite all the species he could identify, the crowd was mostly dominated by those that he could not. These came in single exemplars, which meant that Ouest could not tell whether they were representatives of an unfamiliar species or something entirely unique. Such individuals were many and multiform, dread and vile, wondrous and terrifying, and none more so than that occupying the great throne before him.

One might be tempted to call the thing that rested uneasily on the dais "humanoid," but such a classification would be giving it too much credit. It was swathed in yellow, diaphanous robes that concealed the vastness of form, and a square of the same material draped over its head, concealing the eyes, but revealing the gaunt, lipless mouth and ivory, peg-like teeth that sat amongst a husk of grey skin. Its hands, resting in its lap, were gloved, with only a thin gap between the gloves and the sleeve of the gown. Ouest could see nothing in that gap; no skin or bone seemed to connect the appendages to their terminal digits. Ouest knew that acting as Ythill was a dread task, and that the host was to expect certain concessions, but becoming partially unreal seemed excessive. Above the creature's head, floating like an untouched and untouchable crown, was the ghostly, triple-curved symbol of He Who Must Not Be Named, marking its wearer as the King in Yellow.

Without a prompt, Ouest and Sthast both bowed before the *Regent Giallo*, but their failure to kneel sparked a wave of disapproving chatter throughout the courtiers. The great form strained its neck and peered at them through unseen eyes. When it spoke, it was not in a language Ouest recognised, but he understood what the words, which tasted of ichor and dust and decay, meant. "What fools dare to come unbidden to the Carcosan Court, wearing such masks as these?"

Ouest bobbed his head, respectful but defiant. "We wear no masks, milord, and we come, not at your bidding, but in response to the will of our own Lord, who sends to you this precious boon in hopes that the enmity between you shall no longer rage."

There was an inhuman noise, the sound of something that wasn't quite real laughing. "After all these years, my half-brother sues for peace. He sends two Terrans, a man and a child of Yig, to do his bidding. It has been millennia since I last saw the Serpent Lord. I was there when the Q'Hrell punished him for refusing to bond with the Shining Trapezohedron. He didn't understand that he had been created for just that purpose. His crucifixion was a wondrous thing to witness." The thing on the throne paused, then added, "Despite all their power, the Q'Hrell are so fearful of becoming singular. They want so much to know what would happen, what they could become. How goes the war against them?"

Sthast spoke, proud and defiant, "The Q'Hrell still lie, dead but dreaming, and Nodens still roams free, warring against us where he can, though with the loss of the Great Machine around Altair, their power is diminished. The black crystal remains theirs to do with as they wish."

The gloved hands floated forth and gestured to Ouest. "It must be unbearable, Man, to know that your creators have abandoned you, that they have the ability to raise you up, to make you so much more than you are, but have chosen not to."

Ouest bowed his head. "My people have found new Gods to serve."

"And so, we come full circle. Tell me, what gift does the Sepia Prince think can possible ease my vendetta? The Yellow Sine is not so easily dismissed."

"My Lord, the Sepia Prince seeks to end the conflict through union. He sends to you His greatest possession—His only daughter."

The lid of the great, ebon sepulchre slid back slowly and a great, noxious smoke poured forth, spilling over the sides and roiling over the floor of the chamber. The crowd inched back against the walls, but Ouest and Sthast stood their ground and let the green fog envelop them. With each passing second, the great lid retreated and more of the mist seeped out. Ouest inhaled deeply and let the glowing, green aerosol fill his lungs and permeate his being. Behind him, the tomb had opened fully. From the swirling mist emerged a hand—grey-green and boneless, with vestigial suckers lining the palm, it was more of an imitation of a hand than a real hand. It was large, massive, nearly the size of those possessed by the King in Yellow, but it was, at the same time, slender—delicate, even. With a slow sense of determination, it grasped the edge of the casket and helped raise its owner into the royal chamber.

Ouest and Sthast fell to their knees and, together, announced the arrival of their charge: "Behold the Lady Cthylla!" The thing that crawled out of the mist was as human or humanoid as the Ythill that bore the ruler of Carcosa; a great, tentacled head surmounted a lithe, feminine body with full, robust breasts, a thin waist and wide hips atop two sculpted legs. Like her hands, these features were merely an imitation, an attempt, by something that was not even an invertebrate, to mimic the flesh and bone structure of a woman. The result was surreal and terrifying, and exacerbated by the strategic placing of swirls of gold, in imitation of a sense of human modesty. She leapt from her sepulchre and, with the aid of two massive, tentacular wings she landed, in the space between Ouest and Sthast.

It took a moment for the demi-thing to find her footing, but only a moment. Ouest suspected that it was only he that actually noticed her transition from predator to a demure maiden with a bowed head and large, pleading eyes. It had taken years to train her in the art of such body language and Ouest suppressed a smile as she slinked forward, her breathing exaggerated and her chest heaving rhythmically. Her voice was the dull, howling roar of a black smoker bellowing out of the abyssal plain. "My father sends me as envoy, my Lord, to parlay for an end to the aggression that lays siege to our home. He asks that the Yellow Sine be withdrawn, the integration made whole, and the reputation repaired."

The King in Yellow roared up out of his throne. "You ask much on your father's behalf, my niece, and you offer what in return, yourself? What makes you think that I would be interested in such carnal offerings?"

The Lady Cthylla widened her eyes and strode forward. "You are the King in Yellow, the avatar of Hastur." The court murmured as she spoke the unnamable name. "But under those robes, beneath the crown, you are still Ythill and all such creatures still have certain . . . needs."

The Regent's tattered robes fluttered as he rushed to meet the Lady Cthylla at the base of the throne.

"You know the Prophecy of Cassilda?" His disembodied hand leapt out and grasped her by the throat.

She nuzzled her head against his chest and murmured an affirmative.

If the thing beneath the veil could sneer, then it did. "Then you know that my service in this place makes me immortal. Only beyond the mists of Demhe am I vulnerable and taking leave of these halls is something I have not done for more than a thousand years. Even then, if I were to be mortally wounded, the mantle would merely find a new host, a new Ythill. And I assure you that the vengeance my successor, Uoht, would wreak on the Sepia Prince would be legendary."

The retainers of the great court of the Carcosan Imperium shuddered, as if a cold wind had blown through, and the Lady Cthylla laughed once more. "It is true that the throne cannot be empty, a singularity must reside, and should the mantle of the King be somehow divorced from his crown, the universe itself would bend to fill the void. The Kings of the Yellow Sine would be deposed, relegated to cosmic memory, and Uoht, the Pallid Masque, would be free to roam the cosmos. So, let us assure that nothing untoward ever happens to you, my liege."

Cthylla leapt forward and embraced the Yellow King, let her great appendages and cilia dance around and beneath his robes. She blossomed and enveloped him in the coils of her terrible form. The King moaned, but whether that moan was from pleasure or from the sudden realization of what was happening, none could rightly say. The lady was dragging the King backwards and, entangled as he was, he could gain no leverage to resist her. As they inched back, the shoggoth move forward and tilted the great sepulchre, so as to better receive them both.

Cthylla's tentacles reached backwards and gripped the edges of the ebon box. The victim bellowed as the maw of the tomb grew closer, but another set of those grey-green pseudopods wrapped around the King's head and muffled his protestations. In an instant, the two figures were suddenly lost inside the mists that still seeped from the sepulchre. The lid slowly slid forward and, with a grinding finality, closed with a gasping hiss.

The members of the court cast their eyes about in anticipation, but while they waited for one of them to become King, Sthast and Ouest put their own plans in motion. Ouest withdrew a scalpel—a small thing, really hardly a threat at all to the entities that prowled these halls. He looked at his companion and whispered, "I'm sorry."

The ancient serpent man bared his abdomen. "We don't have time for your human sympathies, Ouest. Do what you must; bring this to an end."

The knife flashed and sliced through the green-scaled flesh, leaving a trail of crimson in its wake. As Ouest's left hand completed its arc, his right plunged into the wound and sank deep. Ouest grunted and twisted his wrist, searching inside the body cavity of his companion. Suddenly, he stopped and a wry look covered his face. With a sense of satisfaction, Doctor Erbert Ouest, Lord of the Ghilan, withdrew his hand from the gut of his dying friend and brought the Shining Trapezohedron into the light.

Some amongst the court moved against him, but the shoggoth, following its master's final orders, lashed out at anything that moved, enveloping its victims in fleshy pockets of digestive juices and rings of restraining tendrils. The others fell back and some made for the exits, in a last attempt at survival. The Hydran Sisters fell to the ground and began swearing allegiance to the Sepia Prince, wailing for forgiveness. Unfortunately, their ministrations fell on deaf ears.

Ouest took the great crystal in both hands and brought it to eye level. His eyes were locked onto its facets. Through them, he could see the billions that comprised the human race. He struggled to speak the words, to perform the rite, to forge the connection with the shard of Azathoth that the Progenitors had secreted within. The chaos thing in the crystal crawled up out of its prison, into the consciousness of Ouest and, through him, nearly the entirety of the human species. For too long it had been confined, forced to assume shapes both many and multiform. Now it would be one with Man, and Man would be one with it and themselves.

Ouest faded from existence, replaced by the great, dark form that rose up in his place. It was no longer human, but rather, a monstrous amalgamation of Humanity. The Black Man strode across the space, his three-lobed burning eye challenging all those who would oppose him. As he claimed the Carcosan throne, the shoggoth finished planting the black, coral tomb in place and sealed it with an Elder Sign. A fraction of the human thing, a facet that had once been Ouest, mourned the loss of Cthylla, but took comfort in the eternal, frozen tableau of the King in Yellow clawing at the inside of the sepulchre, his crown still ensconced on his brow.

And as the Black Pharaoh, the human singular, took his place amongst the god-things of the cosmos, the Yellow Sines fell and the dreaming, five-fold consciousnesses hidden in the wastes of Earth finally woke. They cried out in alien voices the name of their ultimate creation: the Man-God Nyarlathotep!

INKY, BLINKY, PINKY, NYARLATHOTEP

Nick Mamatas

Nick Mamatas is the author of several novels, including *Sensation* and two Lovecraftian works: *Move Under Ground* and, with Brian Keene, *The Damned Highway*. With Ellen Datlow he co-edited the Bram Stoker Award-winning anthology *Haunted Legends*. His fiction and editorial work has also been nominated for the Hugo, World Fantasy, Shirley Jackson, and International Horror Guild awards, and his short fiction has appeared in *Asimov's Science Fiction*, *Lovecraft Unbound*, *Long Island Noir*, and many other anthologies and magazines.

The Old Ones thought they were so smart, tapping the Earth's mantle to make the environment of the planet more amenable to themselves and deadly to their rival species, Humanity. 'Rival' perhaps is the wrong word—'idiot germ-things' would be apropos. Humans were little more than gooey amoebae to the Old Ones, but humans were also progenitors of the New Ones. So, when the Old Ones took the planet, all the humans died, but the one billion New Ones were already gone, safely beamed up toward a waiting spacecraft—one the size of a waffle iron—parked 1.5 million kilometers beyond the Earth in the handy-dandy L2. A little solar wind got to pushing on the sunshield and we were off!

Newspace was a lot like old space. Well, posters of old space stacked atop one another and constantly shuffled and re-shuffled. In the little waffle-iron spacecraft was the thunderous Niagara, any number of mansions on emerald hills, all piled up in a corner with Escheresque staircases going downwise and anti-spinward, marmalade skies and airships in the shape of giant, open-mouthed fish, the Pyramids of Egypt poking out from every horizon, and long, dark hallways in blue and purple neon everywhere, absolutely everywhere, as this is what the New Ones thought VR would look like, back when they were all children.

And the New Ones had fun playing like children. As it turns out, virtually all problems faced by Humanity, save the million-year war with the Old Ones, were resource problems. No Old Ones, no resources, no problems. *Virtually* no problems, anyway, which is an awful pun, it's true. So, the New Ones spent their days naked and immortal, writing songs no fleshy ear could comprehend, inventing new languages to describe disembodied emotional states, engaging in virtual nucleic exchange and reproducing wildly to the humming databases, with beings unheard of and indescribable.

The waffle iron was busy, too. Zipping around space and whatnot, eating dark matter and printing copies of itself, in case something happened to it. And oh, yes, something was happening to it. Naturally, the poor little waffle iron didn't quite understand that the something happening *was* the drive to laze-lathe meteoroids into replicas of itself. Oh, and then, within the guts of the waffle iron, ghosts started showing up everywhere, upsetting and terrifying the New Ones with their googly eyes and their siren howls. And they loved to eat the New Ones. Beautiful, tow-headed, pink children with cloth diapers and bows in their wispy hair. Lovely children with rich, brown skin and smiles to light up a room. Obnoxious children who sat on the couch all day, pretending to kill with their minds for fun. Children who flailed their hands about and slammed their heads against the wall because they saw the wrong kind of penny. Ghosts were indiscriminate—the ugly and the exquisite both were consumed, leaving naught but wrinkled husks behind.

You have to realize that words like eyes and children, and even husks, make little sense; it's being dumbed down for you and the quaint bag of chemical reactions you keep in that bone bowl. We're talking a density matrix, here. So, when a character is introduced, as one is about to be, understand that you'd be just as accurate, were you to imagine her as a blurry, yellow ball of light floating around in a black field, instead of as a person. Which is to say, you'd be much more accurate, after all.

So, let's make our child slightly older than many of the victims. Let's put her in a dark hallway, with lights running in a single row down the middle of the floor. Who is she? It hardly matters. Let's just say that she was a handsome woman—call her "Lindsay." That's a better name than "qubit," one endlessly pulsing about in a Bloch sphere. Chestnut hair, a strong Hapsburg chin, wide eyes. Toned limbs, born without defect, just out of her teens, as that's a very heroic age. Clever, too. Clever enough to turn and run when that great sheet of red turned the corner and swooped toward her, howling like a police siren. She was so clever that she found out the unbelievable truth, or a brief sliver of it, anyhow. Here's what she had to say before her . . . well, not death. (How can a fundamental particle encoded with information based on its superpositions die? Rhetorical question: There's a way, of course. Heat death of the universe, anyone? Wait for it!)

Who won the Second World War? Or, should I ask, who can take credit for winning the Second World War? Americans will point to D-Day and storming the beaches at Normandy, then maybe Hiroshima. The Russians nod grimly toward Stalingrad. Even little Greece has a claim—resistance to the Axis delayed German's invasion of Russia for six weeks. For the nerds, it was Turing and the Ultra Secret that won the war. Everyone's the hero of their own story.

The same with the war against the Old Ones. Was it the armies that held back the monsters for the precious few hours who won the war, the scientists who developed the first Q-chips, or the Indonesian and South Korean workers who mass produced them? The artists and writers who inspired a species with dreams of escape and rescue? In the end, it hardly matters. We won and Newspace was our prize. Humanity couldn't defeat the Old Ones militarily, and their technology was indistinguishable from magic, but we still won, by evolving past the strategic goals of the war. So, they got the Earth and cracked it open. Big deal. So, seven billion people died. Big deal. It's not as though wars are won and lost over a bodycount toteboard. We had everything Humanity ever created up here in Newspace, available at whim and nearly infinitely fungible. We don't need planets, anymore. The Old Ones still do.

The ghosts are . . . problematic. We didn't even realise they were ghosts, at first. We called them "bugs," since they seemed like glitches in programming, the unintended consequences of a trillion lines of code. But I was the first one to get a look at them and live to tell the story, so they took the shape of the story I told. Eyes and a bright jet of light are all I remembered, and that's all we thought they were.

Inky, Blinky, Pinky, and Clyde. There are four of them. We control everything about Newspace, but unfortunately, you can't unthunk a gunk, as it were, so the ghosts continued to appear and consume. We raised ramparts and armies, which were useless. We whipped up proton packs and crossed the streams, which didn't work, either. Then up went the ziggurats and we stained the staircases with the blood of the heartless dead, hoping that, at least, we'd get to choose who died to appease the ghosts. The ghosts didn't rap on tables in our darkened rooms, or move the planchettes under our fingers; they just ate and ate and ate us all up.

Clyde was the key, I was sure of it. He was different than the others, if only because we'd made him different by giving him the name. I was the one who figured out what we had to do. Think more about the ghosts; think more about that old game. Give them an environment to run rampant in, all black and neon blue. I volunteered to change myself—genetic engineering is a snap in Newspace. I would eat the motherfuckers back. That's how I was going to win the war against the ghosts.

Spoiler alert! Lindsay lost. Newspace was overwritten with labyrinths and warp-alleys, and Lindsay lost those toned limbs, had nozzles shoved into every orifice to blow her up into a sphere, and set loose. It was ridiculous, really. A childhood daydream-ritual made out of pop culture she wasn't even around for. Newspace was nothing but an agglomeration of the easily Googlable, after all. Some Rapture of the Nerds this turned out to be . . . for them.

Lindsay boobled down the same ridiculous hallway in which she had first encountered the ghost, but where she was once clever and ran without thinking, this time, she charged bright-blue Inky, who was programmed to interpose itself in front of its target. She knew red Blinky would be chasing her, as was its own fate. But Clyde, he was an odd duck. He liked to wander around more or less randomly, hugging odd corners, shifting directions back and forth, eyes one way then another. It was an obvious clue, I suppose, but the New Ones weren't any smarter for being all that much faster. *Crawling chaos*, come on! *Beyond the worlds vague ghosts of monstrous things; half-seen columns of unsanctified temples that rest on nameless rocks beneath space and reach up to dizzy vacua above the spheres of light and darkness.* Ring a bell? This was all in the library, you know, and every New One had instant access to everything ever written by a human hand, and more than a few scrawled by inhuman hands, as well.

Lindsay survived her second encounter with the ghosts. She slew them handily and, when they regenerated, slew them again in a pointless battle. New Ones don't tire; they don't need sleep, but damn, do they get bored quickly. Lindsay needed to beat the game, she thought, and for that, she needed an army, and for that, she needed a lot of quarters. Things were done to the guts of our poor little waffle iron to make it generate ever more copies out there in 3-D land, and thus, ever more Lindsays to replace the loser. She wasn't so much an altruist as a narcissist, our gal Lindsay—she'd be an eternal subroutine inside Newspace now, and everyone else would necessarily spend at least a little bit of time thinking about her and her ongoing sacrifice. Oh, let's replay that bit, too:

Newspace is only *nearly* infinitely fungible. It's a lifeboat, in essence, and the best lifeboat ever built. "Everybody in, nobody out," that was our slogan. We weren't even allowed to end our lives, not even if we wanted to. Not even for *fun*. That was what made the ghosts so terrifying for us all. The system wouldn't let me change myself if it thought it would lead to my death, so I couldn't die. So, how could I get more of me from the copy-spaces? Simple—swap me out for Clyde. He moved about randomly but without belligerent intent, so he was the one ghost who could be contained. We'd contain him, transmit him to the next closest space and swap me out. Headcount's all the same to Newspace, since it's not as though we could reproduce, nor need to. Then we'd just repeat the process when I needed another life to keep playing, shuffling Clyde around indefinitely. Eventually, I figured that if I played the game enough, I'd hit the famous "kill screen" at level 255 and it would all be over. If not, well, at least I have a real purpose in life. A little something to do that was beyond my control. Competition, a fight. A real war, against real enemies I could sink my teeth into.

What a woman! I suppose you can say I have a thing for electricity and psychology. What's that line again? *He spoke much of the sciences—of electricity and psychology—and gave exhibitions of power which sent his spectators away speechless, yet which swelled his fame to exceeding magnitude. Men advised one another to see Nyarlathotep, and shuddered.*

The old mudball Earth was getting a little hot for me, even though I'm used to the Sahara. The Old Ones, subtle as hammers and twice as dumb, had interfered with my plans once too often. And Humanity thought that *it* was the historical subject of the war? Not even pawns, really. More like the plants crushed, by pressure and time, into petroleum from whence to extract the chemicals, from which to make the plastic pawns are molded in for the cheapest of chess sets. That's the kind of game I was playing. It was the long con, see? I wanted a ride off-planet, so I helped the New Ones come about with my hands that are not hands and then set my thumb that is not a thumb out, to hitch along on their waffle iron. Luckily for me, everyone aboard knew what a pyramid looked like, so of course, a reasonable abode was included in Newspace.

I just had to bide my time for a few grand million years, while the waffle iron reproduced and spread its own matrix of copies out in every direction. I'm not easily reproducible. I'm a *being*, you understand, not a bit of code masquerading as life —not like *some people* I could mention, but who will remain nameless—so I needed to visit each waffle iron in turn, then do my little magick trick in one after the other. Call me "Clyde." Boo!

Lindsay and the other New Ones were handicapped by their past humanity. They thought in human terms. I *healed* them, every one of them. Now, the New Ones don't think like men at all. Lindsay was smart enough that she didn't have to be human if she didn't want to be. Once she came to that conclusion, she realised that she didn't want to be. So, she became an ever-devouring, blurry, yellow ball of light floating around in a black field. Lindsay was the lucky one. She adapted quickly.

From waffle iron to waffle iron I was sent, swapping myself in for the only person who might have been somewhat clever enough to do something about me . . . had she not already unwittingly volunteered herself to work on behalf of my campaign against the Old Ones. I'd be "contained," but the Inky, Blinky, and Pinky I whipped up on the spot wouldn't be. And then the New Ones would die again, and some other friggin' genius would rise up and take the bait, and I'd be off again to the next ship and the next and the next. Slowly but surely, the scales would fall from the eyes of the New Ones.

It's hard to be human. I know, I know. I've been human, here and there, now and again, for a nonce and millennia. What's much harder, though, is being inhuman, immortal, and utterly free. Let me tell you that we cosmic beings don't understand our wars and intrigues any more than any bystander peering through the small end of the big telescope in Ladd Observatory, Providence, Rhode Island. We do it for fun, because we can't die for fun. The New Ones muddled along for a bit because they pretended to still be human, even though humans were little more than gooey amoebae to the New Ones. But after an audience with me, the New Ones had to force themselves to evolve past the pleasing lies of ego and limb, to realise two very important things: One, that their great escape was nothing more than my personal outflanking of my old enemies on their home planet. Two, what they truly were—infinitesimally small fundamental particles floating about in infinite space, purposeless and just clever enough to realise that all their dreams and hopes and loves and tiny glimpses of enlightenment were meaningless, that they were a less-than-meaningless joke I told the Old Ones to cheese them off.

And then nobody ever stopped screaming.

FOR THE WIN!

ᚤᚣᚻᚤᚱ

TRI-TV

Bobby Cranestone

Bobby Cranestone was born in a quiet and ancient part of Germany, spent its early childhood with the beaux arts, and was a devotee student of music, poetry and books, both fictitious and scientific. Following an early fascination with the mysterious and strange, Bobby gave life to scary stories and humorous fables. Bobby is a contributor to both fanzines and discussion boards in newspapers, and also the writer of fiction and composer of weird ambient sounds, with a small fan following in the UK. Author of "The City of Melted Iron," published in *Candle in the Attic Window*.

Commercial

TRI-TV is more than simple 3D television. TRI-TV provides you with the latest hits from anywhere around the universe and even crosses over dimensions.

3D Television was yesterday, TRI-TV is the future and brings you everything (!!!) you want. And that for only 30 crex (1 crexour = 1 delmax, 25 naral, or 10,000 Lemurische pa"c).

Enjoy sports, or live TV shows from around the Solar System, the Dark Zones, or from anywhere in our 15 million subscribed systems.

See your favourite shows like *The House of Nouth*, *The Literary Circle*, or the famous *Extraterrestrial Cook Book*.

Enjoy the brilliance of TRI-TV.

Enjoy the fun.

Enjoy it now . . . .

For fast subscribers: You even earn a 20-week power voucher.

ↃϞϟ

Sports: Mad Head Rally in the Mars Arena

Kevin Haggerty speeds forward on his shoggoth, Marley. He passes Nos. 4 and 13 and enters just into the 42nd round. That's what I call "his olde self". After his longtime absence, there were some who believed in his retirement. After the rumours of doping his shoggoth, he had taken some time off, but I say nonsense . . . A guy like Haggerty doesn't need to cheat. What's that! Collis draws close to challenge the previous year's champ, but Haggerty and Marley show him only a cloud of cold dust . . . .

That's sports; that's . . . .

switch

ↃϞϟ

The Literary Circle

Our guests today are the ghouls clmck, chrmk, mkrmnm, and Dr. Nrmckmnpf. Dr. Nrmckmnpf is winner of the Sacred Leaf of Irem—the City of Pillars—the Max donated by the Venus Foundation and the Pulitzer Prize 2228.

Today, we will discuss the new translation of the *Necronomicon* into Sanskrit, *Die Unheimlichen Kulten of Van Junzt* and the classic, *My world is your world—what are you gonna do with it?*

switch

ↃϞϟ

Welcome to the new issue of the *Extraterrestrial Cook Book*. Today, we will prepare a tasty meal for four and what we need are 100 grams of mushrooms, five kilograms of Stegosaurus *kotelett*, five mint leaves, four juicy tomatoes, one mouldy yoghurt, and three Old Ones. You'll ask, "Four Persons, will three Olde Ones be enough?" You'll see there will be enough left, even to prepare a dessert.

We start cutting the mushrooms and the mint leaves. The tomatoes are cooked over a low flame, while we give the Stegosaurus *koteletts* a hearty dance in the fire; five hours will be enough. Just stop when all the liquids are gone and the meat has a nicely black crust.

We take the tomatoes from the fire, then, as prepared, peel them and push them through a sieve. We put mushrooms, mint and tomatoes into a cooking pot, add the yoghurt, and let it steam.

Now, over to the Olde One heads. Rather tough is this stuff, I can tell you. We use, therefore, a pinch of robust *korund* and open the heads from the flipped-up underside, starting from the middle to the starpoints. We do this five times . . . and again. I prepared this for you. After removing the ganglia system . . . Don't waste 'em; this will make a wonderful desert served with cream and strawberries . . . you can have a good look at the brains, light-blue and semi-liquid to the touch, just as they should be.

Now we fill our mushroom/mint/tomatoes tart into the head, chop the *koteletts* into cubes of seven-inch length, and add them, decorated with a blossom. This won't even just be a heaven for the tongue, but for the eye, as well. . . .

Enjoy!

switch

ꓷꓭꙭ

The Literary Circle

glibber glibber knugk (subtitles, English translation)—In your opinion, does the new issue lack its former esprit? It's charmless. . . . "

glibber knk glib gnub—"Just the opposite. I believe that the Sanskrit translation is another step to a better understanding of what we call acceptance of . . . "

gnib—"Acceptance of what?"

glib glib glib—"Of the art, as such, what it means to adjust to the deeper sense of life."

gub brb blrb—"I always hear 'acceptance'; what about the practical advantage?"

gub blb grb

knub

gub kn brurb
switch

ƆϞⱹ

The topic of today:

"More freedom for the Dholes"

An assemblage of the seven leading races has come together to discuss
the petition of the Dholes to have more rights on their planet, Yaddith.
The problem is that the race of the Nug-Soth also lives there and that the
petition also includes a plea for a healthy lifestyle and nourishment, which
concerns all the other races also living on this planet, because they usually
are the nourishment of the Dholes. We welcome historian Zkauba of the
much-honored guild of Yaddith wizards, astro-sociologist Dr. Arthur
Peterman, the Tolero Brothers, Dr. Rosa Vanderman (who is a specialist on
the physiology of both Dholes and Nug-Soth), Kyle Feld from the United
Army of Planet Earth, philosoph Ka-run Nuats, and the Blateleys from
Wichita. Also, do we heartily welcome Dhole 7459/K.

7459/K, please start with your arguments. You'll have the first word. . . .
switch

ƆϞⱹ

Soap Opera

Klimax Group proudly presents: *The House of Nouth*

In this episode: Will Zathatera face new troubles? Just released from
jail—after he found out that his mother is, in truth, his father and a
vegetarian—he accidentally killed his estranged parent and an innocent
neighbour, while on drugs during a fishing holiday. What he doesn't know
is that his mother/father isn't truly dead, but subscribed to a Malaysian
dance troupe, while his neighbour . . . is truly dead.

But he won't have any rest. Unhappy, he tries to interfere in the marriage
of his stepdaughter, Althera . . . Will he succeed?

We press thumbs.
switch

ƆϞⱹ

Now, you simply break the three legs off, and fill the beetle with the garlic and a bit of Croni liquor . . . I've just prepared this . . . .

switch

glb glib

brb brb

switch

Haggerty and Marley are close to the finishing straight. The decision must come now . . . .

switch

The Dhole seems restless. After the argument with historian Zkauba, he/she/it seems to be losing ground. The sympathies of the public are clearly on the side of the natives, as the voting shows . . .

The new single by the Alhambra Flutes . . .

. . . accompanied by the Tolero Brothers . . .

"You just can't catch me . . . but if you did, I wouldn't care.

Gardening with Modern Cybernetics

The secrets of unique blossoming, and colours simply from out of this world, revealed by the Ythians.

Make your neighbour rip his head off!

Crime on Io

Seven Mooncats and a youngish Zook are dead, but who's the victim?

ⵓⵀⵉ

Documentary: Delve with us into the ruins of Ib and rediscover astonishing revelations of an unknown past.

ⵓⵀⵉ

If you call now, we'll even add this useful pincer at the price of only 30 Crex!

ⵓⵀⵉ

Chemistry for Kids

Part 1—How to build a door between the worlds.
Part 2—Nitrogen bombs in three easy steps.

ⵓⵀⵉ

The News

The price of energy decreases, due through the find of a new crystal specimen on Venus.

ⵓⵀⵉ

Headhunting Live

Who will catch the criminal on the run? Call now . . . McCarty and his team of Old Ones are, as usual, prepared . . . This ain't fun for the juvenile nightgaunt.

ⵓⵀⵉ

Opera

Dubbed in Ancient Egyptian and Modern English.
Kla (Hero): *What do you want of me?*
Ste (Heroine): *Kill him.*
Kla: *I cannot do this.*

Ste: *Kill him.*

Kla: *Don't tempt me, dearest; don't tempt me.*

ↃⅣ⌇

The Dhole broke free! It's rampaging through the conference room. The assembled are panic-stricken. It's breaking down the door and moves out of sight.

Wait for more breaking news.

ↃⅣ⌇

Only metres remain between Haggerty and the final. But what now? A Dhole enters the racecourse. It squeezes two participants into the corners and keeps aiming at Haggerty, simply sweeps him away . . .

What a tragic ending of a gorgeous day in sports . . .

ↃⅣ⌇

News: Dhole heading for the Portal.

News: Energy prices slightly increasing.

ↃⅣ⌇

glrb nub?

grub clrb?—"What does the Dhole here?"

knub crlb—"Take *that* for breaking my headstone!"

ↃⅣ⌇

"Out of my kitchen! Oh, no, the dessert!"

ↃⅣ⌇

Chemistry for Kids

"The portal works and, as suspected, it reveals a Dhole . . . a Dhole?! Argh!"

"It's getting at the bomb!"
"Well observed, Mickey!"
BOOOMB!

⊃⽊⟨

News: Studio Five has mysteriously exploded. Tragically, it also caught an energy depot close by . . . Stay tuned for more news.
News: Prices for energy high as never before!

⊃⽊⟨

Opera
"What do you want me to do?"
"Kill, kill, kill!"
switch
Snow
switch
switch
Shut down due to maintenance.

⊃⽊⟨

Stay tuned.

⊃⽊⟨

TRI-TV was yesterday! Today, we have printed paper!

⽊⟨⽊⟨⼈

DO NOT IMAGINE

Mari Ness

Mari Ness' fiction and poetry have appeared in multiple print and online publications, including *Clarkesworld*, *Fantasy Magazine*, *Shine: An Anthology of Optimistic Science Fiction*, *Goblin Fruit*, and *Ideomancer*. Further small insights into her mind and work can be found at: mariness.livejournal.com, and on Twitter at: mari_ness. She lives in central Florida, and openly admits to being rather grateful that the streetlight at the end of the block keeps monsters away at night.

You, in your long, grey ships
of cold rationality and hard mathematics,
shimmering along the path of light,
bending time in your starswept path:
Do not imagine yourselves free of madness.
Not the rich, pulsing joy of winedrunk dance,
nor the madness that lets poets speak to stars
and hear songs from the dripping waters
of rain caught upon roofs of steel,
or the cold, silent songs
pulsing from the deep.
Not the madness of high towers,
of concrete poured over pulsing grass,

or the frenzy of human dance,
of instruments and drums,
singers chanting in the dark,
collapsing with the sun.
Those are the insanities of earth,
the madness that only earth and water
can beat into bone and brain.

But the madness of the dark,
the madness of the silent stars,
the madness of the dark matter
that will move upon your ships—

Do not imagine yourselves so free.

Do not imagine that in this darkness,
nothing awaits.

Do not imagine that no one
will hear you scream.

In the spaces between stars,
our tentacles pulse.
We see your grey ships
and thirst.

We eat upon human screams,
and in the shadows of the stars,
we hunger,
hunger.

The bright stars in all their frenzy
hide us well.
We hunger. We hunger.
You cannot imagine.

ᚴᚼᚻᚼᚻ

RUBEDO, AN ALCHEMY OF MADNESS

Michael Matheson

Michael Matheson currently resides in Toronto, where he works as an author, freelance editor, and technical and public relations writer. He has been a presenter at the ACCSFF and has served since mid-2010 as the editor of the Friends of the Merril Collection publication, *Sol Rising*.

The stars gleam like polished bone out on the galactic rim, edging up on the borderless black of deep space at the outer reaches of the Milky Way. There are graveyards there, celestial sepulchres of rotted hulks and ruined metal that drift in slow arcs through long orbits. It's deathly cold on the rim. Light from distant stars diffuses before it reaches so far out, not enough of it left, by the time it hits those frigid boneyards of blasted metal, to warm what lies within.

Once, these trackless wastes of accordioned metal were home to smugglers and the kind of pirates who preyed on half-mad colonists keen to dare the endless black of the deeps and claim what lay beyond. But they died out long ago, or were driven off by the kind of men who claim a bounty for killing work. Now, only Eliana keeps silent vigil here, an accidental caretaker in this unhallowed place, where Death has walked with arms outstretched, gathering all unto him.

With the crash and sweep of Debussy's "La Mer" flooding over the *Lacrima*'s speaker system on a loop, Eliana drifts in the arms of morphia, its hot bloom in her stomach and her bowels a balm to wounds that refuse to heal. Slumped, opiate-riddled in the grimy bucket seat of her not-quite-several-hundred-feet-long, decaying shuttle, cobbled together from the skeletal hulks of still-older wrecks, she dreams the face of her dead son.

She sprawls, tethered by fraying straps, in her pilot's seat; enclosed in a full pressure suit of black metal and antiseptic cloth resembling nothing so much as a shroud. Only her helmet is off, the bulbous capstone floating several feet away and suspended in midair in the weightless cabin. Her head lolls one way and then another, hot tears orbing as they hit her cheeks and float off to make a starry sea of the darkness from the blank, black screens for the ship's lateral and aft camera HUDs, arrayed around the closed shutters of the cabin's forward viewport. She drifts between sleep and waking. Her face is grey and lined with age, framed by straggly locks of still-night-black hair. She has been out here on the edge of absolute darkness a long time.

ↄﾊ⅄

Twitching and whimpering in her sleep, struggling against the straps that hold her down in the weightless cabin of her ship, Eliana is awakened with a start by her ship colliding with an interposing object. Her ship tumbles from its orbit, rolling with a groan of warping metal that sounds only within the confines of the shuttle as she comes to, wiping salty streaks from her face and gulping down air.

Debussy's etheric, otherworldly strings and crashing cymbals drum against the cabin's interior as Eliana reaches, bleary-eyed, for the con. She slams her palm down on its smooth, touch-sensitive face and blazing starlight floods into the ten-by-fifteen cabin as the main port's reinforced titanium polymer shutters peel back, opening to the dizzy whirl of revolving space.

Eliana's eyes skitter without purchase across the scene unfolding before her. A large section of her carefully maintained graveyard home is in disarray: Scythed halves of ships that were whole only a few hours before rip and tear at one another as they pass, shards of their ionised hulls floating free in the swirling maelstrom of shorn metal. Light is sent scattering everywhere from still-reflective surfaces in the spiraling, tumbling mess that her ordered world has become.

Shielding her eyes from the brightness, Eliana engages the cabin portal's lumen filter and the light of the distant stars dials down to a bearably harsh brightness. Blinking away the seared patterns still emblazoned across her retinas, Eliana's hands fly over the controls, her ship righting itself along the graveyard orbit's lateral line at her command. Activating the ship's lateral propulsion jets, she brings the *Lacrima* to a cruising halt, the ramshackle, jerry-rigged craft shuddering as it comes to a full stop and drifts into its regular orbit.

Eliana's eyes scan the false horizon of the debris field, her eyes slitted against the stabbing rays of ultraviolet light, calculating the origin point of the disturbance. She has let her body fall to the tender mercies of entropy, but Eliana's mind is still razor-sharp, dulled only slightly by the last vestiges of the morphine high. The simple trigonometric equation is no challenge for a woman who once designed interstellar starships and helped her people defy the laws of physics in their ever-hungering quest to transit beyond the known reaches of space. It has been a long time since her mind wandered these neural pathways, but the slow passage of twenty years falls away in an instant, leaving her mind awake and staggeringly fast.

The revitalisation of her faculties also awakens the grief etched deep in the seat of her hypothalamus. Firming the line of her jaw and forcing it to stop quavering, Eliana sets that pain aside and focuses on the task at hand.

She plots the trajectory of the inciting object that has thrown her celestial cemetery into chaos. She can't make out which piece of debris it is that has been sent hurtling like an eight-ball through the dense debris field, so she settles on tracing its wake back to the point of origin. The trail is easy to follow: A wide avenue of disturbed particles drifts out in an ever-expanding cylindrical radius. Eliana manoeuvres the *Lacrima* into the pathway, the ship's capacious bulk sending small driftwood bundles of metal scattering, as the distorted shadows of tumbling objects trail across the portal and the cabin within like clutching, lingering fingers.

Ↄﾈ𝼁

All light is blotted out by something unutterably immense at the end of the tunneling pathway, the route widest here at the edge of its inception, as Eliana comes to the edge of her debris field. Beyond the field floats the absolute darkness beyond the rim, lit only by the weak blaze of stars distant beyond dreaming, beyond the scope of human lifetimes. Here, on the edge of known light where human understanding falters, time is measured in celestial reckonings.

Eliana strains her eyes to see what thing it is that lies against the light, not backlit, instead obscuring all the light behind it as though drinking it in. Her eyes struggle to focus on the shape, but she cannot wrap her mind around its contours. The interposing object is composed of too many angles and lines that seem to warp and bleed off into the edges beyond seeing as she tries to follow them. It hurts her head to watch those inchoate lines that seem never to actually terminate. She looks away and shuts her eyes until the image clears from her mind's eye.

Rubbing at the bridge of her nose with thumb and forefinger, and opening her eyes once more, Eliana is careful not to look directly at the juxtaposed, form-defying shadow. Instead, she stares at the space around the deeper blackness, calculating size and mass, exhaling in awe.

The object, whatever it is, appears to be several thousand feet in length, and maybe a third of that high. And there is something roughly familiar in the design. A subtle curvature and overall aerodynamic sense to the obscuring presence that makes Eliana think back to the days when she studied propulsion engineering and hull design theory. She drums the fingers of one hand along the con panel before her while she contemplates the alien object, letting her hand fall silent as she decides that the massive, light-blotting horizontal obelisk is a craft.

Determined to prove her theory right, Eliana straightens in her pilot's seat and activates the *Lacrima*'s massive aft propulsion jets, salvaged from a derelict Saturn V rocket. Their immense roar is silent in the frictionless space, but sets the interior of the ship to shuddering violently as Eliana steers her craft around the protruding edge of the alien object.

ꝺﬅ

The *Lacrima* clears the obscuring edge of the alien craft's length while Debussy swells over the ship's speakers, rising into the middle section of the third movement of "La Mer"—the "*Dialogue du vent et de la mer. Animé et tumultueux*"—and Eliana is forced to slit her eyes when a baleful, red glow envelops the entirety of the ship's cabin. On this side of the obscuring object, a deep, crimson pulsing blurs the light of distant stars. Like a breathing eye, the pulsing orb inhales and exhales light, the red shift deepening and paling sequentially.

Eliana screws her eyes shut and turns her face away from the overwhelming ruddy light, blindly swatting at the con panel, her fingers sighted, even in self-imposed darkness, through long practice. The *Lacrima*'s main viewport filters out the burning red shift and Eliana opens tear-streaked eyes, blinking away the stinging salt. Her newly opened eyes focus on the strange shape before her, webbed to the side of the still-all-but-invisible craft.

The thing attached to the side of the ship is hard to focus on, at first. It is roughly circular in shape, rising in an imperfect half-dome from the hull of the drifting, possibly derelict ship, and seemingly translucent. The hazy, ill-defined bulbous contusion on the alien ship's hull runs the height of the craft and stretches over a quarter of its length, the enormity of the canker mind-boggling. The more Eliana focuses on the strange shape, the more she realises that it is not the dome that is red, but something within—something that pulses and breathes. Something that moves within the confines of the space, tentacled limbs roving and thrashing in amniotic dreaming.

With a Pavlovian reaction that tears at her gut and opens the floodgates of her memory, letting loose a torrent of buried images and sensations tied to the child who once gestated in her own womb, Eliana realises that the thing attached to the side of the alien craft is an egg. Her stomach dry-heaving, hand across her mouth, Eliana struggles to subdue the raging floodwaters crashing through her mind: images of her son laughing; his tiny hand in hers; his first step across bare, clattering floorboards; the soft, downy smell of him in the spring air; his first breath in an antiseptic hospital; his last, choking gasp for air as he convulsed and simply slipped away, cradled in her arms, her hot tears running through his hair and down into his staring eyes; his unmoving flesh clutched to her breast.

These and innumerable other moments, captured in refracted amber, steal the breath from her lungs and now, she does disgorge the contents of her stomach, what little there is in it rushing up as bile and sluicing out over her lips to blob and float away. Followed by tears that do likewise and choking sobs that echo in the small confines of the *Lacrima*'s cabin.

As Eliana cries, the tendrils of the thing inside the egg cease moving and it pulses once, deeply. For a few moments, it is silent, utterly still, as Eliana is wracked with the outpouring agony of her long-repressed grief. And then, all the tentacles of the immense, spacefaring entity thunder against the egg's outer membrane at once, releasing a torrent of gravimetric waves that traverse the empty space between the alien craft and the *Lacrima*, slamming up against the pitted, already-cracked surface of the decaying vessel.

Eliana rocks in her straps as her ship shakes violently in the gravimetric storm. And then, one of the straps, long overdue for replacement, tears and she is hurtling through the cabin to smash up against the open viewport at the front of the cabin. Her head cracks sharply against the well-reinforced, poly-paned glass. And then there is only silence.

⊃⪥⪤

In the darkness, in which she floats, there is a voice. It is her son's. She knows this without thinking. It is as automatic a recognition as the ceaseless, effortless work of breathing. Eyes opening on a vast plane of darkness where no stars lie, she sees herself floating, then comes to stand upright on an unseen sense of solidity beneath her.

Her son is before her, rushing toward her, his small legs pumping quickly across illusory, solid terrain that cannot be seen, but is nonetheless felt. But Eliana has been here, before. She knows the illusion for what it is, even in this state, somewhere between dream and memory. Always, always in her mind is the knowledge of his death. Ingrained so deeply that neither sleep nor dream can steal the knowledge from her. She holds herself erect, dream eyes closed as her dead son throws his arms around her and holds her tight. She clenches her jaw and looks away from the small, thick arms cradled around her upper thighs and the warm, soft head nestled up against her navel.

Again, she damns her subconscious mind for thinking this will bring her peace or a measure of comfort. Doesn't her symbol-ridden sense of self understand that nothing will ever be right again?

She keeps her eyes shut against the sight of her long-dead child, but opens them when the arms pull back and the warmth of him moves away. That's new. Confused, Eliana opens her eyes. Before her stands her son, his head cocked at an angle, his body naked and pristine, so unlike the actual state of him in death, when the lesions had blossomed on his rosy flesh and his skin had rotted away in great weeping chunks. But there is something wrong with him, here. Something . . . different.

Eliana stares, unable to take her eyes from her dead son as he twitches, shudders and then convulses uncontrollably. She stands, rooted to the spot, unable to move her body, though every muscle screams to run to him and cradle his spasm-ridden body. Before her eyes, he throws up one tentacle, then two, then three, until his mouth is full with the thickness of a fungal bloom of cephalopod tendrils. He chokes on them, as she screams, and then tendrils are bursting through all of his skin, ripping it aside in order to be free of the cage of still-mortifying flesh.

She cannot stop screaming.

Ɔᛣᚾ

She is still screaming as she awakens, the sound loud in the silence of the *Lacrima*'s cabin. Debussy no longer plays over the collapsed speaker system, the ship's silent collision alarm awake and blaring in swift, repeating, red pulses of light that mimic those generated by the entity now raucously beating at the shell of its cage, drifting between her ship and the debris field far beyond. Blood wells and orbs from a deep gash in her forehead, and her vision swims, but suddenly, Eliana understands, watching the tentacled entity beat at the cage.

It is trying to birth, but cannot free itself. And through the haze of her own floating blood, Eliana sees not the trapped tentacled entity, but knows it for what it truly is. Her son has come back to her. He has found her at long last. Tears well in her eyes, but now, after twenty years, finally, she sheds tears of joy. Her son has come back to her.

Eliana sets her jaw, straightens her spine and pushes off the cracked viewport with one steady hand. She floats her way back to the cabin's pilot seat and settles in as best she can, grabbing for the helmet that dances away from her in the weightless air, everything bathed in the intermingled glaring reds of the struggling entity and the *Lacrima*'s alarm system. She adjusts the helmet over her head and snaps it shut with a violent twist, her suit filling with refiltered air. She closes her right eye against the sudden rush of properly flowing blood as it courses down her face, filling one half of her vision. Strobe-lit orbs of her blood still speckle the cabin, intermingling with the ever-present sparkle of her globular tears, filling the otherwise-empty space.

With the barest nudge on the control panel, Eliana sets the *Lacrima*'s impelling engines roaring to life and the battered ship slides forward, gaining momentum as she revs the hulk up to ramming speed. With a look of absolute joy on her face, Eliana sends the *Lacrima* slamming into the immense, tentacled creature's egg, shattering it. Sheer portions of the collapsing egg fall away and shear sections of the *Lacrima* from the main body of the hull, opening parts of the engine room and auxiliary fuel dumps to the void of space. A thick, black, quickly-globuling leak of engine coolant and fuel bleeds out into space as the ship depressurises and portions of the hull begin to crumple inward.

Eliana is thrown forward from her seat by the collision and slams up against the cabin view-port, this time full-bodied. She lingers there, watching the tentacled foetus within the egg breach, its massive tendrils ripping at the collapsing barrier. With each stroke, it reveals itself more fully until it is free.

She watches as her son stretches tendrils to the distant stars, light radiating from its pulsing, burning core. Radiative heat boils off the stellar entity, its external membrane burning a bright, pulsing red. Eliana forces her eyes to stay open as her retinas burn with the brightness of her son's awesome new form. A swell of pride blooms up within her. His new body will not succumb to the ravages of disease, nor age, nor infirmity. Here, in the limitless black of space, he will live, undying.

For a moment, the tentacled stellar creature swells, drinking in the ambient radioactive energy of the deep black around it. And then it turns its spherical mass upon the wreck of the *Lacrima*, the ship collapsing in segmented stages, one portion of the hull after another crumpling in like an accordion. Drawn by the bleeding heat and light of the dying ship, and the meager warmth of the entity within, the interstellar entity falls on the crumpling hulk and wraps it in a tentacled embrace.

As the cabin is bathed in burning, pure-red light, the tentacled mass of her newly reborn child crushing up against the already-weakened glass, Eliana exults in her son's final embrace. Metal crumples and folds in on itself in sharp, swift strokes, pinning her and crushing the breath from her lungs. And as the tentacles scythe through the hull and find purchase on her form and close tight around her, cracking bone and turning muscle to pulp, one thought repeats endlessly in Eliana's mind.

He has come back to her.

PEOPLE ARE READING WHAT YOU ARE WRITING

Luso Mnthali

Luso Mnthali was born in Malawi, grew up in Botswana, went to university in the United States, and now lives in beautiful Cape Town, South Africa. Luso hikes in the mountains because it helps her get over her fear of heights.

In a room on the top floor, maria typed. And she typed and she typed. After two days, she looked up and saw a man, a short man with a clean-shaven face, standing in front of her. He watched her silently until she looked up, alerted by breathing not her own, when she needed to stretch and yawn at last. On another world, her stamina would have astounded many, but here on the New World, new human feats were always in motion, such that people were constantly re-evaluating what was humanly possible. These humans breathed differently, slept less, did more. They were also capable of retaining more information, and were also able to shut out the world when need be.

When maria at last stopped typing, she was not surprised to see him standing, watching her.

"How long have you been there?" she asked him.

"Oh, a couple of days," he answered. He was face to face with her, as she sat there, at that table, her hands vibrating above the keyboard.

ꗞ

"Why are you here?" maria asked him.

"maria without the capital M. You are making them nervous."

"What do you mean?"

"Punctuation, spelling, all done with a certain…flair, or done differently. Truth and honesty, to the extreme. Killing off characters that we…that we like. Where do you come up with these stories? They're just stories, are they not? And your new word creation. Why can't you stick to the approved list? You're making a lot of important people angry, Maria."

"No, my name is 'maria'. Not…not 'Maria'. Simply…'maria'."

Her large, determined, brown eyes did not waver; there was no perspiration on her bald head.

ꗞ

The man pursed his lips even more, until the straight line blurred with his features. "maria without the capital M. You are making them nervous." With that, he disappeared and she simply continued. She made her spelling "mistakes" when necessary, creating new colours and new words, and new moods to feed a crowd. Soon, her fame spread throughout the land and people wanted to crown her Queen. "Chiphadzua," they called her. The one who kills the sun with her beauty.

ꗞ

She thought and thought about it. How people, even now, after the voyage to the New Planet, insisted on the old languages and ways of doing things. She had all bloods within her, yet people still chose to see her as from the Old Planet. The Old Ways still remained very much a part of their existence. They did not believe that the wars of the past could happen here, that the Old Ways were still very much a part of the New World, on the New Planet. Perhaps her Xhosa ancestor, Maria, for whom she was named, was strongest in her blood. Her Old South African heritage told her of the First People. Maybe this is what the Council feared the most. That the oldest blood was the strongest. Perhaps Mallika of the Iyer in Old India gave her the gall, the necessary courage. Mallika with her long, black hair and big, shining eyes. An intellectual, famed ancestor. And Maita, the Kalanga woman in Old Botswana, asked her to dare and keep on daring. She also knew that Mireille, neither Hutu nor Tutsi, and not fully French, would give her courage, ask her to remember faith and the Old God, and to travel. These were all her ancestors. But somehow, the last country she lived in, Old Malawi, was stated in her bio. She wouldn't escape that, didn't want to, but she remembered what it meant.

ƆЖ₤

In the Old Ways, women were not free to inherit from their deceased husband's estate when they became widowed. In the Old Ways, very few women were educated. Those who were educated, sometimes chose not to show how smart they were. Sometimes, they gave up the Freedom education had given them to have families. They bought into what the Council would eventually build—a New World. They gave up fighting for more freedoms, all around the world, for more women. The reasons for this were varied and she wrote about them often. Telling the people, so they would not forget. New Planet agents wanted the people to forget how unequal the society remained. Your bloods and your past remained with you, were documented in your bio and were used to keep you within a certain level of society. Even though the New Constitution stated that there would be no discrimination based on nationality, race or country of origin, discrimination in the New World was rampant. But maria was a woman with a past. Her bloods and history marked her as a person ripe for dissent. Her bloods marked her as a rebel, even amongst women in other parts of the New Planet. Women who believed maria was to be saved from herself and follow the ideals they espoused. Therefore, she stayed in her prison, built shortly after she had arrived on the New World, and plotted dissent quietly.

ƆЖ₤

The short, bald man with dull eyes and hardly any lips visited her again over a few days.

"I hear you will be crowned Queen," he said to her.

"No, I will be a queen. Just like that girl over there, in the past world, who writes poetry and is still controlled in her tweets. Who does not dance all over the world and all over the place and keeps her face in place. She is unlike me, but she is a queen." maria stopped the tapping across her keyboard and looked directly into his eyes. He backed away a little.

"Who is this girl you speak of?" he asked her.

"No one," she said, lying to him in a way he could understand. "No one." Just like the poor women in her country, she was no one. In a world that liked to stratify, she was no one.

ꙨꝪꚄ

And so, she was given a small crown, a small crown for a tall woman with a fierce look in her big, brown eyes. A woman who wore a long, black, sleeveless dress. The only jewellery she wore were small pearl earrings that glowed against her golden-brown skin. These used to be Mireille's. queen maria wore her small crown of flowers, which were so rare that she wondered where the people had found them. Maybe they grew them away from the Council's prying eyes. She was told they were called "bougainvillea," and their cream colour was the rarest variety. She recalled reading about this plant in Maita's Old Botswana journals.

ꙨꝪꚄ

"Queen of what?" The short man appeared again in the dead of night, clearly agitated. His eyes kept darting about, trying to understand how she made contact with the outside world.

"How is it," he asked, "that you can display such laziness one day, such fortitude and stamina the next, such ill discipline on another day, and still, they love you and crown you queen?"

maria looked up from her work for just a few seconds, but then continued typing as she spoke.

"You give me all the fortitude, all the tools I need to carry on. It is your voice I listen to when I write the character that is a lover. It is your voice that I listen to when I write the character of a ruthless politician or a would-be killer. It is your voice…that drives me. I write about the past so we can all have a future. This is all the Council wants to prevent. A future with a real past. And this is why you are here."

"You give me no choice, maria, but to pull the plug on you. The Council gave me full powers. It is up to me now."

"Go ahead. Are you scared of what I will write or what I have already written? You make me more powerful when you try to silence me. In my absence the spectre of what I could have been will lean heavier and become greater than anything I do while I am free. So, go ahead; make this easy for me as queen. I am free."

"I insist that you issue a statement, asking your followers to respect your privacy and to not commit any acts in your name."

"And what would those be? Pretending to be me? Finishing some of my works in a voice they think I would appreciate? Protesting?" maria stretched her long body at the desk, raising her arms so the tips of her fingers reached out to space. The man moved back so her toes would not touch him. She had no hair and, as she twisted her neck to ease some of her tension, she caught fear reflected in the man's eyes, the kind of fear you see in a soldier's prey,"

"Why are you so scared?" she asked him.

"People are reading what you are writing. It does not make sense to let you go on."

ꝺꝼꞓ

That had been yesterday. Or, so her calendar had told her. In a room where true time does not exist, she could never tell. She only told true time by what the planets told her. And the moons, the moons told true time. She rarely looked outside, mostly within. So, for the most part, time did not exist.

ꝺꝼꞓ

maria got up. Outside, the blue dawn had risen and the planets were aligning. The man, the muse, the Council representative, he of the short stature and nondescript face, of the unhealthy tint to his skin and the follower's demeanour, was really going to do this. She knew that those on the inside, those who lived as her followers, those who were her children, past and future subjects, her characters and those she gave birth to, would appreciate her escape. From the tall filter window of the light-yellow room in which she worked, she could see the rest of her world. In the streets below, an army surrounded her tower. They had been there from the day she started to write. The day she took up residence in the six-story, grey-stone tower, with the single flight of stairs, spiralling inside and outside, they had appeared. The sound of their boots was enough to alert her to their presence; otherwise they never made direct contact. Sometimes, she'd catch a few of them looking up at the tower, at its strange construction and its pointed dome, much like the spindle of an old-fashioned sewing wheel. Perhaps she'd dreamed it up from some photographs of Old India that Great-Grandmother Mallika kept for her children. Or, from books that her own mother read to her when she was very young. Some stories about a little, evil creature who kept a king's daughter imprisoned in a tower. Eventually, she had dreamed up her prison and there she sat. She felt that the Council would never understand her intention and for this she was grateful. Being free—of the Council, of expectation—was something she greatly craved.

ɔ⅄�

The Council knew that a woman from this part of the world, writing, was a greater threat than any other they had yet faced. She had the bloods to prove it and her bio told them that history could repeat itself. After all, it was women who wanted to unseat them. It was women who tried to rewrite the balance of power. It was women that the Old Countries went to war for, in Ancient Times. They had all the excuses to keep women away from knowledge and a better way to lead, and read, the world they lived in. Rather a docile system of Womanhood, anywhere in the world, than any form of a unified and strong Womanhood, in many parts of the known world. Keep them different, docile, weak, and dis-unified.

ɔ⅄ᵳ

As the moons carved a trajectory across the sky, and the light from the ships let it be known that another imposed day was upon the planet, she felt that her people would contact her. And they did. Without knowing how much time had passed, she felt surrounded by a warm energy. She was on the floor, lying down, without remembering how this came to be.

ɔﬠɟ

Soon, one of her own whispered to her. Then, all she could see was a woman dressed in white, opening the filter window. maria got up from the floor and scrambled after the woman, who was clearly about to jump. All maria could grab was cloth and then, finally, a slim hand, as the woman in white slipped from her grasp. Before she let her hand go, on the very ledge from which maria watched the world below, the woman said, "You are everything. I had to die to let you know. Don't let them stop you. Keep writing in yellow. Then send in red. The colour of life." And then she let go, her long, dark hair billowing around her, but her body pliant and ready, not angled in fear. She smiled as her body met the pavement. maria had used the ternary glasses she kept for just such an occasion, to see everything that happened. Below, her follower was the colour of life in seconds, and was immediately surrounded by soldiers. Some looked up. The man appeared to her a short while later. He held handcuffs and talked to her about inspiration.

ɔﬠɟ

"You inspire us to make this more difficult for you," he said to her, his eyes almost catching light, almost becoming alive.

"You inspire me to write. She died for a reason. The part of me that never dies, dies in this world. On another, freer world, she is everlasting. My Followers do not weep for this. We rejoice, because we know Freedom is soon coming."

"You're naïve. Who will you go to? You know your voice cannot carry beyond these walls. We made sure of that. Only the Followers in your head, when they appear, know of you."

"If I told you my plans, I would not live beyond the three moons, and beyond this world. There are many who wait for my shape to enter its chosen space. This is what frightens you. And the more I write, the more ready my chosen space. For you to keep appearing, it means I am close to my goal."

"I have the plug right here, little queen with a small m. What would you tell your followers if I were to pull it? What then would your imprint be like, incomplete, not ready to take shape?"

"You forget I have allies outside of this yellow, cold room. And that sitting, writing all day is an exercise in creation. You forget many things when it comes to women from my part of the world. You forget our power."

"You talk a lot. The Council has agreed. It is time to say goodbye."

ᴐ⪤⪤

The planets were in alignment; the three moons rose that day. Outside the tower, red scarves appeared around the necks and mouths of some soldiers. They started to scale the tower, to the only room it housed, on the top floor.

⪤⪤Ͱ⪤ϟ

HARMONY AMID THE STARS

Ada Hoffmann

Ada Hoffmann is a graduate student in computing who commutes to southern Ontario from an obscure globular cluster populated mostly by elves. Her short fiction has appeared in *Expanded Horizons*, *Basement Stories*, and *One Buck Horror*, among others.

Harmony I: Day 624

There's only so much paper on this ship. I shouldn't be wasting it on a diary, even with my thumbtop gone. But I have to write this somewhere, before the songs of the stars drown it out and I forget.

I found blood on the walls today.

I was lugging garbage from the mess hall out to the recycler. Thumbtop in my pocket, piping *kwaito* music into my ears. Humming along, so I wouldn't hear the stars at the edge of my mind. I kept my eyes on the white-tiled floors, avoiding the windows. The current song ended and I picked up the rectangular screen of my thumbtop with one hand, using my thumb to scroll through to a song I wasn't tired of yet. I settled on a homemade audio file: my sister, Onalenna, back Earthside, laughing and singing a song we'd invented as children.

Then I looked up and saw it: the red-brown streaks marring the wall's white tile, just opposite the window. Angry, dripping Mandarin characters. I dropped my thumbtop with a crash.

I can get by in a Mandarin conversation, but the writing still eludes me.

I don't know what the characters said. Normally, I would have needed to use the detector on my thumbtop even to know what they were. But I've got a PhD, same as everyone, and I knew what it would have said if it hadn't just broken. Organic material. No bacteria. Dissipated proteins. Glucose. Platelets. Erythrocytes.

Blood.

I wanted to pretend I didn't know why anyone would have done such a thing. But I knew. After all, I've been avoiding the stars with all my might since we passed the Oort cloud. They've looked different since then. When I'm not talking or listening to music, I hear them whispering, just past the edge of comprehension. *Blood* is one of their favourite words.

Blood on the walls meant someone else heard them. And someone gave in.

ƆӾƐ

I was halfway done scrubbing the blood off the walls before I realised I might have let them stay as evidence. But there's already enough crazy on this ship and blood's unsanitary. Better to clean.

Cleaning used to make me laugh. I've got a PhD in microbiology. When we get to Barnard's Star, nine years from now, I'll be doing tests too delicate for the antique robots that got there, first. Checking if the local bacteria interact catastrophically with our crops or our bodies. Fixing it if they do. So a plague doesn't wipe out the real colonists.

But the only bugs on the *Harmony I* are the ones we brought ourselves. Until we land, "microbiologist" means "cleaning lady".

I picked up the broken pieces of my thumbtop and tried to hum while I worked, taking up the song where Onalenna's voice left off. But I was so upset I couldn't remember how it had gone.

ƆӾƐ

I thought about not telling anyone, but this ship has hierarchies. There are the glorified cleaning ladies and there are the scientists who have important things to do shipboard. And then there is Captain Hao.

Captain Hao likes to say her door is always open. In Johannesburg, when profs said that sort of thing, they meant they liked to chat. I tried chatting with Captain Hao, once or twice. Got a blank stare, like I was singing about cockroach-headed dogs. I thought maybe it was me; maybe my Mandarin was just that awful. But I asked everyone—even Jason Chong, who grew up speaking Mandarin in Singapore—and they all agreed: Captain Hao is like that with everyone.

When Captain Hao says her door is always open, she means she expects verbal reports whenever anything happens. So, when I'd scrubbed the blood off the wall, I made my way to her quarters.

"Captain," I said, saluting—she likes salutes.

"Dr. Maele."

She was sketching with a sharp pencil in her quarters, which are bigger than mine—bigger than anyone's out here—but still barely the size of a college dorm room. No decorations, beyond some charts and calendars: Even her sketches went in a neat pile at the side of her desk, not onto the walls. She was off-duty, but still in her uniform jumpsuit and gloves, with her hair pulled back to the nape of her neck.

She's beautiful. Her eyes are like licorice candies. She makes me nervous.

"Captain, I found something odd on my cleaning rounds. Somebody's been writing on the wall. In blood."

Even her raised eyebrow was tidy. "Have they?"

"Yes." I took out a slip of notepaper where I'd copied the characters. She frowned at the use of paper, but didn't comment. "By the recycler. This is what it said. I cleaned it off so no one would panic, but I thought you should know."

Captain Hao took the paper and studied it. I wanted to ask what the characters meant, but stopped myself. She knows that I have to look at the English side of the manuals, but I don't like bringing it up. I don't like looking incompetent to her.

"Good work, Dr. Maele. I'll look into this. Leave the next one up so I can study it, if there's a next one. Is that all?"

"Would you like me to do anything? Should I keep on the lookout for blades, bloodstains on pens, suspicious behaviour, anything like . . . ?"

She gave me a flat look, like she didn't trust me to notice suspicious behaviour in the first place. "No. Is that all?"

"That's all."

That's what I mean by hierarchy. Captain Hao needs to know everything. Cleaning ladies don't need to know squat.

But I can't hate her for it. I can't do anything but wish that I was tidy and important like her, and that she liked me. Call me crazy.

Harmony I: Day 625

Ni Nyoman Suardana can fix anything. Except, apparently, a shattered thumbtop. She put on her gloves, took the pieces, one by one, from their plastic bag, examined them critically for a few minutes, then turned to me with her dark eyes wide, like she thought I'd be angry. "I can't do anything, Moremi. I'm sorry. This thing's wrecked."

I must have looked disappointed, because she jumped back like I'd startled her. Suardana was like a nervous little bird from day one. I've been told she passed her psych eval narrowly, but out here, she keeps getting worse.

"It's okay," she said, holding out her hands. "It's okay. We'll get you a spare."

I leaned against the wall and tried to look real casual. If I don't act casual around Suardana, she just gets worse. "I'm not too worried. Is it easy to get a spare?"

Suardana nodded like she was placating a gunman. "Yes, it's very easy. Very, very easy. You backed up your files, right?"

" 'Course."

"Just bring that to me tomorrow, and I'll get one out of storage and put them on. Really, it's easy. It's fine."

I wasn't lying to placate her. I really thought I had a backup. I remember saying goodbye to my family, hugging my sister like a vise and holding my mother more gently, afraid of hurting her. Trying to memorise the smell of the earth, even though it was just asphalt and fuel out there on the launch pad. Walking stiffly onto the ship, praying the photos and letters and music I'd packed onto the thumbtop would be enough. I'm sure I was smart enough to make a backup.

But I've trashed my room. Every space-saving drawer. Every pocket. If we were allowed to keep personal files on the ship's mainframe, I'd have trashed that, too. There was no backup. Finally, I gave up and took out this paper.

I keep glancing out my little window, daring myself to look at the stars. I've only realised just now how much I've kept on my thumbtop and not in my head. I had a diary from Earth, but I can't remember any of what I wrote. I had letters from all my friends, all my extended family, even a few ex-lovers. I can remember a few of their faces but only one name. I didn't know it was possible to lose so much.

I wonder if I'll remember the percussive beat of a *kwaito* song, nine years from now. I wonder if I'll remember Johannesburg. Or the moles on my sister's face.

Harmony I: Day 628

I slept with Henri last night to block out the stars' whispers. To think about something else besides cleaning, blood, and loss. It wasn't our first time.

I like Henri and I don't like him. He has nice hands and nice legs. His hair is going prematurely grey. He's nice to me, in a smarmy sort of way. He's better than being alone.

I don't like trying to cuddle on his little cot. We can do it if we try, but once the endorphins wear off, it feels sweaty and squished. So, when we were done, I sat on the floor, wrapped myself in a blanket, stared into space. He ran his fingers through my hair.

"You can take the spare Suardana offered," he said, when he'd run out of sweet nothings. "You can borrow my music. Borrow everyone's. Better than doing your oh-so-menial job in silence."

Henri gets to tease me about that. He's an organic chemist, so he has one of the only jobs lower on the totem pole than mine: He repairs the composting toilets.

"It's not the silence. You know what it is."

"*Oui*. And the lost files, of course."

"It's the sounds."

I glanced at the window. I'd been hearing it more and more since my thumbtop broke. *We were here when you were prokaryotes,* said the stars. *We will be here when you are dust.*

There was a nervous smile in Henri's voice. "*Oui*, Moremi, but don't say it out loud. Ssh."

I closed my eyes and focused on his fingers in my hair. Normally, I don't like closing my eyes with Henri. Not in the afterglow, when it's only his fingers. I always end up realising, with a start, that the hand I'm imagining in my hair is Captain Hao's.

ว)⅄ɛ

Harmony I: Day 643

Henri's music doesn't help. It's all breathy *chanteuses* and tinkly pop. It doesn't grab me and move me like *kwaito*. I keep drifting off and hearing the stars.

We were here when you were dust. We will be here when you are vapour. And you, in the meantime, will serve.

I'm not sure I have all the words right. I try not to get them right.

I keep finding messages in blood. I don't want to know what they say. I left the second one up for Captain Hao, but after three days, I couldn't stand it, anymore, and scrubbed it off. She didn't say anything about it, good or bad, but the stars got louder. The third one, I scrubbed right away. Too much crazy on this ship, already. We don't need blood.

Last night, I woke up sweating from a nightmare. I couldn't remember anything. Just the terror. Instead of going back to sleep, I started cleaning early. No one gets up early on this ship. The mess hall should have been empty.

But there was Captain Hao, with a razor blade and a calligraphy brush. One glove pulled off, one hand dripping red, the brush redder. Writing a word on the wall.

She turned her head and looked at me. I've never seen emotion in Captain Hao's face before. Today, her eyes went wide; her lip trembled. I think it was fear.

If she hadn't looked scared, I might have stormed in, demanded an explanation. But with that look in her eyes, half of me wanted to hug her, kiss her straight black hair, tell her it would be okay. Half of me wanted to run screaming.

I split the difference. I bowed my head and backed out politely. Hours later, when she was gone, I scrubbed the bloody wall until it shone.

Harmony I: Day 644

I almost didn't tell anyone. I lay awake, tossing and turning, trying to shut out the stars. Told myself it would make no difference if I did. She's the Captain. Even if she weren't, what could we do? Send her home?

We will be here when you are dust, said the stars. *You will serve us. She will serve us.*

I got up and paced, as much as you can pace in a room the size of a closet, taking one step and turning, step and turn, step and turn. I leaned on the poster I'd smuggled up from Earth, a big view of a herd of kudu in Marakele National Park. I stared at it and wondered if I'd been there before.

I couldn't remember if I'd ever seen kudu. I couldn't remember if I'd been to a national park, at all. I tried to think of it and only saw blood.

That was the last straw. I had to talk to someone.

ↃⱵ٤

"Someone" means Mesfin Biniyam, the ship's psychiatrist. At Mission Control in Beijing, when they told me psychiatry was one of the most important jobs in space, I laughed. I wrote an eye-rolling letter back home to Onalenna.

Nowadays, I don't laugh about it.

We each had a weekly session with Mesfin for the first few months. When Henri and I started fighting over whether to call ourselves a couple, Mesfin smoothed it over. When Suardana reported anxiety, he taught her some deep breathing, which helped her keep an even keel—for a while.

But when I first told Mesfin about the stars and their whispers, he got this gazelle-in-the-headlights look. Like, all of a sudden, here was something he hadn't read in a psychiatric journal. Nowadays, he wanders the ship with nothing to say.

When he stopped holding weekly sessions, I just grumbled and wished he'd help with the cleaning. But today, I needed him.

Mesfin's office doubles as his cabin and it's one of the bigger ones. He and I can both sit down and close the door and, if we're careful, our knees don't touch. He's decked out the walls in inspirational posters mixed with traditional Ethiopian art.

I sat down and explained. About Captain Hao. The blood on the walls. The whispers. How I felt like a traitor just talking about it, but worse if I said nothing. How beautiful she was, even writing with the blood from her own wrist. How badly I wanted her to be sane.

He let me finish. He asked the usual headshrinker questions. "How does that make you feel?" Then he closed his eyes. "I can't help with this, Moremi. I'm sorry."

I pulled away a half-centimeter, which was all I could do without plastering myself against the wall. "What do you mean? You're the one who deals with the crazy. You're telling me there's no entry for this in the Diagnostic and Statistical Manual? No little page of instructions in Mandarin, somewhere in the ship's handbook? 'By the way, if the whole crew goes batshit, here's what you do. . . . ' " My voice cracked. That surprised me. I held my hands up to hide my face.

Mesfin's voice had the kind of calm that you only get by doing a real good job of pretending to be calm when you're not. "What do you think, Moremi? Do you think there are instructions for this?"

I didn't want him to see my lip trembling. Like a little kid. "You're the psychiatrist. Make something up."

"I hear the voices, too, Moremi. Maybe they're the stars. Maybe they're a projection of my unconscious mind. My temporal lobes constructing a presence to block out the emptiness that's really out there. How can I know? And if I don't know, how can I give advice? Won't I simply be repeating what the stars tell me? How can I say anything?"

"People are writing on the walls in blood. How can you *not* say anything?"

"I can't say anything." I expected him to show some emotion, to start waving his hands or trembling. He just sat there. Repeated it over and over. "I can't. I can't. I can't."

I stormed out. I cried in my cabin for a minute or two.

But so what? He showed me what not to be. I refuse to sit there, expressionless, while things fall apart. Even if my memory's going and the stars are loud in my ears, I have to do something so we survive until Barnard's Star. I have to, so I can.

Harmony I: Day 645

I am going to have a talk with Captain Hao.

It will be delicate. I can't do it when someone else could be watching. And her door isn't open, anymore. When I come by, she waves pages of Mandarin paperwork in my face. I have to wait for the right moment.

It's awful, waiting. It drove me to distraction all day. Finally, I gave up and went to Henri.

He smirked the way he always smirked. "Ah, yes, love. I'll give you something else to think of." He pulled me close without waiting to see if I liked the idea or not. Half of me hated him for it and half of me wanted to kiss him until speech was not an option. I went with the kissing. Henri's not all bad. His jaw is a good shape. His skin tastes salty, alive.

I'd kissed halfway down his neck before I realised I wasn't thinking of those things. And, this time, not about Captain Hao, either. I was thinking of the pulse in his throat. Strong, heady, rhythmic, saltier than skin. The red, the life, hiding inside him. I wanted to touch that. To taste it.

I pulled back abruptly. Henri raised an eyebrow, not moving. He's learned not to push.

You are ours, said the stars, suddenly loud in my ears. *We can use you.*

I put my hands over my ears. Henri tilted his head. "Moremi, what . . . ?"

I shoved him away and ran back to my room.

I'm not crazy. Captain Hao's the crazy one. I've always had these little uncomfortable moments. One time, I had a girlfriend back in Johannesburg who—

I don't remember her name. I don't remember what she did.

I remember it was awkward, though, and I came home and told Onalenna about it. Once told, it was funny. We laughed and laughed, and Onalenna said—

What did she say?

I can't picture my sister's face, anymore. I don't know what she said. I don't remember our mother's name, only the stick of her wrist as she hugged me goodbye. I remember Onalenna's last words to me: *Don't look back, Moremi. I'll miss you, but . . .*

But what?

I think I remember her voice. I think I remember it cracking. But I don't remember my sister.

Harmony I: Day 646

I don't remember what I said when I got Captain Hao alone. Just the feeling of blood pounding in my ears. I felt sick, but I had to say it, or be like Mesfin forever.

She stared at me. Not a caught-in-the-act stare. Not a repentant stare. She stared like she'd never believed an African cleaning lady could be so stupid.

"Dr. Maele." Her voice was ice. "Can't you *read?*"

I'd pictured her screaming, attacking me in a blood-writing homicidal haze. This was worse.

"Not Mandarin," I said helplessly, my eyes frozen to hers. "Not very much of it. I can speak Mandarin and read English and, for a non-Chinese citizen, that was enough for—"

"I know the personnel requirements of my own ship, Moremi. Fine. Since you're so concerned, let me educate you. The words I've been writing on the walls? They say, *Keep out*."

I stared.

Captain Hao clasped her gloved hands and spoke the way you'd talk to a brain-damaged 12-year-old. "The stars speak to me most of all, as is fitting. They wish to use me, and my ship, for their own ends. I will not let them. They understand blood more than anything else. So, I use blood to let them know they are unwelcome. Haven't you noticed that, when I do this, the voices lessen, if only for a while? Or does the University of Johannesburg give doctorates to those who don't understand covariation?"

I was frozen down to my belly. She was right, and I hadn't noticed.

We will use you, said the stars. *We will use her. Soon, you will see.*

"Captain?" I said. "What do the stars say to you?"

She pointed. "Out."

Call me a coward, but I left.

Harmony I: Day 647

I stewed all evening and all morning, all through my cleaning time. I couldn't calm down. When the *Harmony I* was spotless, I collapsed into Henri's bed.

He didn't seem surprised. "Your little panic attack is over, then?" I was past caring. With him, at least, I could stop thinking for a minute.

The voices slithered into my ears. I kissed him and kissed him. He pinned me against the cabin wall. His skin grew hot with surface blood. The voices sang. I didn't care.

Kisses. *Blood.* The stars. Captain Hao. *Blood.* I was past thinking. I still saw them.

Henri was already inside me when the voices coalesced into words. Too loud to ignore, not even there and then. So loud they drowned out Henri's moans.

He is ours. His blood, his life, they are ours. You will give him to us.

For a split second, I could see it: His limbs splayed, his eyes glassy, red everywhere. The stars laughing.

My stomach turned to ice. The vision, and the voices, went away. He was alive and moving, kissing me, cursing in French. Should I have told him to stop? Should I have pushed him off of me?

He took a few minutes of afterglow before he realised I still wasn't moving. "Love? Are you all right?"

I managed to make my mouth work. "I think so."

"Come here."

I sat on the cot beside him and he wrapped me in his arms. They were not comforting.

"It's the voices, *oui?*"

"*Ee,*" I agreed. He knew as many words of Tswana, by now, as I did of French.

"Poor thing. They speak to me, too, you know."

It was the sort of inane thing Henri would say. Did he think there was anyone who didn't hear them? But, out of some perverse impulse, I asked, "What do they say?"

"They say that I am not worthy of them. That I must die and my blood will consecrate the ship." His fingers tightened in my hair. "But it is foolishness. I have never been suicidal, even out here, and I find them easy to ignore. If they want me to kill myself, they will have to try harder, hmm? So, what do they tell you?"

I was silent.

"Poor little Moremi. Don't think of the stars. Think of home. Old lovers, drinking companions, colleagues, that sister you love so much. Remember we are doing this for them."

I thought of them. Or I tried to.

I could not think of anything. At first, I thought I was still paralysed from the vision. But I could think of Henri, Captain Hao, Mesfin, Suardana, all the rest of them.

I could not think of my sister. Nor my parents. Nor anyone on Earth I had ever known. I could not remember my alma mater, my hometown, my religion—if I had one. I could not remember veldts or rivers or cities. And I had not even noticed them go.

"Did I have a sister?"

"Of course you did. You always used to talk about her. Her name was . . . Oh, let me see . . . It's coming to me . . . "

He trailed off and went very pale. We looked in each other's eyes for a moment. Then he put a hand to his forehead and began murmuring to himself in French, too low and too fast for me to make anything out.

I was in no shape to comfort him. I made an excuse and went back to my room. I read the scant lines in this notebook, over and over again. 'Onalenna'—that was her name. But I only know it because it is written here. It does not ring a bell.

I think we are all going to die out here. I hope we will die.

Harmony I: Day ???

How long has it been since I wrote in this notebook? A day? Five years?

It must have been a long time. Everything is in disarray. Wails and screams echo through the metal halls.

I remember nothing. I am not even completely sure that I am Moremi Maele. My only memory—recent? Or old?—is this:

I held a human heart in my hands.

Blood covered my fingers and stained my jumpsuit. I knelt and held the heart up to a woman, speaking words I no longer remember. She was cold and indescribably beautiful.

I remember a split second of revulsion on her face. And then a change, a sort of crumbling. In that moment, as I knelt before her, she *gave in*. She began to laugh. The stars laughed around us. I felt an odd, surging joy. We were theirs, now. Together, we had crossed the point of no return.

That is all I remember. I don't know what it means. I don't know if it is a real memory or a false vision. I don't know for sure whose heart it was, though I think I know. Call me cowardly. I can't bring myself to go look in his cabin. Instead, I sit with this notebook. Waiting, though I can't say for what.

Is Henri dead?

Is Moremi Maele, in any sense, still alive?

ᚤᛊᚺᛊᚾ

THE COMET CALLED ITHAQUA

Don Webb

Don Webb began writing in a class at Texas Tech University in 1983. Since then, he has had fifteen books in English and one book in German in his name. He teaches creative writing on-line at UCLA. His next two books are a nonfiction book, dark esoterica *Uncle Setnakt's Nightbook* from Runa Raven Press, and a collection of vampire stories, *A Velvet of Vampyres* from Wildside Press.

The first time, it was necessary.

It was centuries ago, during the Belatrin Wars. We were on the scoutship *Fulton*. One of our robots was a Belatrin spy with cunningly faked asimovs. It smashed our hydroponics, our communications, our Dirac drive. Melting it to slag relieved little of our anxiety. Two days without food honed our anxiety to high sharpness. None of us had ever been hungry before. Hunger was an impersonal, historical, statistical thing—so many million in Ethiopia in the 20th century, in Brazil in the 21st, on Mars in the 25th. The personally-new phenomenon of hunger displaced the transpersonally-new phenomenon of civilisation very quickly.

Doc talked about it first. She was probably the bravest of my shipmates. She'd spent hours trying to repair the hydroponics with the few tools the robot hadn't managed to dump. She had also repaired one Cold Sleep unit.

"One of us could take the Cold Sleep. The rest could kill themselves painlessly," she told us afterward.

"Or eat each other," said Vance.

"I'm not getting into the Cold Sleep," I said. "Any of you could raise the temperature a little and provide several kilos of meat."

"Several kilos," said Roxanne, patting my paunch. Captain Oe silenced us with one of his deep-space glares. Captain Oe was always on a distant planet, his quiet voice coming across cold light years. Why didn't he make with the bread-and-fishes routine? Isn't that the function of captains?

Killing Vance was easy. He was bending over a circuit tracer, building a simple radio. He thought the folks back home should know that the valiant *Fulton* was lost. I drove a microsolder into the nape of his neck and out through his Adam's apple.

Captain Oe discovered the body. His mineral calm hid any reaction. I think Doc suggested we cook him. Doc and I did the honours, producing a very serviceable sweet-and-sour Vance.

No one wanted to begin. The Captain ordered us to it. It was difficult to keep the meat down. We had diced the flesh well, so no part would be recognizable. No one mentioned that Vance had obviously been killed. Thus, we became murderers all.

Doc and I had removed Vance's liver and lungs. She feared they might be poisonous—contaminated by Vance's addiction to tobacco.

By our fourth meal, I had overcome my nausea. I viewed everyone else as items for future menus. They were too affected by disgust to notice my change. I left the meal still hungry, still empty, and tried to sleep on my bunk.

I kept thinking of the liver and lungs. Doc had refrigerated them, since we lacked means of recycling our wastes. The refrigerator could only hold so much. The *Fulton* stank like a sewer. If I ate the inner organs, I would either die or be sated. Either would end the gnawing pain of my stomach.

I crept to the medical room to remove the meat. I let it thaw on the surgical table. I collected some of Doc's tools—they might be useful later. I watched the dim light of Aldebaran through the port, wishing the scene would magically change to the grey of hyperspace.

When the liver was fairly well-thawed—juicy on the outside and crunchy ice crystals in the middle—I bit into it. Unfortunately Doc entered the lab at this moment.She viewed the blood streaming down my cheeks with something less than affection. I put the liver down. I pleaded, "Help me." She moved forward and I turned on a scalpel. Laser scalpels only cut a few centimeters, but this is adequate when the heart is your target.

I quartered her and hauled the bits to the in-system probe. I sealed us off. I activated all the sensors.

I felt no need to refrigerate the corpse and, in fact, enjoyed it more as it began to ripen.

They began pounding on the bulkhead hours later. First, they demanded that I surrender. A day later, they demanded their share of the meat. I watched my telemetry, ate, and slept. I did not dream. Dreaming was the first facet of humanity I lost.

Two days later, as I sliced some of Doc's hams—I still used instruments in those days—a green light blinked out. I would need to act fast or I would lose out on the kill. Had Oe honorably committed seppuku? Or had his martial training removed Roxanne as Executive Officer? Or had Roxanne, herself, mastered the murderous act?

The *Fulton* smelled very bad. A hint of sesame oil overlaid the stench—Oe preparing a delicate Oriental dish. Moo-Shu Roxanne? I went deep into engineering. I activated one of our dumbest robots and told it to walk into the kitchen. I called Oe up, told him I would surrender to him.

I followed the robot. The kitchen portal dilated and Oe fired. He must have been crazed. No one would use a ranged weapon within a spaceship. Fortunately, the robot's body absorbed most of the blast and no exterior bulkheads were breached.

The energy weapon triggered internal security. Poor Oe. If he'd only reasoned. Microsolders and scalpels are not weapons. Scores of idiot robots came to restrain him. In the brig, he decided to join his honourable ancestors.

Weeks later, when my meat supply was exhausted, I completed Vance's radio and put myself in Cold Sleep. Fifty-six years passed in the twinkling of an eye. The rescue team was very, very understanding. There had been cases of survival cannibalism in the past. Of course, I would have to undergo therapy to expunge the terrible guilt I must feel. Then I could join the service, again. Of course, I could live pretty well on 56 years of back pay, as well.

They sent me to Tarsis Hospital on Mars. Within a week, I knew three things: 1. Therapy consisted of producing the "right" answers to an AI's endless questions—a job even a moral moron could fake. 2. Their pills— which they gave me in great, multicoloured fistfuls—had no effect on me. 3. I couldn't eat the food they provided. I wasn't hungry or in need. I'd grown a thick layer of fat on the *Fulton*. I vomited up the first few meals and then I asked if I could take my meals in private. Understandingly, they agreed. I kept the food until it was moldy—then I could at least bear to eat it. But it didn't satisfy. Something was missing.

As my therapy progressed, I was allowed the freedom of the city. A small congregation followed the teaching of the blessed Zoroaster and placed their dead in a Tower of Silence, to be devoured by genetically engineered buzzards. I visited the Tower by the light of the double moons to cut hunks of flesh from the Zoroastrian dead. I couldn't eat them there in the thin Martian atmosphere, but carried the slices back in my total environment suit to the domed city. Needless to say, I shot all the pseudo-buzzards. Who needs competition?

The hospital had a huge library. I read endlessly about cannibalism and ghouls. Certain Arabic texts were helpful. I wasn't alone. There was little biology—no clear information to aid me in my survival. What were my vulnerabilities? What were my strengths? If I wrote a manual for future ghouls—who would publish it?

One legend touched me more than the others. It turned me as I have never been turned before. Certain Amerindians spoke of the Wendigo.

A party of hunters becomes lost in the snow. They find a cave. Eventually, they must kill one another for survival. One of the party loses his disgust at eating long pig. He warns the other survivor(s), "You must go. I am a Wendigo." They flee in pious terror. The rogue warrior lives on, becoming like a wild beast—long of tooth and claw. Eventually, the tribe destroys this raider with many arrows.

Other legends said that the Wendigo was Ithaqua the Wind Walker, a terrible god of storms and ice. This being could only be bought off with human sacrifice. They would lead the wretches deep into the snowy forest and leave them there to freeze. The remains were found miles away. Fiery, cold eyes could be seen among the trees, the true spirit of deep space—of pure Hunger as a ball of mind-wrenchingly-*cold* fire. *Iä Ithaqua!*

There was no attempt to match the legends of Arab ghouls and Canadian cannibals with whatever lived in my soul, but I felt they were connected.

I began to use makeup to cover the dull grey of my complexion. Bright light—a blessedly rare commodity in the domed cities of Mars— discomforted me greatly. I thought I might have a mutated form of pellagra, a disease that causes its victims to desire blood, but decided I suffered from a deeper spiritual change. Unlike most spacefarers, I had no mystical side, no prayer, no meditations—I had an emptiness inside where the Cold Hungry One could live. It ate my soul in the Great Dark and now, it would eat everything. I was happy. I finally had a purpose.

I had no social life, but my warders felt that was because I was a man of the last century—I simply had no one to talk to. Would that my estrangement from humankind were so simple! I began to stalk the streets at night, but I knew this was only a temporary solution. My killings didn't fit in their computer yet, but as the problem expanded from computer to computer, my research would be discovered.

I visited the Tower of Silence, having noted the death of a Parsi merchant in the weekly data. As I sliced into his corpulent paunch, I knew I was not alone. I looked up.Far away—to the west—I saw two carmine stars where no stars should be. A red haze swirled about them. It was Ithaqua, my soul. I removed my respirator.I could breath the thin Martian air. I thanked my new god as I greedily feasted on the corpse.

An opportunity arose soon afterwards to ship out on a deadliner ship. With my seniority, I got on easily. A "deadliner" is a term invented by the 20th century philosopher Barrington Bayley. It's a spaceman gone for decades at a time, a victim of time dilation who has become totally removed from human warmth and kindness. When they're in port, they know everyone they see will be dust before they return. I felt at home among those dead souls. Deadliners go deep into the galaxy, further than I'd ever been. Some of the crew actually had birthdates decades before mine. In a ship of such individualists, I could stalk easily. I signed on as 'Albert Donner,' a famous miner and cannibal of the 19th century. Even a ghoul can have his little jokes.

A light month past the solar system, I began to let my claws grow. They were semi-retractable. I could pass in human society. Especially in deadliner society—for deadliners never look too closely at their shipmates. They're always spiraling inwards.

A young-looking computer tech with magnificent red hair would be my first target. I stalked her quietly, waiting for my moment. When the moment came, I ripped her tender, white throat open with my claws. I carefully placed the bleeding body on plastic to avoid telltale bloodstains.

I hadn't taken the security of a deadliner ship into account. These people often kill each other. The stresses of the long voyage overcome all of their civilised traits. The ship was ready. It snared me in hundreds of tiny robot arms.

They didn't give me a trial, didn't ask me anything. They came into normal space and shoved me through the airlock.

I felt all the air sucked from my lungs. I screamed the call in the silence of airless space. Ithaqua came and filled me and changed me. *Oh, my burning feet of freezing fire!* As the ancient wind god, long since banished from the Earth by disbelief, filled me, he changed me into a burning ball of hunger and hate.

I travel through the void at great speeds. I will return to Earth. I will eat you all, every one.

PHOENIX WOMAN

Kelda Crich

Kelda Crich is a new-born entity. She's been lurking in her host's mind for some time, but now, she wants her own credits. Find her in the intestines of London, laughing at the status quo, or on her blog, (It's about time she got one of her own): keldacrichblog.blogspot.com.

Rising phoenix, garmented in
plumed rust-red feathers,
groomed with persistent
nano-mites.
Gene-modded eyes stretched endlessly
into infinity's seeing vision.
Iron talons flexed,
a promise of rendition.

Warrior-women-bird.
See dust-eyed, endless men
chant and dance
to bone flutes' tunes.
The priest masked in yellow silk
on a gold throne,
spanning altar stone.

Phoenix arch over
dust-dry plains,
sucked dry by thirty, thirsty gods.
Shapes of chaos, crawling slowly,
digesting our colony bones.

Metallic-bird-woman,
seek the wind-walkers,
seek crowded chaos,
the ocean's spawning flesh,
rise over jungles' colossal shapes,
ancient teeth,
fed by fluttering mouths
grown in marrow-wood stars.

Seek the space of things.
Fly, phoenix,
born in our end of days.
Hosanna hunting song
that will not be stilled.
Over endless factories,
Where our recurring flesh
quivers in Fibonacci sequence,
Mandelbrot tentacles around our necks.
Rise, phoenix.
With down-blind-cast eyes, we watch you.

POSTFLESH

Paul Jessup

Paul Jessup: Published in a slew of magazines (in print & online) and a mess of anthologies. Has a short story collection out (*Glass Coffin Girls*) published in the UK by PS Publishing. Have a novella published by Apex Books (*Open Your Eyes*) and a graphic novel published by Chronicle Books.

1. Captain Found Us a Ghost World

Shadrim. It was a grave of space, a planet of bones. It was the endless all and everything. Shadrim. When we discovered it, we found it full of ruins and corpses. Shadrim. When it discovered us, it was thinking. Shadrim. It had the grave thoughts. Thoughts that only the dead could or would want to think. Filtering through the entire planet.

When we found it, we were lost. It sent out beacons, psychic signals across the radio waves. Old Gray Mack thought it was perverse. We all laughed at his thoughts. Mack could fly the darkness like no one else. But he didn't know anything about the human mind—the world between the waves.

When we landed, we saw the big, bronze skull-city-states; we saw the machines they had left behind. Large spider beasts. Evolved, transfigured. Machines with alien skin stuck to the grindbones, scuttling through those ruins and making the corpses dance. First time we saw that sight, we wanted to leave. Big alien bones with zombie skin still stuck on them, prancing around in nightmare waltzes. We ran like hell away from them. They didn't follow. They stayed behind, dancing and staring with ghost eyes.

When we got back to the ship, it was dead. Buried in the ground with a grave on top. All that was left was ash and skeleton. A breathing thing that sustained us, gone and dead now. Like Manhome, itself.

Carit wept and Sunday Jay said a prayer in Pascal. It was the way Sunday Jay talked to the onboard systems. Through Pascal. Sure, it was an old language, but we are an old people, wandering the restless void of space and searching for ourselves in the reflection of the cosmos.

The next day, we found that dog that did our ship in. Giant machine thing that kept piecing itself together out of the ruins of the world around us. It was a sea of corpses and machinery. It looked at us with alien eyes, and Good Day just smiled at it and offered it a smoke.

Carit cursed it. Claimed it killed the ship and kept us trapped here. We couldn't look at that alien thing, covered in ship blood and the strings of organic machinery. It kept trying to talk to us, talk to us over the radio sounds of the dead. It was so lonely.

But we couldn't. Not now. Even though it promised us so much. Faster-than-light travel. Becoming transhuman. Existing beyond the realm of mortality. We couldn't let it know how we felt. How it hurt us and stranded us in the depth of space. The Captain even went out and got the zox box and shocked it around. This machine seemed to love it. It squealed with delight and then asked us if we had anything yet for dinner.

Good Day stepped forward and told it we were all starving. The creature had a few nanokin whip us up some good stuff. It tasted all right, for alien metal food. And we thought, this giant postflesh spacecat couldn't be all that bad. Sure it killed our ship, but that space trawler was dying anyway. Maybe it was a mercy killing.

Later that night, we slept under the frozen, purple light of 14 distant suns. They were moon-sized in the distance, spread across the sky and shouting out the light of the stars. The pull of this world was dizzying and complex. It weaved through the orbits of so many planets and suns. It was like a drunk, fractal nightmare of astronomical physics.

When we dreamed, we dreamed in ghost voices. We dreamed of ghost algebra on a ghost planet. This world, it spoke in our sleep and screamed in our waking hours through the radio towers broadcasting around us. The bones were restless, dancing. When the last hour of sleep washed away, we were greeted with the beating of techno drums and the dancing of the alien corpses.

And this time, they sang.

2. We Discuss Ghost Dreams

Spillgal was the first to do it. She just sat up like a white cat with black eyes, stretched out her tail and started talking. Her voice meandered at first, wandering over our heads. But then we realised what she was talking about, and we leaned in and listened.

Even that big A.I., that giant shipkiller corpse-monster, it bent the massive head down, dripping with columns and garbage and rotting, alien flesh, and listened. We had to filter out the screams of the dead in order to hear her properly.

Her voice was like static, noise in the broadcast of Shadrim. "I dreamt of endless space, and vacuum tubes. I dreamt of a doll without eyes and a lady without teeth. I dreamt that I licked the feet of secrets and they gave me bones to pay for a ship. I think I dreamt memories, but I can't be sure. So many voices, lost in my head. Even as I am awake now, I am almost certain I am still dreaming."

We talked about her dream for a bit, discussing its contents but coming to no conclusion. Whisper Kid went next, talking about smoke and a guy named 'Kagaratz'. Each of us went in turn, and each dream was discussed, but without any answers. Finally, at the end, the Captain sat up and proclaimed that he would build us a new space ship, one to take us home.

The dead aliens scuttled away, screaming. Our dreams were a gift. They felt insulted that the Captain would not stay and experience more of them. The giant machine that was our host ticked his head to the side and sighed, getting the nanokin to make us a meal of tin and scraskin. It tasted worse than it looked, but we ate it.

After that, we were less welcome on the planet of the dead. Our host kept ignoring us and the broadcast screams of the lost world got so loud that we became just static and noise in the background. It was hard to think like that, but we had to. It was a learning process, a way of filtering ourselves out from the void that tried to swallow us.

3. Skullchic Finds Material

We scavenged the world for parts and pieces, but of course, we couldn't go too far. There were a lot of alien machines, but we couldn't make sense out of any of it. And our host wasn't talking to us, anymore. He kept towering over us, watching and recording us with thousands of nanocams. We could see them scuttle about his massive body like living dust.

And the corpses—they were mad. They hung on the edge of our vision, running through the ruined city and howling in a dead tongue, their voices projected just barely above that load broadcast of ghost voices and ghost memories.

And we starved. Hunger laced through our veins, spilling over into our thoughts. All we dwelled on was the memory of food. Of great things like pancakes and waffles and syrup and strawberries and tomatoes. No vegetation was on this planet, nor any living meat we could kill and fry up.

In the hour of our greatest hunger, Skullgirl found some parts. At first, we weren't sure what she had—it looked like some skeleton from an alien body, with a glowing, orange heart. But metallic, and carved with cold, foreign pictographs.

The Captain knew what it was, knew what to do with it.

He kissed her in joy and we all screamed. The voices got louder and that AI started to crumble into smaller pieces around us. We fitted each part in and assembled it right and proper. The Captain got Old Grey Mack to study the controls and then to figure out a way for us to interface with it.

Old Grey Mack was great at that sort of thing. He was a xenoarcheologist, a regular alien retrofitter. He could sew these things into the right pieces of his mind, find out exactly how their propulsion system differed from our ion drives. He was used to this sort of thing—rearranging his mind into alien shapes and geometry.

Soon, we had a working model up and running. Time for a test drive and then off to freedom.

4. We Gasp, We Sigh, We Say Goodbye

It was a rough-looking space vessel, made from the alien boneparts we found and some old stuff from our ship, strapped on so that Old Grey Mack could pilot it without a problem. More like a shambling, half-dead animal than a cruiser, it spun around the atmosphere and screamed as it flew in chaotic, messy lines. Our host watched, his body slinking into sludge parts, the air filtered with his nanodust. He tried to get the alien corpses to dance a goodbye dance, but he could not get them to come near us.

In the moment of the test departure, those dancing corpses came out again, screaming and running towards us. Mack was flying low in the sky, looking down. The machine worked, leaving trails of blue light behind it in whirling vapours. Mack smiled and gave us the thumbs up to say that everything was okay. He flew a little lower, getting ready to find some open ground to land on.

Our host collapsed into thousands of tiny bodies, trying to restrain the living dead's nanosystems. They surged and came forward, crying out and scurrying across the floors of the world, with many thin and angular limbs. Like undead spiders, with big, bulging eyes and tiny, puckered lips.

The planet shook; the radio systems picked up. It was all one voice now, the voice of Shadrim, that zombie planet that wanted us to stay here and be assimilated into its nightmarish ecosystem. The voice of the planet spoke in strange tongues and the nanomachines obeyed. We tried to get Mack to land, to drop down something we could cling onto and escape. He only hovered low, a look of shock and horror on his face.

The dust of the world poured into us. Living things, tiny AIs, pieces of that host that kept us here for so long. Mack just circled about and watched as we were disassembled, our parts and pieces connected to the ruins, now. They strung up our bodies like art, our intestines and bones collected with bacterial computers and small nanomachines, that somehow preserved us and made us do what the world told us to.

In our minds, we could hear it all the time. The thought, running through our veins like the whispers of space. Commanding us. Telling us what to do. Our We had gotten bigger, engulfed us. We had one mind now, the mind of the world. The mind of the ghost planet. It sang in our skin, set our nerves on fire.

And now we danced. We danced and our voices broadcast from those old radio waves. This was the radio song, the voice of Planet Shadrim. This was us and who we were. Mack sped off and we would have, too. But now we were dancing, our corpseskin cold. Soon, we would transcend. Transcend and be like our host, postflesh.

꓾꒐ꖸꙄꓵ

THE LIBRARY TWINS AND THE NEKROBEES
Martha Hubbard

Martha Hubbard lives on an island in the North Baltic Sea. For thousands of years a place of strange gods, mysteries, tragedies, and wonder, Saaremaa Island provides the perfect bedrock for a writer of dark fantasy. Previously, she has been a teacher, cook, stage manager, dramaturg in New York City's Off-Off Broadway community, a parking lot company bookkeeper, and a community development worker. Recently, she put aside some of these activities to concentrate on her writing, but is still the Consulting Chef for the local Organic Farmers Union. Her story, "The Good Bishop Pays the Price," appeared in Innsmouth Free Press's anthology, *Historical Lovecraft*, and "I Tarocchi Dei d'Este" is in their *Candle in the Attic Window*.

All around their hiding place, towering stacks of books careened upwards, their tops vanishing into murky darkness. Iris and Thyme Carter were on a late-night stakeout in the National Library of France because something was disturbing *their* books after hours, making them whimper and cry like hurt children. During the day, automatic lights flashed on if any moving object larger than a butterfly intercepted the infrared sensors. At night, these were switched off to save money, which meant that any creature entering these cathedrals of dust and paper then had to navigate in the dark. This was no problem for the 'library twins,' as one of their genetic abnormalities was ultra-keen night vision; darkness was their friend. Now, at almost 23:00, the twins were hiding in a section reserved for French and Italian fiction.

One of Iris's sometimes-disturbing genetic gifts was the ability to hear the voices of inanimate objects. Chairs, plants, street lamps, and bridges had, at one time or another, spoken directly to her. The pitiful moaning of tortured books had been disturbing Iris' dreams for days. When the painful cries of her precious charges finally made sleep impossible, she insisted that Thyme join her in uncovering what was distressing them.

Iris was slumped on the floor, her back against a shelf of Italian mysteries, a first edition of Emile Zola's *Thérèse Raquin* on her lap. Wearing disposable, white, cotton gloves, she was turning the brittle pages one by one, trying to discern any changes in the text as she remembered it. Lately, some of her favourite novels had begun to seem strangely . . . *different*.

ɔﾄɜ

By the end of the 21st century, most reading material was read on electronic devices, when it wasn't injected directly into the neurological pathways via learning tubes. Real books, of cloth and paper, were the cherished artefacts of a vanished era. To preserve these, librarians had gathered most of them into a scant handful of libraries in the Western world. The BNFP (Bibliothèque Nationale de France, Paris) held works from Continental Europe: France, Italy, the Low Countries, Greece, and Germany. Harvard held American and Canadian literature, and technical and early medical texts. Berkeley—Micronesia and Australia, Maori and Aboriginal; The British Library—British and Russian—a bow to Karl Marx; the National Library of San Paolo—South American, Mexican and Spanish. There were smaller collections in Helsinki for Nordic works and Budapest for Central European. Reprieved from destruction at the last possible moment, these were considered the foundation blocks of Western thought.

Human hands were not normally allowed near any of the books protected in these specialised archives. Scholars who had been able to demonstrate a need to consult the originals used hermetically-sealed, climate-and-light-controlled boxes. Inside these, internal robotic fingers turned the pages, when instructed via touch pad. It wasn't like holding a real book in your hands, but it was better than having the pages disintegrate from careless handling.

Curator of this section, Iris was one of the few allowed to touch these books. While they waited for intruders, she methodically reread the pages of *her children* for anomalies. Possessing photographic recall, she remembered by 'seeing' things—pages of books for example—in her mind-viewer, and could instantly detect any textural alterations. As the minutes ticked towards midnight, she was wondering if it had all been a bad dream. "Great Goddess, how did we get here?" she whispered to her sister.

ᗑᛸᛠ

Good question. As the famous frog once said, "It's not easy being green." While not green in appearance, the twins had grown up profoundly committed to the repair and protection of the environment.

By the middle of the 21st century, any thinking person, by then a declining species, understood that the pernicious effects of extensive agribusiness farming was transforming the residents of wealthy countries into slow-moving, cancer-ridden, dull-minded robots. The proliferation of foodstuffs assembled from refined corn syrup had created a sub-class of citizenry no longer able to discriminate healthy food from toxic. Soya derivatives mixed with reconfigured corn syrup, flavoured by e-numbers, were mashed and extruded into an endless variety of products. Diets consisting of little more than sugar, cellulose and food colouring made consumers sluggish and unhealthy. Sugar-induced torpor meant that, as people moved less and less, bones became dangerously brittle. Physical education programs in schools had long been abandoned because even the youngest children could not run or jump or risk the fractures that ensued from the smallest of accidents.

Early on, some people had developed Multiple Chemical Sensibilities (MCS)—in other words, they had become allergic to almost everything in their surroundings. Forced by their illnesses to escape the dangers presented by polluted water, air, soil, and food, many had retreated to guarded rural enclaves, as far from the centres of toxicity as possible, where they produced their own food, tried to live more sensible lives, and campaigned for more sensible farming and food production practices. America had become that dreaded hydra—a two-tiered society: one part, physically and mentally active and healthy; the other, physically incapable, diabetes-ridden and mentally incompetent.

Others, recognising the dangers before irreversible damage had been done to their biosystems, voluntarily removed themselves from the locations of greatest pollution.

Iris and Thyme's parents had been among the first wave to recognise these growing environmental hazards. When Mama Carter learned she was carrying twins, she insisted they move to an island off the coast of Maine to gestate their babies. There, with other like-minded families, the community grew its own vegetables, raised sheep and chickens, and fished. Mama had been determined that her children's minds and bodies would not be compromised by the toxicity of American supermarket offerings. As with so many well-laid plans, there had been a glitch. The elder Carters and their community had not anticipated the changes wrought in the seas by agricultural run-off.

When the twins were born, they seemed perfect: healthy bodies, smiling faces, prodigious lungs, which they demonstrated when annoyed or hungry. However, as they grew, they began to display some unusual abilities. For one thing, they could talk to each other without words across vast distances. They could also change their shapes and, in the form of any winged creature, could fly. A call of distress from Thyme would produce Iris leading a swarm of threatening birds in seconds.

They had other skills, as well. Iris could see events in the past, and project herself and her sister into them, while Thyme seemed able to project into the future. Papa Carter had been so concerned about the twins getting lost, injured, or trapped in other time periods that he made them promise to not use these powers—at all—until they were older and, hopefully, wiser. They loved their Papa, so they promised. Safe on their beloved island, the twins grew up convinced of the need to respect and protect their world. The environment responded by making them tall, beautiful and clever. "If only they weren't twins and could have had individual styles, their lives would have been perfect," they said but only to each other.

Time passed. Outside their secluded enclave, awareness of the need for healthier food and respect for the environment had increased in some places, so it became safe to leave Maine. Besides, the twins needed more of an education than their isolated haven could provide. Iris chose to study at USC Berkeley, while Thyme remained on the East Coast and went to Harvard. When both elected to study Library Science, no one was surprised. During their years on the island, books, real paper books—not electronic tablets—had been their dearest companions.

While they were studying on opposing coasts, their parents, worn out by coping with an earth in turmoil, elected to take BDL (Bodily Life Cessation).

The twins were alone. When both were offered positions at the BNFP, they accepted. *What a lark,* they thought. They were twenty-four years old and had never left the States.

 כוﬡ

Relocation to France was blinding—a full-on blast. As so often in her past, Paris in the late decades of the 21st century had become a mecca for the world's wannabe creatives and misfits. Not that these incomers were incapable—far from it. The variety of physical presentations and unusual abilities that had made them outcasts in societies composed mainly of sugar-munching trolls, made them ideally suited for life in 21st century Paris. These genetic newbies, who were too active, too lively, too noisy—too alive to be comfortable neighbours back home, found a warm welcome on the *rues* and *boulevards* of Paris.

Paris has always attracted a diverse collection of colourful immigrants. In the 20th century, refugees from France's colonial past, from Tunisia, Algeria and Morocco, from Viet Nam and Cambodia, had transformed certain *arrondissements* of the often-stuffy city into vibrant bazaars. Now, again, the streets teemed with a visual, aural and olfactory cacophony of colours, styles, foods, and music. Not since the 1920's had Parisian cafés vibrated with such a glittering array of gorgeous people and lively discussions. Her throbbing heart was the seedy, graffiti-decorated rue Belleville—far from the staid bourgeoisie of the riverbanks. Within a week, Iris and Thyme had an apartment on a high floor overlooking the *parc,* its creaky, wrought-iron-curlicue cage lift operated by state-of-the art computers. They dove into their new life, ugly ducklings transforming into swans as they fell.

Work-wise, it was perfect. The library most called the "TGB" (*Très Grand Bibliothèque*), Mitterrand's monument to his ego, was also in the east of Paris, so required only one line change on the Metro. These were much less crowded than in the past, as so many people, unable to deal with stairs and walking long distances, worked from home. Mitterrand's *Very Big Library* had tottered along into the future, its concrete towers chipped and mouldering, without losing its cachet amongst scholars, or any of its over twenty million volumes. This became their second home, its books their *raison d'être.*

אלץ

Midnight found them sharing a sandwich. "Maybe we should give up," said Thyme. "If I don't get at least a little sleep, I'll be comatose during Monsieur le Directeur's scintillating presentation tomorrow."

"That's okay," said Iris. "You go home and catch up on your beauty sleep. I'll stand guard here."

"No way. Whatever this is, we're facing it together."

"That's the sister I know and love." Iris beamed her most radiant smile.

"You stay here. I'm going to take a quick flit around."

By down-shifting until she was as weightless as a hummingbird, Thyme could fly. Darting from shelf to shelf, up and down lightless rows of books, she was virtually invisible. Speeding round a corner, she had to backpedal her wings furiously to keep from colliding with a lighted flying object. Ducking into a space between two books of differing heights, she exclaimed, "What the . . . blathers is that?"

The glimmering purple thing buzzed and growled as it explored the shelves. It seemed unaware of her. Stopping near the end of the row she had just exited, it turned and hung, briefly motionless, before emitting a piercing, saw-like whistle. Out of the gloom behind, a phalanx of glowing, flying creatures appeared, moving up the rows and fanning out in groups, violet lights flickering on and off inside their rotund bodies. Clearly, they were looking for something—a book, perhaps. *I'll be damned*, thought Thyme. *They're bees—sentient, purple, light-producing bees.*

As soon as the last of the platoon had passed her, their buzzing communication mode and regimented behaviour marking them as soldiers on a reconnaissance mission, Thyme headed back to Iris as quickly and soundlessly as her tiny wings could take her. "Iris, Iris, wake up. We're being invaded by bees."

"Huh! Killer bees? . . . I wasn't asleep."

"I don't know about the 'killer part,' but they're purple, smart, and they're looking for something."

"Our books! They're after our books. *Merde!* Those . . . those . . . " Iris couldn't think of an expletive harsh enough. "Thyme, we have to stop them."

"Shh . . . quiet! You're right, but let's think about this before we rush in like Wyatt Earp at the OK Corral."

"No rushing, there—it was a standoff, one gunman against another."

"That's just what we could be facing—a standoff between a regiment of killer bees and two defenceless young women," said Thyme.

"With special powers—don't forget our special powers."

"They have special powers, too. Have you ever looked at that book they keep locked up in M. le Directeur's safe?"

"The one we're not supposed to know is there . . . the *Necronomicon*?"

"That one. I think they have something to do with it. I have the feeling these flying terrorists are Nekrobees."

"If that's the case, we could be in way over our heads." Iris flopped onto the floor, her head in her hands.

"When has that ever stopped us? Come on. We'll think of something."

The sisters put their heads together, to communicate telepathically. Wanting to make surprise one of their weapons, they decided to follow a single bee, in order to determine what the group was up to. Downsizing to the dimensions of baby dragonflies, they zoomed to the top of the stacks, so they could hover over the entire collection. From there, they watched the bees moving through the stacks. They seemed to be reading the book titles on the spines. "I didn't think bees could read French," whispered Iris.

"We've already agreed that these aren't ordinary bees."

"No, they're not . . . but . . . ah . . . look there, that lazy one . . . it's falling behind the others."

No matter how well-drilled an army, even of rampaging sentient bees, there's always at least one who can't or won't keep up. Iris and Thyme had found a slacker.

Taking advantage of their diminished size, they flitted and darted behind the lone, lazy bee as it fell farther and farther behind the main group, stopping every few shelves for several seconds before moving on. "What a lazy plodder. It isn't helping its fellows at all," said Thyme.

"I think it's looking for a place to sleep until the pack comes back."

"You could be right. Look at that."

The slow, and really, rather-size-challenged nekrobee had slipped between two books, its violet glow dimming to a memory. "What do we do now?" asked Iris.

"I'm not sure. I think we've got company. Look behind you."

"They look angry. Do they look angry to you?"

Five flashing purple bees had appeared behind them. Another group materialised around a corner, while a third cluster zoomed down from the top of a row. As the twins attempted a tactical retreat toward the front of the stacks, still another group appeared, cutting them off. They were surrounded.

"Yes, Iris. They look angry to me."

"Damnit, we've been ambushed. . . . "

"Led into a trap . . . "

" . . . by our own carelessness."

"Now what do we do?"

That question was answered by the bees. Buzzing, they circled the girls, who had retaken normal size in hopes of improving the odds. Not a chance. The bees darted in, stingers first, trying for an arm or a cheek. To avoid them, Iris and Thyme waved books pulled from the shelves. It was hopeless. Any attempt to deviate or escape was countered by a cloud of angry, purple insects. Inexorably, the bees manoeuvred the girls deeper into the darkness. After five minutes, the twins had run out of stacks, books and ideas. All the while, in the far back, an eye, set into an opaque black circle, watched the melee.

"Iris, that wasn't here the last time I checked."

"It's here now, sister, and we're about to go through it."

Unblinking, it had followed their frantic attempts to escape. Once they were flat against it, the eye swirled open. Surrounded by irritated buzzing, the girls exploded through the sable pupil into a lightless cavern.

Behind them, the eye clanged shut. Far ahead, violet lights glowed in the darkness. The bees pushed them towards it. "They really like this colour," mouthed Iris.

"When we get out of here, I'll never look at a lilac bush in same way again."

"If we get out."

They were moving down a tunnel with smooth, slippery sides. Deeper in, it was lit by flashing bees nailed at intervals to the ceiling.

"I wonder how often they change the bulbs," said Thyme.

"Don't joke. Those poor things."

"Those 'poor things' may be herding us to our deaths."

Ten metres ahead, the tunnel widened into a chamber, its walls covered in markings that looked like writing, but indecipherable. A short, man-like creature, dwarfed by four angular stick insects, waited in the centre.

"Iris." Thyme poked her sister. "Check out the vertically-challenged dude with the basketball-player bodyguard?"

"My, my, he is short. Looks like a jack-o'-lantern plopped on top of a pumpkin."

"His mother must have had a mega case of carotene poisoning when she was carrying him."

"I don't fancy the look of his bodyguard, either. Green stick insect is not this season's best fashion choice."

Mr Pumpkin Man strutted up to the twins. "You two have caused me a very great amount of difficulty. That wasn't nice."

"What funny noises it makes," Thyme said. "They sound like they're being generated by a machine."

"No talking," he barked. "When I want to hear your voices, I'll tell you. Now, be quiet and follow me."

"Why should we do that?" Thyme demanded.

"Because, if you don't, I shall have one of my very tall and very hungry friends crunch off your sister's arm."

"You and what army?" Iris shifted from human form into a small, stinging creature. "They'll have to catch me first." She swooped in and landing a dart, right on the creature's shiny, orange head.

"Ouch! Get her! Don't kill her!" Pumpkin Man screamed. "IT wants them alive."

The tallest of the Praying-Mantis creatures waved a raptorial leg at Iris, its mandible clicking commands. She darted away, but was soon cornered. With all four trying to grab her, she wouldn't hold out for long.

"Leave my sister alone!" Thyme, shifting as she screamed, swooped at the Mantis Leader's eye. It roared and thrashed in pain, all four pairs of legs flailing, lopping off feelers and bits of other mantises. Iris tried to escape the melee and flew straight into a wall of nekrobees. Ominous, saw-like buzzing broadcast how angry they were. Once again, they herded the twins, pushing them deeper into the cavern until the girls teetered on the edge of a cliff. Behind them gaped a long drop into nothingness. "Are you ready, sister?" said Iris.

"Ready when you are." They jumped.

Endless hours, or seconds, passed. It was impossible to tell. All perception of time had vanished. The bottom, when it arrived, did so without warning. They landed—Splot!—in a puddle of sticky, foul-smelling, purple goo.

"I'm really beginning to hate this colour," said Iris.

"Me, too. What's that stink?"

Iris leaned closer to the puddle and sniffed. "It's from the Dragon Arum (*Dracunculus vulgaris*), I think. Euch! Disgusting! The things I do for you."

"Is it dangerous?"

"Probably. I don't know. Never touched one before."

"Then I think we should get out of here as fast as possible. Damn!"

"Now what?"

"I'm stuck. Can you lift your arm?"

Iris jerked her arm upward; rubbery strings wrapped around her forearm pulled it back.

"Damn!"

Taking a deep breath, she bent over suddenly and pulled a knife out of her boot. Bouncing back up, she slashed at the tentacles holding her arm. The puddle creature writhed and hissed, releasing her. As it backed away growling, she moved to cut her sister free.

"That's better," said Thyme, rubbing her arm. "That was gross."

"You two are becoming very tiresome. First, you blind my avatar's guards and now, you've frightened my poor little dragon flower."

The twins swivelled around to discover an enormous, squishy-looking thing with waving tentacles and beady, purple eyes.

"What the . . . who or what are you?" Thyme demanded.

"More purple," muttered Iris.

"Many people have called me by many names; all were wrong and all were right."

"First, it tries to kill us, complains when we protect ourselves, and now answers our questions with stupid riddles." Thyme detested inconsistencies.

"If you must possess something as trivial as a name before answering my questions, 'The Elder God' will do as well as any."

"Thank you. I'm relieved we have that settled," said Iris.

"Now, will you have the courtesy to answer me? Whatever are you doing here? Why have you invaded my home?" While the creature was saying this, oily tentacles had extruded from hand-like appendages and were slithering across their faces, caressing their hair and examining their ear-cavities.

"Argh! What in the name of bastard kittens do you think you are doing?" Thyme barked.

"I'm trying to discover your weaknesses—your price. Everyone has one."

"And you think that rubbing slime and squid spit in our hair will make us reveal it?"

"Do you know a better way?" The mouth part of the monster smirked.

"Stop that!" Iris pushed an intrusive tentacle away from the corner of her eye socket.

"Yes. Why don't you just ask us what our price is?"

"What an intriguing idea. No one has ever suggested *that* before." The monster leaned back, appearing to be deep in thought. "All right, what is it that you care about more than all else in this life?"

"Books!" they shouted in unison.

"Ouch! Not so loud, if you please." Several tentacles clutched the places on its head where—in a humanoid—ears would be, and grimaced.

"Books, book, books!" they screamed again.

"Books on paper, whole books, old books, new books, books between cardboard covers . . . " shouted Thyme.

"With leather bindings," added Iris. "Unexpurgated, uncut, undoctored, unelectronic—real books!"

"Books for children—that they can hold."

"And young adults and students."

"All right, I get the point. So, tell me how I can use that to get you to leave my pets, my sweet little nekrobees, alone."

" 'Sweet little nekrobees,' " Thyme mimicked the Elder. "About as sweet as a tarantula crossed with a rattlesnake."

"You don't like my little pets?" it asked, as one settled on its frontal area. A tentacle reached down and caressed the bee before popping it into a mouth. Crunch and it was gone. The Elder belched a stench of rotting violets.

"Euw! Don't you ever brush your teeth?" Iris complained.

"My, you are a silly girl. Answer my question, please. How can I persuade you to stop persecuting my bees?"

"Keep the damnable, flying vermin out of our library," said Thyme.

"Oh, but I can't do that. They have work to do there—important work."

"What's that, then?" said Thyme.

"And what kind of work causes my books to cry and scream?" demanded Iris.

"Surgery is always painful—is it not?"

"Surgery! What kind of surgery?" They cried, this time in unison.

"When something is diseased or broken or wrong, it should be cut out, like a cancer. Don't you agree?"

"There are no cancers in my books, only ideas," said Iris.

"Ah, my dear Iris, I'm sure you would agree that ideas can sometimes be dangerous, that wrong ideas can spread like disease until they infect entire civilisations."

The creature's beaming, oily smile made Thyme want to smash her fist right into the middle of that blubbery gob.

Iris thought about The Elder's words before she answered. "I believe, if people read enough, are educated enough—think about hard things enough, they can protect themselves against dangerous ideas."

"My darling Iris, you are so idealistic. "

"I'm not your darling."

"And who gets to decide which ideas are good and which are dangerous?" Thyme demanded.

"In this case, I do."

"Wait! No . . . I get it." A shining yellow globe lit up above Iris' head. "That's what those horrid bees are doing. They're changing texts—to suit . . . YOU!"

"What a clever child you are."

"That's monstrous."

"Why bother? Nobody reads these books—nobody but us, anyway. The rest of the world gets its ideas from electronic libraries." Thyme, muttered.

"That's right. And where do you think electronic libraries get their texts from?"

"Huh?"

"Your books, and those in the other central depositories, are the foundation texts for all the world's electronic media."

"So, if you change our copy, you change all the rest."

"What smart little girlies you are."

Growling and hissing, Thyme was temporarily beyond speech, so Iris took up the cudgel.

"Let me see if I understand you correctly: You're not re-writing history . . . "

"That's so passé. Nobody believes what's in history books, anymore."

"Because monsters like you have re-written them so often."

"I'll ignore that, but yes, history books have become irrelevant. Facts don't influence individual actions—except for soldiers, anyway."

"And you think novels do?"

"Certainly. The world's great books form the underlying paradigms of all human behaviour."

"At least we agree on something. What's wrong with our books the way they are?"

"Oh, Iris, are you really so naïve? Your books are so nice . . . so moral. They have nothing to teach us about how to live in a modern world."

"You're saying that if Madame Bovary hadn't been so guilt-ridden, she wouldn't have ended up riding around the French countryside with her lover's head on her lap?"

"Exactly. Had she been more pragmatic, she'd have lived a long and happy life."

"Next, you'll say Anna Karenina shouldn't have thrown herself in front of that train."

"Stupid, stupid, stupid . . . a sorry waste of human resources."

"You think that, by changing the plots of great novels, you can influence how people behave? That's nonsense—nobody cares about literature these days."

"Not necessarily. Even if very few have read a particular book, everyone knows the basics. The ideas in them permeate our global consciousness."

"You think altering the core ideas in our books will change human behaviour?" said Thyme. "It won't work. Nobody but people like us reads, anymore. The general population won't be exposed to your changes," said Iris.

"That's because *your books*," the Elder sneered, "are so removed from real life. But if I and my bees bring these into line with current realities . . . Do you have any idea how many people think popular media—novels, TV, films . . . ARE the truth? Remember the flap back in the 'oughties caused by Dan Brown's *The Da Vinci Code?*"

"Yuck! Unfortunately." Iris looked as if she had bitten into something rotten and very bad-tasting.

Thyme said, "You want to Dan-Brownify our classical heritage?"

"Please." The creature looked affronted. "Nothing so egregious as that. I like to think I'm a better writer."

"Irrelevant. We can't allow you to pervert our books."

"How do you plan to stop me?" the monster sneered. The effrontery of these two simple young women delighted him.

"We'll burn the *Necronomicon*—all the copies, in all the depositories. How many copies exist? Five?" asked Thyme.

"Six," prompted Iris.

"You can't . . . you wouldn't do that," it said, horrified.

"We can and we will, if you don't leave our books alone."

"I . . . I will have to consider that . . . " The Elder retracted all its tentacles and humanoid features. The twins were facing a massive, featureless, stone obelisk.

"What's to think about? You leave our books alone or your book is a goner!" Thyme shouted.

"Dead, splat . . . ash," added Iris.

An eye and a speaking tube appeared. "I could kill you, or keep you here—turn you into ice statues."

"You could, but you won't," said Iris.

"Why is that, pray tell? Please enlighten me."

"Because our colleagues know we were looking for the source of the books' distress. If we don't return, they will initiate a meticulous search of the stacks." Iris was lying baldly, hoping the monster wouldn't guess.

"They'd find your eye into our world," added Thyme, smiling.

"Humphf!" grunted the Elder. "We seem to have reached something of an impasse."

"I would say so."

"Let me see if I understand this correctly: If I don't stop altering the books in your library, you will destroy the foundation document of my world, left for safe-keeping—and in good faith—in your TGB."

"That sums it up," said Thyme. "And all the other copies."

"If I promise to leave your books alone and return you safely to your blasted library, you promise to leave my books alone?"

"Done," said both.

"Do you promise never to come to my world again?"

"Definitely! I'd offer to shake on it, but I might vomit all over you."

"I'd rather you didn't." The Elder produced a high-pitched humming sound that continued for several seconds, bringing a phalanx of gangly mantis creatures at a gallop. "See that these two are delivered intact back to the portal from which they entered.'"

High, fluting voices responded. "Yes, Your Evilness! Nothing will happen to these ugly creatures while we clean them out of our home."

"Good. Now get them out of here."

The Mantis Guard, forming a tight square around Iris and Thyme, marched forward. There was no escape and nothing to be done but move with them. After about ten metres, the ground under their feet disappeared. They were flying upwards though what seemed to be a giant wormhole. As on the downward journey, time ceased to register until they were propelled through a membrane in the tunnel. Pop!—and they were back in the library.

"Ow, that was weird," said Iris. "Are you okay?"

"I think so."

"What time is it?"

Thyme looked at her watch, which had started working again, "It reads 22:00 hours. Can that be right? We're back before we left?"

"Let's go to the front desk and check."

As the twins walked through the tunnels of stacks towards the reception area, a soft, melodious humming began. "Iris, what's that?"

"I think the books are thanking us."

"Oh, how lovely."

In the cavernous, marble reception area, everything looked just as it always did. The brass clock above the main desk read 22:15. "Look at that," said Thyme. "It felt like we'd been gone for hundreds of years."

"But it was less than nothing . . . minus an hour. Weird."

"Seems so. I don't care right now. Let's go home."

"You took the words right out of my mouth."

"Didn't change them, though—did I?"

The twins went through the routines for securing the building; recalibrating and turning on the sensors, checking that all peripheral doors were closed and locked; setting the alarms; and, finally, locking the main entrance doors with their bronze bas-reliefs. Someone else could open them tomorrow. They were going to call in sick. They'd earned it.

Just as the heavy doors were clicking shut—way, way back at the end of the oldest, dustiest stack—a black eye opened and closed; a tiny violet light winked on and then out.

꓄ꕜꓱꖜꕯꓭ

GO, GO, GO, SAID THE BYAKHEE

Molly Tanzer

Molly Tanzer is the Managing Editor of *Lightspeed* and *Fantasy Magazine*. Her debut book, *A Pretty Mouth*, is forthcoming from Lazy Fascist Press in late 2012. Her fiction has appeared in *Running with the Pack*, *Historical Lovecraft*, *Lacuna*, *The Book of Cthulhu*, and other places, and is forthcoming in *Andromeda Spaceways Inflight Magazine*. She is an out-of-practice translator of ancient Greek, an infrequent blogger, and an avid admirer of the novels of eighteenth century England. Currently, she resides in Boulder, Colorado with her husband and a very bad cat. You can find her at mollytanzer.com More frequently she tweets over at @molly_the_tanz.

> . . . human kind
> cannot bear very much reality.
> Time past and time future
> What might have been and what has been
> Point to one end, which is always present.
> —T.S. Eliot

Wriggler lived in the lake, and when you didn't throw stones at him too much, he would bring up purple-scaled *balık* and tiny scuttling *yengeç* for roasty crunchings. Feathers lived in a hut in the treetops and she would help pick the highest-up *kayısı* when they were ripe and juicy—sometimes.

Feathers was mean. Half the time, if you so much as looked at her funny, she would open her mouth wide like an O and birdy squawks would come out, *eee eee eee*, which, true, were the only words she ever said since she changed, but she could make them sound so *angry*! No one cared if she was angry, though, because even with the wings, she couldn't fly. Wriggler could breathe underwater, and Whee! could swing from branch to branch with his long fuzzy tail, and Mister Pinch could bruise you with the handy claw on his extra arm, if he ever got mad at you. Ouch! Feathers, she looked like a birdy, but wasn't, quite. Everybody said it was because she didn't pray hard enough when she went on pilgrimage to Tuz Gölü, to see the Mother in the Salt.

Dicle was still a two-legs, two-hands, two-eyes, upright skin-wearer, so she still had her cradle-name that said nothing at all about who she really was. Bo-*ring!* But that would change soon, she knew it. When she went to fetch water, she could see, in the shiny surface of the well, two of the protuberances mammals and mostly-mammals got when they were ready to give live birth and suckle their young, and she'd had a dream about Wriggler coming to the surface and touching her between the legs with one of his long, bendy arms. Those were the signs, Whee! had said, but then again, Whee! couldn't be trusted, not completely. Whee! wanted to be the one Dicle took as a snuggler, once she was given her true shape by the Mother in the Salt. But Dicle knew she'd rather snuggle with Wriggler, even if they had to do it mostly underwater, so he could huff and puff through his gills.

But Stag-Face said Dicle wasn't ready for pilgrimage, or for huff-and-puff. Stag-Face said she was still a baby-girl and, since Stag-Face was the boss of everybody—those who'd visited the Mother in the Salt, those who hadn't yet, and *especially* those who failed—she had to heed him. She hated it, though! Ugh! Kids like her, they couldn't dance in the nightly revels, and they had to do all the worst chores, like climbing up the burning rocks to every single one of the hill-caves to dump out the piss-pots, or sweeping away the rubble to find the empty meat-shells when the earth shook and there were cave-ins, or weave reeds into wind-shields so people could sleep out of the dusty, gusting breezes. But Dicle didn't like climbing, and she didn't like to clear away rocks to find meat-shells, and she didn't like weaving, either. She liked to run as fast as she could and she could run so fast! Stag-Face said maybe she could be a messenger, once she was old enough. But she *was* old enough and that was why she'd come up with the secret plan.

Well, it wasn't a *total* secret. Wriggler knew, but he'd promised not to gurgle it to anyone else. In fact, he'd helped her by catching *balık* a-plenty, just for her. Dicle had built little fires and smoked them so she'd have food for the overnight journey to Tuz Gölü. She knew it was wrong to disobey Stag-Face, but ever since her mama had been crushed to death in the cave-in during the shivery months, Dicle had been restless. She was going to go on pilgrimage, whether mean old Stag-Face liked it or not, and when she went, she'd take her mama's bones to the Mother in the Salt, so Mama could really rest. The Mother in the Salt would be so very pleased she'd change Dicle just how she'd always wanted, and then Dicle would come home and snuggle with Wriggler and everything would be wonderful.

Ↄⴴ⟊

The morning she left, early-early she awoke, after the revelers were all in bed and before even the dawn-time scurriers were out and about. She snuck away at a run, the rucksack she'd stuffed full of Mama's bones and smoked *balık* bouncing on her back, the skin full of water slapping her hip. She'd also strapped a gleaming knife to her arm, so the beasties of the wood and the ghouls of the salt flats would see she was one dangerous girl. She bared her teeth as she ran, *grr!*

The path was made of cracked black stuff, and was smooth from ages and ages of people going to Tuz Gölü and elsewheres. Dicle wasn't scared, though—at least, not at first. Back during the shivery months, right after Mama had died, she'd gone down the path a fair way before Whee! had caught her and told Stag-Face. Stag-Face had beat her, bad, and Whee! had laughed at her. That, more than anything, was why he'd never-*ever* be her snuggler.

Everybody, even little, unchanged girlies like Dicle, knew that time and space were the same thing, except when they weren't. There were a few places around K'pah-doh-K'yah everyone knew to avoid, where, if your eyes worked right—which was no promise!—you could see how the trees grew backwards in time and would gobble you up, if you got too close to them. Stag-Face said those places were holy because, if you looked at them too long, or thought about them too hard while you were there, you'd get a nosebleed and that was the sign of the Mother in the Salt. Also, if an animal or person went there and he or she had a baby inside them, the baby would grow so fast it would tear its way out and make its mama or papa a meat-shell instead of a mama or a papa, and the baby would be a ghoul and never know anything except hunger. That was a bad thing and it happened a few times a year, even if everybody was careful, since time isn't always the same and, therefore, neither is space.

Dicle ran through a few of those Mother-places the first day of her pilgrimage (She ran as fast as she could, so time didn't slow down too much for her and make her journey take too long), but she saw more and more of them on the second day, as she drew closer to Tuz Gölü. She knew she was getting closer because all the trees had gone away, and she could taste salt on her lips when she licked them, and she was thirsty. She wasn't scared, though, because she didn't have a baby inside her and, if any of the ghouls said *boo!* to her, she showed them her knife and they slithered away back to their hidey-holes.

Then Dicle crested a hill, as the sun climbed as high as it could in the white-hot sky, and when she looked down into the valley, her eyes started to hurt from too much brightness. Ouch! But that was what Wriggler said would happen, so she knew she was in the right place. Below her stretched endless white: the Tuz Gölü, at last. When she shaded her eyes with her hand, she could see the altar at the edge of the pale lake, sitting a bit back from the shore. It was a rectangular box the size of the meeting-cave, with all these poles jutting from the top, holding up a big empty circle. The rectangular part had lots of holes in the side that Wriggler said weren't caves but little peep-holes covered in clear stuff that kept the wind out better than woven reeds. That was strange, but Dicle fought her urge to explore. Her business was with the sacred stair and what was at the top of it. She'd show the Mother how dedicated she was by staying focused.

So, Dicle ran toward the altar, her bare feet pounding the earth, every cut or scrape on her body smarting from the salty wind, but as she drew closer, she saw something and stopped so quickly she almost stumble-tumbled—something was crawling out of the Tuz Gölü and nothing was supposed to come out of the Tuz Gölü except the Mother!

For the first time, Dicle felt scared, but she also felt curious. The thing—no, she realised, as she peered slit-eyed and scuttled closer sideways, just like a *yengeç—things* were not happy, not at all. One was screaming and flailing, and seemed to be missing a leg at the knee, and the other one was dragging the first as fast as it could away from the shore of the Tuz Gölü. As the

dragger dragged the screamer farther from the edge of the lake, Dicle saw
they were leaving a big, brown blood-smear behind them. But Dicle had
seen wounds that bad before and knew just what to do. She ran closer to
help them, only to feel more scared and curious than she ever had in her
whole life when she realised that the things looked *just like her*, even though
they were obviously long past the time when they should have made their
pilgrimage and been changed by the Mother in the Salt.

Still, Dicle remembered her manners.

"*Merhaba!*" she called, approaching them cautiously.

"Get away from the lake!" shouted the dragger and Dicle understood
what she was saying, even though she spoke the words in a funny way.
"There's something in there!"

"Of course there is, silly," said Dicle. "That's the Mother! Don't you
know?"

The screamer looked up at her and spat up a big bubble of blood, then
went limp in the dragger's arms. The dragger, who wasn't dragging anymore,
fell to her knees and vomited everywhere. Then she looked up at Dicle.
Her mouth hung open, making shapes but no sound, and her eyes were
glassy, empty, and bulging. She looked just like a *balık*! Dicle laughed and
unsheathed her glinty knife.

The dragger wiped her mouth. "But we just left *yesterday*," she said.

When Dicle's mama died, Stag-Face had comforted Dicle in her distress
and helped her perform the rituals after they'd dug out her meat-shell from
underneath the rocks. Dicle was happy to do the same for the dragger.

"Don't worry!" said Dicle and she patted the dragger on the shoulder,
to comfort her in her distress. Then, as was proper, Dicle plunged the knife
into the right thigh of the (now quiet) screamer, slicing through skin and
flesh. Working quickly, she cut a long strip of meat from his shell.

"What are you doing?" whispered the dragger. "Oh God, oh, *God*, what
are you *doing*?"

This person *must* be a stranger if she didn't know the sorts of things
even the littlest babies knew! Dicle decided to be Teacher and help her to
understand. Leading by example, Dicle dipped her thumb in the (now quiet)
screamer's cooling blood and drew the insignia of the Mother in the Salt
on the dragger's forehead, then adorned herself the same way.

"The Mother knows our hearts and loves us all, her children," said Dicle,
and then began to gobble up the meat.

ᗡϞϟ

Once Dicle had given the stranger some water to rinse out her mouth—she'd vomited again as Dicle gobbled—she'd told Dicle her name was 'Yıldız,' and forbidden Dicle from cutting the rest of the (now quiet) screamer's flesh from his bones, even though that was what was supposed to happen.

"I don't understand," she kept saying, over and over and over again. Bo-ring! Dicle didn't know what there was to understand, so she gave Yıldız a roasted *balık* to munch on. It looked so good, Dicle ate one herself.

After Yıldız ate, she said, again, "We just left yesterday."

"How can that be?" Dicle was getting impatient. The sun was hot and she wanted to clamber up the sacred stair to summon the Mother in the Salt, so she could pray and change and then start home again. "You could not have left yesterday. You are all grown up, but you don't know about the Mother and you haven't changed. Did you fail on your pilgrimage?"

Yıldız laughed, but it wasn't a happy-sounding laugh. "Maybe so," she said. Then she pulled her knees into her chest and put her forehead on them. "This looks like the Tuz Gölü Research Station, so maybe . . . " Yıldız looked up at Dicle. "Where are you from?"

"I am on pilgrimage from K'pah-doh-K'yah," said Dicle. "Where are *you* from? There's not another village for a million billion klickers."

"*Cappadocia?*" Yıldız looked upset. "Where in Cappadocia?"

Dicle frowned. She *must* be from far away.

"K'*pah*-doh-K'*yah* is how you say it," she said, Miss Matter-of-Fact. "I live in the caves, of course, and Stag-Face is our boss. Everybody lives in the caves unless they're like Wriggler, who has to live in the lake, so he can breathe."

"No one's lived in those caves for centuries," said Yıldız, as if she knew anything! "There were too many earthquakes; they were unsafe to live in. The Turkish government forced everyone to evacuate."

"Turkish?"

"Yes, Turkish. Turkey. That's where we are." Yıldız got all glassy-eyed again and went quiet. Dicle wondered if she'd have to slap Yıldız to get her to wake up, until Yıldız started talking again, but it was like she was a tiny baby. "Tuz Gölü is an endoheric basin, so if there was any runoff from the Hypersaline Resonator, it wouldn't get into the rivers—"

"The Music brought the Mother, who came here, but was always here, and she gave us our true shapes. The Mother knows our hearts and loves us all, her children," recited Dicle.

"The music what? The Mother?" Yıldız bit her lip. "I saw something down there . . . too big, it was too big, though. The lake should be less than a metre deep in the summer, and yet. . . . "

"Come with me!" Dicle grabbed Yıldız's arm and yanked her to her feet. "Space and time are the same thing. The Mother has always been there, forever and ever through time, so it's deep and big enough for her! Don't you know *anything*?"

Dicle took off running toward the altar, dragging Yıldız behind her. She was jitter-jumpy and restless, and anyways, the Mother would explain better, once she was summoned.

"Where are we—"

"Just come *on*!"

"What the hell is that?!"

Even though Dicle had reached the bottom of the sacred stair, which was made of hard rusty-crusty iron and ran zig-zag up the side of the altar, she turned around to see where Yıldız was pointing. There, at the top of the hill, terrible and looming against the bright afternoon sun, was Stag-Face. Dicle could see his antlers. He'd spotted her, and was running pell-mell down the salty sand to get to her. She began to tremble.

"Stag-Face," she whispered. "Oh, no!"

"That man has a deer's head!"

"Come on!" Dicle would not be thwarted. She yanked Yıldız up up up the sacred stair, until they reached the flat top of the altar. She heard clomping on the stairs behind them as Stag-Face's hooves rang on the iron. Mean old Stag-Foot! He wouldn't stop her, not now!

Dicle rummaged in her bag and, under the roasted *balık*, found the sack of her mama's bones. She placed those at the base of the big circle and found the thing that Wriggler said was called a *lever*—it was just where he said it would be, on the left-hand side.

"No!" cried Stag-Face. He had reached the top and was pointing. "Dicle! Whee! told me you'd be here! Such a bad girlie! You don't know enough, yet! You haven't purified your heart; you haven't learned the right songs! The Mother will *not* accept you for changing! She will punish us all!"

"The Mother knows our hearts and loves us *all*, her children," shouted Dicle, as she wrapped her hands round the lever.

"Stop!" cried Stag-Face and Dicle heard his hooves pounding on the roof.

"He's got a knife!" shrieked Yıldız. She was fumbling with something hanging on her belt. "Wait! *Wait!*"

But Dicle wouldn't wait, even if Stag-Face had a knife. She yanked on the lever and big, crackling shafts of lightning began to curl around the circle, writhing and touching each other, just like Wriggler's arms, and they were even the same purple-blue colour. Dicle felt a burst of heat behind her; she heard the angry sound of Stag-Face in pain, and then the salt began to sing. It was so beautiful, it made Dicle's heart shudder and her skin crawl all over, and she felt a sudden gush of sticky hot wet over her face as she pressed her hands to the sides of her head in agony. It was blood, flowing from her eyes and ears and nose—*ugh!* But that was the sign of the Mother and, as the Mother emerged, Dicle began to pray, harder than anyone had ever prayed before.

ƆƳƐ

Yıldız, who was now Spots, came back to K'pah-doh-K'yah with Dicle, who was now Jackrabbit. Spots took over bossing everyone because she had teeth and claws like a leopard, and she'd also killed Stag-Face with what she told Jackrabbit was called a "laser pistol". And that was okay, because the Mother had made her understand, and afterwards Spots was the smartest of them all.

"Ahmet and I went through the Hypersaline Resonator, thinking we could visit this other place, a place up there in the sky that the star-watchers had said was okay for us to breathe and see," Spots had explained. "The Resonator was supposed to help with the problem of too much time passing here while we were gone. But when we got there, we saw a Mother—a different Mother, or maybe the same one, I dunno—and we were afraid it would come back here through the Resonator, because we didn't understand that the Mother loves us all, her children, and that would be a *good* thing! Silly us! But now everything is better."

Jackrabbit, who had been Dicle, was sure that Mother loved everyone, but she wasn't sure everything was better, even though she had finally changed. It was true that the Mother had granted her prayers to be the fastest of everybody, but she was now also the scaredest and rarely wanted to come out of her hidey-hole in the caves. All the sounds were so *loud* in her big ears! She'd almost gotten gobbled by the ghouls on the journey back home because, every time she heard something or saw something, it terrified her and she couldn't always control her urge to run away and get deep underground.

But, she reminded herself every day, at least she could dance in the revels and she could jump higher than anyone. Not that she felt like jumping or reveling much, even for the sake of the Mother. She was very sad, all the time. Wriggler hadn't lived more than a few months after snuggling with her. When he'd seen her true self, he'd said she was so pretty and they'd done the huff-and-puff a lot, but only for a few weeks. All of a sudden, he'd gotten sick and pale and told her to go away, so she'd gone away. When she next worked up the courage to bolt down to the lake, she'd found his corpse washed up and rotten on the bank. No one had eaten his meat and that was sad. All Jackrabbit could do for him was clean his bones and put them with the rest, for the time when the next little babies grew up and made their pilgrimage to the Mother in the Salt. And nobody else wanted to be her snuggler, not even Whee!, because Wriggler had put a baby inside her, but when it had come out, she'd gotten so scared when everyone had crowded around to see it that she'd gobbled it right up!

Being changed was sure not like she'd thought it would be. Jackrabbit was always frightened and always alone. Nothing was wonderful. Not at all.

ᛎᛁᚻᛁᚪ

SKIN

Helen Marshall

Helen Marshall is pursuing a PhD in Medieval Studies at the University of Toronto, for which she spends the majority of her time in the libraries of London, Oxford, and Cambridge, examining 14th-century manuscripts. Her poetry has been published in *ChiZine*, *NFG* and the long-running *Tesseracts* anthology. "Mist and Shadows," published originally in *Star*Line*, appeared in *The 2006 Rhysling Anthology: The Best Science Fiction, Fantasy and Horror Poetry of 2005* and her poem, "Waiting for the Harrowing," has been nominated for a 2011 Aurora Award. Her poetry chapbook, *Skeleton Leaves*, was released by Kelp Queen Press in 2011 and her collection of short stories, *Hair Side, Flesh Side*, is forthcoming from ChiZine Publications in 2012.

Colleagues, as many of you know, I have been at some pains over the last months to complete the research which your very kind donations have made possible. If it has taken a toll on me—if you can detect something of a dreary languor in my demeanour—I beg your indulgence. The archives can be an unkind place and History, herself, the cruelest of mistresses.

But I must tell you that it is more than the simple rigours of study that send a wild light to my eyes; it is far more than that. As you know, I have been engaged for some time in a study of a certain manuscript come to light recently in Biblioteca Estense in Modena, a small volume written on a fine vellum, much-damaged by fire, but still clearly one of the earliest copies of a Latin work thought to be attributed to Aristotle. Recent research has indicated—and my colleagues in Harvard have verified the results, checked transcription after transcription and traced both dialectal and paleographical evidence—that the book can be reliably placed near Heliopolis in origin, and may once have been housed in the lost Library of Alexandria.

The ramifications of such a find are far-reaching and will require far more study than I myself in a lifetime could ever hope to achieve, even with such generous donations as you may wish to give toward the endeavour. Nevertheless, it is not the contents themselves that disturb my composure. No, it is the parchment—the stretched and tattered skin, barely readable, discoloured by fire, yet still beautifully resilient after all these years.

In May, I departed for Cairo at the request of this esteemed governing board. My passport was stamped, my visa checked in triplicate, and the manuscript eyed hairily by authorities who neither understood its value nor my own purpose. "Where is the *usstaz*? The professor?" they would ask, ignorant of my protestations that I *was* the professor.

Finally, a small, svelte man with immaculate English arrived to take me to the Museum of Egyptian Antiquities. 'Khaled Nassar,' he said his name was and he was a godsend, though, no doubt, he'd dispute the term bitterly.

It was at the university that my true work began, and an intoxicating blend of excitement and curiosity drove me forward, even as exhaustion threatened to drag my mind from those soaring pinnacles of knowledge that we have glimpsed in the gelid mists of our studies. I was alone, utterly alone, but for my rescuer who—it appeared—was to be my liaison. He helped me negotiate the streets of that wretched city, sweat crawling down my spine, and taught me the few words of Arabic that helped me survive. In the evening, he would bring a strong, sweet coffee, which we drank to the dregs together, discussing the struggles of research, the petty bureaucracies that exist in all universities. Between us, there was that flash of friendship that comes when two minds strike against each other, flint on steel; it was a friendship that would bring many rewards.

Mister Nassar, you see, had a brother in Giza who worked as a phylogeneticist with a team of French scientists. He had agreed to sample the manuscript and perform the necessary tests to verify its authenticity.

It took five days for the results to arrive from Giza, five days of the breath of Hades on my neck as I tried to fill my time reviewing my students' Michaelmas papers in a hotel infected by fleas and Americans, five days of cryptic responses from my liaison: "Soon, *usstaz*, it will be soon." The paper, when it came, was heavily worn and bore many official stamps. I opened it carefully, reverently, and it is that which I found inside—the words Mister Nassar translated for me from Arabic—that I present to you today. For indeed, I learned that this book *had* been housed in the Alexandrina Bybliothece—and there must have been many others like it—but even this, colleagues, members of the governing board, is not why I come before you.

The fateful words of dear Mr. Nassar are burned into my mind forever: "The skin," he said, "the skin, *sahib*. It is not sheep." And then he touched my hand. "Human."

A chill still runs up my spine when I think on it. I have been a scholar for some years, and I have given all of my career and most of my eyesight to the study of books. When I sleep, I smell the musty scent of their pages; when I wake, my fingers explore them, probe their bindings, the threads that stitch them together. I know the soft velvet of the flesh side and the smooth, oiled surface of the hair side. I have studied the pattern of follicles, traced the network of veins that undergirds our most precious documents, the records of Western civilisation, the rise and fall of human knowledge. I have devoted my life to recovering the irrecoverable and rebuilding what was lost, searching out its ghosts and giving them flesh within monographs and articles.

But to learn that the skin I touched was human skin, the network of veins cousin to mine, and that the knowledge I had sought to reinscribe in the hearts of my students was written on the fleshly fabric of their would-be ancestors. . . .

It was a shock whose subtle charge still haunts my nights.

I looked to Mister Nassar, and he to me, and in our blank, uncomprehending gazes, we knew we shared a secret that would shake the foundations of the Academy.

That was six months ago and it could have been six years. He and I, joined by the strange bonds of discovery, left Cairo that day, clutching the codex, but shuddering at the weight of its presence, for we knew, deep in our hearts, that it was not just one book.

Indeed, Mister Nassar's connections were invaluable. Discretely, we were able to obtain samples of manuscripts from across the country—from Plato, Pythagoras, Aristophanes of Byzantium, Apollonius of Rhodes. For one and all, the answer was the same. "The skin, the skin," he had said. "Human." The Great Library of Alexandria was a charnel house whose secrets had been hidden in the fire that immolated all those stretched, disfigured bodies.

In the intervening months, we have visited many archaeological sites, studied the ancient midden heaps of Heliopolis, Sharm El-Sheikh and Aswan. Beneath the layers of refuse were bones, bones, bones, so many of them that it sickened me. Whole villages had been wiped out, their inhabitants sacrificed to the altar of the great gods of our civilization. A single codex could have required as many as three hundred hides and it was becoming increasingly clear that those of the young were valued most highly for their smoothness, their freedom from blemish. Children. A seven-year-old child could provide enough for twelve folios; an adult, perhaps sixteen, though the quality would suffer for it.

'The unspoken holocaust,' we called it, as we huddled in tents that clung to the skin of the desert. We were as thick as thieves, he and I, whispering our secret again and again. "Human," he would say, until the words meant nothing and the charred midnight air snatched them away.

Three days ago, an ancient bus knocked its way over potholes and hard rock, depositing us at last in the village of Deir el-Bahri. It was there we received a second letter, this one even more dishevelled, the number of stamps seeming to have taken to heart God's commandment to be fruitful and multiply. Mister Nassar opened it, fingers shaking, but his face turned strange as he read the Arabic within.

For a second time, he took my hand and I wondered at the calluses on his finger, the rough texture of them, the way the pads were paler than the coffee-coloured knuckles. They were beautiful, those hands, the skin of them.

"It is my brother," he said. "He must speak with us."

We boarded the bus for a second time, proffered bills to the surprised driver, who made a sign and ushered us aboard. The ride to Cairo was long and, try as I might to question my companion, he would reveal nothing of our new mission and what might await us.

His brother could have been a twin. They had the same deep-set eyes, the same nervous manner about them. But whereas the one had the tongue of a linguist, the other spoke only in halting English, stumbling over words until he and his brother turned to a guttural Arabic, with only occasional breaks for breathless translation.

He led us into the university science complex where the smell of formaldehyde drifted in clouds from behind shut office doors. A rattling elevator brought us to the bottommost level and there, following him as Theseus followed his ball of yarn through the subterranean system of tunnels, we saw a machine—a great beast of a thing, a wonder of modern mechanical genius. I don't pretend to understand most of what the second Nassar told us, only that he had been shocked by the discovery as much as we had, and that there was a way—perhaps—for something to be done. . . .

What would you do, colleagues, with the weight of that knowledge hanging upon you? What would you do if you were offered a chance to set it right? The press of a button and that slaughter of innocents prevented? Would you have the strength of will to silence Aristotle, to let the words which shaped civilisation go unremembered, unpreserved, reduced to whispers and empty air? Would you preserve instead the genetic code of that dead, forgotten mass of bodies? For they *are* dead, those slaughtered children, flayed for the libraries, flayed so that we might—

They are *dead*. A plague could have taken them and history would not have cared one jot. They would still be dead today.

But it was not a plague. It was men. Men who desired books, who knew these things must last, that it meant more than those hundred thousand lives . . .

The pyramids were built on such sacrifices. Who are we to say?

The three of us—myself and the twin Nassars—took wine that night, though I had never seen my companion drink a drop in all our time, despite everything. We swallowed morbid thoughts with every draught, drank down our fears, our apprehensions. But as the sun sent pale fingers of light creeping through the window, across the table and its scattered papers, its empty bottle, I hailed a taxi to the airport and left Mister Nassar and his brother to their grim duty.

We had come to something there, a decision.

Members of the Academy, colleagues, I know much of what I say is doubtful and I can already hear the murmurs of my detractors. You do not believe me and I do not blame you. It is a horrid business.

But you need not believe me; you need not ever publish these findings; you need do nothing but wait.

We decided, you see, the three of us there with our forbidden bottle. We decided.

The second Mister Nassar and his machine—that damned machine. I cannot say how it will work, only that he has promised—sworn—that it will. That the past could be unwritten if we so choose.

And we did.

I stand before you, not to accept laurels for my findings. I stand here in shame, for a terrible thing will happen soon.

This is a vigil, you see.

Soon, even as I speak, the button will be pushed and we shall face a brave new world, a *tabula rasa*, with the guilt of sins wiped clean. What the world will look like, I cannot say. I cannot imagine a universe without those learned men, those sages—the words of Aristotle and Plato like a light for us in the darkness. Their words, written for us, on the skins of children. It is a terrible thing we have done, and I do not know if Mankind will be the better for it.

But I *saw* their bones and I have flayed myself of every pretension, every mark of civilisation, of academic certainty and distance. We live in a world in which a life must be measured against more than the length of a page—mustn't it? Mustn't it?

That is why what follows must happen.

They are dead.

The children are dead.

And so, colleagues, I ask that we wait, together. The button has been pushed. The world is changing. It will only be a moment now.

THE OLD 44th

Randy Stafford

By day, Randy Stafford practices the dark arts of tax collection for his master and counsels his minions in the same. At night, after the anguished cries have faded from his ears, he cowers in his Minnesota domicile, comforted by his wife and an extensive collection of books and DVDs. He writes many a book review for Amazon. Every few years, he writes some poetry and, besides being an American Academy of Poets award winner in his long-ago-vanished college days, he has published poetry in *National Review Online* and *2001: A Science Fiction Poetry Anthology*, and book reviews in *Leading Edge*.

There is a geometry of Death.
I have seen its streets and paths
In the records of my father,
From the old 44th.

Krasten's streets were open
And straight like their minds,
Calling for our wares
And for our human ideas.

So, they baited their minds for the Hounds,
Pack predators from forests outside spacetime.

They came and killed, as did my father,
With comrades, to add another legend to the old 44th.

And as he, the last of the 44th,
Lay dying, his kit listened,
Watched as the last of the Hounds
Loped past the terminus of the city.

Right there, where the mesa ends,
And their blue, frothy Hound blood
Shone under the moons,
Is where they're kenneled.

The Angles, kinks of rectitude,
Hide them in the Beyond,
And in our world of circles,
There's always more like the old 44.

IRON FOOTFALLS

Julio Toro San Martin

Julio Toro San Martin resides and writes in Toronto, Canada.

I fled Him, down the nights and down the days . . .
I said to Dawn: Be sudden–to Eve: Be soon;
With thy young skiey blossoms heap me over
From this tremendous Lover! . . .
Halts by me that footfall;
Is my gloom, after all,
Shade of His hand, outstretched caressingly?
—"The Hound of Heaven" by Francis Thompson

Year 562 NNPE

She crouches alone in a corner, waiting quietly for you, her prosthetic reader barely registering her enclosed environment. She waits and remembers when her father first told her the dream of you. You were the embryo, the idea, the fixation in his brain, throbbing constantly like a metronome. How many versions of you there were, at first, she can't now remember, but when something finally like yourself—*your terrible self*—emerged from the compass of his craft, his workshop cocoon, she naively marvelled at the sight.

From somewhere, she hears the powerful disemboguements of the Ion-Plasma weapons. The tearing of metal. What a strange sound metal makes when it rips like paper. Tremors shake the walls. Loud blasts set air particles quivering. Then comes the silence. How many station drones have you destroyed now, Brother? Perhaps hundreds? She places her one biochemical hand against the cold, metallic sheen of a wall and thinks she can feel the steady, diminishing pulse of the CompuMind, retreating into itself, like a lanky, frightened tentacle into a deep hole. And then she hears your footfalls again.

Steady. Steady. Moving in her direction.

She wonders if you wonder how Father felt when you were almost complete. She wonders how he felt, too.

As a young soldier, her father could remember being taken to the peripheries of the Oort Cloud. There, in the Rim System, where human habitation barely penetrated, from the windows of an interplanetary carrier, he could see the silent spaces beyond, stretching to eternity, where, in unfathomable distances, lay the cluttered stars, eons old. Stars, that had never known human passions, sickness, evil, war. Staring into those abysses of beautiful darkness and uncountable time, he had felt peace, awe, silence, and all the ages of strife had seemed as nothing to him, then. This is what she imagines he felt then, looking at you, as they both stood on this lone asteroid hurtling quietly through open space, around a star that's been its companion since before life ever appeared on Earth: when the first planets were formed in early times out of the primordial, galactic ooze; when the stardust first touched the nascent valleys and mountains of his homeworld, and the first sunrises were there to be recorded by no one, until mankind had come.

Do you grasp the sublimity of the image, the awe of time and eternity, the feeling of vastness, of grandeur—do you feel anything at all, she wonders, *Brother?*

She's lost. The only difference she can imagine between you is that her darkness is the blackness of this station, where the lights have all gone out, while your darkness is the blackness of the soul, where no light shines and perhaps never shone.

She says, *This darkness, this nutshell, this being locked up, inside and out, this claustrophobia is becoming maddening.*

She reaches out with her mechanised hand and cybersynapses instantaneously make her realise she's touching blood. Dry blood—her own.

Your footfalls are getting closer.

From the corridors and the nearby airlock, she hears snippets of her absent father's recorded mad talk, disjointed and emanating from the comm centres scattered throughout the station. They say:

ↃⱧↃ

His name was Talus, made of iron mold,
Immovable, resistless, without end;
Who in his hand an iron flail did hold,
With which he threshed out Falsehood, and did Truth unfold.*

ↃⱧↃ

War. Drudgery. Pain. Death. Hopelessness. Destruction. War. Mankind. I will soon put right a mistake that never should have happened.

ↃⱧↃ

Oh, how I long for you to live, Talus!

ↃⱧↃ

His footfalls are coming faster, now, girl. Unstoppable. The booming echoes—gigantic. Like a mad-brained, moonstruck hound, he's homing in on you.

ↃⱧↃ

He will walk, breathe, and learn by uncontrollable compulsions like great, heaving seas of lava.

ↃⱧↃ

Time is running out. She, however, has not given up hope. She believes some message will reach her father, the planets, or at least a stray ship.

Sadly, no help will ever reach her. *She is alone*, too far from anyone.

We see this all and laugh.

Close now are your iron footfalls. With majestic instancy they beat.

Crouching, she uncoils the segments of her cyborged arm, which then part and configure into two snake-like appendages that input into a wall panel nearby, joining metal to metal. Direct communication with the central brain of the CompuMind is now possible. She feels the totality of the station and, in cyberspace throughout it all, lurking, *a foreign mind*, hunting and sniffing for her. She bypasses this *presence* whenever she senses it and secretly whispers with the CompuMind in a shut psyche-lock. Her waiting is almost over, she tells it. The CompuMind warns her it hasn't stored enough energy, yet.

Her hastily-attached synthetic reader, resembling a goggle, retracts and re-lenses. Visual images, albeit poorly, allow her to focus more closely on the end of the lightless corridor.

Your footfalls have stopped, Brother.

A small scoutdrone is suddenly thrust into her line of vision. The drone makes a horrible screech and red lights begin to flash violently around it. She quickly tries to re-lens, to get a better optical reading, but before she can, we feel the drone's insides ballooning with your meaty metal, Brother, until it explodes, leaving your gleaming feelers quivering with excitement.

Shards of the scoutdrone hit her, cutting and jabbing into her organic parts. She loses her balance and falls over, hitting her plated head, yet still, she manages to remain hooked to the wall panel.

Though dazed, the primitive lizard brain in her humanity causes her to involuntarily send a shocked, lightning-like panic signal to the CompuMind. It answers in kind.

Reams of corded electricity shoot out from capacitors hidden throughout the corridor and impact on you fantastically. Energy illumes you, flashing and exploding in blinding, brilliant lights. Erratically, you still advance, like a dark planet rising within a molten sun. Her lens refocuses and she sees your shape, full of wrong angles and impossible edges and strangely moving contraptions that should not fit together. You heat up like the core of a red-hot star.

She begins to feel pain. *Terrible, burning pain.* Her flesh bubbles. Her metal heats.

We hear the CompuMind say, in a tone too emotional for a machine,

"Impossible! Impossible! Nineteen dimensional spaces! Curved space collapsing, inconceivable angles surfacing!" And then it goes silent. The charges cease, darkness comes and, at long last, ends the chase.

Now your *being* is upon her like a looming horror. She feels your electrified presence. She sees your terrible hand reach out to her. She awaits her death bravely.

But nothing happens.

She feels, above, your hand swing past her, like a bird of prey swooping for the kill and then leaving. You pass by her like a planet swing. Uninterested. Walking around her.

She turns to see your footfalls recede and then vanish into a wall. You are now on the outside of the asteroid. Your massive shape is moving away. Your alien intent and intelligence are incomprehensible to her. *An intelligence more like ours.*

How you yearn to set us free. The blessed impurity of angular Space-Time will soon enter her dimension.

Once, there was a God of love and spirit; now they have fashioned a god of metal and of the outer hells. Her father wanted to destroy those responsible for their ceaseless war and then start anew, yet through our influence he created instead a sentient machine, designed to perpetrate genocide on its own creators.

You are like a scapegoat, Brother. In times long gone, when her species was as yet young, they would lay their sins upon a goat and send it into the wastes to die. This creature bore the sins of the people and they would be cleansed of their sins. You, the Talus Machine, are the last scapegoat come back out of the wastes, bearing their sins back to them.

As she prepares to hunt for you on the asteroid, she hears your voice inside her head, metallic and scratchy, say the ultimate incomprehensibility to her mind: *Witness as I fall into the sun and pull the worlds down.* Then your heavy feet push away from the asteroid. *Senseless,* she thinks. *Utter, complete senselessness.*

Seconds pass and then she begins to feel the pull—the great, gravitational pull of the collapsing sun that will soon form into a fast-burgeoning black hole, from which nothing will escape.

These are the last hours of her species. Unbeknownst to her, on Earth, a few days past, the Great Old Ones rose in madness from their sleep and plunged with worshippers and slaves towards the blasphemous, ultra-dimensional, black planet of Yuggoth. And now, the last portal to Tindalos will soon be opened.

Sasana Xavi VI rushes to a window, horrified. The stars in the night-black sky begin to burn out. The celestial bodies move. The asteroid shifts forcefully towards the sun. She looks one last time and then the lights of the universe go out.

We will soon howl free from *the other side* of our prison-home. It will soon be time for a new arrangement.

Ƴ𝈙ᚺ𝈙ᚹ

*From Edmund Spenser's *The Faerie Queene*, Book V, Canto I.

THIS SONG IS NOT FOR YOU

A.D. Cahill

Avery Cahill has worn many hats in his life, from working at a cheese factory to Lecturer of Classics. He's lived in Japan, Italy and Norway, but currently awaits the End Of Time while waging a losing war against fire ants in Florida. He is a graduate of the Odyssey Writing Workshop, and his fiction has appeared in Dog Oil Press and Innsmouth Free Press. Tweeting as Falcifer9000 or blogging at scythe-bearing chariot in the 2D world, he shouts into the meaningless void.

This song is not for you.
The golden pipes sound
Flat fifths on alien scales
Around the all-consuming sun.
A black sun.
Their notes are not for you.

He is pleased.
His writhing, festering pleasure
Strikes a ten-dimensional cord.
He consumes himself,
Excretes himself.
Weaves space, weaves time.

A star. Galaxies. Light.
These endless forms are not for you.

DAL NIENTE

The pitch shifts.
The dance pauses,
And in the rests between
That awful melody,
In the emptiness,
In the void,
In the inhalation before the note,
you.

On dust, you stand
And laugh, and sing
And lust, and cry,
And slay and rut.
And build your cities,
And fight your wars,
And gaze longingly into the void.
A great, sordid emptiness
In the song that is not for you.

The screaming ant
Clamps a morsel,
Dragging it home along
A hormone leash.

Your blood burns.
The sun is warm.
The sky blue and cool.
You know with a vengeance that
I am I.
Yet, this song is not for you.

PERDENDOSI . . .

A voice in the centre,
The very centre,
Away and down,
Deep, deep down,
Infinitely far away.

The black sun answers the trilling pipes.
The pipes fall silent.
The strings relax.
The terrible dance winds down.
Galaxies rip.
Stars fade.
The eve of atoms has come.
Quivering in entropic ecstasy,
The song is done.

. . . AL NIENTE

You follow in the wind,
wherever the played note goes,
a node on a silent string.
None of it was for you.

TLOQUE NAHUAQUE

Nelly Geraldine García-Rosas

Nelly Geraldine García-Rosas is a Mexican writer and a freelance copy editor. Her stories have been published in independent magazines and anthologies. Some years ago, she struggled with the decision to become a writer instead of a physicist; she has no regrets, but she loves to read, write and discuss about physics, cosmology, astronomy, and weird science. She can be found online at: www.nellygeraldine.com.

> If you wish to make an apple pie from scratch,
> you must first invent the universe.
> —Carl Sagan

I—The Particle Accelerator

They built an underground temple. A well of Babel sinking into the gloomy ground at 175 metres of depth. They wanted, like the Biblical architects, to know the unknowable, to discover the origin, reproduce Creation.

The desire to unravel the nature of the Everything floated permanently in the controlled environment of the laboratory. Hundreds of fans and machines emitted a constant buzzing, which the investigators called the "silence of the abyss". This, combined with the smell of burnt iron, gave the ominous sensation of finding oneself in space. Doctor Migdal lay upon a nest made of coloured cables and, with eyes closed, fantasised that his body, weightless, floated, pushed by the breeze of the ventilation.

Sometimes, he would imagine that he was being attracted by a very narrow tube, a cafeteria straw, the ink container of a pen, or a bleeding artery. His feet, near the edge of the conduit, would feel a titanic weight that would pull him and make him push through the small space. Migdal could see how he would turn into a thick strand of subatomic particles that would extend forever.

Most of the time, he saw himself arriving slowly at the union of the circular tunnel that formed the particle accelerator. Before the accelerator, Migdal was tiny. The machinery attracted him softly, although with such an acceleration that he lost no time in approaching the speed of light. He knew that, the faster he travelled through space, the slower he would through time, so that, if he looked forward, he could see the rays of particles that preceded him—sent during the morning, the previous day, or the month before—and if he looked behind, he could see what would come—tomorrow, the next day, or the next month. As he advanced into the confines of the accelerator, the scientist felt eternal, for he was capable of appreciating the complete history of that point in time and space: from the Big Bang to the most distant future.

Migdal left his daydream, trembling and sweaty. He distanced himself from the other scientists and spoke to no one about his fantasy because, each time he imagined himself floating in the particle accelerator, he knew He was there, shining, in all the instants and all the places.

II—The Dream

I dreamt I was in a penetrating darkness, without limits, without time. One could hear a sinister music of pipes, whose interpreters adored a gigantic, amorphous, inert mass in the middle of nothing, the primordial chaos. From all the confines of darkness there surged a conglomerate of iridescent bubbles and one of the terrible musicians announced the arrival of the door, the key and the guardian.

It is impossible to describe with words how He filled the space, was omnipresent, he knew everything and could see everything. With a movement that reverberated in the infinite, he gave matter to the darkness. A blinding explosion surrounded the drooling chaos.

I do not remember more.

ᗡᚻᘓ

They say an accident occurred in the underground laboratory where the particle accelerator is found. The say that is why we cannot connect to the Internet; that is why the electricity comes and goes. Estela, my neighbour, thinks these are government lies. "Come on, my child, how can a problem in Europe make the lights go out here in Mexico? That's very far away. I think this is politicians trying to rob the people again. Accident, my ass!"

III—The Lord of the Near and the Nigh

"What did Migdal and the other scientists seek in their well of Babel?"

"The elemental particle of the Standard Model of particle physics."

" . . . "

" . . . "

"They would have to reinvent the Universe."

"They did. Well, in a way."

"They would have to make a universe. Any universe. Make apple pie."

ᗡᚻᘓ

Estela knocked on the door as though she wanted to tear it down. Her hair was uncombed; she sweated. I offered her coffee, which she swallowed in gulps as I watched in silence her trembling hands. At last, she confided in me that she had had a horrible dream: Monsters with the heads of snakes walked towards the house of Doña Iluminada, her friend; they played flutes that looked like phalluses, but moved like the tentacles of a squid.

I tried to calm her down. I told her that it was just a dream, that she need not worry, that we were all uneasy, due to the electrical failures and the telephone grid, which was now inaccessible. But Estela interrupted me and said, "No, my child, it's not that. It's just that, this morning, I went to visit my friend, Iluminada, since there's no phone. When I was about to turn the corner at Donceles and República de Argentina, I heard a music that gave me goosebumps and I remembered the dream. I approached slowly, to see where it came from, but the ones playing were not monsters, no. They were my friend, Jacinto, and his children. Imagine: My godson walked as if possessed, as if he could see something that was not there. I ran to my friend's house to see what was happening and I found her very calm, making tamales. She told me they were for the Tloque Nahuaque, because he supposedly came to our world, thanks to the scientists in Europe that had found his *nature*. She also told me other insanities, like, she wanted to go to the pyramid of the Templo Mayor to adore the *spheres of the beginning*, or something weird like that. How can I not be afraid? She is my friend and she is going insane, my child. Who will look after my godson if Jacinto is also wrong in the head?"

Doña Iluminada had lived for more than thirty years just a few metres from Templo Mayor in the centre of the city, but she had never visited it; Estela assures me that her friend had not heard of the experiments made inside the particle accelerator until there was talk of an accident, and that this might have caused the electricity and communication problems. Nevertheless, she prepared tamales and thanked the subterranean discoveries, for she believed that what had happened in Europe was not a tragedy but a wonderful encounter with what had been long sought after.

Ↄﬧⰻ

"One time, I asked Migdal if there existed the possibility that, following the theory of the multiverse, we were always in a branch where the Higgs does not exist. He asked me to take out my gun and find out.

"Migdal did not believe that the probabilities would ramify to create many worlds. He would say particles exist in all their possible states at the same time, but that, when we interacted with them, they would be forced to choose one possibility, the one we would finally observe.

"What would happen if one particle would not respond to either of the two theories? What would happen if it would exist in all its possible states and, like this, we observed it? What if, also, it multiplied to be in infinite universes?

"You'd have to make apple pie."

Ↄﬧⰻ

Estela explained to me that Tloque Nahuaque, the Lord of the Near and the Nigh, had been to the Aztecs the Master of the Near and the Far, for they believed he is near all things and all things are near him. They had given him many names and representations, such as 'Tezcatlipoca' or

'Ométeotl'; however, his greatness was such that there is no single word that will contain him, for he is in everything.

IV—The Higgs Boson

Imagine the origin, the primordial chaos, the instant in which none of the primogenial particles had mass. He, who shines in all instants and in all times, manifests, touches the chosen, and provides them with mass. That is how everything begins.

Imagine your weightless flight, Migdal. Now look at the monitor and see the results of the test. You found it.

つれと

"The Tloque Nahuaque can also revive the dead, my friend. It's so good that you came to help me with the tamales," said Doña Iluminada, as Estela amassed the dough in a strange state of disturbance: The meat which would be used to prepare the dish for the god was none other than that of her godson.

"They say He demands sacrifices now that he has given us knowledge of his *nature*, miss. Carlos Guarda, a university teacher, came to see us and said the Higgs (He calls him like that) has shown us already how the universe began, that we should thank his wisdom. That is why we will deliver him Danielito," Mr. Jacinto said as he played with a wooden flute and continued: "Carlos Guarda told us we should let him drop from a very high place, so he could achieve terminal velocity (God knows what that is), but the steps of the Templo Mayor are broken and the highest we have is the roof. That is why my wife thought we should make more tamales, so the Tloque Nahuaque does not get mad."

V—The N-Sphere

The last report from Migdal was confusing. He talked about iridescent spheres and the representation of a being of four dimensions in our space of three, how it is possible to draw a sphere on paper because the tridimensional figure can be sliced to form circles. "Our tridimensional universe is immersed in a sphere of four dimensions and, at the same time, in another more complex. Until infinity," the document reads. "That is why He can manifest in this space, but remain outside of it; be in all points and instants, touch a particle, give it mass, create and recreate the Universe."

᠌ᠤᠠᠵ

The electricity fails more and more. Slowly, I adapt to the idea that we might never again have telephone service or an Internet connection. All I know of Europe and the particle accelerator is that they lost contact with the surface and the efforts to descend are useless. The rest is speculation. I've learned of many suicides and violent deaths. Estela says that they are sacrifices to the Tloque Nahuaque, as they call him in Mexico City, but that, in every town, he has a different name. "There is no word that can contain him, my child. He, inside and outside the world, sees everything and knows everything. It is impossible to distance oneself."

Somebody bakes apple pie.

ᠨᠵᠻᠻᠵᠢ

DOLLY IN THE WINDOW

Robyn Seale

Robyn Seale was born in 19-diggity-7, at a time when the nation briefly outlawed the 8. After short periods called "childhood" and "college," she created a Lovecraftian webcomic, and illustrated a number of print comics. She lives somewhere in the Midwest, where she hopes Dagon will be summoned on a flood plain to help explain the number of bait/tackle-shop-and-restaurant combo businesses.

Hey. New girl. Im Joelle. Welcome to the Nabrinious official Orphan Asylum Fer Girls. Lemme be the first to welcome ya. As you can see here, youll be bunkin in this gurgeous, six-by-eight room with me, your lovely host. Whats yer name?

Annabelle? Good name. You an offworlder?

Yeah, i can always tell. Yer bones are soft. S okay. Itll make this arm easier to break. Yer what, six? Seven?

Ghaaaaaaad. Dont whine like that. I aint gonna do it now. Gotta get some other girls up here. S a hard job, yanno? Generally, we get this girl, Carolina? Yeah. Shes built like a tank, that girl. Has a hard job gettin through the ducts, but does all right.

Well have to cut yer hair, too. Shame, really. S so pretty. My hair was like that once, yanno? Not all gross and mouse-brown and braided up. Youll have to learn to do it close to yer scalp, so's it doesnt get caught by accident in the fans n stuff.

Ghaaaaaad. Shuddup. Yer jus like Mary, all puffed up about yer hair. Itll grow back. The tooth weve gotta knock out wont, though. Which side are you partial to chewin on? Left or right?

Left is the L side if you make it with yer thumb. Hold up both your hands n' make Ls out of 'em. The one what looks like it ain't backwards is your left. Like loser.

Stop yer cryin. Wont hurt but a minute.

Pshsshshshshs. You think yer the first one Miz Bensons told that to? Think agin, buttbreath. You know where youll end up? Not offworld, livin the posh life. Youll get adopted by the Dollmakers, all right. Then youll regret it.

Did I knock some teeth out? Naw, I don come from good stock, yanno? Mdad wholloped mosta my pearly whites out fore he kicked the bucket.

You dont believe me? Well, you dunno about Mary.

Mary was like you, some snot-nosed fancy brat that comes in here all snooty, like this colony was too good fer her. Bit older, though. Had differ'nt hair.

Miz Benson told her the same thing. She didnt listen to us. You see all these girls in here? Notta licka us pretty or all dolled up. Were the smart ones an keep ourselves useful, cleanin up these air ducts.

It aint a nice job, sure. Sure, we gotta few teeth missin and some bad skin. But were here, yanno?

Now, you know the Dollmakers an how theyre so proud to get all their dolls unique? Howdya think they do it? Huh?

Ill tell ya.

These girls. That come in through here.

Mary didnt believe me. Went off with those creepy mouth-breathers and their fancy masks. Theyll give you somethin too. Somethin' thatll make you sleepy fore you even leave here. Yell be givin yer goodbyes through crazy, off-matched eyes.

Then well never see ya agin, cept through the Dollmaker shop winda.

Serious! Dont look at me like that. You can see Mary down over there in that winda. The one with the red hair, nitpick. Kept her velvet dress on, too. Recycles, I guess.

Why, doncha believe me? Cross my heart, hope to die. Thats the gods lickin truth.

Hey. Ill give you more proof, if you want. Gimme a candy or two you got in yer bag, an Ill tell ya.

So . . . I aint told the other girls; I dont think theyd go back in the air ducts after what I saw. Man, how olds this candy? Takin forever to chew.

Anyways, after Mary was taken up by the Dollmen, I went ahead and did my shift. She werent here but a day or so, an there aint no sympathy in Miz Bensons cold, withered mummy heart.

Anyways, here I was, doin what would be her route had she listened. And then I hear a noise.

Its this weird gurglin noise that I havent heard before. Like . . . like, yanno how cats get all drippy an stuff? Like they was yowlin and drippin all over each other.

So's I went to go take a look-see. Got all up in some vent that hadnt been cleaned in a minute. I dunno whose route its on, but it werent any of ours. Someone woulda said somethin', yanno?

Anyways, I get to followin this duct and somethin awfuls comin from it. Really horrible. I mean, I smelled poop and theres dead critters comin' in from outside that get trapped and die, and sometimes, you find them rottin . . . but this rottin that you aint find nowhere.

I start peekin in some vents and I realize, Im lookin at the factory! The Dollmaker factory! You aint never seen nothin like it. Theres this big ol room, with these huge drainage vats and somethin' right awful is livin in them. Theyre just . . . blobby things with faces and eyes and mouths all poppin up like bubbles boiling.

An theyre huge, like . . . whatcha call em . . . elephants! Elephants on the videoprompter. Giant blobs of gross jus rollin' and boilin' and yowlin'.

You aint never heard sucha sound they were makin. Jus thinking bout it gives me the willies. Thats when I realizedtheyre cryin like babies. Theyre hungry.

I know, cuz the Dollmen start roundin girls like you up. Theyre all naked as the day they came inta the world, and weird.

I mean, weird as in drugged. Not like they did anythin' like the perv down the street does, with his huggin too long and bribin with candies. They were all sleepy-eyed, like when they leave here. An they gotta be, yanno? Im here, lookin at these things, and I nearly lose my lunch over it. Those girls are just . . . standin' there. All glassy-eyed and dumb. I spotted Mary and she was all smilin like she was on a picnic or somethin.

Anyways, these Dollmen start leadin these girls up these stairs to the edge of the drainpipes, big ol gargantuan things, all filled to the brim with these slippy slidin monsters. AND THEN THEY JUST WALK IN. These girls just take a step and bloop! Right into the mess they go.

Whats really nasty is that the girls dont pop up for a minute. The bodies churn and theres more mouth bubbles and these vats are makin' a happy noise, I guess, cuz it sounds like a weird, keenin song. And all the vats are makin' it. The dollmen are just standin there, not movin'.

When they do pop up, theyre just skin and hair. Everythins been taken out. You can see it when the Dollmen take these long hooks and skim the surface. The mouths and eyes and stuff just slip under or over the metal.

And then what? Whatchoo think, girl? I got the hell outta there. I didnt wanna poke around and see how they stuff em. How they pop some glass eyes in there. If they wait around for some teeth to pop up, so they can replace them pearly whites.

Nooo. I just went my way. Came home, pretended I was sick. Miz Benson didnt like it, but it wasnt hard to fake. I threw all up on her when she tried to whup me. All's I had to do was to think of those things in the factory.

The next day, Mary Mary Quite Contrary was up in that windasill, lookin finer than when she left here. Left in that pretty velvet dress.

So, Im sayin, cut yer hair, break a tooth or two. You dont wanna end up like Mary or the other girls. You gotta do it quick or—

No, Miz Benson, I ain't tellin' tall tales agin. Annabelle here was jus' sayin' how she didn't wanna go with the Dollmen. She wanted to learn the fine trade of air duct cleanin', didn't you, Orphan Annie. *Didn't you?*

Oh . . . You didn't? I swears, Miz Benson. I didn't tell her nothin'.

[In a low whisper] You ass! You brat! Youve done it in now!

Youre right, Miz Benson. I am late to my duties. Well, goodbye, Annie. Guess Ill see you in the shop winda, sometime. Besta luck.

ᚤᚥᚺᚥᚦ

A COOL, PRIVATE PLACE

Jen White

Jen White is an Australian author of speculative fiction. She lived for some years in the tropical north of Australia, but has since moved to the gentler climes of country Victoria (Australia, that is, not Canada). Her work has been published in various magazines and anthologies. Most recently, her stories have appeared in the anthologies, *The Tangled Bank: Love, Wonder and Evolution*, *Bewere the Night*, and *Dead Red Heart*. She also has a story in the e-book anthology, *Extinct Doesn't Mean Forever*.

When we signed the papers on our property, they gave us a map of all the known time wells in our district, and a pamphlet on how to live safely in their vicinity. Our friends thought us crazy to buy in one of the abandoned towns, but what else could we do? With Tamsin unable to work full-time any longer, and my own poor showing at employment, we could never afford the city, or even the fringes of the city, so it was one of the abandoned towns for us. Besides, here we'd be safe from the rising oceans for a good, long time.

We chose Hills Point for the sheer beauty of it, a mountain town ringed by other mountains. It was hard to get to and, because of that, solitary and still, a cool, private place of reflection and contemplation. It consisted of a main street, and a few other, smaller streets running off it, and that was it. Population 30, a few abandoned shops and falling-down shacks. And a pub, of course, a huge, white palace of a pub. The only shop still running was the general store, owned by Ruby Langdon, 15 years resident and as wide as she was tall.

Our own place had once been the local boarding house, a weatherboard maze of rotting carpets, cast iron beds and washstands. It was the first thing of any significance we had ever owned. At night, we would climb up to the top floor and gaze out at the wildness, listen to the scuffling and snuffling of the animals, drink our wine, and imagine how it used to be. A mining town, a working town, a coarse, noisy, stinking town full of energy and self-importance, the very life of it ripping great holes in the quiet of the bush. And now all but dead, life seeping away. Hills Point, and other such towns, had grown so still and silent after such clashings and clangings that the very air had begun pooling, settling in great, suppurating clumps, past and present overlapping unhealthily, creating time wells. Hills Point was full of them.

The nearest well, fenced off for safety, was down the end of Welcome Lane, a short street of ancient shops that had been boarded up decades ago; it was a smallish well on the right side of the road, right in the middle of the footpath, the air around it puckered and torn, as if it were grieving the loss of all those smart, busy ladies dressed in their fineries, marching up and down with their packages. The deepest well lay down near the creek, hidden amongst some giant ferns. Tamsin and I decided that this must have been where sweethearts went to find privacy and, when the town died, this powerful space had yearned so much for blood and warmth and movement that a time well was born. Sometimes, when I walked down that way (which I did often, for I liked solitude and quiet), I would glimpse things in this well—old things, ancient creatures, staring out at me—and I would wonder how far back this well went, for we had no history, no conception, of animals with six legs or four heads or a hundred writhing tentacles.

How could you not explore the time wells? our friends asked us. *Touch them, push at their skin, pass through?* And we would have, but for the deep sense of unease that came upon us whenever we ventured near them, a sensation akin to that of standing at the edge of a bottomless abyss, of falling into the terrifying unknown. We could go so close and then no further. We were glad, on the whole, to give these wells a wide berth, even averting our eyes whenever we neared one.

I found the shallow ones hardest to bear, the ones that held your own grey day from a few months ago, where all you could think was: *What's the point?* Or the ones that showed you bright, blithe ignorance before bad news. There were a lot of those. But all the wells were bad. We are creatures who look forward. To look back goes against all our instincts.

I was up on a ladder one evening, painting the lounge room wall a pale green, when I felt it. I nearly fell with the strength of it and I had to hold on tight for a minute or so.

Tamsin came running in. "Can you sense it, Jamie?" she called out. "Something's shifted."

We headed towards the front door and peered into the darkness, as if we'd see a change, but everything was still and quiet, as always. And yet, we were sure we had not imagined it. Something had happened; something was altered. But we managed to settle down. We had our dinner and forgot about it for a bit.

It was when I was on my morning trek to Ruby's, to grab some milk and get a sense of the day, that I first noticed the Welcome Lane well had healed. The shimmer and shift of it that I normally glimpsed out of the corner of my eye was gone. Cautiously, I moved closer to the site. Only concrete path and grass tufts and a forlorn wire fence. It made me uneasy. Were we living in some kind of boiling time soup, where wells bubbled and popped continuously? I had hoped for a bit more stability.

Ruby wasn't about when I arrived at the shop, but this wasn't unusual. She could be out the back having a breather, or taking a quick walk. She knew she could trust us to keep her up to date with what we took. I collected my supplies and was about to write out an IOU at the counter when I saw Ruby's stockinged legs on the linoleum. It was such an incongruous sight that, at first, I didn't understand what I was seeing. I moved around to the other side of the counter and there was the rest of Ruby, sprawled across the floor, a rich, red liquid pooled under her head. I bent down, took her wrist. No pulse. She looked like she had been there for some hours. The doorbell behind me rang. It was Malcolm, another long-term resident, ex cattle man.

"It's Ruby," I croaked. "She's had a fall."

Malcolm joined me, squatting down beside Ruby. "That's no fall," he stated. "That's a bashing. See how the head's all caved in? She's been murdered."

I called the police. Malcolm said he'd stay with Ruby till they arrived, which could be hours, as they were based a couple of hundred kilometres away. Then I hurried back to the house, feeling distinctly uneasy, what with the time well and now Ruby. Who on earth had done it?

I headed for the kitchen, following the bitter aroma of just boiled coffee. We loved our kitchen. It was huge, industrial-sized, built to accommodate vast vats of scone mix, mountains of mutton. We had nearly blown ourselves up with the stove when we first moved in, but we'd got the hang of it now. I relished the smoky flavour of our morning toast, the thick, oily coffee that stayed with me all day. I found Tamsin standing at the table, vigorously stirring a bowl of pikelet mix. She gave me one of her looks.

"What?" I said.

She shook her head, flicking the wooden spoon up so mix went all over the table.

"Milla reckons her shed's been broken into. Her gun and ammunition's been stolen."

"Jesus," I said, pulling up a chair and falling into it. I told her about Ruby.

"But it wasn't a shooting. Malcolm said her head was bashed in."

"Gotta be connected, though," Tamsin said.

But who?

We knew there were some odd ones living around the place, people searching for absolute solitude, people who could not live within society for any number of reasons. Tamsin and I had always prided ourselves on our tolerance. Milla herself was a Satanist. Another resident, Jeff, had worked most his life in the abattoirs and carried his own, personal aura of tension around with him at all times. A little difference, after all, was no big deal. But how far do you go, how much do you tolerate, before it becomes dangerous?

Like any small community faced with a crisis, we gravitated to the pub. By about mid-afternoon, a dozen of us had arrived.

It felt calming at first, comforting to be with others, drinking and yarning in bar, a reminder that most of the world was ordinary and predictable and safe, and that talking about it usually helped. Although, after a while, it didn't seem like such a good idea at all. Fear and alcohol are a terrible combination.

"We need to search every house," Jeff stated firmly, his voice louder and louder. "That's all there is to it. That way, we'll know for sure who's done it."

"Now, let's not get carried away, said Malcolm. "Could be someone who passed through."

"Can't be," Jeff argued. "We haven't heard a car in days."

That was true enough, I had to admit.

"So, it's gotta be one of us. We've got to search the houses."

Jeff had started banging on the tabletop. He stood, leaning forward. I could see that things could very easily get out of hand.

"Hey, hey," I said. "We're not the enemies. We're all worried. But it's not for us to decide. It's in the hands of the police. They're at Ruby's shop right now, working out what to do. We'll hear soon enough. All we need to do is look after ourselves in the meantime. Lock up tight."

Tamsin and I left for home soon after.

Life changed for a while. We lived behind locked doors. I didn't take my usual walk down Sweetheart's Way. And I kept a cricket bat beside the bed of a night. Not much use against a gun, I know, but somehow, the thought of having a gun in the house scared me even more.

"Is it worth it?" Tamsin asked. "All this uneasiness, this fear, just to own some property? It was supposed to be a beginning, but it doesn't feel like that, anymore."

I knew what she meant. I didn't pick up a paintbrush for days, not able to see a future here, not sure where we were heading.

But we did settle. You can get used to anything, I found, even finding a dear old neighbour dead on the linoleum. You can't live on high alert forever. It's just not physically possible.

And it was a fine place, really. This part of the world felt ancient, prehistoric. Giant ferns, skittering marsupials, the air clear and fresh, the quiet addictive. Despite the time wells, I felt centred here. Much more than I ever had in the city. At least once a day, we'd go walking in that clear air. I'd had a lot of struggle and complication in my life, but this place was helping to give me some space between me and all that. We'd had a glitch but now, we were on our way again. It was senseless to lock ourselves away when we were surrounded by all of this.

It became our habit to take a morning walk together, a different route every time. We found trees that must have been a thousand years old, creeks full of jumping trout, old miners' huts made of hessian and lime, still containing a bed and shelves and a bench full of dusty tins of food. And we found the skins. We smelled them before we saw them. Round a bend and there they were, a dozen or so rabbit skins hanging from the branches of a eucalypt, sinister flags twisting slowly with the breeze.

"What is it?" Tamsin whispered.

It felt threatening. It was clearly mental. Hell, it was both. Whoever had done this had some agenda I couldn't even begin to grasp. That made it dangerous. "C'mon," I said, "Let's go." Whatever it was, there was something wrong about it, a wrong feeling, a wrong sense. Just wrong.

Later, at the pub, Tamsin asked Malcolm about it.

"Sounds like someone's camping around here, using old-time skills, things my grandad taught me. Only, why hang them up like that? They'd be flyblown within hours, ruined. No, when you think about it, it doesn't make sense."

We thought it might be witchcraft, but Milla said no, didn't seem like anything she was familiar with. It set our teeth on edge, all of us, and we grew wary and afraid again. Tamsin and I began to talk about moving. We had no place to go, people like us didn't have much choice, but it seemed clear we couldn't stay here. There were too many things we didn't understand about this place, too much dissonance going on for me, creating an almost unbearable tension. I could see it was the same for Tamsin. She wore a constant frown and a faraway expression, and held her body rigid as if she were becoming uncomfortable in her own skin. When we made love, she held on to me so tight it hurt, as if she were trying to stop from sinking, drowning. We kept close to home after that, only venturing out to get our supplies. We might as well have been living in some apartment in the middle of one of the cities, for all the countryside we saw. And we checked on each other constantly. If I hadn't seen Tamsin for half an hour or so, I'd go wandering, searching all the rooms, make sure I'd placed her, that she was safe enough for the next little while.

Whenever I was at the shop, I made sure Tamsin locked herself in. But you can only make a place so safe, can't you? I'd forgotten the milk that morning, so I'd had to go out for the second time if we wanted our morning coffee. I'd found croissants and had bought a dozen. They were frozen, of course, but exotic enough for a town like Hills Point. I couldn't wait to show Tamsin. Only, it wasn't just Tamsin in the kitchen. She had company. An odd-looking man, bearded and black-hatted, wearing dirty, white oilskins and a dark waistcoat, and from the stink and colour of him, he hadn't washed in months.

It was him, I knew, as soon as I saw him. He was the shift. This man had come through the time well and it had closed up behind him. Is that what it took to close a time well? Human sacrifice?

I tried to place him in time. Somewhere in the mid 1800s, I thought.

"Get you there," he spat when he saw me.

I froze. Too many shocks piling one on top of the other.

"Get you there!" he yelled, "or you won't be able to. I'll do the same to you as I done to the shopwoman."

So, he had killed Ruby.

"And that stupid girl who tried to bewitch me."

Milla? Brave Milla.

"Oh, no!" Tamsin gasped.

"What do you want?" I asked him.

"Tell me," he said. "Where be this?"

"Hills Point," I told him. "You're in a small town called 'Hills Point'." I could feel myself consciously slowing my speech, enunciating more clearly.

"Where be this?" he said again. "What country have I come to?"

I saw the tremor in his hands, the size of his pupils. If this man had come through the well, the passing through had changed him, you could tell. The symmetry of his face, his body, was slightly off, his colour wrong, his hair, up close, far thicker than normal hair.

And he blurred. I thought it was my eyes, at first, but no, holy hell, it was him. That's right. When he moved he blurred. He got all pixelated and smeared-looking, almost as if he were lagging behind himself, as if, all around him, space, time were unstable. God, it was weird. Creepy weird. Scary weird. I wondered if it hurt, blurring like that. I was terrified he'd touch me and suck me into his pixelated lag space, almost more afraid of that than of being shot. But, most of all, I was afraid he'd hurt Tamsin. We had to be careful. This was a desperate man, a scared man, and probably an insane one. He had killed Ruby and Milla. Who knew what he was capable of?

"It's Australia," Tamsin whispered.

"Then why your foreignness?" he shouted. "I don't believe you. You are not Englishmen."

"We're Australian," I said. "Not English, Australian. And you, what are you?"

"British, of course, brought out here for something that weren't my fault. And now, stuck here and hating the damned place. But towns like these. Why do we not know of these places?"

Tamsin slid down to the floor.

"Up!" he shouted.

"She's afraid. Let her be."

"If she don't get up, she won't never," he threatened. I could see by his eyes he meant it. He was a man with nothing much to lose.

I helped Tamsin to her feet and held her there.

"Then, if this be Australia," he continued, "this is where I stay. Not in that godforsaken, backbreaking wilderness I came from."

"Yes," I agreed. "You will probably have to stay. The, ah, road you came through has closed up."

"But am I dead?" he muttered to himself. "Is this Hell?"

God only knows what private torment he was living in now.

"No, you're not dead," I said, trying to keep my voice as steady as I could. "But you probably shouldn't stay in Hills Point. We are only a town of 30. You need to go somewhere bigger."

I had no other plan but to get him away from us as far as possible. I had to get him away from Tamsin.

"Eh, bigger, you say. And where would that be on this lonely continent?"

"A town of thousands," I said. "There are lots of towns like that. Somewhere you can be lost in the crowd. Somewhere no one can find you."

"What you say makes good sense," he said slowly. "So, I'll need me a horse and a map and some supplies."

And then I realised what I had just done. We had no horses, only cars. And this man couldn't drive. He would need to be driven. He would need someone to drive him. He would need me to drive him.

"We don't have horses," I began.

"What do you take me for?" he yelled. "If you have no horses, how do you get around? Tell me!"

So, I began to explain cars and how things were different here.

"We are very advanced. Our carriages don't need horses. But they are hard to drive. I will have to take you."

He insisted on tying Tamsin up and locking her in the pantry before we left. I knew she was a resourceful woman. I hoped she'd be able to find some way to get out, for God knows when I'd be back. Or if. At least he hadn't insisted she come with us.

Our car was just an old Falcon, but he seemed impressed enough with it. Afraid, even. He took a turn around the car several times, touching various parts of it. I opened the bonnet and showed him the engine. I tried to give a cursory explanation of how it worked, but I saw his eyes glaze over.

"You will need to sit in the back," I told him. "And wear a belt."

"Why must I?" he enquired belligerently.

"It is to keep you safe. These carriages go much faster than a horse."

I settled him in and put his belt on, being very careful not to actually touch him. Up close, his stench was overpowering. What was it? Sweat, of course, months, years of drying, stale sweat. And a godawful diet of rabbit. And something chemical, too, that I couldn't readily identify. But it was definitely the worst thing I'd ever smelled in my life.

"Your name," I asked. "what is it?"

"What's it to you?" he snarled.

"This will be a long trip," I said. "We might as well get to know each other."

He nodded. "William Stanley," he said. "And you?"

"Jamie Straughan."

If he knew me as a real person, I reasoned, he might be less likely to bash my head in.

"Get me to the next town safely, Jamie Straughan," said William Stanley, "and I will let you go free."

I had to wonder whether that was true.

I started the engine and headed off down the main road. *It's now or never,* I thought. Just before the intersection, I veered left, doing a hairpin turn and taking the dirt road as fast as I could down towards Sweetheart's Walk, dodging trees and flying over rises, the old girl feeling every bump. I only hoped William Stanley would not realise what I was up to in time to shoot a great hole in the back of my head. I took us straight for the deep well, only jumping from the car at the final moment. I had made sure not to put my own belt on. I rolled over the long grass, winded and dazed. I watched as the car crossed into the well and, once in, push through what appeared to be dense grasslands, on and on. I continued to watch as the air heaved and buckled and the well popped, and man and car vanished. What would William Stanley find, I wondered, in that place, that time?

It took me an hour to get back home. I'd done something to my knee and could hardly put weight on it, and I could feel blood gushing from the back of my head.

"Oh, God," Tamsin said when she saw me. "I felt it. I thought you'd been taken. Oh, God."

"I lost the car, Tamsin," I told her. "Sorry."

"You silly thing," she laughed, hugging me, crying. "I never liked that car, anyway."

I looked his name up later. He had come through wrong, all right, but he had been wrong to begin with. He had been convicted of murder and sent to Australia for life. But he had been suspected of many murders. These days, we would call him a serial killer.

Tamsin and I still think about leaving. But others are joining us here, people like us, couples, families, those with few options. Soon, the town will be a real town. It will have more shops and, eventually, a school and its own police station. But time still overlaps. Once, I heard the clop-clop of a large horse behind me. I turned to see nothing. And some nights, I swear there's a carriage driving right past our bedroom window. And I'm sure I saw something hovering one night, all still and silvery, right above our roof, only to veer off sharply, disappearing in an instant into the dark sky. Who knows what will come next? In this damaged part of the world, we walk lightly.

꿁ꇰ

VENICE BURNING

A.C. Wise

A.C. Wise was born and raised in Montreal, and currently lives in the Philadelphia area. Her stories have appeared in publications such as *Clarkesworld, Daily Science Fiction* and *Strange Horizons,* among others. She is co-editor of the online 'zine, *The Journal of Unlikely Entomology.* She can be found online at www.acwise.net.

A floating city, a sinking city, a drowned city; there isn't much difference, really. When R'lyeh rose, it rose everywhere, *everywhen*. Threads spiral out, down, in, stitching past to present to future.

There are ways to walk between, not particularly hidden, if you're willing to lose a part of yourself. Most people aren't; it's my specialty.

I stand on a pier, eyes shaded against the water's glare. It's 2015, by the smell—diesel and cooked meat, early enough that such things still exist—and the particular pale-jade of the canal. It might as well be 2017, or 3051. But this year is where my client is, so I wait, sweating inside a black, leather jacket, watching slick weeds stir below lapping waves.

The sun burns white-hot. Across the water, atop a basilica whose name no longer matters, Mary stretches marble arms over a maze of twisted streets. Legend claims that, when the basilica was built, the statue turned miraculously toward the water to guard the boats in the canal. The day R'lyeh rose, she turned her back on the water forever and wept tears—sticky and ruby-dark—that weren't quite blood.

A hand touches my arm, nails perfectly manicured and painted sea-shell pink. I'm surprised the Senator came herself. A frightened mother looking for her lost son is one thing; a politician desperate to protect her career is another. I wonder: Does the Senator know which she is?

Sunlight catches the diamond net of hairspray holding every blonde strand in place. Her lips press thin, leaving unkind wrinkles at the corners of her mouth, marring otherwise-perfect skin. Nails, lips and suit all match; only the Senator's eyes betray her.

From her perspective, it's just beginning. R'lyeh is a shadow beneath the waves and there is still hope. But I've seen tendrils slide through the canals of the city, sinuous, licking the stones and tasting the ancient walls. They want nothing. The Senator still thinks she can bargain with the Risen Ones, strike a deal and become a new Moses to her people.

I focus on the Senator's nails, striking against my black leather. I know this about her: Her life will end in a church, green water rising between the pews, light reflecting against the ceiling in shifting patterns. She will die screaming, bound hand and foot, while her blood is pulled through her skin by sheer force of will.

I don't offer to shake her hand. "Do you have a photo of your son?"

The slim case tucked beneath her arm matches nails, lips and suit. She hands me a glossy, professional-looking headshot. Her son looks nothing like her. Mr. Senator is an actor, younger than the Senator by at least ten years, dark of hair and eye like his son, but prettier by far.

Marco, the son, gazes back at me from the photograph. Slick-oiled hair hangs to the collar of a leather jacket, an open-necked white shirt beneath it. He has deep-brown eyes and the faintest of scars—acne, despite the medicine and the cosmetic surgery his parents could easily afford. I hide the edge of a smile at Marco's tiny act of rebellion.

"You understand this is a matter that requires the utmost discretion." The Senator holds out an envelope. She tries for frost, the same control she displays on the Senate floor, but her voice fails.

"I'll be in touch," I say, looking at a point beyond the Senator's left shoulder.

A subtle tugging wraps threads around my spine. I'm amazed at the Senator's self-control, her talent for denial. How can she not feel what the world has become? How can she resist the temptation to slip into the future? She has the perfect pretense—looking for her son. She could see how it all ends.

I pocket the envelope and Marco's photo, and step past the Senator. Her mouth opens, snaps audibly closed; she isn't used to being dismissed. My bootheels click as I walk away, thinking about her son.

A family vacation in a city of masks and illusory streets—the perfect place to hide, the perfect place to disappear. Twenty-six and vanished—of course Marco doesn't want to be found. Even photographed, the desire to run shines clear in Marco's eyes. Desperation and fear, they bring a flicker of memory, which I push aside. There is no place far enough, but he'll still try, fleeing forward to test the notion that the future is infinite.

I know where to start—Harry's Bar. I step forward, and slide crosswise, surrendering to shattered light, burning stars and the aching space between. Tentacles as insubstantial as breath slide beneath my skin. They want nothing, but they take what I have to give. Cold, cold, cold, they grip my spine, caress my skull, and scoop out the heart of me.

If they were beings to be reasoned with, I would ask them to take everything. It doesn't work that way.

Firelight flickers. My scars itch, stretching tight across my back. I hold the memories up as an offering, but the tentacles find their own prize. I don't know what they take from me; I only feel the familiar, hollow ache when it's gone.

It's 2071 when I enter the bar. The light is green, but the waiters still wear immaculate white jackets and ties, a terrible joke. I slide into a seat.

"A double." I don't specify of what, but it hardly matters.

Behind the bar, where mirrored shelves used to hold bottles of liquor, pendulous nets hold a jumble of perpetually dripping starfish, conch shells, mussels, and clams. Breathing, wavering things cling to the wall. Occasionally, the waiters pause, offering their fingers, as if feeding choice morsels to a favourite pet. Fragments of shadow stretch in tacky strands, linking the waiters' hands to the creatures on the wall as they draw away. The air smells of brine. Things at the corner of my eye shift, skirl, unfold impossible dimensions, and retreat—deep-sea anemones shy of the light.

The bartender slides a drink in front of me. Misery haunts his gaze. This is our life now, our life then—this is the life to come. His mouth doesn't move when he breathes. His nostrils don't stir. If I didn't know to look, I wouldn't see the gills slitting his throat above his starched collar, nictating almost imperceptibly. His eyes bulge, moist, blood-shot. I place a bill on the bar and add a stack of silver-gold coins, a generous tip.

I wait a moment, then place Marco's picture next to the coins. The bartender's skin sweats oil and sorrow. People determined to vanish come to Harry's Bar and, for the right price, the miserable waiters in their starched, white uniforms show them how.

"When?" I ask.

"Can't say." The bartender's voice is frog-hoarse.

I know he means 'can't,' not 'won't.' Everything can be bought and sold here: sugar-sweet cubes that melt on the tongue and bring oblivion; death; pleasure; escape; even answers. The man behind the bar taught Marco how to leave, but didn't ask questions—a good bartender to the last.

"Thanks." I down my drink in one shot.

The liquor unfolds in my mouth, sending a spike through my lungs. My eyes water. I walk back outside.

It's dark. The stars are right. But the stars have always been right.

Where would I go if I were Marco? A useless question. He knows what he's running from—a suffocating life of expectation, his parents' blind oblivion a shadow pressed between his shoulder blades. Some people can feel the future coming; others refuse to believe in anything but the infinite Now. The future reached out blind tentacles, snaring my heart. Marco chose R'lyeh's ways; R'lyeh's ways chose me.

Firelight flickers. A horse whinnies—a soft, breathy sound. The scent of wet leather and dry hay overwhelms me. Lips trace mine, arching my throat, shivering across my belly. I gather sweat on the tip of my tongue, briny-sweet like the sea. The horse's whicker turns to a scream. My scars tingle, hot and cold at the same time. Fragments tumble, edges sharp like splinters of bone lodged beneath my skin. Some things can't be outrun, taken, or let go.

Suddenly, I don't give a fuck about Marco. And I have all the time in the world.

I walk along the water's edge, where there used to be a restaurant. Once—after R'lyeh, but before now—the entire city burned. The canals turned to oil and fire swept from rooftop to rooftop, sparing nothing.

Centuries of human existence, wiped out in the blink of an eye. I was there. I will be there again.

Venice, as always, survived. It rose from the ashes, born anew in brick and stone and marble, in deference to the old ways. It was also resurrected in glass and steel, in deference to ways old-yet-new. Finally, it shambled back from the dead, with walls that bled and seethed, flickered and writhed, in deference to the way things are now and always will be. Venice—an impossible city, impossible to kill.

I turn inward, crossing a bridge made of glass. A canal creeps, sluggish, beneath it. Lights glimmer on the water's surface; things sleep in its depths. Venice floats, it sinks, it is drowning, it is drowned. And it survives. So do I.

I've been to the underwater city where Venice used to be. I've kick-pulled through cathedrals lit by the unearthly, phosphorescent glow of things best left unseen. I've worshiped at unholy altars, caressed by tendrils of night, studded by unnatural stars. I've witnessed the twisted images of saints spider-walking up church walls, their mouths open in silent screams. I've kissed the greened marble lips of the Mary who wept tears that weren't blood, as she watched the fish nibble her children's bones. I've seen Venice in all its guises, peeked behind all its masks, witnessed all its states of decay. Venice survives, no matter how ugly its scars.

My feet guide me through twisting ways to a little restaurant off Calle Mandola. It's almost unchanged since the old days, except for the light, and the sick-green smell, and the taste of salt in the air. They still serve a killer martini—an olive *and* a twist. Inside, the sound hits me like a wall. My heart skitters, painful.

Guilt persists, even when I've given up love.

The place is nearly empty, but Josie sings as if the restaurant is full. Her voice is heartbreak: smoke and burnt amber and chocolate so dark it draws blood. It suits the restaurant's mood, and mine. Waiters move listlessly between tables, bringing baskets of bread, plates of limp vegetables in heavy, oily sauce, and pasta—everything but meat, which ran out long ago, and fish, which is forbidden.

I tried to bring Josie fresh meat once—unspoiled, untainted. She wouldn't touch it. The thought of anything that had been in-between made her shudder and gag.

I remember—as much as I want to forget—how I held Josie's hands. Her moss-green eyes glowed with fear. I asked her to trust me. We stepped in-between.

Just as soon, we were jerked back, as if R'lyeh's ways had spit us out. Josie pulled away from me, the brief touch of *otherness* enough to shatter her already fragile mind. I followed her back. I could have kept running, but I didn't even think twice.

We were staying in a hotel next to the theatre on Calle Fenice, in a room with walls the colour of blood, patterned in threads of pale gold and delicate lines of mold. The shower had stopped working long ago, but the toilet still flushed and, against all reason, the sheets were clean. When I stepped out of the between, Josie lay curled on the floor, clinging to the Turkish carpet rucked beneath her folded body as if it were the only thing holding her to this world.

"It burns. Ara, it burns."

I crouched beside her and touched her, feeling the sharp ridges of her spine through clothing and skin.

"Make it stop." She rocked and whimpered.

I lifted her sweater, peeling it as though from a wound. Tattoos, inked long before R'lyeh rose, writhed across Josie's flesh. Black ink against skin the colour of fired clay, lashing, twisting, moving in ways nothing ever should.

"Make it stop. It hurts. Make it stop." Josie turned her face, just enough to show tears and stark terror.

"I'm sorry," I told her. "I don't know how."

There were so many places I wanted to show her. I wanted to take her deep—somewhere off the coast of Mexico, to another drowned world full of turquoise water and old bones. I wanted to hold her hand, even through thick rubber gloves, and gesture to her through the enforced silence of breathing tubes and masks, hoping she'd understand.

She shuddered at the mere mention and I went alone. I let the stillness envelop me; I drifted. Vast things floated beside me; an eye the size of Luxemburg opened below me in the deep. I should have been terrified, but I felt only peace as it looked into me and through me.

I used to think there were some sins too terrible even for R'lyeh, some offerings the spaces between would always refuse. But in that moment, I understood: Sin is a human concept. I did what I did to remain human. I buried sin deep at my core. I could walk the ways between a hundred, thousand times, and it would never change the deepest, most fundamental part of me.

In the end, I never took Josie anywhere. For a while, I tried to hold her when nightmares shivered beneath her skin, when her tattoos writhed in their own dreams. My touch made it worse.

The day I left, she sat on the hotel bed, head bowed. A red-glass heart from Murano lay cupped in her palm, brilliant as blood. Bubbles ran through its core. I touched it with one finger; the glass was warm from her skin.

"I don't know why I have this," she said.

Her eyes held hurt, raw as a wound. Whatever I'd taken from her, trying to guide her through the between, was something I could never replace. Some wounds never heal. I left. I didn't ask her to forgive me.

Here and now, a ruby spotlight pins Josie—an American girl, singing Southern standards and bluesy jazz in a drowned and drowning city half-way across the world. Her song cuts knife-deep, touches bone. I can't help remembering the last time we lay, cooling in each others' sweat, windows open, listening to the crowds leaving the Teatro. The breeze raised goosebumps on her skin, skin the colour of Tuscan hills, of earth, of a time before the Risen Ones.

That was the last time salt tasted good.

Josie's voice is sandstone, rubbed against my skin. It is coffee, scalding hot and poured into my lap. In the ruby spotlight and the green seeping from the edges of the world, she's beautiful.

I sip my martini, slid without asking across the bar by the loyal bartender, Lorence. His skin is damp, his eyes as pained as the poor boy who served me in Harry's Bar. No matter that it hurts him, he still labours to breathe with human lungs, shunning his gills.

Josie leaves the stage. Her dress swirls against legs encased in nylon, blooming roses. The skirt catches light in its folds, red on red, pooling blood. She wears a flower in her braided hair. Once upon a time, I may have given her a flower the same shade—a real one, not a silk monstrosity with hot-glue dew-drops clinging to its petals.

Her eyes meet mine, their moss-green accentuated by the underwater light. A smile touches her lips but not her gaze.

"Ara." Josie brushes her lips against my cheek, making sure to catch the corner of my mouth.

She smells of powdered lily-of-the-valley, dusted heavy to hide the reek of fear. Someone very wealthy must have bought it for her. Scents like that are hard to come by.

Guilt spreads patterns of frost across the surface of my heart, but it doesn't touch the core. Pain flickers in Josie's eyes. I've forgotten; she hasn't.

I tip my head towards Lorence; it's the least I can do. Josie orders something as blood-red as her dress, but with far more kick.

"What are you doing here?" Josie asks.

Her fingernails are ragged, as if she's been raking them across the walls in her sleep. A tendril of ink slips from beneath the strap of her dress, a questing tongue tasting the air. She shivers. The ink-shadow stains her eyes for a moment, too, turning them the colour of lightning-struck wood.

"I was lonely," I say. It may be the most honest thing I've ever said; I don't know.

"Oh?" Her eyes are green again, sparking mockery.

She lifts the long, black braid lying over my shoulder, running it through trembling hands.

"I wish I could do something for you." The words fall, a numb rush over my lips.

Josie is the most breathtaking woman I've ever known. Why can't I feel anything for her? I know what she meant to me, what she means to me, but I don't *feel* it. Not anymore. Her skin flickers, the ink shivering across its surface and underneath. I mimic the motion unconsciously, my body responding to her hands on my hair.

"There's nothing you can do." She drops my braid, a soft slap against my leather.

Josie finishes her drink and orders another, her mouth set in a hard line that reminds me of Madam Senator and the case I should be on. What am I doing here?

"There's nothing I can do for you, either." Josie steps back, eyes as hard as the line of her mouth.

She's right. There's nothing I can do except buy her drinks. And isn't there a selfish hope that her inhibitions will drop and we'll end up back in that decaying hotel room, listening to the remnants of humanity leave the Teatro while we fuck?

Once, in the space between midnight and dawn, in the half-dark—an unnatural glow belonging to caves and never aboveground—I tasted the nightmare-sweat slicking Josie's skin. I traced the writhing lines of her tattoos with my tongue. She didn't wake. That sweat wasn't sweat—it tasted like the oil born of the rotting bones of prehistoric beasts, oozing beneath the skin of the world.

Josie's next words send my pulse into the roof of my mouth. "Do you remember what you told me about your stepbrother and the night you got your scars?"

"No." The word comes out hoarse, terrible. Josie's smile is worse. I can't remember if it's a lie.

What did I tell her? What if I took her between, trying to make her forget?

Josie leans forward, her lips against my ear, her breath raising tiny hairs on my skin. Her voice is smoke, rough whiskey, shattered amber. "He called you his angel. They're shaped like wings, your scars."

When she draws back, I feel the absence of her breath.

"I don't think you're even human, anymore." Her hips sway as she walks back to the stage.

God help me, I'm wet and trembling. I want to throw her over the bar and bury my head between her legs, nipping the soft flesh of her thighs till she bleeds. Maybe she's right about me. Maybe I'm not human. Maybe I'm too much so.

Josie grips the microphone like she wants to throttle it. Her voice is steel wool, scouring flesh; her eyes are fixed on me.

The blood-and-seawater light fills my mouth with salt. The world rolls. Firelight flickers, throwing shadows against the thinness of my eyelids.

"The world is going to end." A voice speaks against my ear.

"It's already ending." I smell wet leather, tangle my fingers through wheat-gold hair, and pull wine-stained lips against mine. Rain drums. Hay prickles bare skin. "So, fuck me,"

I bite down hard, yank fabric roughly over hips; a body pushes into mine. A cry of pleasure and pain, and after, the world burns.

Josie's voice wails. Her smile is blade-edged, her tattoos unmistakable, now. They slither across her shoulders, beneath the neckline of her dress, chasing the ghost of my fingertips across her skin. Josie tips her head back, throat working. The song becomes a scream, her body shuddering, eyes rolling white between agony and ecstasy.

The bar squirms in murky half-light. Tentacles unfold. They undulate across the walls, wrap my arms, lift my hair. I drift in the green deep and they caress my bones.

I stagger for the door, retch on fire-scored pavement. Chill air slaps my face; I shift without meaning to. The threads binding past to present catch me, hurl me forward in time. My bones nearly shatter, filled with desire to part company with my flesh. I want to scatter wide enough that I don't have to remember anything ever again.

In another reality, following another skein of time, I follow Josie back to her tiny, hot apartment, overlooking S. Francesco della Vigna. We listen to distant water lap. We fuck. Her tattoos writhe; she whimpers with pleasure and fear. I taste her while she screams. She tells my future in her sleep. I say goodbye. And she forgives me this time.

I brace myself against a wall, trembling. Damp, heavy breezes push air through the narrow, winding streets. My skin cold-sweats with borrowed dew. Where am I? When?

I walk, boots hushing over time-worn stone. I sympathize with Marco. I wonder why I'm hunting him. The Senator's envelope presses against my chest. I want to get this case over with and pretend there's a place I can go to that will feel like home.

Blonde hair, the smell of leather in the rain. I survived; he didn't. Fire scored my back with a thousand whips, tracing the shape of wings.

I walk along the waterfront, fighting memories that insist on surfacing, no matter how many times I try to give them away. I've begged the dark spaces teeming with star-ripe tentacles to take them away, but they never do. There are no refunds on the price of survival, once it's paid.

I pass a nightclub where a church used to stand. Tentacles—half-seen— lash the night. Shadows obscure the stars and they are just right. The club-beat is a heart-sound, a pulse-thump. The building sways. It shivers. Pigeons weep and mourn in cages embedded in walls of slick, trembling flesh. Overhead, gulls still scream their laughter, but then they would, wouldn't they?

I know where I'm going now. Farther down the wharf, where, once upon a time, goods used to be delivered in rusting, corrugated containers, is the man I need to see.

Vincenzo sits at the end of a pier jutting out into the water. The piles are ghosts against the lapping dark. Each weed-slicked piece of wood is topped with a creature with too many arms, suckers gripping rotten wood. They *sing*.

The eerie-sweet sound licks my spine, too much like the timbre of Josie's voice. But instead of smoky-hot, the tentacles sing cold. How can things without mouths sing?

Their voices—if they can be called that—are vast, reaching distances but also reminiscent of the deeps, of cavern-glow and waving fronds. Their tears—should they ever cry—would taste of copper, iron, sulfur, and flame.

Vincenzo cocks his head. He hears me coming, but he doesn't pause. His arm moves, his brush stroke jerky, involuntary.

"Ara." He doesn't turn.

The scant, pulsing light falling from behind me illuminates the rotting pier. The dark water shimmers, bioluminescence touching the waves but never what lies beneath. It shows Vincenzo's face and the gaping spaces where his eyes are not.

I was the one who found him. The bathroom tiles—staggered white and black—slick with blood. Vincenzo's head rested against the edge of a claw-footed tub. He wept.

Rather—his body shook with sobs and his eyes lay next to the drain in the otherwise-spotless tub, darker than the most cerulean sea and incapable of tears. Blood had spattered where they'd fallen, but otherwise, the porcelain remained white, white, white. His palms were stained rust-dark; so were his clothes. I nearly slipped in the blood covering the floor, but in the vast, arctic space of the tub, there were only a few drops, trailing from the drain back to the eyes.

"I can still *see*." Vincenzo's sobs turned to laughter while I held him. I couldn't make his dreams stop, either, but at least I resisted the urge to taste his bloody tears.

"Hello, Vincenzo." I can't tell if he flinches or not when I lay my hand on his shoulder.

"You smell like her," he says. Did I tell him about Josie? My stomach turns.

"I need information." My soles should be hard after years of running; my soul should be hard after years of leaving myself behind. Some things R'lyeh will never cure. Not in any place—not in any time.

It's what I was counting on.

"Watch the painting." Vincenzo's voice holds the same quavering tone as Josie's song.

Pain flickers through the space where his eyes should be, stars shifting through black, bloody caverns. I see blue, crimson-tinged spheres against porcelain-white; I feel him shaking in my arms. It's too late for apologies.

Vincenzo sets aside a canvas of writhing blues and greens. The paint is still wet, fresh and thick. I want to run my hands through it and feel it between my fingers like river mud. I want to drift in it and be seen by a vast, opening eye. I want to be told I did the right thing.

Vincenzo places a fresh canvas on the easel. His arm jerks, spastic. I watch over his shoulder as he paints. Flames. Venice burns.

"Thank you." I put my lips close his ear. Vincenzo's body hitches; he might be bleeding the paint—crimson, saffron, umber. He doesn't stop. I leave him to his colours and his pain.

I shift. Sideways, cross-wise, moving through a cold space as crushing as the deepest parts of the sea. My lungs compress. I could not scream if I wanted to. Tendrils wrap me, loving me. They lap my heart, sucker-hold it; they caress every part of my spine. They take a bitter-sweet song sung in a smoky voice like burnt almonds. I shiver as it fades; salt lingers on my tongue. It leaks from my eyes and I don't bother to brush it away.

Venice burns.

Heat batters my cheeks, drying stinging eyes. I throw an arm up to shield my face. Inhuman tongues hiss unknown words, shiver laughter, babbling inside the flames. The stars spin. The canal heaves. Angles and rounded nubs of stone-not-stone—worn by untold eons—rise, dripping. The city would shudder in revulsion if it could; instead, it screams as it burns.

Against all reason, I turn toward the city's fire-wrapped heart. Sweat pools beneath my leather. My scars itch, pulling tight between jutting blades of bone.

Marco is here. I was wrong. He wasn't seeking the end of the world, just the end of *his* world.

I find him in the little restaurant off Calle Mandola—Josie's restaurant. The soles of my boots have almost melted. Heat-cracked, multi-coloured glass from the shop across the street crunches under my feet.

The restaurant's walls are black, curling with smoke-wrought shadows. They don't shift and unfold yet, but they will. Everyone else has either fled or burnt to death. Only Marco remains, belly-up to the bar. His hair, greasy as it is, should burn. Instead, it clings to his collar, loving. I think of water-wet tendrils cupping pale skin.

He turns a pock-marked face towards me, unsurprised. Flame makes his already-dark skin ruddy. His eyes shine, and not only with the glow of alcohol. He mimes a toast, lifting his glass, and throws the liquor back, grimacing.

"I knew my mother would send someone."

I don't bother to answer. How long until the flames reach us? I pour myself a drink, and refill Marco's glass. Nothing unfolds against my tongue as I drink. My eyes don't water. It's only alcohol.

"She wants you to come home." I pour again.

Marco slugs the drink in his glass. His eyes shine empty, staring into a middle distance only he can see. When he ran, how far did he go? Has he seen the end of all things? Did he watch his mother die screaming? His eyes are unsettling. Not burnt-wood, something else.

"What are *you* running from?" he asks.

My stomach lurches. I try to pour another shot, but most of it spills on the bar. It will evaporate soon; the bar will go up in flames. All this alcohol—we're a Molotov cocktail, waiting to happen. "What do you mean?"

"You wouldn't have chased me this far if you weren't running from something." Marco's eyes fix me. I know the colour now—river-mud brown.

I shudder. The sensation goes all through me. I don't taste what's in my glass; I taste cheap wine stolen from a funeral table the day we buried our parents—my father, his mother.

Jason. My stepbrother.

I saved his life once, pulled him out of the river after he slipped on a rock. He was nine; I was ten. Lying on his back, rocks darkening with the water running from his skin, squinting up into the sun, he called me his guardian angel.

I breathe deep, and draw in a lungful of wet leather and hay. Firelight flickers from the old trashcan we dragged into the barn. Rain drums the roof. Our feet hang over the edge of the loft, heels kicking dust-pale wood. A horse whickers softly.

"I hate them," my stepbrother says.

"Who?" I drink straight from the bottle, bitter tannins clinging to my skin, staining cracked lips red.

"All those people at Mom and Dad's funeral. They're all a bunch of fucking phonies."

He takes the bottle from me. I nod. A storm hangs over us that has nothing to do with the rain. A weight presses between my shoulder blades; my skin itches. I know Jason feels it, too. There is something waiting to rise.

Then, there, I am pulled out of myself. I am in Venice, looking at Marco across the bar, watching the world burn. I am floating above the vastness of a star-filled eye. Time means nothing.

I know what I will do to survive.

My stepbrother finishes the rest of the wine, tosses the bottle against the far wall where it shatters, spraying glass. A few droplets fall into the fire, making it snap and sizzle. I retrieve another bottle, pen-knife out the cork. We stole a whole armful as we left the funeral.

My stepbrother says, "They're lucky they aren't alive to see what happens next."

I don't have to ask what he means. He feels what's coming, but has he seen the end of the world? Does he know what I'll do to make sure I will?

"What's the worst sin you can think of?" I squint into the dark on the far side of the barn. "Not that Bible shit. Something real."

Shadows shift, fold and unfold. Jason looks down, heels drumming the wood, dust spinning up every time they hit.

"Hurting someone you love and meaning it."

I nod. The stars shift. They've always been right. They prick the sky, prick my skin, and draw blood. I know what I have to do to survive. Tendrils reach for me, the colour of starlight and as cold as the moon. I have to wrap myself in a sin I can never forgive, the worst thing I can think of, a pain I can never forget or give away. It's the only way to stay human.

I reach for Jason's hand, squeeze fingers as chill as ice.

"The world is ending." Jason's breath is rapid, wine hot.

I nod, lean close. Our faces almost touch. He understands what's coming and he wants me to save myself because I once saved him. I could refuse his gift, but I don't. My heart beats, cracks, and salty water rushes in.

"It's already ended," Jason says.

"So, fuck me." I pull him close, bite down hard on a kiss. I taste cheap wine and blood.

It would be mercy to say I slid into oblivion, but I felt every minute. I tasted every drop of sweat. I cherished every tear, cradled it on my tongue. After, Jason slept. I drank half the remaining bottle of wine, and threw the rest into the trashcan—a spray of glass, a gout of flame, the horse's soft whinny turning into a scream of fear.

The fire traced wings on my back.

And I flew.

Dizzy, I grip the edge of the bar. "Your mother paid me a lot of money." I force the words out through clenched teeth.

Marco's image doubles, sways. I see other eyes, reflecting flame—eyes so pale they would pick up the colour of whatever was around them, flaming gold like the setting sun, or silver like the rising moon. River-coloured eyes; rain-coloured eyes. Jason's eyes, weeping love.

I swam in marble corridors, in drowned-green canals. I tried to let tentacles steal the best of me, the rest of me. It wasn't enough. My sin kept me safe; it kept me whole.

"Your mother . . . " I try again.

"It doesn't matter." Marco shakes his head.

The ghosted memory of a smoky voice, tasting of bitter chocolate, threads the air and fades away. Scratchy hay presses a pattern of almost-words into my skin. I hold a blind man as he sobs. Shadow tendrils touch the deepest part of me, stripping my bones clean, taking everything except what matters.

I could cash in. I could make the biggest paycheck of my life. I could keep running and test the theory that the future is infinite. Or I could stay this time. I could burn.

Marco's gaze meets mine. Flames reflect between us. Inside the flames, impossible angles rise dripping from the canals. An eerie, piping song needles me with remembrance. Stars draw blood from my skin. Marco lays his hands, palms up, on the bar—an invitation.

Ragged-nailed hands grip a microphone, cup a glass heart. Palms slicked with blood drop eyeballs near a drain.

There are many possible futures; I see them all in Marco's eyes. Two charred corpses decorate the remains of Josie's restaurant, one in front of the bar and one behind. One charred corpse sits slumped against the bar. An empty, charred husk of a bar dies alone, with no one to witness its end.

It will come down to a battle of wills, my will to survive against Marco's will to die. I know what I gave up to survive; what did he give up to run? Which matters more?

My scars itch and stretch tight across my back, shaping wings. Wings for flight, or wings for salvation? Maybe this time they'll stay stitched beneath my skin, folded tight around my body like loving arms.

My wings have always been there; the stars have always been right. R'leyh rose everywhere, *everywhen*. I have always been what I am now. I have always survived.

For the moment, I take Marco's hands. And together, we watch Venice burn.

A DAY AND A NIGHT IN PROVIDENCE

Anthony Boulanger

Anthony Boulanger is a French author living in Paris. He writes most often about the dark paths of Fantasy, but also makes frequent excursions into Space Opera. Among his favourite subjects, you can find birds (which come in many forms, with a marked preference for the Phoenix) and maledictions. Among his favourite authors, Tolkien, Glen Cook, Roland Wagner, Orson Scott Card, and Mathieu Gaborit occupy the top spots! You can join him on his blog: anthony-khellendros.blogspot.com, his Facebook page, or by email: mithrilas@wanadoo.fr

The group was one of the most heterogenous that Philips had ever led into the Providence basilica: some Asians, ears already glued to their guide; some Europeans, apparently wondering what they were doing there; and some American compatriots. *Among all these people, how many came only because the building is listed on the tourist routes?*

"Ladies and gentlemen," Philips began, "welcome to the Most Holy Church of Our-Lady-of-Lothlorien. The initial structure was first constructed in 254 Before Tolkien by a pagan community. The conversion to the Saint's cult dates to the fifth century."

The young guide did not turn toward his group. He refused to contemplate the children who preferred to play on their portable consoles, rather than look at the glass windows representing the creations of the

Master-God, or the parents trying to masticate popcorn in this sacrosanct place.

"The planned visit passes by the catacombs, in which you will be able to see a letter from Tolkien to his son, Saint Christopher the Messiah. But first, I draw your attention to the papal altar. Sculpted from a single block of white marble, it is decorated with gold veins of flowers and of niphredil of Seredon. But the magnificence of this altar is assuredly nothing in comparison to the Chapel of the Holy Trinity, where there are services every day from 18:00 hours to 22:00 hours, the Father, the Son and the Holy Spirit."

In finishing his sentence, the young man knelt on one knee on the ground and put his hand to his head. *But what am I doing?*

Delaying for one last moment, he put his hand on his heart, then on his mouth. Behind him, only three other people took the trouble to make the sign of the Saint-Eru Illúvatar. Philips remained in this position for several minutes, masking behind his pious attitude the fear inside him. He had been inattentive several moments; he had almost made the evil Sign: the head for Madness and Horror, the lungs for Tuberculosis, and again to the head for Suicide.

If the Inquisitor is in the basilica, or is viewing the screens right now, I risk a maximum...It will be necessary that I do the change in prayers tonight... Perhaps volunteer myself for the lecture on Saint Silmarillion. Pardon me, you of whom I carry one of the Holy Names.

Philips stood up. Behind his back, sighs more insistent than usual made it clear to the guide that he was falling behind schedule. People like those he was leading today did not like to be late. This happened to be a peak hour for fast foods . . .

"Ladies and gentlemen, we are now going to make a tour around the side bordering the nave. You can see here the portraits of the different saints, from Saint Gemmel to Saint Bradley. You can also . . . "

He was stuck in automatic mode. Another hour and a few specks of minutes before the end of the tour, then another four hours of prayer before leaving this place. Philips was eager—oh, how eager—to return home. Once there, he shut himself in what he called his "chapel" and began preparing himself. This night was indeed one of the biggest nights of the year for the Shadow Cult, in which the Inquisitors of Tolkien ruthlessly pursued him . . .

"Before the *Necronomicon*, today we call you. In the Name of the Madness and the Horror of our Father Lovecraft, who leads us and destroys us. In the name of the Decline and Misfortune of his Son Smith, who heard and read the Holy Words of The Father. In the Name of the Duplicity of the Corrupt Spirit Howard. We call you, you Great Old Ones: Cthulhu, Chtuga, Yig, Glaaki, Chaugnar Faugn, and Y'Golonac."

Philips was in trance. In a few moments, his group would take over the litany, the prayer to the Outer Gods. On this night of the 15th of March in the year 655, seven centuries after the death of the Father, the faithful ones of the Shadow Cult reunited in the city of Providence.

The city in which he was born and in which he had died . . .

The city in which he had revealed to the world the existence of the Great Old Ones, and of the other Gods.

The chants reached a peak and would soon fall, to give the floor to Philips and his brothers and sisters. The chants did not act like constructed melodies, melodies that one could follow on a song sheet. They acted like a chaos of sounds, grave flights that chained themselves to magnificent, acute angles. In the spirit of the young man, colours devoured themselves, images of tentacles emerging from a cocoon of human flesh, succeeded to those of gigantic orbs, swirling about themselves. For a few heartbeats, Philips was Lovecraft. There appeared before his eyes the Revelations, the images which had enabled the Father to describe Cthulhu and all the others. He felt the fatigue that the Master had accumulated each day of his life, then the energy that ran through his body when he wrote out the Scriptures.

This night, the adepts of the Shadow Cult would invoke the power of the Trinity so that the city of R'lyeh might arise from the waves and, with it, He-who-Dreams-and-Waits.

"*Ph'nglui mglw'nafh Cthulhu R'lyeh wgah'nagl fhtagn!*"

With this phrase, the first group concluded their part of the incantation. Screams of terror punctuated the litany as the adepts were haunted, one after another, by nightmarish visions.

"*Ph'nglui mglw'nafh Cthulhu R'lyeh wgah'nagl nafl'ftaghn,*" answered the second group, including Philips.

The phrase that he pronounced in that moment, the words of Saint Derleth, was one of the most powerful keys for the Call of Cthulhu. They marked the commencement of Horror!

ƆϾϏ

Over Providence, clouds gathered. Black clouds, charged with lightning, charged with hate, carriers of a creature rampant and magnificent. With the aid of bursts in his perpetually changing body, he attacked Reality, aided in this by tens of humans who prayed to him and the other Outer Gods. He was All in One and One in All. In this rhythm, there remained only a few hours before Yog-Sothoth infiltrated our world and ravaged it!

Some kilometers from the city, the ocean was agitated by gigantic mountains of putrefying flesh. Columns suddenly pierced the waves. Rocks reddened by blood even the seawater could not efface. A white building, made of bones, suddenly appeared.

A dome of tibiae and femurs, of skulls and ribs.

A sudden explosion. A flood of chaos, of abyssal monstrosities.

An opened tomb from which escaped indescribable creatures.

Then two wings. A head of an octopus.

A gigantic body of a man.

Cthulhu was walking.

Cthulhu was walking . . .

ƆϾϏ

Great Old Ones and Outer Gods massed around Providence, more numerous with each word that Philips and the others pronounced. Creatures nebulous and bloody, horrors born from the Chaos Primordial and the Infinite Madness. Beings the sight of whom blinded the spirit and annihilated all forms of life . . .

In a world locked in a straitjacket of rules and pre-chewed thoughts, in this world where the Holy Fantastic Literature imposed its laws on creation, restricted the imagination of the most original, men and women still dared to defy the Church and the Inquisition. Persecuted for centuries, ever more fiercely and cruelly, they had decided to revolt in the most extreme fashion possible.

In the name of Lovecraft, of Howard and of Smith, their Sombre Trinity, they called in, with all their body and soul, the End of the World.

And on this night, the anniversary of the 15th of March, in this sacred city of Providence, It was at their door . . .

A WELCOME SESTINA FROM CRUISE DIRECTOR ISABEAU MOLYNEUX

Mae Empson

Mae Empson has a Master's degree in English literature from Indiana University at Bloomington, and graduated with honours in English and in Creative Writing from the University of North Carolina at Chapel Hill. Mae began selling short stories to speculative fiction magazines and anthologies in July 2010, and can be found on twitter at @maeempson, and on the web at: maeempson.wordpress.com.

"So, the Arctic is changing and it is changing faster than most people have predicted. This is leading to increased activity. As some of you know, last year, several German cargo vessels navigated the Northern Sea route unaided by icebreakers. . . . In fact, this is about year three of the Arctic becoming essentially an adventurer's playground, with yachts, cabin cruisers, folks seeking excitement and death in unusual ways . . . . Fortunately, they have yet to find death in unusual ways, but we know that will happen, eventually; it is only a matter of time."
—Mr. Dana Goward, Director of the Office of Assessment, Integration and Risk Management of the United States Coast Guard, speaking at the Proceedings on Climate & Energy: Imperatives for Future Naval Forces, March 23-24, 2010.

This private cruise to Svalbard was financed by
adventurous foodies, by gastronautic dreams
Of incomparable and illicit sights, aromas, and that
first brave promised taste and swallow.

With the Arctic melting, icebreakers have widened
the ship lanes further, and the roving eye
Of food frontier fashion has turned north,
watching, hungrily, as the monster squid,
(As the tweeters named them) began to be
found frozen beneath the melting lid
Of Arctic ice, where they'd apparently once,
long ago, gathered to spawn and die,
The ice between them riddled by acres of unanchored
egg cases. Spawn, freeze and die.

But are the eggs dead? You're here because you've
heard our claim, dream of dreams,
That Norwegian scientist-opportunists asserting
their national rights over the icy lid,
Beneath which the frozen treasures waited, have
experimented and, hard to swallow,
Hard to believe, but true as toast, the eggs can
be hatched, live paralarvae god squid,
Infant monster squid, big as a man's fist,
miniatures of the adults, with each eye
No bigger than a man's thumb. You know the
largest of the adults found so far has an eye
Big as the TV screen in our standard cabin. These
hatchlings are revived in order to die.

To die by the most delicious means possible. Sure,
you've had calamari before, mundane squid,
But the god squid paralarvae preparation is in the
Ortolan Bunting style; every Frenchman dreams
Of that taste, of the songbird first caught and
fattened, force-fed, required to swallow

Twice its size in food, drowned in brandy, and
tossed whole beneath the roasting pan's lid,
To be eaten whole, bones and all. The diner covers
his head and face with a towel, before the lid
Of the serving plate is lifted, so the rich aroma is
trapped, and the diner's face is hid from the eye
Of God—at least that's tradition, *mon Dieu*, our
tradition. The same God who counts the swallow
Before it falls. The sparrow. The songbird. But will
he mourn the hatchling, the next to die?

I think another eye is watching. The dead, frozen,
monstrous mother. I see her in my dreams.
Of course I dream of squid. It's our livelihood now.
Nothing to it. Just you wait to see the squid,
The Mother of All Squid, waiting in the ice hotel
in Svalbard. They took the largest squid,
Carved the ice around her to a thin layer, an extraordinary
ice sculpture. The base forms the lid
Of the dining room table. You literally eat on the
ice that houses her carcass. In my dreams,
Her huge eye, that would look out upon the table,
were it not closed, that hideous shut eye,
Turns to face me wherever I sit, no matter how
I hide behind my towel. Better to die
Than know what happens when that eye opens.
Better that the seas rise up and swallow
Our ship. Better that you jump overboard and
freeze than wear the towel and swallow
The hatchling, the paralarva, the spawn of the mother,
and let the tentacles of that tiny squid . . .

That tiny squid . . . What? Forgive me. I've lost my
train of thought. A momentary lapse. Die,
Indeed. Folly. Better to eat. Better to taste. Better
to know the forbidden. Open the lid
And swallow the forbidden food whole. Fear is

part of the savour of the illicit. Let the eye
Of law be blind. Let risk be our reward. We are
adventurers. We will live our wildest dreams.

If by live, I mean die. Or, rather, live squid-ridden,
like me. The hatchling will swallow
Your brain. Your will. Your dreams. Her will. My
Lady. My Mother. The Mother of All Squid
Is hungrier than you. Watch! The lid opens. It's all
been worth it. Her glorious, dinner-plate eye!

ᛉᛁᚺᛁᚾ

LOTTIE VERSUS
THE MOON HOPPER

Pamela Rentz

Pamela Rentz is a member of the Karuk Tribe and a graduate of Clarion West 2008.

"I thought the Space Barn had its own cleaning crew," Lottie said, trying to sit up straight. She'd come straight from her shift and her old bones ached for the mattress.

"We don't call it the 'Space Barn,' " Phyllis said.

Phyllis came from a family of tall, humourless Indians. Her first job at the United Tribes Space Travel Center had been on Lottie's cleaning crew. Now she was Special Assistant to the Vice-President of Facilities, with an office like a museum. Lottie sat in an uncomfortable leather chair with polished wood armrests. Must be nice to have your brother elected to Tribal Council.

Lottie rephrased the question, "I thought the Moon Hopper Storage and Refitting Hangar had its own crew."

"Used to," Phyllis said. A wall-sized calendar behind her highlighted the monthly missions in bright yellow.

"Then what happened?" Lottie asked.

"Thirty percent pay raise," Phyllis said. "I'd bring you on permanent. If you're still interested."

Why wouldn't Lottie be interested? Everybody who came through the front gate wanted to work on the Moon Hopper, even the janitors and lunchroom cooks. "Why me?"

Phyllis folded her hands on the desk. The smooth surface reflected an upside down image of her tight smile. "Why not you?"

"I applied for Moon Hopper crew a bunch. You told me I couldn't keep up," Lottie said. She'd given up a long time ago, but she could still summon the weeping fury she felt over that tangle with Phyllis. Phyllis had said everything except the words, "You're too old."

Phyllis pressed her fingers to her mouth as if trying to remember. "Huh," she said, at last. "Well, I need your experience. You've seen it all. I know you won't let me down."

It was Lottie's turn to say, "Huh."

"I got new workers. A space vessel can have unexpected . . . " Phyllis flapped a hand up by her head.

Lottie had no idea what the woman was going on about.

"You have to make sure the entire crew looks good. I need the whole thing to not be fussy." Phyllis gave Lottie a knowing nod.

"Not fussy?" Lottie said, not sure what she was being asked.

"It's a tough job," Phyllis said. "But you're unflappable."

"I can flap," Lottie said.

ᎠᎻᏓ

If prodded, Lottie would have confessed to a trembling, schoolgirl thrill over going to see the Hopper for the first time. She'd cleaned at the Space Center for years, but only in the offices, never the Space Barn.

A well-scrubbed girl waited at the security entrance next to the Barn's giant, rolling door.

"You the crew?" Lottie asked.

"I'm Hazel," she said. "Do they let elders clean the Moon Hopper?"

"Elders that want to," Lottie said.

Hazel had dark hair that reached to her elbows in one smooth sheet. She wore slacks and a long-sleeved blouse, like she expected to sit at a desk. She looked like she'd never gotten her hands dirty in her life.

"You work cleaning crew before?" Lottie asked.

"Oh, no," Hazel said. "I've been at Stanford." She paused here and Lottie understood that she was supposed to be impressed.

Instead, she said, "All that fancy college to clean the Moon Hopper?"

Hazel's brightness faded. "I intend to do Moon missions. *Lead* Moon missions. This is the entry-level step."

"Small wonder I never done a mission," Lottie said.

"I'm not qualified," Hazel said. "Yet. But Aunt Phyllis sneaked me onto this job."

" 'Aunt Phyllis'?" Lottie said. So, that's what this was about.

"It's not just because she's my aunt," Hazel said. "I work hard. I told her I could keep up with anyone."

"I'm old; I'm not slow," Lottie said. "I've been cleaning around here since you was nothing but a dot in the Creator's eye. What have you done?"

"I worked at a pastry shop near campus," Hazel said. "I utilised my people skills to communicate with customers and meet sales goals, and I initiated clean-up in the seating area."

"Great," Lottie said. She wondered what other halfwit relatives Phyllis was going to foist on her.

At last, the security door opened. A big Indian with movie-star looks jumped out and gave Lottie a hug.

"Finally! You made it to the Big Time," Clem said.

"I hear they like to promote from within." Lottie handed over their information fobs. "More crew inside?"

"I think you're it," Clem said. He gave Hazel the once-over then flashed her a panty-dropper smile. "I know you?"

Hazel blushed. "No, I've been to Stanford."

"Ah," Clem said. "Applying for a Moon mission?"

"I have far-reaching goals," Hazel said. "I'd like to see more of our people getting to the Moon. Bigger missions."

"Good luck," Clem said.

"She's Phyllis's niece," Lottie said.

"Oh," Clem said. "No luck needed."

Hazel offered a bland smile.

"Two of us cleaning," Lottie said. "Doesn't the Hopper usually have four?"

"Usually," Clem agreed. "You want me to call someone?"

What had Phyllis said about no fuss?

"Nope," Lottie said. She could already see the long night stretched ahead of them. "Send us through."

Clem led them through a long hallway to a second security station. He pointed at a heavy door with a small window.

"Your fob will get you through from here. Cleaning station is stocked. Sometimes, there's weird stuff. Be sure to wear the full Hazmat suit."

"We're not helpless," Lottie said, waving him away. "We'll see you in the morning."

The door shut behind them with a sucking snap. A green light came on, indicating they were sealed in.

Clem waved through the tiny window. Hazel waved back.

"He's cute," she said. "What do you think?"

"If I dated men half my age, I'd hop right on him," Lottie said.

Lottie opened the cleaning station and they dug through the shabby Hazmat suit collection.

"They send a barrel full of Indians to the Moon every month. You'd think they could spare a few bucks for new Hazmat suits," Lottie said. She picked the smallest one and struggled to pull the thing on.

"Is there another small one?" Hazel asked, digging through the rack.

"This ain't small," Lottie said. "You'd think they was expecting a six-foot Indian with a hundred-pound ass."

Once they were zipped in, Lottie showed Hazel how to stock her cleaning pack with the anti-bacterial, anti-viral, anti-germ, anti-dust, and anti-dirt mops and swabs they would need.

"I don't mind doing basic work like this," Hazel said, sorting her supplies. "I feel like I'm learning, already."

Lottie used her fist to cram the last items into her pack. "Don't get lost," she said as she headed for the hangar.

Hazel lurched to her feet and stumbled. She grabbed at Lottie's pack and they teetered for a few seconds before catching their balance.

"Careful, you," Lottie said.

"I can't move right and I can't see," Hazel said. "These outfits aren't made properly."

"Tell it to Aunt Phyllis," Lottie said. She grabbed a handful of Hazel's suit in back and put a plastic cleaning tie on it. The fabric puffed out like a big white rose.

"I guess that's better," Hazel said.

One last security door stood between them and the main hangar. Lottie waved her fob at the ID pad.

"Nothing's happening," Lottie said.

"Did you hear the old crew quit?" Hazel said.

"I didn't hear that," Lottie said, wondering why Phyllis failed to mention that.

"We're not supposed to know," Hazel said, lowering her voice. "I overheard. They said the Hopper made them feel funny."

"What else you hear?" Lottie asked.

"Something about the astronauts and the Space Center shrink."

"What does that mean, feel funny? Like they ate something bad?" The last thing Lottie needed was space flu.

"I don't know," Hazel said. She took the fob from Lottie and tapped it against pad. "What's taking so long?"

A low buzz sounded and the door slid open.

"Oh, see?" Hazel said. Before she should go on, Lottie pushed her through the door.

The Moon Hopper sat in a pool of dim light, looking like a shiny grasshopper built from blocks and tubes. A long ramp led up to the main hatch. A bluish glow came from inside.

Lottie had been looking forward to seeing it for years, but now that she stood in front of it, she was overcome with a sense of disappointment she couldn't place.

"Wow," Hazel said, walking toward it. "What an accomplishment for our people and—" She raised her hand to the face plate. "Gross. What's that smell?"

"You can't smell nothing. These suits have all kinds of layers and filters." Then it hit Lottie, too, a wave of thick and terrible smell, like rotten green vegetables and burned rubber. Lottie thought she might put her hand up and stick her fist through it.

"What is it?" Hazel asked.

"Someone must have forgotten a cheese sandwich," Lottie said.

They walked up the ramp and peered into the main work station.

"I thought it would be more impressive," Hazel said.

Looking around at the yellowing panels, the torn storage pouches and the carefully placed strips of duct tape, Lottie found it tough not to wonder how the Hopper made the roundtrip each month.

"Looks lived-in, is all," Lottie said. She stepped inside and her feet skidded on the floor.

"Is it supposed to be wet?" Hazel asked.

"Just leftover something," Lottie said. She bent to one creaky knee, keeping a hand on the wall for support. She dragged a gloved hand through it and the smell bloomed up from the floor. For a moment, she thought she might gack and she had to rest her head against the wall.

"You okay?" Hazel asked.

"Get the floor clean," Lottie said, pushing to her feet. She held up a wide scraper, which she fitted on an extending plastic pole. She swept it back and forth, pushing the muck into one corner. The pooled liquid had a grey tint to it.

"Too bad we can't see any experiments," Hazel said. She scraped half-heartedly at the floor, her cleaning initiative nowhere to be seen.

"Grab these," Lottie said, pulling out a wad of absorbent pads and throwing them to the floor.

"I didn't think it would be nasty," Hazel said.

"Cleaning is like that," Lottie said. She explained the Moon Hopper cleaning protocol. Every storage pocket, every compartment, every pouch had to be opened and emptied. Viable items were placed in clean, white bags to be re-sorted for possible future use or distribution. Everything else went into garbage bags.

"That gets sorted more later, too," Lottie said. "Nothing from the Moon Hopper leaves without being accounted for."

"How does the re-sorting work?" Hazel asked.

"Not your problem," Lottie said. She would have liked to explain that certain families benefited from this, but no doubt, Aunt Phyllis would fill her in on that.

"This is the composting bin. We leave it and the HazWaste for another crew. You got all that?"

"It's not rocket science," Hazel said.

The two women got on their knees to get the floor liquid up. The goop left sticky stains on their suits.

"How do you know this isn't hazardous?" Hazel asked, taking her time putting the dirty pads into the trash.

"Just mission muck," Lottie said. "We'll see more before the night is over."

A sound came from the next room, the gentle slap of rubber against a hard surface.

Lottie's heart surged in her chest, but she kept her mouth shut. She went to the narrow opening and checked the next section.

"Is someone there?" Hazel asked.

"Can't be," Lottie said. Nothing in disarray. Her breath sounded loud in the suit. She pressed her palm to her chest to calm down.

"Just ship noise," she said.

The two women set to work, going through each compartment and scrubbing everything down. Lottie was accustomed to heavy workload late at night and kept a good pace. At one point, she thought someone was watching and she turned, expecting to see Clem, but no one was there. Now that she was inside the Hopper, swimming in strange smells and substances, she had an idea what "feeling funny" might mean. Her skin was cold and her dinner didn't sit right.

"Do we have time to rest?" Hazel asked.

"You barely move," Lottie said. She'd been watching Hazel from the corner of her eye. She had house pets that could do better.

"This is super hard," Hazel said.

"No whining," Lottie said. "Next area is the sleep station. It's smaller." The sleep station was a series of cocoon-like pods, one for each astronaut. The section was lit with a few dusty lights that cast a dingy glow over the worn cloth of the pods.

"What do you think?" Lottie said. "The Moon mission lasts over a week. This is where you'd sleep, strapped in so you don't float around."

Hazel's eyes got big. "How do they relax, stuffed in like that?"

"That's the job," Lottie said. "We gotta pull all this stuff out for laundry." She leaned into the first pod to release the sleep gear. A muffled pop came from inside and a wave of spoiled smell boiled up.

Hazel gagged. "I can't stick my hands in there." She tried to back away, but she didn't get far in the cramped quarters.

"Nothing to worry about," Lottie said. She pulled the girl to her side and showed her how to untangle the straps and sleep cloths. Hazel's hands jabbed in and out, like she was reaching into a box of spiders.

"I'm so sweaty," Hazel said, in a shaky voice.

Lottie noticed it, too, a cold, uncomfortable damp in her armpits and crotch. "Hard work is good for you," she said.

Lottie had to do the last pod by herself. She cinched the laundry bag and left it on the floor.

"One section left," Lottie said, urging Hazel to the control room. This was the tiniest room yet. The two women squeezed in side-by-side.

"Just got to wipe all this down," Lottie said. "Then we're done."

"All this?" Hazel said, a creeping despair in her voice. Lottie knew how she felt. The room was nothing but giant consoles, with racks of buttons, dials and display screens. Switches stuck out from tiny shelves. Anything that wasn't a gadget was a window facing into the dark of the Space Barn.

"Grab a cleaning pad," Lottie said. "Sooner we start—"

"I can't stand it in here," Hazel said. She stared up through the windows.

Lottie didn't know what to say. Her joints ached and a fiery pain flashed through her back. She was dying to sit down.

"How come you don't you retire?" Hazel asked.

"Usual reason," Lottie said. "Money." Admitting it to this girl was especially discouraging. She eased herself into a command seat, her legs slick with sweat.

"My Mom wants me to go to the Moon," Hazel said.

"Every Indian wants their kid to go to the Moon," Lottie said.

"I'm too tired to finish," Hazel said. She sat in the other command seat and crossed her arms.

In the sleep section, a cluster of sleep fasteners clanked together, followed by a quiet flop.

Hazel grabbed Lottie's arm.

"It's more afraid of you than you are of it," Lottie said. That's what her Daddy had always told her about bears. And it was mostly true.

"What is?" Hazel whispered.

"That's not our worry," Lottie said.

Hazel stood and peeked out the opening. "I'll be right back." Before Lottie could stop her she sprinted out to the main hatch. Her boots clomped down the ramp.

"No safer out there," Lottie called. She wondered if she should chase after the fool. Clem would probably let her out and Lottie was stuck with walls of tiny doodads to be cleaned.

The smell flared up again with a rhythmic, liquid noise, like a tiny fountain.

"Settle down, you," she called. She grabbed a cleaning pad in each hand and worked the panels at a brisk pace. Hazel didn't return and Lottie's head baked in fury. No doubt, she had Clem holding her hand, and utilising his good looks to ensure she remained calm and the centre of attention.

Lottie finished the control room, her poor arms like limp noodles. She made her way back to the main work section. A long, black tail snaked into a floor vent and disappeared. The grey goo was back, possibly thicker and more syrupy.

"That's enough," Lottie hissed. "Old woman trying to get a job done. Leave it alone."

Her boots stuck to the floor. She could barely lift her feet. She yanked a few last pads from their packaging, tossed them down and wiped up the last of the fluid. Then she sat on the floor, finished. She wondered how long it would be before someone came looking for her. She would have cheerfully strangled Hazel at that moment, though she doubted she had the strength.

She closed her eyes and counted to three. When she opened them, she saw the compost bin. She crawled to the floor switch and, after a couple of tries, the thing came open with a mighty SHUCK.

She tossed the gunky pads in and used the sides of the bin to climb back to her feet. She took her time getting down the ramp.

Hazel's Hazmat suit was wadded up on the floor. She had her purse out and she brushed her hair.

"I thought you'd be rubbing against that security guard by now," Lottie said.

"He wouldn't let me in without you," Hazel said. "Did you see that thing?"

"What thing?" Lottie asked.

Hazel tossed her hairbrush into her bag. "I don't think I'll ever get that smell off me," she said.

"No," Lottie agreed. "I don't think you will."

⟨⟩ ⟨⟩ ⟨⟩ ⟨⟩ ⟨⟩

THE DAMNABLE ASTEROID

Leigh Kimmel

Leigh Kimmel lives in Indianapolis, Indiana, where she is a bookseller and web designer. She has degrees in history and in Russian language and literature. Her stories have been published in *Black October*, *Beyond the Last Star*, and *Every Day Fiction*. You can see more information about her current projects at her website: www.leighkimmel.com.

Transmission from Asteroid 37,101,191 Urtukansk, mining-pod leader Seryozha:

I have only a little time. I must get this warning out for all mining outposts throughout the Asteroid Belt.

Two weeks ago, Urtukansk acquired a companion. From the moment the smaller asteroid became enmeshed in Urtukansk's gravity well, it aroused our profound distaste. With each passing day, we found it harder to maintain our work schedule. Crossing the asteroid's surface from our habitat to the uranium pits and the breeder reactor meant seeing that scabrous lump rising and setting in its rapid orbit overhead.

We started finding excuses to stay inside. There is always more maintenance than a single pod of miners can keep up with and still make its production quota. Fix the balky valve in the 'fresher, lay new circulator lines in the algae ponds, run tests on the electronics in the life-support monitors—all legitimate tasks, but also all ways to avoid making that trek across the surface and having to see that horrid thing sweep across the starlit sky.

But there is only so long the mind can avoid a matter, however unpleasant, that remains in close proximity. There was the issue of our unmet quota of refined plutonium to drive us forth to extract the radioactive ores and prepare them for the breeder reactor. But that foul body orbiting overhead exerted its own pull upon our minds, relentless as gravity. Like an itch under a spacesuit, it grew more intense the harder we tried to ignore it.

Alyosha was the first to investigate what we all had agreed to ignore. When I confronted him, he responded that he had done nothing more than the gravimetric and spectroscopic observations that are standard whenever a body of substantial mass approaches an occupied asteroid. However, his demeanor—a direct challenge to my authority as pod leader—was at such marked variance with his usual disposition that I felt no inclination to examine his data. Instead I bawled him out, a punishment he took with a display of resentment atypical of his character.

Three days later, we received a hail from an approaching spacecraft. It belonged to Sally Nguyen, an independent sutler we'd done business with before.

I don't know why I didn't follow my initial urge to order her to pass us by. At least I won't have long to regret my decision to tell her to note our new satellite when laying in her approach.

We welcomed her with the traditional bread and salt. I was as happy as my pod-brothers to see a new face. Although we could've traded and sent her on her way, none of us wanted to lose the opportunity to socialise.

Over vodka, we talked and, as it loosened our tongues, the conversation turned to our unwelcome companion. Sally had done her own analysis of the satellite asteroid during her approach and believed its peculiarities indicated the presence of valuable materials. However, by her people's law, it became our property when our asteroid's gravity captured it and she could not explore it, except as our business partner.

The vodka had clouded our judgement, as well, for we agreed without a second thought. We spent the next two hours planning our venture before turning in to sleep off our drunk.

The next day, we ate a hasty breakfast before suiting up and piling into Sally's ship. Our asteroid's escape velocity is so low that a layer of padding on an empty cargo hold sufficed for acceleration couches. It actually took longer to lay in the course and get our launch window than to make the trip, since the satellite asteroid's orbit fluctuated in response to Urtukansk's local mass variations.

As we landed, and I got a better view of that leprous-yellow surface, I regretted the previous day's bravado. But I squelched the urge to bail. I was not going to look weak in front of my pod-brothers, much less an outsider. So, I put on my brave face and led the way.

Stepping onto the asteroid, I noted the crumbly texture of the surface stratum. It resembled rock exposed to high levels of radiant energy, but with a tendency to clump together, which suggested a strong static charge. However, electrostatic measurements proved negative, leaving us to speculate what unknown force might produce such an effect.

When we reached a safe distance from the spacecraft, we set to work digging that yellow matter that grew spongier the deeper our hole became. All my misgivings returned in force, and I was just ready to call everything off, when the robot excavator teetered, then tumbled through an unseen opening.

Alyosha scrambled down the slope, sending dust spraying in all directions. As he approached the place where the digger had disappeared, his whole body went limp. In the tiny asteroid's gravity, his fall looked more like a bit of paper fluttering to rest, but I knew something had gone very wrong.

So had Volodya. He and Alyosha were always close, although not enough to unbalance our pod's brother-bond.

Before I could caution him, Volodya scrambled down the slope. He got within a meter or two of Alyosha before he, too, went limp and fell.

Even as I struggled to make sense of what I'd seen, Sally brought a tool from her ship—an extensible pole with a grip-claw at the end. Its internal structure kept it rigid, even when fully extended and, with our help, she pulled both our stricken brothers back to the edge of the pit. I knew the worst when I saw the darkened life-support telltales on their helmets, but my heart could not yet encompass it.

Sally's shipboard autodoc was smaller than our habitat's medlab but more sophisticated. Still, it could offer no aid, only information—neither Alyosha nor Volodya had died from life-support failure. Instead, the cellular mechanisms of their bodies had shut down in the same moment as the electronics of their spacesuits.

At that point, I knew we had no business continuing to explore. "Let's get off this rock and leave it to somebody with the equipment ... "

Before I could finish, the deck set to vibrating. All of us hurried to the nearest viewport.

The scabrous surface of that damnable asteroid bulged upward, as if a balloon were expanding just beneath it. Cracks formed at the highest point and spread across the bulge. Dust and debris rose, flung out with such force that they struck the spaceship's hull, hard enough to make it ring like a bell.

I shouted for Sally to get us out of there, even as the whole ship lurched. In so little gravity, we went tumbling in all directions and, by the time we found handholds, even that gravity had gone. The violence of the eruption had thrown us back into space and freefall.

But only for a moment before the engines fired, this time a jolt strong enough to make me wish for proper acceleration couches. Improperly restrained objects pelted us as they fell.

Weightlessness returned and we pulled ourselves to the viewport. It took some seconds that stretched to subjective eternity for the relative motion of the three bodies in our micro-system to bring the damnable asteroid into view.

Our makeshift mine had become a maelstrom of dust, so thick it obscured the landforms around it. From within came a pallid glow reminiscent of certain growths that invade a habitat's waste-reclamation system. It aroused a profound sense of revulsion, which I forced down in my determination to see what had just killed two of my pod-brothers.

Even now, I cannot describe the shape which emerged from that dust cloud. I had the impression of a great bulk, yet of a putty-like flexibility possible only in a microgravity environment. From it extended translucent surfaces of improbable size and thinness, fluttering as if on some cosmic aether from those tales that predate even the semi-legendary First Age of Space.

A touch on my shoulder pulled me free of that thing's grip on my mind. I turned to find Sally waiting just behind the window.

"I've put the ship onto a parabolic trajectory that should buy us enough time for the computer to work out a solution for an inhabited asteroid."

My mind was still befuddled enough that it took a moment to understand. Asteroid miners don't work with orbital mechanics on a regular basis, so we don't think about how individual asteroids' orbits around the Sun make for constantly changing positions in relation to one another. The haste of our escape would have made matters worse, because the computer would first have to derive our new location.

On the other hand, our course had removed the damnable asteroid and its hideous inhabitant from our line of sight. One by one, my pod-brothers came out of the trance that monster had put them under.

Before I could answer their questions, an alarm began to whoop. Sally punched a button on a nearby terminal. As she read the data it displayed, her expression hardened.

"There's a problem with the computer. It can't resolve a course anywhere and it's starting to degrade performance on other systems."

I asked her what other options we had.

"No good ones. I can aim for an asteroid that's transmitting, and hope I've got our trajectory right and don't send us on a slow orbit to nowhere. Or I can return to Urtukansk on visual and we can try to fight—"

More alarms went off. Life-support telltales went yellow and red. We re-sealed our spacesuits.

"I think that decision's been made for us." I gestured for my pod-brothers to brace for the necessary manoeuvers.

Throughout the series of thruster firings, I waited for disaster. When we landed and gravity resumed its pull, it took a moment to believe we had returned safely to Asteroid Urtukansk.

Or not-so-safely, I realized, as we exited Sally's spaceship, just in time for Urtukansk's companion to rise over a horizon all-too-close. Except it was no longer a solid mass but a cloud of fragments that continued in the same orbit as their parent body. Within it rippled the eye-twisting form of the monster that had killed two of my pod-brothers.

A panicky voice came onto the suit-radio circuit. "It's coming after us!"

Before I could calm my pod-brother, Sally came on. "I'm taking the ship back up and trying to distract that thing long enough for you guys to blow your breeder reactor."

There was no time to argue the wisdom of that plan. At least the task of running across an asteroid's surface, without launching ourselves into orbit, kept our attention on the ground.

We were within a dozen meters of the reactor complex when Mirosha shrieked, "It's got her!"

Behind us, a light flashed, casting our shadows in sharp relief on the rocks. I squelched the urge to turn and see what had happened. Sally had bought our chance and we mustn't waste it.

Only at the airlock for the reactor complex did I pause. I pushed three of our surviving pod-brothers safely in, but even as I reached for poor, lagging Mirosha, the writhing mass overhead extended a tentacle that wrapped like a sinuous rope around his waist and lifted his feet right off the surface.

His shrieks of terror over the suit-radio circuit made my ears hurt, but there was nothing I could do for him. I shut the airlock behind me and hit the controls to cycle us in. When the screaming stopped, we knew Mirosha had met the same fate as Alyosha and Volodya.

Once inside, we hurried to disable the safety systems. All the time, we could hear that thing clawing overhead, trying to break in.

We had just shut down the coolant pumps when the roof gave way over the reactor. Atmosphere vented into space and, with it, everything not fastened down. I hit the buttons to withdraw all the control rods from the reactor.

The explosion threw me against the wall so hard I thought sure it would break the faceplate of my helmet. A flash of light filled the area and in that moment, I saw the hideous thing torn apart, reduced to a dust of ash so fine even photons would scatter it to the farthest reaches of the solar system.

Although the control room shielding did protect me, I still took a lethal dose of radiation. It just bought me enough time to transmit this account before my body fails altogether.

Now you must see that my warning gets to every mining outpost in the Asteroid Belt. There are things undreamed-of by our science, that can lie encysted for so many millions of years that the accretion of space dust upon them can form an asteroid around them. And when disturbed, can reawaken to a life inimical to our very existence—

[Choking sounds, followed by an open carrier for fifteen minutes]

ᛉᛁᚻᛁᚾ

MYRISTICA FRAGRANS

E. Catherine Tobler

E. Catherine Tobler lives and writes in Colorado—strange how that works out. Among others, her fiction has appeared in *Sci Fiction*, *Fantasy Magazine*, *Realms of Fantasy*, *Talebones*, and *Lady Churchill's Rosebud Wristlet*. She is an active member of SFWA and senior editor at *Shimmer Magazine*. For more, visit www.ecatherine.com.

Abeni Baba was accustomed to things falling apart in her hands: grains from distant worlds, the dead in autopsy, her marriage. As *iyaloja* of Aphelion Station, she found that things fell apart less than they once had, yet still, these corridors with their people and goods could surprise her, as happened when she took the palm-sized copper pendant from the opened sack of nutmegs. How had it come to contaminate the goods? This was her first thought, being that her purpose was to ensure clean and equal trade among the people; she was Mother of the Market, these traders her children, these goods her grandchildren. And this pendant—

It was marked with a figure: upward man and downward fish. When her thumb moved over it, the pendant came apart, silent and sure, and Abeni closed her hand around it so that none might see. Her dark eyes lifted to the vendor before her. Bolanle bowed her head, spreading broad hands toward the bounty of nutmegs she had procured this journey. Such goods were worth more than gold on Aphelion, yet Abeni would give them all up for a taste of sunlight once more.

"You journeyed to . . . ?" Abeni's voice trailed off, wondering from where these sacks had come. She knelt before them, one hand sliding over the canvas sack, finding it had no mark upon it. In her other hand, the pendant warmed, seemed to send tendrils of sunlight up the length of Abeni's arm. Her fist tightened.

Bolanle's answer didn't interest Abeni: It was a common trade route, the nearest planet to the Aphelion Station. However, the dark man who emerged from behind Bolanle *did* interest Abeni. She watched this man, overly tall and thin, peer around Bolanle's slender bare shoulder, borealis eyes widening as he looked down upon Abeni and the sacks of nutmegs. He reached with one impossibly long arm—Where was the joint for his elbow, for his forearm seemed to reach entirely to his shoulder?—black spindle fingers sliding with a whisper against Abeni's own, holding a startling coldness that seemed like the very depths of space to her. So, too, his skin: black abyss, like that which stretched around and out from Aphelion.

"Mother Baba."

The dark man dwindled and faded to nothing more than Bolanle's shadow as she rounded her goods and knelt beside Abeni. Abeni felt the pulse of the thing in her hand and slowly rose, shaking Bolanle off. "It has been a long morning of arrivals," she said, nodding to the traders who cluttered the docking ring and cargo bays. "And I've more to tend." Her voice snapped and Bolanle withdrew. Abeni took one nutmeg with her and fled Bolanle's stall without marking the requisite forms to allow her goods full entry to Aphelion. And if Bolanle opened her mouth to cry a protest, Abeni took no notice, so intent was she on leaving the docking ring.

Aphelion Station spread in five concentric rings, rotating on the edge of known space. Abeni had never been troubled by its motion before, for her work consumed her. But as she hurried away now, she caught sight of the whole and infinite black beyond the arched station windows, and she cried out, as if looking into the face of the shadow man. And then, Aphelion faded.

Abeni felt the pulse of the thing in her hand and found herself standing in a field of grain. Sun drenched the space and her. Abeni thought she would melt, that her entire body would liquefy and flood the ground beneath her. Her death would feed these grains until they were strong, until they—they whispered against her fingertips as she walked and under her passage, they grew. They changed. These grains, once green, flushed to gold and thickened. These grains, once only knee-high, pressed their roots into the soil and surged upward, until they reached skyward. Abeni lifted a hand, but could no longer touch the grain tips. And these tips, once gold, now burned under a flaring sun, turning black, the charred fragrance falling onto Abeni's shoulders like snow. The grains closed over her then, pressing her to the dirt, until its darkness filled mouth and nose, until the shadow man snatched a hand out and pulled her into the earth.

She woke in the depths of the station, humid, fetid air rolling over her sticky skin. Painlessly, one palm had been marked by the pendant, the fish figure curling inward, as if huddled. Abeni sat up, the small pendant gleaming a step away from her nose. It was sealed shut once more, though the nutmeg she had taken was cracked in half, revealing its labyrinthine innards, brown curling through ivory; its sharp scent carried to her, seemed to clear her mind. Abeni rolled herself to sitting, crossing her legs and finally reaching a hand to claim the strange pendant. Moisture coated its case, making it slick within her grip. When she picked up the nutmeg next, it withered in her hand, yet Abeni took it with her as she climbed her way out of the maintenance levels and returned to her private room.

It was a small room, unassuming, decorated with very little, save small trinkets that merchants brought her. Three books, two miniatures, a dried flower from a riverbank on a planet she would never know. A figure that looked like a blue jellyfish, a small plate with an off-center fish painted upon it, three jars of soil. It was the soil she sought, knowing she needed it—though not knowing why or how. She broke the seal on one jar, releasing a fragrance that seemed like sunlight to her; the air sounded like whispering grains as the lid came away. She stuck her small hand through the mouth of the jar, burying the withered nutmeg in the black soil. After a second thought, she planted the pendant, too.

Come morning, Abeni returned to the docking ring, wishing to pretend all was normal and well. But she knew she had left her work unfinished and unhappy merchants greeted her. Goods lined the pathways, awaiting proper entry to the station. One by one, Abeni worked her way through them, last of all to Bolanle, who sat atop her nutmeg sacks, as she had the whole night through. Abeni made no apologies and none of the merchants were openly hostile. As *iyaloja,* her methods were beyond scrutiny; she would work as she worked and their goods would only be allowed entry by her word. Bolanle worked at her side in comfortable silence, shifting her approved goods to the pallet so they could be moved into the station proper. When Abeni claimed one sack of nutmegs for herself, Bolanle only looked at her.

"I have need of these," Abeni said and Bolanle said nothing, for it was not her place. She considered herself lucky to lose only one sack. Everyone knew that larger tithes had been taken by *iyaloja* prior to Abeni.

However, not even Abeni could say why she took the entire sack of nutmegs. She cradled the sack against her side, as she might a child, while she made the last of her daily rounds and checked the following day's schedule. The sound the nutmegs made within the canvas sack calmed her: click, click, click-click. She pictured their small brown shapes, pressed against each other and her; their veined insides, worms coiling through flour. These things pleased her, but she could not say why. Later, in her room, she would look at the quantity of nutmegs she now possessed, and her meager jars of soil, and she would mourn, not understanding.

Neither did she understand how, in the depth of night, she came to discover the pendant pressed against her breast. It came away with a puckering sound of sweat, the image of this fishman pressed again into her skin. Soil clung to her, as well, proving that she had truly buried it, but now it was here, with her. Abeni held the pendant between her fingers, stroking the fish until the pendant slid open.

It was not a locket as she understood lockets; there was no place for a mirror or an image. Inside, there was only yawning blackness, as if the pendant were a portal. When Abeni pressed a finger to the darkness, it was as though her finger went inside a space she could not otherwise see. Her finger did not come out the backside of the pendant as it should have. It was simply gone.

And inside? That darkness was warm and wet, vaguely like a mouth, she thought, though it contained no teeth. She drew her finger out and, though it felt wet, she could see that it was not. *All the ocean in this little ornament,* she thought, and closed her eyes. This was not her sunlit grain.

The darkness belonged to Bolanle, as surely as the shadow man did. This thought came to Abeni upon waking. The day had not yet begun on the station; its crew slept on, tied to the rhythms of the ancient world that had envisioned this place. Did that world exist, still? Abeni often wondered, for to her, Earth was but a dream, a place for other generations. Her place was here, Aphelion in deep space, and she roamed its corridors barefooted, heading toward Bolanle.

In Bolanle's room, Abeni pulled her to the decking and showed her the pendant, cradled in both hands, opened, the darkness yawning. Bolanle stared. "This is for you," Abeni said, and pressed Bolanle's hand to the dark.

Bolanle vanished. It was not a sudden thing; Abeni wished it had been. The woman disappeared bit by bit through the small opening of the pendant, as though she were a piece of paper, folded in on itself over and over. Bolanle shrieked once, as the shadow man ripped himself free from her then pushed her—pushed her as he might a boulder from a great height, hands and feet of abyss pressed against her backside—pushed her until only a toe remained poking out, and then that, too, was swallowed by the darkness. Abeni stared, expecting to see something—there was only that small, yawning circle of dark—then lifted her gaze to the shadow man, now crouched across from her.

"Feeding me will not stop it," the shadow man said. His voice was a terrible thing, the sliding of oil down Abeni's throat, and she felt she would be sick. "If you plant all the nutmegs . . . there will still be the water. Even they cannot drink it all."

Abeni wondered if she could drink it all and the shadow man laughed. His laughter was like a flood—she wished for that field of grain, so the water might be stemmed, but it rushed onward, over her, into her. She was drowning now, in a water thick like oil, which filled her nose and mouth and ears, until she was mute and could only watch herself float away. In this floating, there was no peace, no peace until Aphelion, herself, bent under the pressure and exploded.

Abeni's hand snatched out to grab the shadow man. His borealis eyes went wide and she laughed, bubbles streaming through his oily flood. She latched onto his impossibly long arms and held to him, and then—

He vanished as Bolanle had. Folded up on himself, until he could be folded no more, and poof! Abeni fell to the decking, the pendant rattling beside her. She half-expected Bolanle to be vomited out, but no, the pendant had closed and there was no Bolanle. Abeni grabbed the pendant and opened it, but even the small darkness has closed upon itself, no more than a pinprick within the metal. Abeni stroked a finger over it—oily wet—but it did not expand.

She closed the pendant and stood on shaking legs, moving out of Bolanle's quarters, toward the docking ring. Most of the station was still not awake, but merchants would arrive soon, early ships on clocks different from station time. Even now she could feel the slight vibration in the station as a ship docked. By the time she reached the docking ring, they were unloading and Abeni watched from a shadow. As the goods came onto Aphelion, the *iyaloja* wondered what else she might have let slip through. All these years, how many pendants? How many shadow men folded inside merchants? She saw nothing out of place, yet—until there, there! Her eyes went wide as a trio of shadows slid out of a shipping container over the wall, creeping upward on obscure feet.

If you plant all the nutmegs. . . .

His words came back to her; Abeni shook them off. Of course, she could not plant all the nutmegs, for she lacked the soil—Or did she? Abeni's mind turned to the place where she had awakened and that awful, fetid smell. Compost, she thought. Station waste. But he had said no—that even planting them would be of no use. She could not see what was coming, only knew there was something—something in these shadows that crept from the containers of distant worlds. What was Aphelion becoming gateway to? What?

As Mother of the Market, it was her job to stop it. Abeni knew this the way she knew her own heartbeat, the way she knew she craved the light of a distant sun. Sunlight on grain, she longed for it—but no, not yet.

Yes now, sweet Mother.

The whisper startled her and the shadow man curled his hand around her throat. Abeni no longer felt inside the station; the docking ring and its cargo bays seemed far distant, only a smudge of light on the distant horizon. The shadow man pulled her backward, through stars and planets, through nebulae and across black holes. Flashpoint, she thought, and squeezed her eyes shut, but even then she could see the places he showed her and all their terrible creatures. The darkness writhed, reaching for her with questing limbs that were sun-warm and slick. Abeni could not breathe for the horror that spread before her, this rotting land with its dying gods. These creatures reached for her, for Aphelion, to live yet again though so many had forgotten.

The sunlight here was sickly, throwing into shadow more than it illuminated, but she could see winged horrors moving within that light. Abeni tried to make sense of what she saw, but could not; she found that when she stopped trying, she could see more, more that made her want to shriek, but she had no breath, for the shadow man kept firm hold of her. She supposed, in a far distant corner of her mind, that he hoped to intrigue her. These goods, if they could be called such, were like none Aphelion had seen; wouldn't the universe marvel that Abeni had found such wonders? Wouldn't they herald Aphelion Station as the new dawn, the beginning of an entirely new life?

Abeni wrenched herself free. She stumbled to the decking, hands smacking the metal before her shoulder could. She sucked in a breath and startled when she felt a hand touch her shoulder. She rolled toward the wall, expecting the shadow man, but it was a different man who stood there, the merchant Esmail, whom she slowly recognized. Abeni took his hand and pulled herself up.

"Little Mother, are you well?"

Her eyes moved past him, to the shadows that coated the walls of Aphelion Station. "I am not," she said, seeing no reason to deny it. She was not well and neither was her station, but she wondered how both might be so, again.

"You speak in riddles, Abeni," Esmail said, after she told him of Bolanle, of the nutmegs, of the writhing darkness. She could not make better sense of all that she had seen, did not know how to stop what she felt coming. "You speak of things that are not so. These shadows do not move and nutmegs are but nutmegs."

The worst thing of it, Abeni decided, was not Esmail disbelieving her. It was that she longed for the things the shadow man had shown her. She wanted these creatures to come through Aphelion Station and make their mark upon it. How wonderful a discovery these great and terrible things. This corner of the universe had never seen their like. The curious child within Abeni responded to that, wanted to see these creatures in the light of the sun, wanted—

No. What she wanted did not matter. She could not allow it. Would not. "Esmail, I need your help," she said. "I need the containers of your ship and the compost of this station."

The shadow man said it would not matter, but Abeni moved forward, anyhow, claiming one cargo bay for her experiment. Sunlit grain, she wanted a forest of sunlit grain. She would have to make do with nutmegs and so, did, planting all that she had in the malodorous compost the engineers gave her with mocking smiles. They thought she had finally lost her mind, for nutmegs were not grown this way. The horticulturists told her the same, insisting she come to their deck to see how they did their work—one must splice, one must graft!—but no. Abeni paid to house her experiment within one of the cargo holds and waited, ignoring everyone who told her she was wrong.

As the hold began to warm over the coming days, Abeni wondered if perhaps she was wrong after all, but something within her said to keep on. Never had she heard such an insistent voice and so, she tended the nutmegs as she might children, often forgetting her normal duties as she walked among the growing trees. This could not be so, the arborists said, walking down the neatly planted rows; how could these poor nutmegs be growing as they were? Abeni did not know, but watched as they soared upward and reached for the ceiling with its artificial sunlight streaming downward.

Harvest, and Abeni welcomed those who would see what she had grown. Esmail came to help her gather the nutmegs and it was he who opened the first of the pods to reveal the spice inside. Thus, it was Esmail who suffered the first horror as the creature unwound itself from the nutmeg and crawled out of the pod, latching onto the nearest arm. It was, after all, hungry, Abeni supposed.

The creature was a thing she had seen in the writhing darkness, a dozen lashing limbs and one hungering mouth. As it suckled at Esmail's arm, he staggered backward. Below his moan, the cracking of other pods was heard within the cargo hold. Beneath Abeni's feet, the decking rumbled. She moved to the doors, knowing then that Aphelion was lost. All that it had been, gone. Her mistake. Her vain hope. She pushed the arborists into the main docking ring, sealing the cargo hold with herself and Esmail inside. All around them, pods broke open, creatures writhing to escape their confines.

And then, the shadow man came and laughed in Abeni's ear as he wrapped his arms around her. Abeni leaned back in his embrace, wanting to let these creatures out, wanting to show them to the world, and yet -

"Told you, there will still be the water," the shadow man whispered.

She thought, *Oh, but I miss the sunlight.* "Let the water come."

The shadow man flooded the compartment with his warm, oil-slick water. Abeni felt herself float upward, amid the creatures who swam and seemed to grow within the disagreeable water. They moved effortlessly, bobbing and darting, swarming over what remained of Esmail, drifting closer to Abeni and the shadow man. She pressed closer to him, into his darkness and beyond.

"Sweet Mother," he whispered—and then his eyes flew wide.

Abeni had reached beyond him, to the control panel, where slick fingers skimmed to vent the compartment. Water and creatures alike were blown outward, into the abyss beyond Aphelion Station, into the darkness between the stars. Abeni felt the shadow man release her, felt his scream as his children died, amid boiling water which then exploded in a shower of ice. Did it snow between the stars? That day, it did.

And Abeni . . . Abeni reached until she could reach no more, and dreamed she felt sunlight trailing over her cheeks, her throat, and into the hollow of her fish-marked palm.

{ᘿHᘿ↑

DARK OF THE MOON

James S. Dorr

James Dorr has published two collections with Dark Regions Press, *Strange Mistresses: Tales of Wonder and Romance* and *Darker Loves: Tales of Mystery and Regret*, and has a book of poetry about vampirism, *Vamps (A Retrospective)*, that came out this August from Sam's Dot Publishing. Other work has appeared in *Alfred Hitchcock's Mystery Magazine*, *New Mystery*, *Science Fiction Review*, *Fantastic*, *Dark Wisdom*, *Gothic.Net*, *Chi-Zine*, *Enigmatic Tales* (UK), *Faeries* (France), and numerous anthologies. Dorr is an active member of SFWA and HWA, an Anthony and Darrell finalist, a Pushcart Prize nominee, and a multi-time listee in *The Year's Best Fantasy and Horror*. Up-to-date information on Dorr is at: http://jamesdorrwriter.wordpress.com.

"Houston," the voice crackled, "we've completed our separation. We're starting our descent to Tsiolkovsky now." Tasha monitored the transmission, only half-glancing at the flickering control panel screen as she fired her own rockets. She didn't need to follow it word for word, anymore than she needed to check the adjacent monitor's feed from Earth, with its pre-dawn view of the Moon's hair-thin crescent—the dark of the Moon—just above the horizon to know, more than anyone else, what was happening. The voice was that of Gyorgi, her husband.

"Commander Sarimov, we read you in Houston. All systems A-OK?"

"Gyorgi Sarimov here. Yes, Houston. Tsiolkovsky's below us, brighter than Tycho on your Earthside. Its central mountain—you'll see for yourselves once Natasha has brought her C.M. to a higher orbit. Meanwhile, to north, we can see the Sun glinting off the peaks of the Soviet Mountains while, southeast of us, Jules Verne Crater, the Sea of Dreams. . . . "

Tasha heard NASA's reply, mostly lost in static, perhaps a result of her shifting orbits, or, more likely, because the Command Module that she now piloted alone was itself passing behind the Moon. It would store the pictures that Gyorgi sent to it, waiting until it passed once more into sight of the Earth, where she could transmit them to the International Space Station and, thence, to Houston. But, for now, she could still hear Gyorgi's voice.

She shut her eyes. Listened.

. . . *Fancies such as these were not the sole possessors of my brain. Horrors of a nature most stern and most appalling would too frequently obtrude themselves upon my mind, and shake the innermost depths of my soul . . . .*

Why had she thought that?

She thought, instead, of when she had first met Gyorgi, at what they then called the Baykonur Cosmodrome, over tea at the enlisted men's mess. She was, technically, a civilian and he still in training, so that the officer's sector was barred to them. Back when the U.S.S.R. still existed.

Such horrors as she herself had experienced that dark night, when she'd felt a loneliness such as she felt now—separated from her then-future husband, with nothing that she could do. The night of the accident.

And then she chuckled. Gyorgi had found the words now to speak to her, perhaps just in a whisper over the uplink. For her ears only. And Gyorgi remembered. He quoted to her, not the words that she had thought during the accident nor words of his own, but those of an American author, Edgar Allan Poe, from a story she'd shown him in Florida after he'd started his training with NASA.

The story had had to do with a balloonist who'd gone to the Moon.

ↁⱡⱦ

When she began the transmission again, she already knew of the Lunar Module's safe landing, of Gyorgi's careful step out onto Tsiolkovsky's smooth floor. She had seen, as if through his eyes, the other two follow: one man American, one a Frenchman. There would have been another

American, too, in orbit in the C.M., had he not taken ill just before their launch window. She had been a last-minute substitute for him. In her mind's eye, she saw herself still on Earth, standing outside in the dim, winter air to watch the nearly invisible Moon rise, where she *would* be, had it not been for Gyorgi's powers of persuasion. And she thought that, in the imagination of another Frenchman, not far from where she and her husband had lifted off scarcely four days before, other lunar cosmonauts had launched themselves in a shell from a huge gun.

So many authors, and not just Americans and Frenchmen, had been enamoured of the Moon for centuries. Even the namesake of her husband's landing site, their own Tsiolkovsky, had written among his scholarly papers a novel, *Outside the Earth*. Others, too—Oberth, Goddard, the Englishman H.G. Wells—wrote fact and fiction about lunar travel or travel to planets beyond the Moon. Or, in the case of Wells and another American, Lovecraft, of alien beings beyond the Moon, who, turning the premise on its head, came to Earth to do evil.

Horrors most stern and most appalling . . . .

Tasha shuddered. As if Mankind couldn't do evil enough itself.

She thought of Russia. Its people. Its sorrows. Its myths, also, though they, like the Western science-fictional myths filled with their own wonder, had helped bring her and her husband together.

And now *he* had landed, part of the first expedition to the Moon's far side. The side that was dark when you could look up and see the Moon—always faced out to space. And light when you couldn't, so that now, when the Moon was hidden from Earth, Gyorgi had light by which to explore.

" . . . We're setting the cameras now on the crater floor." This she brought up on the C.M. monitor to watch for herself, to compare the camera eye "reality" with such deeper truths as her mind's eye might show her, again almost as if she might see through *his* eyes. So well did she knew her husband, by now, and his way with descriptions.

And she saw a graveyard . . . .

꒐⼦

Her mind snapped back to the Baykonur Cosmodrome. To a metal table and glasses of hot tea. "You," Gyorgi had said, "you know the myths, too, then?"

"Yes," she answered. "The Sun and the Moon. The stars their children. You, Cosmonaut-in-Training Sarimov, brought up in Krasnoyarsk"—they'd known each other that well by then—"are the image of Dazhbog, of the Sun."

He chuckled. She gazed at his sun-bright hair—her own was pale-brown, at best its dim shadow—as he smiled and answered, "Then you, Mechanical Engineer Tasha, must be that strangely named beauty 'Myesyats'. Named as a man, yet entirely a woman, the Goddess-Moon." He chuckled again. "You know, they were married."

She blushed. By then, they *had* slept together, but still . . . talk of marriage? She frowned as she answered, "True. They were married. But then he abandoned her."

Gyorgi laughed. "Yes. But the following springtime . . . "

And then, a week later, he *did* leave her, though not by his own choice. The KGB was still to be feared then and when, one evening, he didn't show up with the others at the mess, she imagined the worst. She knew what he had been trying to do for her, to get her into the cosmonaut program. Fearing, to be sure, that as an engineer, she might at any time be re-assigned to some other location, something she didn't wish to happen, either. But she knew, too, that, while Gyorgi had a way with his superiors, a way of usually wheedling successfully what he asked for, one could not push the system too far before it would push back.

And that was when she'd found out how much she really loved him.

ↄﾊエ

"Houston, do you read? The cameras are working, but possibly, we've made a miscalculation. We've set down on the southern side of Tsiolkovsky's central peak, since that's where the ground seemed the smoothest, but as a result, our landing site is in shadow. Perhaps in a few days, when the sun has shifted somewhat. . . . "

She watched the pictures on the TV monitor and saw what Gyorgi meant. When they turned away from the mountain they were to explore, she could see the far crater wall, brilliant in sunlight, and the L.M. itself, where it sat on its landing struts, half-lit, half-shadowed.

But back toward the mountain, the strange, jagged peak that, so the scientists said, could only mean that Tsiolkovsky itself was an impact crater—and what an impact, the scar it left nearly three times as wide as the Earthside's most prominent feature, Tycho!—back that way, all that the cameras could pick up was darkness.

She *looked* through Gyorgi's eyes . . .

Darkness. A jumble. Shadow and darkness—the realm of Chernobog. And yet, in the darkness, this side of the mountain, what looked like small hillocks, yet pointed and craggy.

"The central peak's children?" she whispered, half to herself. Realising, of course, that even if she were trying to contact him, Gyorgi, outside the L.M., couldn't hear her.

She watched as if through his eyes, as if her sight, too, were confined by his helmet as he and the others peered into the darkness.

The hills were still far away from the L.M. and the men wouldn't go to them until the next morning—Earth morning, that was, after they'd had another sleep period. Yet, they *did* look a little like gravestones.

Huge, sharp gravestones, patterned in rows. And between them—did she see what Gyorgi *really* saw?—what could almost be mist if the moon had an atmosphere.

Shadow and darkness. Her thoughts went back once more to that evening in Baykonur, when all her inquiries about Gyorgi had turned up nothing. She'd lain in bed in her room that night, claiming she felt ill, and tried to concentrate on Gyorgi.

She thought of the Sun and the Moon and their mythic love—the cause of the seasons. Dazhbog and Myesyats. Thought of their quarrels that, so the myths claimed, also gave birth to earthquakes. Dazhbog's abandonment of his Moon-Bride every winter, but—here, she concentrated the hardest—his coming back each spring. And . . . .

She joked about it afterward, saying it must have been the special sensitivity of her Russian woman's soul. Or perhaps just stress. But she *had* seen it.

. . . the vision . . .

. . . white walls. An accident ward in a rural hospital outside of Baykonur, where Gyorgi had crashed his motorcycle. The doctors had not yet informed the officials—or, rather, as her vision widened, she realised they *had* told the Cosmodrome's commandant, but, although she'd asked, he had not told *her*.

The shadow. The brightness. The earlier myths of primeval Man, of evil and goodness. Chernobog and Byelobog, gods of the Dark and Light. Light of truth, withheld even when she had asked . . . .

Gyorgi had come back the following morning, little the worse for wear. And, of course, what she thought she had seen could have been a coincidence—she knew he drove too fast. She had even argued with him about it. But in the meantime, she'd made two decisions. The first was to officially ask for a transfer to the cosmonaut program, to become a cosmonaut-in-training. This, she knew, was what Gyorgi had wanted, but up to this moment, she had always held back.

And the other, when Gyorgi was better, was to insist that they get married.

ↃＷↄ

She lay on her couch, remembering now, while, on the moon's far side, Gyorgi was sleeping. She had read the Western myths. Fantasy. Science fiction. Books she had purchased to read, alone, in the Florida nights while Gyorgi had been away on training.

She knew about training, and nights spent alone, even after her and Gyorgi's marriage. Even though, by then, she was a cosmonaut, too, "to follow in the footsteps of Tereshkova," as her husband had put it to those in command, there still was no question of her being actually sent into space, herself. Even Valentina Tereshkova had been a symbol, making that one flight in 1963, but, as a woman, thereafter perpetually grounded—so, too, her own job had continued to be primarily that of a mechanic.

But then the Soviet Union collapsed and they'd moved again, first to Luga, where her family came from—here, *she* could find work, whereas he was idle—and then to America, as a package with the great *Energia* rockets that NASA had bought from the Russian Republic, to help in the rebirth of its Moon program.

And while Gyorgi learned the ins and outs of American space capsules, Tasha had read Western authors and wondered. She'd wondered at all the authors' obsessions with reaching the Moon. For all, it seemed the ultimate mystery, especially its dark side. And even, for some, it seemed also the key to a deeper mystery.

The Russian myths, before the Sun and Moon, spoke of gods of light and shadow. Of Byelobog and Chernobog. She wondered if Lovecraft had known the Russian myths—

Why had she thought of H.P. Lovecraft? Rather than Verne or Poe or the others?—yet, surely he had known, if not directly, as surely they all had. His vision sharper, perhaps, in some respects, just as the others' was sharper in others. It was her belief that all human thought was ultimately based on identical truth, on some all-but-forgotten memory of Mankind.

Yet, the myths were, at base, simply metaphor. The evil of shadow was surely *Man's* evil. That she believed, too. Just as the *Energia* rocket was her metaphor-child—she and Gyorgi had proved unable to have their own children, despite the myth-union of Dazhbog and Myesyats spawning the stars. But she'd helped assemble the *Energia* on its new American launchpad, so Gyorgi could ride it, and then, when Captain Brechner came down with the flu and she was assigned to the C.M. in his place, they *both* could ride it . . . .

The ship to the Moon's far side—*through* its darkness. Opening mysteries to reach to the stars beyond, past the planets, stars shrouded, yet burning bright in their own darkness. The children of Sun and Moon.

God and Goddess, one in the other.

ɔﬁƐ

Tasha dreamed of the moon and stars, her mind metaphorically one with Gyorgi's. It was while she slept in that way that she often felt she understood the most.

Tasha dreamed of the following morning—no need for TV, now—as the L.M. opened and three men dismounted, bulky in spacesuits. She walked with the first of them into the shadows.

She saw the balloon first, the one Poe had dreamed of in his chronicle of the Hollander-Cosmonaut, Hans Pfaall. She saw its bent hoop, its tangled netting, its bag-covered gondola—more than even her husband could see because her eyes were clearer. She saw the projectile that Jules Verne envisioned, fired from the giant columbiad cannon, which, even if it had not achieved touchdown, still lay on its side in the shadow before her.

She saw other shapes, too, arrayed in long rows. Rows that converged on the central mountain. A bicycle-like frame, surrounded by skeletons of long-dead geese; another, surrounded by metal spheres. The V2-like slimness of Robert Heinlein's and Willy Ley's coupled dream, made into cinematic flesh in a film she'd seen once when she was a child, *Destination Moon*. And yet other shapes, too, saucer-like nightmares, the visions of men like Jessup and Scully that lay, side by side, with truly *non*-human dreams. Shapes to fit truly non-human proportions . . . .

She blinked.

. . . and yet, all dead. The ships crushed and broken . . .

She *heard* Gyorgi thinking:

. . . *Let us put bones, then. This plain would be nothing but an immense cemetery, on which would repose the mortal remains of thousands of extinct generations . . . .*

She woke. Yes, a graveyard. A graveyard of spaceships. The words were not Gyorgi's, though, but—she thought back—those of Michel Arden. The French adventurer in Jules Verne's novel.

She blinked. On Earth, in Houston, the Sun would have just gone down—she'd slept the whole day through. Far to the west, the Moon would be setting, too; this time, she wouldn't see even a sliver.

The TV monitor was still on, the equipment functioning automatically. She heard its static. She sat up to look at it, seeing the images, shadowy, fleck-filled.

" . . . Tomorrow, we'll rig lights that we can take with us," her husband was saying. NASA was gentle, unlike the Cosmonaut Corps of her own nation—first, they must have rest. "Those, with the portable camera we have now, may give more information on those oddly shaped rocks we've found." Then, he had *not* seen.

She sank back to the couch as he gave his description. A cemetery, yes, laid in rows, but still *only* stone and dust.

Only she saw what was buried beneath it.

ꝯﬞﬗ⚹

Gyorgi! she screamed—knowing he couldn't hear her, not outside— watching her husband step from the L.M. the final time. Half-dreaming, half waking-in front of the monitor, she waited as the three astronauts, in blazing light now, walked through the ships' graveyard, her own space-craft having swung back around the Moon too late to do anything more than just watch them. She saw, with her vision, the L.M. itself, in the line of corpses. The crushing of Men's dreams.

But Gyorgi could *not* see.

During the night, she'd recalled, in her mind's eye, those last days before the launch. Her husband's arguments with NASA that not only had she had cosmonaut experience—something of an exaggeration, at best—but also that, as a woman, with a woman's patience and natural steadiness, her presence in orbit around the Moon would impart a steadfastness in those that were on its surface. But he had been wrong. She did not have patience. Not for the sort of waiting she did now, wanting to see, *straining* to see, what, even with the aid of their cameras, her husband could at best describe only dimly.

Except . . . .

Except that she *did* see. The loneliness and stress produced visions in her mind. She'd looked to her instruments first, of course, the "Christmas tree" panel lights all still glowing green, just in case it might be some bad mix of air. She'd checked and re-checked again, thinking at one point she might call NASA to ask *their* opinion, but, no, she had best not—why cause needless worries? It was only the loneliness, after all, that and the fitfulness of her sleep habits, despite the schedule of sleep-times NASA had asked her to follow.

But how *could* she have slept otherwise, now that Gyorgi and the others were on the Moon's surface?

And so, the visions came, these from the books she had hoarded that autumn. The dreams of a Heinlein, naive and hope-filled, mixed with the more cautious, Gallic optimism of Verne. And the darker, although still ambiguous, visions of Wells and Poe—Poe, with his bleakness, his soul-searing horror, still having his astronaut dream, too, of fields of Selenite poppies. Of lakes and forests.

But, then, Lovecraft's *colours*. His dreams of far Yuggoth. Her own dreams, no less terrible for their having been lived once, of Hitler and Stalin, of KGB horrors. Poe, at his worst, still foresaw *some* brightness, some faint trace of Byelobog. While the other, his fellow American prophet of darkness . . . .

She didn't complete the thought. Something was happening. Lights played on rock spires—spaceships as *she* saw, but still looking stonelike to the others. And now behind them, as they climbed the talus of Tsiolkovsky's mountain.

"Over here, quickly!" The voice was not Gyorgi's. Rather, the Frenchman's, also with an accent. She watched as the camera panned, saw his lights sparkle. And then . . . deeper darkness.

"I don't know, Gyorgi." The voices crackled. "What do you think, then?"

"A cavern of some sort."

No, Gyorgi! she thought. But he could not hear her. Nor could she call down to the L.M. to warn them, because there was no one inside to receive the call, and their suit radios were designed only for communications between one another.

And so, she could only watch as they entered. Half-seeing, half-dreaming—was it a cave mouth? Some huge sort of airlock?

She still heard their voices, that much of her still tracking them on the monitor.

"Sloping down . . . "

"Smooth-floored. Almost circular in its cross-section . . . "

"Almost—what do you think?"

"Almost as if it were artificial . . . "

She dreamed of Gyorgi, her vision widening, while, at the same time, she still stared at the TV. The sudden swirling beneath the men's feet, as if their descent took them into a mist . . . .

"Some kind of gas, maybe. Do you know what this means?"

"That the Moon has an atmosphere of sorts. But so thin, so tenuous that it exists only beneath the surface. Look, you go out—check the wire antenna. Make sure we're still broadcasting up to the C.M. Then bring back a container of some sort for a sample."

She dreamed of Gyorgi, her vision widening. She saw a huge comet, and yet, not a comet. A spaceship itself, crashing into the Moon.

Blasting a crater two hundred and more kilometers wide—the aftershock throwing up its central mountain. The occupant, wounded . . . .

Byelobog shattered. Dead. Chernobog crawling out, once the Moon's floor had cooled, finding a cleft in the newly formed mountain. A hole to bore into. To bide its time . . . hiding.

And on the TV screen, the mist coalescing. Shadowy, whirling.

Forming tendrils.

The vision of H.G. Wells' *War of the Worlds*. A hollow stone turning, revealing metal. Tentacles reaching out. Except . . . .

Except, *much* vaster.

Edgar Allan Poe's *horrors most stern and most appalling*, yet vaster and darker still.

What *she* saw now, her mind's grasp expanding . . . .

To bide its time from the time the Moon was young, over the eons, until it was stronger. And while it was waiting, to draw others to it.

The children, perhaps, of spores it had scattered on its mad journey—some, even, that came to Earth—to draw their strength back into its own body.

And, even it, perhaps the *smallest* of entities . . . .

Coalescing. She *saw*. In her dream, she tried to *send*—somehow—some warning to Gyorgi.

That *something* stared back at her.

Knowing. Not knowing. The myths *were* metaphors. Human and nonhuman, all of the same spawn. Dazhbog and Myesyats. Byelobog. Chernobog. All of them part of the same dark evil . . . .

ᗞᚼᛁ

Tasha woke, crying, to NASA's frantic calls via the Space Station, demanding to know why she had stopped transmitting. Outside, she could see the Earth, bathed in full sunlight. Yet, cold and colourless.

On the TV, static. There was no picture.

She closed her eyes, *straining*. Trying to dream again. Trying to find some trace of her husband.

Then, slowly, she sat up and straightened her clothing and opened the C.M.'s own, separate transmission link, wondering, as she did, what exact words she could use to tell NASA.

ᗞᚼᛁ

There would be no springtime.

ᚠᛁᚻᛁᚷ

TRAJECTORY OF A CURSED SPIRIT

Meddy Ligner

Meddy Ligner was born in 1974, in Bressuire, a small town in the western part of France. He spent his first 18 years there. He goes back frequently to see his family and to play baseball with the famous Garocheurs. He studied history. Afterward, he taught French abroad: in Finland, Russia and China. Since 2003, he has worked as a teacher of history and geography in Poitiers (France) where he is living with his wife, daughter and son. His website is: meddyligner.blogspot.com.

War and Punishment

They would finally land. Expected and feared at the same time, the end of the voyage was very close. Surrounded by his companions in misfortune, who, like him, were backed to the metal wall, Maxim Brahms scratched at length his salt-and-pepper beard and reflected on the past.

He remembered the war that he had led in the course of these last few years. A war implacable, without mercy. A crusade against those who were called "the enemies of the people." A devoted servant of the regime, he had fought the plotters, spies, saboteurs, and other counterrevolutionaries of every kind. In the course of this ferocious battle, Brahms had jailed them with a vengeance, separating whole families, deporting innocents, and obeying orders with zeal. *For nothing. Or rather, to end up here, as one of the damned.* He nearly retched.

Like so many others before him, he had ended up engulfed by yet another purge. His Party card, his advantageous position in the apparatus of the State, had done him no good. When they came to find him in his apartment, cozy in the middle of the night, Maxim had understood. *The swine.* He had barely time to kiss his wife and his son. *Natasha and Alex, what are you doing right now?* By the time he was brought to an unknown prison, he realised that he had seen them for the last time.

They accused him of deviation. Confessions obtained under torture. His trial was even more expeditious. He didn't know why, but he'd escaped summary execution and was condemned to deportation in perpetuity. On Mars. *But is that better than death?* For a long time now, Siberia had gone out of fashion. That region, which had become a zone for the privileged population, had given way to another hell: the Marslag. The final step for those who disrupted. The asshole from which one never returned. Mars the Pitiless.

To reach this charming corner, the prisoners had to pass two months in the interior of a rotten cabin in the vessel *October*: a ruined engine that, for three decades, had watered insatiable Mars with new detainees. These miserable ones were stuck there, penned like cattle, packed like sardines, for the long and punishing voyage across the cosmos. They had become damned souls, errant spirits, empty of their human substance. *In coming here, we have won a one-way ticket to the abyss.*

With a terrible din, the *October* finally landed on the Martian soil.

Their chains were connected at the feet, as in the time of the tsars. The prison guards barked, violently pushing the slower prisoners. The aggressiveness oozed from every pore of their skins. Cudgels rained down. The guards drove the procession of phantoms to the exit of the spacecraft. With each step, his irons cut his foot, but Maxim said nothing. He knew that it was useless to complain. They were brought along an immense corridor with immaculate walls, connecting the *October* to the Martian base. Their metal chains rattling, the convicts trudged along the vast corridor. At the mid-point, they passed under a huge, red banner, on which stood out letters of gold:

"ДОБРО ПОЖАЛОВАТЬ НА МАРС. ЗДЕСЬ
МЫ СТРОИМ СОЦИЯЛИСМ."

"Welcome to Mars. Here, we build the new socialism." *Such bullshit* . . . .
They arrived, finally, under a vast dome whose walls were totally

transparent. There, for the first time, their haggard eyes could contemplate a Martian landscape. Shacks were planted in the middle of a crimson valley on the cracked surface. They noticed immediately that there was no line of barbed wire, no watchtower. The Martian environment was the antidote to any attempt to flee. An unbreathable atmosphere, a sterile world situated millions of kilometers from Earth. This was explained to them, shouted out, by the head of the base, under the guise of a welcoming speech.

A little farther to the left, in the region of one hundred metres, the prisoners could see the cyclopean profiles of the Fathers of the Revolution, which had been carved in the rock of a cliff. Marx, Engels, Lenin, and Stalin stared down at the pestiferous unfortunates, which included Maxim. The scene immediately evoked for him an old, dog-eared postcard given to him by his father when he had been only a child. The image, which had risen from his memories like a bubble of air to the surface of the water, represented the American presidents sculpted onto a mountain.

The filthy mass of men was then pushed toward the decontamination rooms. They were washed, dressed, then directed to the refectory.

There, while they ate, slogans to the glory of the empire echoed. *Obviously, brainwashing was part of the treatment inflicted in the Marslag . . . .*

Then, once they had finished, they were sent to the boarding area. Now, their lives as pariahs could begin.

It remained to exploit the riches that abounded on Mars, and of which the Motherland was fond. As no volunteer was crazy enough to come here, the authorities had decided to create a new paradise from forced labour. The Marslag. The prisoners represented a mass of free and exploitable labour, even if their life expectancy was not very high. Between the beatings by prison guards, the lack of food, and work to the limits of human capacity, the existence of a convict did not weigh very heavily with the authorities.

They brought the prisoners into a locker room with cracked walls, filled with outdated and dirty lockers. There, they put on their spacesuits and then, under the watchful eye of supervisors, they boarded the craft that would lead them to the mine.

Once inside, Maxim stuck to the glass porthole. The desolate land of Mars marched under his wide eyes: stony hills, speckled with brown stones and cutting the horizon out of sight, fields of somber rocks in jagged shapes, a sky reddish and sad. A little farther, cliffs plunged toward an immense, scarlet plain. Immobile and silent.

"Look over there, at the bottom."

These words emanated from a stony voice. That of an old man, sitting next to Maxim. *Dirty-looking, the Ancestor . . .* His face, cracked and weary, reflected the many years abandoned here, but in his grey-green eyes still danced the flame of intelligence. Max did not blink, leaving the stranger to continue:

"That's Mount Olympus. An altitude of 27 km. The highest summit on Mars. And in the Solar System."

Max did not know how to respond to the stranger. They always said to remain on guard and say nothing of import to anyone . . . The Marslag had a reputation as a nest of crabs, each one ready to eat the others. Finally, it was the grandfather who decided to continue:

"We're braking. We're arriving at our destination."

Max opened his eyes wide and what he saw unmanned him:

"Jesus Christ!"

 Jﾄￇ

Faced with the immense, open-pit mine, he believed he found himself at the mouth of Hell. The spectacle was enough to shake the strongest of souls. There, resembling an army of insects, worked thousands of men, turning the soil over a surface, and at a depth, that was staggering. Their effort was colossal.

The prisoners were hustled outside. *My first steps on Mars . . .*

"You risk having some difficulties in adapting, but you should master your movements pretty rapidly. Here, it's necessary to move in small steps that are facilitated by the weak gravity. On the Red Planet, you weigh three times less than on Earth."

Always the same old man. This time, Maxim decided to respond to him.

"Okay, thanks, Comrade."

"Spare me the ceremony. In Marslag, we are all pariahs. The only goal that drives us is summed up in one word: 'Survive'. My name is 'Fyodor'. Welcome to Hell."

"Mine is Maxim Brahms. Everyone calls me Max."

The guards gave their orders. As he did not know what to do, Maxim imitated his new companion. There ran, some steps away from the condemned, a four-wheel-drive, diesel robot. Its steel legs methodically searched the red soil and mined ore. The mission for Brahms and his comrades was simple: to transport the ore to cargo containers. They then had to push carts weighing several tons over hundreds of meters. Despite the feeble gravity, it was exhausting work. A grueling task that shriveled the brain and reduced those executing it to the state of a machine. Turning back and forth like hungry wasps, the warders perched on their quads, which functioned on solar energy, keeping a constant eye on their charges and ensuring that the cadences of labour did not decrease.

"Your spacesuit is your best protection. It allows you to deal with the radiation and dust. Ensure that your water supply and air ventilation systems remain in perfect condition in your backpack. The equipment is often obsolete and mortal accidents are legion. So, take good care of . . . "

Old Fyodor had definitely wanted to talk. . . .

"You seem to know a thing or two. How long have you been here?" Maxim asked.

The exhausted face of the convict stared so hard at him that Maxim was embarrassed.

"I've been in this shithole for almost seventeen years . . . accused, without proof, of counterespionage. And you? Why are you here?"

"Shut up, Old Man! Concentrate on your work!"

One of the guards came over to strike him with a rifle butt. The old man sank to his knees. He began to implore this cerberus for mercy. The other insulted him. Max believed the guard might execute the old man, but finally, he was called away to other tasks.

"Those guards are garbage, scum, dogs that have the taste of blood, said Fyodor. Always ready to fuck you over. Watch out for them like the plague."

꒐ㅼ

In the evening, when they returned to their Spartan dormitories, the convicts ate and were directed immediately to their bunks, exhausted as they were by their life of slavery. Maxim Brahms was no exception. This first day in the Marslag had exhausted his strength. *I will never last several years. . . .* Here, no Sunday, no weekend, let alone any vacation. The Marslag worked round the clock, with no stops.

Some men already slept, but Max joined the group around an old samovar that smoked in the corner. Tortured by curiosity, he started the discussion.

"Hasn't anyone ever succeeded in escaping the Marslag?"

The other prisoners stared at him, flabbergasted as if Max had suggested they take their vacations on a sandy beach.

"It's impossible to get out of here," said one of them, whose face was streaked with a huge scar. "It's said that two or three convicts managed to stow away in a compartment and get off this cursed planet. They left and were never caught. But how did they do it? The rest is a mystery . . . "

The other detainees regarded him in exhaustion. Fyodor took the opportunity to speak.

"In every prison, and since their birth in the dawn of Man, there have existed such tales, touched perhaps by myth. These legendary escapes have a base in reality; I'm sure of it."

The man with the scar could not repress a grin. In contrast, Maxim became curious.

"What have you heard about that, Fyodor?"

"Don't listen to him. He's just a crazy old man."

Scarface does not appear to agree with my friend. Fyodor was uncowed. His face radiated calm. He replied:

"I believe in less-rational explanations. In times immemorial, Mars was a world as joyous as Earth, with forests, prairies, seas, and oceans. It possessed a fauna and flora both rich and diverse . . . In this antediluvian epoch, some kind of Gods ruled on the surface of Mars. One called them the Great Old Ones."

"You're completely cracked, Fyodor! You've said all that before. It's just bullshit!" the scarred man insisted.

"But where did you hear all this, Fyodor?" Maxim asked, curious to know more.

"I'm just repeating what someone told me. It was a long time ago."

"But how do you explain that, today, there is nothing left of that time?"

"I don't know. It was a very long time ago. That time has been forgotten by us."

"And where did these Great Old Ones go?"

"They live hidden in the entrails of the Red Planet . . . "

"I've heard enough for tonight! I leave you now. Until tomorrow."

The man with the scar stood up. He persuaded a goodly part of the audience to imitate him.

"Same for me. All this nonsense has exhausted me. Good night, everyone!" said another man.

Finally, only Max remained with the old man, who went on, murmuring:

"Watch yourself. Here, you can be betrayed by the most unimportant thing, especially if you speak of escape. Be on your guard . . . "

"All right . . . and these histories of the Great Old Ones . . . do you truly believe them?"

Without responding, Fyodor stood up slowly and headed toward his bed. He lifted his dusty mattress and pulled out a piece of rock.

"Look. I found this one day, not far from the mine."

With curiosity, Max inspected the object. It was a red rock, typical of the Martian surface. On one side, it was cut in a chaotic fashion, but on the other, it was smooth, flat, almost . . . polished. And on the surface, there was painted a design representing a sort of mouth. Or rather, the mouth of an animal, almost reptilian, with teeth pointed and large.

"What is it?"

"The proof of the existence of the Gods."

Stunned, Maxim didn't know what to say. It seemed that reality was collapsing under his feet. It was too feeble to face the rantings of this old *mujik*. He decided to flee.

"I'm going to sleep. Good night."

Maxim retired and went to bed, yet Fyodor, himself, remained sitting near the samovar and candle with its flickering flame. Alone, he calmly drank his tea, while the plumes of smoke drifted through the obscurity of the dormitory. Under the rough sheets, Maxim watched him for a long time without attracting his attention. *I like you a lot, Fyodor. That doesn't prevent you from being an old fool.* He turned over in his bed and abandoned himself to sleep.

Crime and Peace

Maxim admired his *dacha*, planted on the edge of a birch forest. The sun shone down from heaven in long, golden firmaments. In the sky without snow, he noticed a blue planet . . . *Could that be Terra? Where am I? On Mars? In Paradise?*

He pushed the door open and entered the house. The interior was not particularly rich, but was decorated with taste. Slowly, he advanced across the floor, which creaked as he passed. On the wall, he found photographs of his family. Photos in black-and-white of his parents, of his brothers, of beautiful Natasha and of little Alex.

"Papa . . . Papa, is it you?"

The call came from the foyer. Max turned on the carpet. The door opened and Alex appeared, running. He threw himself into the arms of his father.

"My little boy! Oh, I'm so happy!"

"Papa! I love our *dacha* a lot, but without you, it's not the same. Why did you abandon us?"

Maxim knelt in such a way as to hold his offspring in his arms.

"But I didn't abandon you!"

"Why did you leave us, Mama and me?"

"But I told you . . . ALEX! What is happening to you?"

The face of his gamin child engaged in a monstrous mutation. It swelled visibly, transforming into a creature most disquieting: His skin was covered in scales, his traits taking the form of a snake. In his mouth, there quivered a tongue, pink and forked.

"WHY, PAPA?"

Max recoiled, horrified by the terrifying spectacle. Then a feminine voice came from upstairs.

"MAXIM! MAXIM!"

Terrorised, Maxim ran and mounted the stairs to the second story, from where she continued to call.

He recognised the voice of the woman.

"MAXIM! MAXIM!"

In a rage, he ran and opened the door from which came the incessant cries.

Inside, he saw Natasha, his spouse, tied to a bed. She struggled while, around her, stood monsters from the abyss of time. Dinosaurs with the feet of goats, birds with brown fur, hydras issued from the worst nightmares of Humanity. Their yellow eyes nailed him with terror.

"MAXIM! WHY DID YOU ABANDON US?" cried his wife.

While the beasts growled, a sort of hideous mouth appeared from the shadows, just above the head of his wife. Four hooked mandibles chattered with ferocity.

"NO! There's nothing I can do, Natasha! NOTHING!"

"Max! Max, wake up!" A voice from beyond the grave hailed him. And dragged his limbs from sleep.

When he opened his eyes, he saw the weathered face of Fyodor looming over him.

"What is . . . What happened to me?"

"You were screaming in your sleep. You woke up everyone!"

Maxim sat up on the edge of the bed, his face still marked by his dream.

"I had a horrible nightmare."

"Everyone has them here, you know."

"There were these unclean monsters . . . "

"The Great Old Ones have visited you."

"What? Stop it with all your legends . . . "

"So, you, too, you take me for an old fool?"

"No, Fyodor. I have always listened to you with great attention, but . . . "

"Know that, for all of these years, I was not simply relating stories from a long oral tradition."

"I just find it difficult to swallow all these stories . . . It's not based on any concrete proof."

"We are mystical creatures. We need to believe in something. Of what material do you make yours?"

Fyodor paused, as if to catch his breath from panting. This gave Max a chance to describe his nightmare.

"I saw my . . . my wife and my son . . . It was disgusting . . . "

"I had the same kind of dream in the beginning. And then, little by little, it faded. Time effaced all memories."

"You know, Fyodor, that makes four years, to the day, that I haven't seen them again . . . four years that I've been in this hell."

Fyodor fixed him with his empty stare. Any speech was unnecessary.

"Registration number 25B43!"

A guard had just entered the dormitory with a crash. He was shouting, spit flying from his mouth.

"Yes, that's me," said Maxim, who got up and mechanically followed the guard. Here, he was only a number.

Max was simply designated. The fruit of hazard. The whim of a bureaucracy. Should he rejoice or worry? He hesitated. But he quickly accepted his part because, in any case, he had little choice.

He must accompany a geological expedition into the zones as yet unexploited. The guy in question had need of a flunky and they had assigned Brahms to this utterly thankless task, but it would change his monotonous routine. And that was priceless.

'Leon Kelonen'. That was his name, inscribed on his suit. With a gruff air, blond hair, and skin like milk, his name indicated that he was certainly of Finnish origin, but Maxim couldn't verify it.

The two men practically didn't communicate and when the other spoke to him, he used a sort of rumbling, tinged hatred that Maxim only understood half the time. No species of consideration transpired in his words and in his scientific spirit, devoted body and soul to the regime. The convict must be reduced to a simple beast of burden.

The two of them left on an exploration trip, far from camp. The prison guards were very confident of them: They could leave the prisoner alone with this stranger. He would make no attempt to escape, even though, of course, this possibility passed through his head. *But go where? Escape to where?* In any case, his reserves of air were not inexhaustible, and in less time than it takes to say, he would have eventually suffocated after a few hours, if by chance he had wanted to run. *Escape from this hole would be impossible.*

They took a six-wheel-drive jeep, setting a course straight toward a region situated farther to the west. They attained their objective after three hours' journey. The place they had to explore was streaked by large canyons that wound through the middle of a vast, reddish plain. Deep ravines with vertiginous slopes. Kelonen stopped the engine near one of them and ordered Maxim to help him get out all of the paraphernalia that would permit them to use the levels and measures. There were a lot of electronic devices of which the convict was ignorant about their true value. Although fascinated by science, he had never been very gifted in this domain . . . .

He obeyed promptly each order from his new master because he savoured with delectation this little moment of liberty that was offered to him. He was happy. Happy to be out of the camp, happy to see something else. *If I behave myself, who knows? Perhaps I could gain the right to be called again for another mission. Better to be here than in the mine, slaving away like a donkey!*

Gusts of wind raised the reddish dust, which evaporated in elegant swirls. Encumbered by all their material, the two men roamed the border of the principal canyon, which was run through by ravines, giving the impression of ripples on the surface of a sea. Souvenirs of an epoch when water streamed across the surface of Mars.

Max then lifted his head toward the sky to try to find Phobos, one of the two natural satellites of the Red Planet. It was Fyodor who had taught him to spot the moon. The old man knew a lot about this desolate world.

Kelonen ordered his acolyte to quit daydreaming and pick up the pace. It was at this moment that a detail drew his attention to the geology. On a sort of natural platform, in a slight depression, stood an opening in the rock. The convict immediately thought of the entrance to a cave.

"We'll go take a look in there. It could be interesting," said the other man into his microphone.

Maxim obeyed and followed the scientist, who had already descended into the cavity.

It was necessary to take care not to slip on the stones, at the risk of falling down the hill to the bottom. The two men advanced with the greatest of prudence, then reached the edge of the hole.

"Go in first and tell me what you see," said Kelonen, holding the flashlight.

Max wanted to protest, but a hateful glance from his interlocutor through the plexiglass of his helmet, and the severe air of the geologist, showed to what extent he was serious. The prisoner knew it was useless to argue. With the help of a rope, he entered the crevasse and was immediately engulfed.

A few silent seconds passed before that silence was broken.

"So, what do you see? Describe to me what you're observing," demanded Kelonen.

"Ah ... it's necessary that you come see, Comrade ... it's ... it's incredible ... I believe ... I am not sure ... It could be that I'm delirious. ... "

"Wait. I'm coming. But I warn you, buddy. If you're playing me a turn, I'll freeze you, here and now."

And, removing the safety on his weapon, Kelonen descended for his turn in the grotto. Flooded with light by the grace of the torch that he had just unhooked, the cavern revealed was vaster than he could imagine. It made him think of a sort of natural cathedral. He went down the slope, four by four, and joined Maxim, who was standing there, some steps away from him.

Before them stood a colossal door, carved into the Martian rock. They remained silent for a long time, mouths agape, totally absorbed by this thing that they found before them and which, normally, would not have been there.

Max thought of the city of Petra in Jordan. *Though less monumental, perhaps.* Of course, he had never visited that architectural jewel—only some of the privileged could go abroad and, most of the time, only to neighbouring countries—but he remembered the photos of the site that he had seen in the pages of his geographical manual, laminated onto the school benches. All he had before his eyes was measured within the environ of fifteen meters high and inevitably evoked the antique style. Two pairs of enormous, crenelated columns guarded the entryway on each side. At their summits, the pyramidal heads bore a tablet decorated with a carved frieze. The convict remembered the fantastic animals that had haunted his dream, the monsters of his nightmare. It seemed to him that these creatures moved on the infinite steppes or on the grey ranges. He also noticed the suites of signs and of designs, recalling Egyptian hieroglyphs. *Who? Who could do such a thing?* If he had been on Earth, he might have thought of some Greek or Roman *œuvre*. But something didn't work, a detail wrong, giving the impression of an edifice all askew. The top of this entrance constitutes a sort of circular crown, from which flowed, at regular intervals, a dozen pinnacles with roofs of scales. This gave a strange impression and resembled nothing that Maxim knew.

It evoked a species of artistic melting pot, an architectural catchall where were mixed different styles and many epochs. Finally, there was no door, proper, to speak of. Nothing obstructed the entrance, but long, iridescent ribbons, constructed of an unknown material, floated in front of the opening. They undulated slightly, carried by mysterious currents of air, sometimes out of the eyesight of those who regarded them, to intrude on *the other side.*

Max tried to see what was happening *out there*, while Kelonen prudently held back. The convict approached with small steps, overwhelmed by such majesty. As far as he advanced, he could perceive some of the colours as he traversed the forest of ribbons. Some green. Some blue. But all remained unclear.

"Do you have any ideas concerning this *stuff*?" Kelonen asked him.

This phrase, which resonated through the headphones of the prisoner, had the same effect as that of pulling him from a dream. Since the two men had discovered this strange building, no word had been pronounced. Too medusaed to be able to discuss what they saw. Once his stupor had passed, Max realised that his guard had spoken to him as if he were a normal being. No aggressiveness, no hate. This unexpected spectacle devastated all codes.

"I don't know a fucking thing!" he said. "We have put a finger on something that will revolutionise our knowledge of Mars."

The two men remained silent for several seconds. In their capsised spirits clashed curiosity and fear of the unknown. All their bearings on which they could draw seemed to crumble and fall into an unknown abyss.

"The solution resides in here," said Max, indicating a passage where the glittering curtain moved in arabesques.

"It could well be. But I don't want to take any risks. We'll return to base and I'll make a report to the captain. They'll advise us what to do next. Hey, come back here! *Let's go!*"

"Wait. Look," Maxim said, showing him the opening where the silver filaments fluttered. I see something on the other side.

And he was not lying.

"Stop! Stop, or I'll shoot you down!" the other man cried, pointing his weapon at Max.

Maxim hesitated and looked again toward that other place which he had at his fingertips. Through the shimmering stripes, he glimpsed green landscapes. He could not believe his eyes . . . On the other side, a savage nature, almost original, held out its arms.

He temporised, clenching his fist before making an about face and turning back to the scientist. In a few seconds, he was level with the man who menaced him with his sidearm. He faced him down without flinching and it all went very quickly. In a flash, animated by a mad rage that increased his strength tenfold, the prisoner succeeded in disarming his attacker. In an ultimate gesture of despair, the other man tried to protect himself, but Max had already torn his hose that connected to his oxygen supply. The other man panicked and tried to replace it. It was already too late. His flushed face twisted in agony. He succumbed in only a few seconds, asphyxiated by the impure air of Mars.

Abandoning the corpse, Maxim then turned his steps and walked cautiously to the door. *Where are you going to take me? Toward the past? The future? Or another world?* All these questions of course remained unanswered, but the convict had already made his decision. For him, there was no way to return to Marslag. In any case, his crime would send him right to the gallows.

He thought back to the mine, to his family, to his comrades, to Fyodor and his legends. *At last, you were right, old friend* . . . Then he passed his gloved hands through the filaments of silver. He sensed a delicate flux, as if a liquid cotton surrounded him. Something warm and padded. On the other side, he thought he could see a prairie, which undulated in gusts under an unknown wind. He smiled as would a child.

And then, in an instant, everything tilted. In a fraction of a second, a tentacle haloed in suckers wrapped around him, crushing his arms against his abdomen. The cyclopean limb almost immediately threw him into an enormous mouth that emerged from the shadows. Maxim did not have time to wonder from which monster this foul mouth had appeared because, already, ferocious teeth slashed him; implacable mandibles crushed him. His ordeal lasted no more than a brief moment.

Natiusha, Alex, where are you?

TRANSMIGRATION

Lee Clark Zumpe

Lee Clark Zumpe, an entertainment columnist with Tampa Bay Newspapers, earned his Bachelors in English at the University of South Florida. His nights are consumed with the invocation of ancient nightmares, dutifully bound in fiction and poetry. His work has been seen in magazines such as *Weird Tales*, *Space and Time* and *Dark Wisdom*, and in anthologies including *Horrors Beyond*, *Corpse Blossoms*, *High Seas Cthulhu*, and *Cthulhu Unbound Vol. 1*. Lee lives on the west coast of Florida with his wife and daughter. Visit: muted-mutterings-of-a-mad-poet.blogspot.com.

On that blistering October evening—
in the days of smoldering skies
when pale little ghosts foraged for food
in junkyards on the city's fringes—

I enlisted with the multitudes
seeking out the supposed prophet.
We disfigured pilgrims quit our dwellings
amidst the fallen monuments

and, in sewer dungeons fouled
by fetid darkness and ageless filth,

climbing the dizzy stairways
of some crumbling old cathedral

whose long-dead worshippers
had doubtless found an apathetic god.
He spoke of the sanctity of technology
and of salvation through transformation—

the sparks of his divine machinery
danced above the roofless temple
beneath the swarming, callous stars.
I saw inappropriate shadows

congregating in the midnight streets below,
the moon sporadically glinting against
gold-anodized, aluminum alloy casings.
Sickened by the ghastly prospect

of forfeiting the residue of my humanity,
I recoiled in horror when his metal minions
began to harvest reluctant volunteers
to undergo radical reconstruction—

I fled as their appeals for clemency
drifted, unreciprocated, to the pallid twilight.
The prophet drives his drones, still,
amidst the ruins of this charred world.

ᚤᛁᚻᛁᚪ

CONCERNING THE LAST DAYS OF THE COLONY AT NEW ROANOKE

Tucker Cummings

Tucker Cummings has been writing strange stories since the day she developed sufficient hand-eye coordination to hold a crayon. Sadly, her handwriting hasn't improved much since then. She is the author of a 365-part microfiction serial about parallel universes, which can be found at MargeryJones.com. Her work has won prizes in fiction contests sponsored by HiLoBrow.com and MassTwitFic. Her stories have been seen frequently on OneFortyFiction.com and she is one of the contributors to *The Thackery T. Lambshead Cabinet of Curiosities* (HarperCollins, 2011). Her upcoming publications include *Grim Fairy Tales* (Static Movement, 2012) and *Stories from the Ether* (Nevermet Press, 2012).

According to the Bureau of Colonial Records, the abandoned remains of the New Roanoke settlement were discovered on Independence Day, 3916 (Year 475 under the revised Imperial Calendar). The settlement was located on the northwest coast of Idris, the largest island on the surface of the planet Iranon.

Founded just 18 months prior to the tragic event (or so it was estimated), the colony of New Roanoke was the 5th colony to be established on the planet. The location of New Roanoke was selected because of proximity to both fertile soil and rich mineral deposits.

The proposed location of the colony had been contested by the regional governors, at first, as the site earmarked for the settlement was over eighty kilometers from the nearest sister colony. Ultimately, however, the board of governors gave Osiris Smith the charter and groundbreaking at the colony commenced in February of 3915.

The following items were removed from the site and catalogued by a team led by DCI Shane Yang and Lieutenant Colonel John Chastewick (assisted by Arianna Armitage, Professor Emerita of the Oread Theological College), and are currently housed in the Colonial History Collection at the college.

Our entire understanding of the New Roanoke Event is based on these 17 items.

ɔＭ£

Exhibit 01: Child's stuffed bear, brown-and-white fur. Approximately one-third of the animal has been burned away, with the remaining portion of the toy covered in heavy smoke stains. The button eyes have been removed. Examination of the remaining threads under magnification showed a clean cut, indicating the eyes were deliberated removed from the bear, rather than lost due to normal wear and tear.

ɔＭ£

Exhibit 02: Cracked ceramic serving platter, blue-willow pattern. Stamped marking on the back reads: "Bell & Dobson 6871."

ɔＭ£

Exhibit 03: Twisted lengths of metal (6). Believed to be the wheelchair of Dr. Thurston. Five of the fragments appear to be from the frame of the chair, with the last piece of debris resembling a modified tread-style wheel. Thurston had been paralysed from the waist down since her mid-thirties, and had preferred to use a wheelchair with tank-like treads, which allowed her greater mobility on the uneven terrain of the settlement.

Exhibit 04: The field journal of Dr. Zulema Thurston, partial. Some pages believed missing, or possibly out of sequence. Handwritten notes on bound pulp, transcribed below:

Day 471: *Several days ago, the engineers tried unsuccessfully to dig a new well. After Mr. Farre's team abandoned their previous dig site, they attempted to draw water from a site farther to the east. However, the efforts at this site were also unsuccessful. Rather than uncovering more red water, however, the team broke ground into an underground cavern that the initial survey team must have missed.*

There is still further digging to be done at the site, but Mr. Farre and Mr. Tydway brought me into the conversation, as some type of ancient writing adorned the walls of the cavern. As the debris is shifted, they say they will bring me images of the walls and any artifacts they find.

Who would have guessed I'd have a chance to use my doctorate out here in the colonies?

I'd expected my retirement to be boring. This could be the making of me.

Day 492: *I got fed up with the digging team today and blew my top at poor Ananais. It's no damn fun at all for them to bring me stray bits and pieces, so I've convinced them to increase the diameter of the dig and create an angled ramp into the cavern pit, so I can catalogue all of the findings myself.*

It's a testament to Mr. Farre's character that he's making way for me. I know, by rights, his priority ought to be finding more water, but, truth be told, I think he enjoys a good mystery more than most.

Except for books and the occasional show on the wi-vane, there's not much in terms of entertainment out here. I think he likes this almost as much as I do.

Day 517: *We had no idea. Or, at least, the survey team gave us no indication.*

This planet, this whole planet, and our settlement in particular, had to have been populated. If not by an advanced civilization, then, at least, by a people who had a religion, writing and architecture.

There's so much under our feet. There must have been a whole city, once.

I can't translate it. Not yet. We need more text.

Day 533: *The last bit of rock got chipped away, today. We found the source of the river, but more importantly, we found the center of the ancient city.*

There is a stone ziggurat at the centre of the centre, a sacrificial altar at the top of it all. The altar is carved with circles and spheres, and it appears to be made of a red stone, while the rest of the pyramid is moss-covered greystone.

Translation is getting closer. Ananais is coming over, later tonight, to help me cross-reference the inscriptions against some of the books he brought. He says his great-grandfather left him a strange, antique book that has odd writing in it, too.

Exhibit 05: A rubbing from a bas-relief, graphite on butcher paper. Pictured are a series of concentric spheres with beams of light emanating from them, hovering over a cityscape. A border of skeleton-shaped keys frames the entire image. There is some text in an unknown language along the bottom-right-hand corner of the rubbing. Red pencil has been used to write initials on the upper left corner: "YOG."

When questioned by DCI Yang and Lieutenant Colonel Chastewick about possible meanings of the initials, Professor Armitage declined to speculate.

Exhibit 06: Unopened bottle of Tokyo-style whisky. Ju-On brand single malt, aged 12 years. Slight moisture damage to label and minor tears on the wrapper around the cork, but otherwise in excellent condition. In fact, the condition is quite impressive, given the disarray the settlement was found in and the state of many of the other New Roanoke items enumerated here.

The only unusual markings on the bottle are five bloody fingerprints, too smudged to be matched with any certainty to any of the colonists.

Exhibit 07: Damaged solid state drive. Files include the following:

A: Translation.txt: Contents: jibberish symbols, letters, and numbers, save for one fragment in English text, which reads, "He no longer lurks."

B: Video file of iridescent glowing spheres, four seconds in length. Thought to be some sort of meteorological phenomena.

C: Image, likely from a colonist's personal library. Depicts a naked shoulder with a key-shaped tattoo.

ƆѪϟ

Exhibit 08: Polyphasic rifle, damaged in such a way that it appears to be melted like a candle. Yang and Chastewick identified it as Bell & Dobson Mark Seven, making it the second artifact from this conglomerated firm to be salvaged from New Roanoke. Both investigators were at a loss as to what sort of environmental conditions could cause this level of damage.

ƆѪϟ

Exhibit 09: Femur. Likely from male in his mid-forties. Remarkable in that it is the only human remain recovered at the site. It is unknown whom the femur belonged to, as many of the men in the colony were around that age.

ƆѪϟ

Exhibit 10: The diary of Ananais Farre, lead engineer for the colonial dig expedition (incomplete). Partial text follows:

Day 460: *We attempted to dig a tertiary well to increase the amount of potable water available, and also with hopes to increase water pressure at the South facility. However, when we began the dig this morning, we found that all water brought to the surface for testing was a blood-red, as if tinged with ochre or a microbial bloom of some sort.*

As the samples sat waiting for analysis, they turned brown and began to solidify. I would say, "to clot," since the water was so vibrant and red, but, of course, it was water and not blood we extracted from the ground. Testing was inconclusive, but, for obvious reasons, we stopped drilling and will not consume the water from the area.

We will begin digging at an alternate site in several days' time, after reviewing the remaining candidate sites.

Day 490: *While we initially thought the underground cavern was completely useless (except as a diversion for our resident academic), further* *investigation showed that there was an underground stream of clean, fresh water at this site. My team will aid with the clearing away of debris at this site, in an attempt to find the aquifer from which the stream stems.*

This news is of course pleasing to Dr. Thurston, as it means more strange linguistic puzzles for her to pore over. I often think she must be very bored out here in the boondocks of the galaxy. She must miss the libraries of the old great cities, since she's always asking to borrow my books.

Day 507: *Dr. Thurston has full access to the cavern system. The team hasn't found the source of the water yet, but the doctor has begun her attempts to translate some of the writing on the walls and on the artifacts we've turned up during the ongoing digs, as we follow the river underground.*

Zulema was particularly intrigued by some of the wall carvings, at least, the ones further down, where there starts to be art and not just text.

The look in her eyes . . . I'm not sure I'd seen her smile once since we settled here, not until today.

Day 520: *We found a door, today.*

Or a seal. A big slab of rock used, Zulema and I think, to act as a final barrier between the outside world and what we think we will find beyond.

There's so much text on the slab that Zulema is sure she can crack the code of the language today. And it's the funniest thing. I think I recognize a bit of it from an old book.

Another odd thing: the further we go into this cavern, the more slime is accumulating on the walls. It has the most peculiar odour.

Day 541: *What have we done?*

We never should have translated the inscriptions out loud.

The moons are down.

I can't find her anywhe—[End of log]

ꝺﻪﻉ

Exhibit 11: Hutch, the New Roanoke mouser. During this period of colonial expansion, it was common for colonists to bring a cat to their new settlement. The cat was something of a communal pet for the community, but its main role was to kill pests in the fields or in food storage areas. The cat was alive and seemingly healthy at the time that the abandoned New Roanoke site was discovered.

However, when the cat was removed from the surface of the planet (along with the rest of the salvaged items), it coughed up a hairball, went into a paroxysm, and died shortly thereafter. One of the crewmen on the transport ship, whose father was a taxidermist by trade, stuffed and mounted the cat for posterity.

ƆЖ҉

Exhibit 12: Heart-shaped locket, nickel plate. Clasp damaged, chain found knotted three times. No pictures within the locket. Testing revealed trace amounts of a gum adhesive on the interior of the locket, suggesting that there were once images of one of the colonist's loved ones within.

ƆЖ҉

Exhibit 13: An antique leather-bound copy of *Dire and Akashic Chronicles* by John Dee, with certain passages underlined. The notations seem to be in two hands: One uses red ink and a single underline, while a reader who used a blue pen (and much more pressure when writing) underlined certain passages twice for emphasis. While some sections are underlined by both parties, most are not.

It is worth noting that all of the sections containing dual underlining are written in Duriac, with one exception: "July 13th, Mr. Talbot came abowt 3 of the clok afternone, with whom I had some wordes of unkendness. He confessed that he neyther heyrd or saw any spirtual creature any more and left my howse."

The Duriac passages remain untranslatable, according to Dr. Armitage.

ƆЖ҉

Exhibit 14: Partial map of New Roanoke, hand-drawn on butcher paper. What remains of the map shows the location of the settlement's water wells, mineral deposits, and nearby geographical features.

A green ink square has been used to note the coordinates of some important locale, but the missing section of the map is positioned just under this green marking, prohibiting the reader from determining what this mystery location could be.

כאל

Exhibit 15: Gamer's dice (3). Hand-carved from bone. Six-sided, roughly cubic in form, approximately fifty millimeters tall. No further testing has been done on them to determine what kind of bone was used to create the dice.

כאל

Exhibit 16: Signet ring in 10 carat gold. A lion is formed from three initials, though there is some dispute as to which letters are used. Armitage believed the intertwined letters were BCH, while Yang argued that the letters were, in fact, PCD. Neither set of initials matched the name of any colonist, leaving Yang and Armitage to concur that, whatever the initials were, they referred to an ancestor of one of the colonists: possibly Elyoner Dare or Dyonis Harvie.

כאל

Exhibit 17: The "Eldritch Slime." So named by Professor Armitage for its strange volumetric properties. The slime is semi-opaque and pale-green. Collected from the ground at New Roanoke by the salvage team, it has been stored in a liter storage jar (pharmaceutical grade).

Armitage found the slime unsettling for several reasons, the most prominent being that the slime has the ability to increase in volume by approximately ten cc every eleven months.

No plans are currently in place to "re-plant" the slime in a larger container, as no consensus has been reached regarding the proper procedure for safely doing so. Professor Armitage estimates that, within the next four years, the slime will have grown too large to be contained within its original storage jar.

ﬧﬤﬨ﬩

THE KADATH ANGLE

Maria Mitchell

Maria Mitchell writes. H.P. Lovecraft taught writers the importance of self-sufficiency. She is learning.

Innsmouth, MA. 5510 A.D.

Cosmic shores aren't so distant when they nestle themselves between the synapses of self-sacrifice. Or what Amy thought to be self-sacrifice. She followed the zodiac into the sea and stood before a crystal promise. Glancing at the darkness over the Gilman House, she walked back to her house. Her mother, having never fully come to terms with her age, sat desolate in the corner.

"I've told you before not to go to the waterfront. It makes you stink of rot," her mother said, and plucked a flea off her scabbed arm.

"The whole town stinks of rot, Mom. It's been that way for thousands of years."

"Or maybe not so little." Her mother wheeled herself over to the window. "What do you see when you go out to the waterfront? All you see is the litter and dead fish that clog the shore."

"Filth can be seen everywhere. It is inescapable."

"That's no reason to keep going back to see more of it, Amy."

Amy turned away. She didn't want to hear any more. She knew what it was that really bothered her mother, but it was pointless to bring the issue to her mother's attention. Silence was always the best response.

Silence, however, teaches one to brood, but not to think, and therefore, is detrimental.

She had remained by her mother's side for many years. She liked to think it gave them both a purpose, since they were of little consequence to anyone else. Innsmouth hadn't changed much since the most recent war with Asia, but for the fact that it had grown more impoverished. Disaffected, unemployed, burly youths, fresh home from the war, wandered the streets like sharks prowling the water, looking for any scent of blood on which to feed. For a withered, shadowy person like Amy, their incessant sauntering through the neighbourhood was a constant dread. Worse was when the church women would stroll up to the door and ask to see her mother. Their lickerish eyes loved to feast on the deformity. The hags would squeeze their rolls of fat into their pale cars and drive away, searching for another fresh victim. Amy and her mom weren't fresh enough, after having lived in Innsmouth all their lives, but the church women still liked to smell the deformity.

When her brother didn't return home from Asia, Amy thought about leaving. Living in Innsmouth had never been pleasant for her, yet it seemed that Innsmouth was everywhere and, therefore, there was little point in leaving. A dull rain began to thump over the attic window. Amy knew rain always pleased the jars, so she glanced over to her mother, just to make sure she had fallen into stupor before she crept upstairs to talk with them.

They stood at the east wall, facing the window. A few raindrops trickled onto the wormy chest they stood upon. She knelt before them and began arranging the stones around them.

"I don't want to stay here, anymore. I want to leave. When will I be able to go?" she asked the jars. The magenta one snickered unpleasantly.

"You could always kill someone and go to prison. Then you'd be gone from Innsmouth."

"I'm not sure anyone goes to prison for murder, these days. It is 5510, after all. Now, speaking freely, that's a different story," said the green jar.

"Will I never change? Will I always be like my mother?" Amy appealed to them desperately. The blue jar snorted.

"You knew from the time you were small that your mother was defective. That she would never change enough to take to the sea. There's no hereditary reason why you won't end up the same way. The same thing happened to your aunt. That's why she starved herself. She couldn't go on living, caught between this world and the sea." The blue jar expelled a deep, philosophical sigh. "I remember Irene very well. She was such a vibrant scrap of a thing. I used to love thinking about the day she'd change and begin her new life among the anemone. She was so found of beachcombing when she was your age. I just knew she'd have the most impressive anemone garden in all of Innsmouth Harbor. Fancy my horror when she turned 17 and we saw the mark of defection rise on her. You think you've got problems, Amy? You can't even imagine how disappointed I was. She had everything going for her. She was well-educated in the texts; she was in regular contact with Cthulhu every time she shut her eyes. She had cursed the entire state of Massachusetts with a plague of raining human excrement for three days on her 16th birthday. We were so proud of her. But then, one year hence, it turns out that she's basically human, after all. She doesn't have enough of the Innsmouth blood to take to the sea. Somewhere along the way, the bland, indifferent God of Baptists must have wrenched her boundless potential for the *Necronomicon* into a skulking subservience for the mortal plain. As a consequence, Cthulhu can do nothing with her and she will never be a part of the sea."

"She won't be a part of anything, now, because she's dead."

"Well now, don't go too far, Amy. I mean, who are addressing right now?" the blue jar said.

"No one. I am mad," Amy replied. She got up and went back downstairs. This staircase was so old that it seemed it must fall, soon. The paneling needed to be mended, but there was no labourer Amy was willing to let in the house after one brawny workman had broken the pale-pearl jar when trying to fix the hole in the attic. Amy looked about the house and wondered how it had fallen into such disrepair. There wasn't any reason for it to be like this. It had been beautiful, once. It was the only thing that was. The last few years had aged it to an ugly, leering edifice that echoed with the sound of creaks magnified to a feverish dissonance. She steeled herself to try and fix a few of the panels, herself.

While she pulled at the planks, and pathetically tried to wrench the bolts off to reset the configuration to a more acceptable level of stability, she imagined how the house could look again if she succeeded. She was too busy thinking about this to notice that she'd plunged her pick too deeply into one of the posts. It gave way with an angry thrash and she stumbled back, terrified. The staircase somehow remained standing, but now, before her, stood a yawning blackness. There was a pocket behind the stairs. She tentatively looked inside, but found nothing. Returning to the scene with a flashlight, she shined it into the depths. She could see nothing except the gauze of spider webs and the miserable muck of water-damaged drywall. The mildew of dust pervaded her nose and she stumbled back from it, angrily. She could not define the purpose of this space, so she quickly tried to cover it back up with the paneling, but her mother wheeled into the room before she could conceal the damage.

"What have you done, you stupid fiend?" her mother yelled.

"I was trying to fix the stairs. I'm tired of living in filth, among fleas, rot and dust. I never could depend on you to clean anything, even when you could still walk. All you ever do is sleep and yell, scream, and cry."

Her mother rolled to her and slapped her across the face.

"Don't you ever speak that way to me again, you little snot. You know I am weak and limited in what I can do."

"You're not so disabled you can't thrash me whenever you like."

"That's right, because I know how weak and stupid flesh of my flesh is."

They stood before each other in a tableau of mutual hatred that seethed with barbed, suppressed rage.

"I don't ever want to look at you again. If you continue to live in this house, you will stay clear of me," her mother finally said, and turned away from her and wheeled back into her room. Amy surprised herself by not crying. She had shed so many tears in her life. Tears for her lost brother, tears for her lost aunt, and all the snide, unrepentant treatment she'd received. Yet, through it all, she did not cry. It was the first time that tears would not come since she could always cry so easily. She was always so easy to break. They didn't come. For the first time in a great many years, she felt a sense of relief. Maybe she would never cry again.

After her mother had gone to sleep, she went back to the staircase and opened the pocket she'd exposed earlier. It didn't have anything in it, but it seemed like it might be part of a larger network. She crept inside. She longed for the peace of dust, but that peace was unrequited. It did not want to give solace to her. It only wanted to be dust. She sat under the panel and in the darkness. She felt like she could sit there for a million years, without compunction about not getting to see what was happening outside. She did not want to know. Certainly, the entire town of Innsmouth already knew enough about all of them, from her drunken father marauding through the streets like a fool, blasting his idiocy to anyone who would listen. If Innsmouth had a dark reputation, then the Gilmans had a particularly slurred stance in a town in desperate need to make something worse than its own blackness.

Would gossip never tire and would burly brutes never be silenced? Would they continue to skulk through the streets outside her door? She lay down on the mildewed floor inside the stairs. She huddled into the corner amidst fungi and rot. She clutched herself. In a few moments, she felt something change. It wasn't anything which she could readily identify. She breathed long, gasping breaths and felt something in her suspire that was alien in its comfort. She breathed deeply and, in her mind, she felt an azure rapture. Pale blue. Electric. The fleas stopped biting her. The tears would not come. She breathed again and felt it bubble in her blood, again. It was unlike anything she'd ever felt before. Suddenly, she could envision the horrid church hags forgetting who she was. Not only forgetting who she was, but having their gossiping tongues ripped off by some invisible spectre, if they ever dared to speak of her or her family again. She could envision the plutonian trash she'd worked for many years ago, now having to take back everything they'd forced her to cover for them. She could envision the tormentors of yesteryears gone, by melting away into a new light from which their evil was bound. If mortal she must remain, then mortality would not be her enslaver. It would be her liberator. She breathed in the rot and, instead of being repelled, she was delighted. Gossip may be a measure of power in some circles, but it was nothing compared to this: great, fabulous, azure light beaming inside her thoughts.

The seeds had been implanted inside her mind. Now began the countdown.

ᗡℋϨ

Diary of Amy Gilman:

Day One

I have had the most incredible experience. I have no words for it except: azure rapture. I can't define it as anything else. It is the most wonderful feeling I've ever known. It comes over me like a wave of light and sea. It washes away all my fears, all my anger, all my hatred. This morning, a punk kid plunged a rock through my window. I didn't even get angry. I didn't even feel abused. I felt as I do now. I felt incredible.

Ɔ𐤉Ɛ

Day Two

Many in my life have indicated to me that a woman's only real power is that of procreation. That, if she cannot conceive, she is nothing but a slab. I can't conceive because I have no interest in doing so. Not a mortal child, anyway. But something has happened. There were strange growths on the inside of that staircase. I breathed them in. I felt something change in me. I am pregnant now with something I cannot define. Not in my belly but in my mind.

Ɔ𐤉Ɛ

Day Three

The change is growing more voluminous. It scares my haggard mom half to death. When she saw me this morning, she screamed herself into unconsciousness. You see, journal, the wires are growing.

Ɔ𐤉Ɛ

Day Four

Space is no longer of the sky. It is of me. 5510 A.D.? Ha! Try 15,510 A.D. and you may have the more accurate year. But the year is of no consequence. Not without my blood to guide it, anyway. Give me all the centuries untold and I'll give you the gluons of a million universes, ten million years in the future. Innsmouth is quaking under the overcast rain of a sneaking, summer deluge. It's uncommon for Innsmouth to have this much rain this time of year, but then again, there is no time, anymore.

Ɔ𐤉Ɛ

Day Five

I went to the waterfront. They were waiting for me. They know what's happened and are proud to say they knew it would. They assured me that they would not forsake me. Cthulhu knows how valuable I can be to his dreams. They would not let me remain a skulking mortal, to rot to dust. The change is still happening. My flesh is starting to slake off in scaled fragments. The town of Innsmouth is truly now one belonging to the Deep Ones. The human fraction that has caused me discontent for so long is beginning to quake with fear, because now they are seeing, as if for the first time in their whole, benighted history, that there really are beings that stalk their shadows that are far more powerful than they. And I am now one of them. The fungi growing in my head are sprouting exponentially. Soon, like Athena bursting forth from Zeus's head, my dreams will give birth to the Kadath Angle: the angle of dream that will engulf the future with my azure rapture.

ᗐﾂᙏ

Day Six

Genesis is always painful. Parthenogenesis, in particular, because we virgins have no one to give a hoot about us in the waiting room. That's not really true, though. At least, not anymore. The Deep Ones are ecstatic. All night long, I hear their yelps and cries echo over frightened Innsmouth. They know what is coming. When the Kadath Angle bursts forth from my head, it will be the birth canal for all star spawn upon the Earth.

ᗐﾂᙏ

Day Seven

God forgive me.

ᗐﾂᙏ

The Kadath Angle burst forth over Amy's prostrate form on the floor. Her mother had starved to death in the upper room, thus she was not disturbed. Like a great serpent, it burst from the Gilman House, shattering the roof. Star spawn rained down over Innsmouth, over the world. The atrocities in Asia whimpered and paled before the spawn of Kadath. The Earth tilted under them as they littered the sky with the protoplasmic slush of universes born many eons before. 5510, 7510, 125,510, 750,500, 5,000,000,000.

Ͻϟϟ

Innsmouth, MA. 5,000,000,000 A.D.

My name is Amy Gilman and I am a monster. I didn't think about the ramifications of what was happening to me when I first experienced what I can still only call 'azure rapture'. I have allowed myself to become Mankind's exterminator, simply because I did not believe my own humanity was fair. I had Deep One ilk in my background. I believed I deserved to live with the Deep Ones. I would have done anything to make them accept me, as no one else ever had. They accepted me, all right. Strictly for their purposes, as these things always go. There is not one trace of humanity left, for they have been undone. My mortal blood touched that which should never be touched and now, not only has Mankind been exterminated, but it has never existed at all. The Earth is what the accursed Necronomicon always hinted it would be if star spawn ever regained control of it. Now their cities are laced upon the barren world. There is no water, save for the terrariums that the Deep Ones constructed to meet their occasional, water-frolicking needs. The Fungi from Yuggoth, which I now know to have been the fungi I suspired from under my staircase, though how they grew there, I am still at a loss to define. Now, I am the fungus that grows under the stately staircase of a Deep One. Winged visitors from Vermont, or what used to be Vermont, are staying over tonight and I have been instructed not to say a word, which is why I'm recording my thoughts on a beam of light in a distant part of the universe. It is my sincerest hope that some passing explorer may find this haphazard message in a bottle and learn from it. Learn that the only way to save mankind is to kill me before I have a chance to become impregnated with the Kadath Angle. This will be most difficult and I can't think who, or what, lifeform that may even have the technology to decode this message would even bother to do so. Even if they do, who can reach that far into the past and rewrite what I have done?

Forgiveness comes slowly.

ϒϟϞϟϞ

THE LAST MAN STANDING

Ezeiyoke Chukwunonso

Ezeiyoke Chukwunonso is a promising young writer of twenty-four. His short story was among the long listed stories in the Golden Baobab Prize, 2010. His poems have appeared in *ANA Review*, a literary journal and *Sowetan Online Magazine*. He was born in Eastern part of Nigeria. He lives there. Currently, he studies Philosophy, with much interest in the Philosophy of Arts.

When the government announced their ban on what they termed 'non-essential foodstuffs,' I didn't fully understand the implication until two weeks later, when I went to buy a Sprite, a drink I was addicted to. My father had been, too. When he was still alive I remember people calling him "Mr. Sprite". If you were near, he would shake hands with a smile. With children, he stroked their hair. When he was in a hurry or a distance apart, he waved. He only rushed when he was going to the coal mine at Coal Camp, Enugu, the site that had first attracted white men to Enugu City. They had then established their house at New Heaven, leaving peasant workers in Coal Camp. My father had preferred living in Abakpa, a town on the outskirts of Enugu City, with a lot of indigenes of our own tribe, but this was where he could find work. That was before independence.

At the store, they said Sprite was not in the stock. Not in stock? That was silly.

I was still battling to comprehend this when they made subsequent bans. Numerous food items were added to the list. Indo-mie, Spaghatti, Macromie, Bobo, Biscuit, all were given their final funeral rites. The Minister of Information, said that we were in a state of emergency, fighting ADAIDS. The production of those banned foodstuffs was a waste of manpower and would not help the majority of the citizens suffering from the epidemic.

Advanced Acquired Immune Deficiency Syndrome (ADAIDS) had a long, complicated history. Rumour had it that a couple of scientists from Germany and America were sponsored by UNICEF to conduct a genetic experiment, using an AIDS virus. The experiment allegedly took place in the Sahara Desert, near the northern part of Nigeria, in an underground lab. Nobody has ever given a correct description of the place. Most people believed it was destroyed immediately after the experiment failed. The experiment, aimed at producing a cure for AIDS, instead ended up producing a mutated type of AIDS that could be contracted from sexual intercourse, even when one was wearing a condom. Worse, the disease remained dormant until three months before death, making it easier to spread. Once someone contracted it, the person never lived beyond three years. After the experiment was shown to be a failure, UNICEF came in and silenced all who needed to be silenced. Some said that all those who had anything to do with the experiment were assassinated. Others believed they were heavily bribed.

I do not know if this is true.

The most popular, story of the origin of the disease was that some Fulani nomadic cattle herders in northern Nigeria, victims of HIV, had intercourse with their cows. The HIV virus in their bodies reacted with another virus in the cow's body and it resulted in a mutated AIDS. The ADAIDS was transmitted to Igbo prostitutes in the southern part of the country (The tribal people used to believe they could literally march through hellfire if money were discovered in the Devil's hand) by those nomadic cattle herders, and to their women when they went home. With time, thanks to sex, as a fire that catches a cluster of palm thatch roofing spreads, the disease spread everywhere.

To worsen matters, the government stretched out its hand to non-foodstuffs. We were constrained to watch only one local TV station and also to listen to one radio station. Two of my favourite programs, *Hyper Fear* and *Dance like the Dead*, were struck off and their producers reassigned. They gave us the same reason: "lack of manpower."

One amusement park was permitted in each state and a maximum of three secondary schools. All the universities were reduced to one, with only two faculties: Medical Sciences and Engineering. They believed that the medical academics were the only relevant faculty that could handle the plague of ADAIDS. As for Engineering, they kept the infrastructure from breaking down. So, we still had electricity. For the rest: "a waste of manpower."

I found out from afternoon broadcasts of the BBC and Radio Nigeria that the UN had abolished the flow of aid workers to the country. Soon, I ceased to hear any further pronouncements made by the government. One day, like a joke, the government was dead! Gone. No more announcements, no nothing. It dawned on me that, with the death of the government, other things, like electricity, would follow suit.

I decided to place an announcement at Radio Nigeria, the only surviving station and the first to be established immediately after the independence.

The announcement would invite everybody living in Enugu City to come and live in Uwani Town, to fight loneliness with 'African communalism,' since the disease was winning every other battle. I was sure not all of us had contracted the disease. I hadn't.

I was not at risk. My illiterate mother had not taken prenatal vitamins during her pregnancy. So, I had contracted a disease in youth that had rendered me a eunuch. But I had hopes that married couples who were faithful to each other and children would also survive.

At first, I was optimistic. I walked out of my bungalow, where I lived alone on Nnaji Street in Uwani. The street was empty. One could hardly recognise the black colour of the road tar. Mud had painted it red.

I walked to the major road, where I would get a bus-taxi that would take me to the station. For hours, I stood waiting. No taxi came. A Peugeot pickup drove past me. The back was loaded with a corpse. Two young men were sitting in the front with the driver. I didn't need any person to tell me where they were going. I had done a similar thing in my street many times. The corpse was going to be disposed of in a big pit dug at the outskirts of town. They would then incinerate it.

It eventually became clear to me that taxis had died a natural death, just like our government. I decided to go back home and use my car. I still had gas.

When I got to the radio station, I was lucky to see the studio manager, Mr. Dudu, standing, arms akimbo, in front of the building. A man as short as Zacchaeus. God forgive me; I hope that is not a cliché. We shook hands.

I told him of my mission. He accepted, but quickly informed me he had just broadcast an announcement: The disease had developed a more virulent strain. Any person who remained with a victim of the disease in an enclosed area for about two hours would also become infected. He said that a Professor Dimbo Theresa from the University of Nigeria had brought him these findings and asked him to air them. The manager then warned me of the dangers of gathering a large crowd of people with my intended announcement.

I considered his warning. There were few of us left in Uwani and plenty of houses for the remaining people, if the mortality rate here had been the same as in other Enugu towns. I was sure there wouldn't be any risk of transmission.

He agreed and my announcement was a success. People turned out, though few in number. To my surprise, Professor Dimbo Theresa was among those who came to join us.

The few of us who remained eagerly waited, listening to the news to hear which new government would seize power, but none came. We were still waiting when the last surviving radio and TV stations vanished. The first day I turned on my radio and was confronted by the reality that the station was no longer working, it seemed to me like a doomsday. But weeks later, we had all become accustomed to the new reality.

As time went on, and people died out, I had to drive my car from where I was living in Uwani to New Heaven, Abakpa and Emene to see if anyone was still there. I usually did that with an old Peugeot pick-up. The reason was to avoid disease transmission. If I saw anybody, that person would have to stay in the open, in the back, during the journey.

But apart from the few of us who were still living in Uwani, I found no other human life in the other cities.

I decided to expand my search. I moved from Enugu City to nearby towns. I headed towards faraway Ninth-Mile, at the other end of Enugu State. Dominated purely by Igbo tribes, the indigenes there had been converted to Christianity, like those who had lived in Enugu. The difference was that, in other towns in Enugu, apart from Abakpa, there were also non-Igbo tribes and Muslims.

I stopped along the way to fill my tank. When I reached a filling station, it was deserted. I remembered, just a few years ago, how boisterous the place had been. I could still recall how I had maneuvered to get my tank filled first, especially during times of fuel scarcity. Such actions usually elicited howling and shouting from other drivers. I lusted for those times now.

There was no attendant to refill my tank. It occurred to me that, if the fuel was exhausted, there was no one to ask for more. There was also no electricity and I soon found I couldn't refill my tank. I looked around, hoping for a lucky break.

Some parts of the roof of the filling station had been blown down by wind. The white paint of the walls had been washed by the rain. Green lichen had started to grow on the side of the building.

I went into the building and pushed a door open.

I was surprised that the door wasn't locked. I had been thinking I would have to break it down. Under the dust and cobwebs, the pink paint on the wall remained intact. I guessed that it was the manager's office, because, sitting with his head bent on a table, was the decaying, stinking corpse of a man. Beside his head were bundles of money. "Igbo and money, just like bread and butter!" I murmured, as I quickly closed the door.

The next door was locked and I had to search for the key in the manager's pocket, holding my breath. Inside a small room sat the station's generator. Thank God it functioned, as did the fuel pump—a miracle. I got my tank filled and drove off. The road was lonely. Not a surprise. I knew it would demand another miracle for another car to drive by. If that ever happened, I would celebrate.

When I reached Ninth-Mile, I had to slow down, peeping through the windshield. No one was in sight. I then took a path that led to the heart of the town and parked at a village health center, a house with green walls. In the old days, the place would have been crowded with people waiting for a doctor. By now, tall, elegant grasses were already overtaking the area.

I left the building and followed another path. The only sounds in the town were the cries of wild animals: monkeys and, sometimes, hyenas and carrion birds like the kite and the owl.

The path brought me to a primary school. Beside it stood a market already in ruins. The shops seemed like anthills of the savannah, telling the new grasses about last year's bush burning. I entered the school building, painted yellow outside and white inside, and moved from one classroom to another, praying for luck. Each door I opened, I either saw lizards playing or rats making love.

I looked at a board in the last classroom. Despite water damage, 'Class Five' could still be read, although faintly.

There was a noise. If I hadn't been fast, I wouldn't have seen it. A long, coiled black snake, at least four feet long, nested among the empty desks. It raised its head. Its neck was dim white with black stripes. A cobra. The type our villagers called "Tomorrow is far," because you would not live to see the next day, once bitten by it. It seemed to say, *Who is this man who is treading on my territory?* Before I could leave the room, it came at me.

I backed away quickly, unsure if it was attacking or defending. It recoiled itself and sprang, throwing itself at me. I managed to dodge and it missed the target.

I saw a broom lying nearby. I picked it up.

The snake sprang erect, spat its venom. But I was far from it, so all the saliva poured on the ground.

It was now my turn to attack. With my stick, I reached for it. It then recoiled itself and threw itself on me another time. I dodged again. It landed on the ground and my stick was on it. I never gave it a chance. I kept on striking till it was dead. Then I walked away, sweating. I was breathing heavily and I was sure my blood pressure was high.

I wanted to go home.

I ran through the town, shouting, asking for someone to come out. I found myself on the path again. Part of me kept telling me to just get in my car and drive back home. The other part insisted I continue with the search. Perhaps someone remained in the village. I listened to that part.

I went through the village. Most of the buildings were intact, though with peeling paint. At every house, I shouted, "Is anybody there?" Getting no result, I moved on. I hoped that, if anyone survived, they would answer me. However, due to the encounter with the snake, I was afraid of entering any house.

I gave up. On my way back to my car, I heard a voice.

A child stood in a doorway, a girl of about thirteen. I ran to her and held her tight. I was overwhelmed with joy. A joy that knew no bounds. She was weak and looked famished. She began to weep. I consoled her and took her to the car, kept her at the back.

Back home, we had a celebration as never before. One of us, I can't remember who, said that this was a sign that God had not abandoned humanity yet. But amidst the celebration, some were skeptical of her. They wondered how a little girl could be the only survivor in her village. What did she have that others didn't?

Rumours began, the most popular being that she was a witch. I think Mrs. Chioma, a woman living across the street, originated this version of the story.

Mrs. Chioma claimed to be a witch doctor. According to her, she never knew that she had the gift until a crisis rocked her family. It began when she gave birth to her fourth child. She had employed a nanny to help her look after her baby, so that she could still meet the demands of her housework. But unknown to her, the nanny was a blood-tasting witch.

A few months after the nanny arrived, Mrs. Chioma's children got sick. Her first child died. She was still recovering from this shock when the second one also died, just six months later. As if that were not enough, the two children left were critically ill. None of the seven hospitals they were taken to could diagnose the problem.

Then a friend advised her to try a native doctor. The native doctor told her that she had the power to heal herself and her children, and that he could help her learn how. He gave her some herbs, which she was to boil and mix in her meals. Three days later, her inner eyes opened. She then saw how her children's nanny turned into a big mosquito at night to suck her children's blood, which she would, in turn, transmit to other witches in their nightly meetings as their meal. She had to exorcise the nanny before sending her packing. She had since lost her husband and remaining children to the disease.

I heard Mrs. Chioma, more than once, telling people that the little girl had a big tooth on her forehead. She even said it was the girl who killed her parents, not the disease.

I asked her, "If the little girl was truly the cause of her parents' death, what of the rest in the village? Was she also responsible for that?"

She retorted, "The girl helped the disease in escalating the death rate in their village." According to her, "When the girl saw what the disease was doing, she availed herself of that opportunity and started sucking blood as much as she could."

If people had only seen her as a gossip among those of us who were living on Nnaji Street, I wouldn't have considered it a problem. The problem was that she instigated people.

At first, it began with people being afraid of the girl. From that, it escalated to direct verbal abuse. I can't now precisely remember the person, but I can still recall hearing somebody, one day, exclaiming to her that she was a witch who had come to kill us all, as she did to her people. The peak of the whole thing came when an angry mob stormed my bungalow. They needed to exorcise her. Unsurprisingly, the mob leader was Mrs. Chioma.

I refused to yield to their demand. But they threatened that if I didn't release the girl, they would certainly catch her.

As this was by no means an empty threat, not only was she now living in my bungalow, I took her with me wherever I went. The accusations never stopped. On the contrary, they got worse! Whenever anyone died, she was the cause. As each day went, the pressure of her potential exorcists increased. I would have yielded to their demand, were it not for the timely intervention of Professor Dimbo Theresa.

Professor Dimbo offered to carry out a test on the girl. She saw the case in another light. For her, it was a step towards finding a cure to the disease, if one could actually find out what made the girl different from the rest of her village. And, although she was fiercely warned that this was a case beyond science, Professor Dimbo was not one who would easily go back on her decision.

Within a week after this test, Mrs. Chioma, herself, died. With their worst instigator gone, the mob faded and the pressures on me subsided. Professor Dimbo later revealed her findings. It was as startling as it was ordinary: The little girl had sickle cell anaemia. Anybody blessed with this ailment has a greater resistance to the ADAIDS—similar to the immunity they had to malaria.

In the subsequent days, I went on more searches. None yielded results. After a month, I became tired and abandoned the project.

The survivors in Uwani dwindled.

They all died.

I became worried for the girl, because she was still so sickly, and hoped I would die first, but it was not to be. She died yesterday.

I have burned my dead. My suitcase is in the car; my supplies are packed.

I am heading to no destination in particular.

One day, I will find another living human.

But for now, I am the last man standing.

ᛣᛠᚻᛠᚻ

EXHIBIT AT THE NATIONAL ANTHROPOLOGY MUSEUM IN TOMBOUCTOU

Andrew Dombalagian

This is the first professionally published poem for Andrew Dombalagian, a long-time amateur writer. His other poetry, inspired by Lovecraftian illustrations, anime characters and everyday observations, has previously appeared in collegiate publications.

Inscription on Plaque, Titanium-Gold Alloy, ca. 2250—2300 C.E. This artifact, showing evidence of prolonged exposure to the conditions of space, was recovered by Professor Amadou Sangare in a folk market outside the New Lagos Desolation Zone, although its true origins remain unknown. The inscription is etched in a dead language, not native to Africa, believed to have once been a trade language prevalent on Terra. Translation has revealed the meaning of the prayer poem, though elements such as rhyme and metre have been lost in transition.

The plaque bears a prayer offered by early starfarers to the Elder Gods, pleading for protection and safe passage between planets and star systems. The crude mysticism and superstition once applied to space travel parallels the rudimentary nature of technology and knowledge of that bygone epoch. Note the childish optimism expressed in the verses, reflecting a primitive belief that the long-dead Elder Gods yet possessed any influence amongst the stars. This artifact represents both an infantile step in starfaring history and a remnant from the Dark Ages, when mortals yet doubted, and even challenged, the supremacy of the Great Old Ones.

The flapping of heavy, grey wings against the
membranous thickness of the void
Echoes in the thundering roar of our thermonuclear
heart, pounding against its carbon bonds.
Humble are we who sail the satin tapestry of night, ever on the verge
Of the Pit, where sleeping lies the Blind Idiot of all Oblivion.
May the sheen of Bast's smile, though never so warm as upon her brood,
Find our voyage safe from the burning cold wrath of the aether.
Before Hypnos closes all eyes forevermore, for another day,
May we yet gaze with awe and horror unfettered.
Protect your servants from the ebon, bilious
hearts that throb against the crystalline
Chains that bind them to the orbs and spheres that pulsate brightly in the
Eternally Yawning Gulfs. Their noxious, chromatic radiations pollute the
Eons with the foul beneficence of their Great Old Masters.
The narrow, blanched roads between worlds
that our vessel travels overhang with
The looming, glassy canopy of galaxies and
nebulae fertile with Three-Lobed Eyes.
They watch with a patience as icy as the void that cradles their bower.
Though our voices are mere flecks of cosmic dust adrift between eons,
Please heed this plea from your vassals, O Elder Lords.
May the dying light of the cosmos find our hull
shining with the might and majesty
Of the vast shell that ferries Lord Nodens across his abyssal kingdom.
From the hearth fires of one sacred star to the next,
may we lowly souls find safe passage,
And in our journeys, may we find comforting respite
Against the Old Ones who dream in their deathless slumber.

ᚼᛌᚻᛌᚼ

THE DOOR FROM EARTH

Jesse Bullington

Jesse Bullington is the author of the novels *The Sad Tale of the Brothers Grossbart* and *The Enterprise of Death*. His short fiction has appeared, or is forthcoming, in various magazines, including *Beneath Ceaseless Skies*, *Chiaroscuro*, *Jabberwocky*, and *Brain Harvest*, as well as in anthologies such as *Running with the Pack*, *The Best of All Flesh*, *The New Hero II*, *Robots vs. Zombies: This Means War*, *Historical Lovecraft*, and *Candle in the Attic Window*. He currently resides in Colorado and can be found online at www. jessebullington.com.

I

When Pipaluk, the chief engineer of Hiurapaluk's Peril Containment Plant, together with 12 of her most well-armed and efficient underlings, came at flickering, artificial dusk to seek the infamous Professori, Laila, in her amphibechanical facility on the lower-most substreet of the city's underlevel, they were surprised, as well as disappointed, to find her absent.

Their surprise was due to the fact that Professori Laila had made much to-do about her expedition not taking place for another fortnight; all of Pipaluk's plots against the Professori had hinged on there being sufficient time to gain the rest of the Quorum's approval before confronting the rabble-rousing academic. They were disappointed because their formidable warrant, with symbolic fiery font glowing on an antique digital tablet, was now useless; and there seemed to be no earthly prospect of wiping the smug expression from Laila's hairy face, to say nothing of confiscating her domestic warrens for the use of the Engineers Guild.

Ingeniøri Pipaluk was especially disappointed, for Laila was her chief rival in the Quorum's science bloc, and was acquiring altogether too much fame and prestige among the Voormis of Mhu Thulan, that ultimate peninsula of the Grænland subcontinent. Pipaluk had been glad to receive certain evidence corroborating her suspicions that Laila's expedition through the Eibon Gate could be catastrophic, and not just in terms of heightening the Professori's already-dangerous popularity.

This evidence suggested that Laila was not, in fact, a devotee of the state-god, Tsathoggua, whose worship was incalculably older than the Voormi race. No, it seemed that the Professori instead paid tribute to Tsathoggua's paternal uncle, Hziulquoigmnzhah, with whom the *true* god of the Voormis had suffered a falling-out sometime in the previous millennium or three. This schism, which had something to do with the fall of Humanity, or perhaps the rise of the Voormis of Grænland and sundry other peoples in sundry different places, had resulted in the sealing of the Eibon Gate.

Walling up the entryway between the worlds of the benevolent, bat-furred toad-god Tsathoggua and that of the much-less-attractive demon prince Hziulquoigmnzhah seemed a surefire means of reaffirming Tsathoggua's favour. The Quorum's vote on this matter had been unanimous, and so the pit where the portal was located was closed off using a variety of fail-safes, and then the whole area was surrounded in a series of airlocks, cultural heritage be damned. Until Professori Laila started in with her insane theories of interstellar harmony and pan-theological unification, no one had given any thought to reopening the portal of ultratelluric metal that lay buried in ruins of black gneiss beneath Mhu Thulan's capital city.

Pipaluk had suspected the worst as soon as she discovered the Professori's new laboratory was directly adjacent to the outermost airlock housing the gate to Cykranosh that the warlock Eibon had used to escape Earth in ancient times, if the mytho-historical record was to be given credence. Alas, the Quorum had dragged its feet, despite Pipaluk's warnings, and now it was too late—she would have given her musk glands to kick the Provost in the *kanaaks* for postponing his vote as long as he had.

Pipaluk's subgineers bustled about Laila's laboratory in their glistening salamander-suits and, behind a tarp, they discovered where the Professori and her team of graduate students, clone servitors, and formless spawn had hacked into the municipal pipe that made up one of the facility's walls and plugged in their plasmaborers. The tunnel they had excavated led—surprise surprise—out of the lab, through a mega-support column, and directly into the first airlock bay, the dull-metal doors towering some thirty meters tall over Pipaluk's team.

"Airlock initially opened, Aggusti Second," the voice of one of the subgineers crackled in Pipaluk's pulsing, yellow bio-helm. "Breached on average twice daily each day since."

"*Hymirbjarg*," Pipaluk cursed, and several of her underlings grinned to themselves to hear their normally unflappable superior use such strong language. "I trust this is sufficient?"

"Fall back, Ingeniøri," Provost Ole answered over the Quorum channel. "We'll hold an emergency meeting. Politibetjent Chief Malik is on his way up, so extract your team and—"

"Wha—shhhack?" Pipaluk held down the garble button she'd installed onto her com-panel as she addressed her subgineers on their private channel. "Right, we don't have time to deal with more dawdling by those *kanaaks*. Ane and Nuka, with me. The rest, seal this airlock after us and don't open it, no matter what. I trust you all remember what happens when you open airlocks, yes?"

They did. It had been Pipaluk's team, after all, who designed the last batch of *svataarsualiartartoq*-suits for Mhu Thulan's formless spawn commandos—space stations tended to lack many gaps for the polymorphous spawn to flow through, so infiltrating the interstellar strongholds of those Yig-worshipping Valusians and Ithaqua-kissing Gnophkehs necessitated finding another way to get the formless spawn inside. Spacesuits that matched the design of those used by the targeted station, save with opaque helmets, did the trick quite nicely—fill a few suits with the spawn, trigger a rescue beacon on the station's frequency, and float the formless commandos through the void until they were retrieved by drones and taken inside the airlocks. Then, total havoc as the deadly children of Tsathoggua swept through the station, a sentient tidal wave of ichorous death.

"How will we get back, Ingeniøri?" subgineer Nuka asked, his voice cracking.

"Have some faith, son," said Pipaluk. "We'll recode the locks as we go.

Things were built by your ancestors; think their primitive programming is beyond your skill?"

Nuka straightened his shoulders, his three-toed foot snapping up in salute. Through the faceshield of his bio-helm, Pipaluk could see the lad's umber fur bristling straight out from his face in embarrassment. Good, he *should* feel like an idiot.

"—stunt," Provost Ole was saying as Pipaluk relaxed her finger on the garble button. "Is that clear?"

"Perfectly, sir," said Pipaluk, and quit the channel altogether. "Right, let's go."

Nuka whined, long and low; Ane prayed, fast and loud; and the other subgineers all saluted as the ancient airlock opened into the deep.

II

There were three airlocks in total, and the trio had reached the control panel beside the second by the time the first had ground shut behind them. Before advancing any further, Pipaluk had Ane explore to the left and Nuka to the right—the Ingeniøri had been over the schematics a dozen times lest just such an emergency entry become necessary, but it never hurt to confirm what the blueprints had already told her.

"Dead end," Nuka reported through the bio-helm's thrumming com-membrane. "Basalt. Dry. No cracks."

"Same here," Ane said, as she hiked back across the bay.

"Good," said Pipaluk. "Everything matches up. The reports state that the Eibon Gate was interdimensional, so they were able to completely surround it. Basically, they built a giant basalt box around the thing, with only an airlock leading in or out. Around *that*, another stone box with an airlock, and then another. So, through this door is another bay and across that is the final airlock, which opens into the ruins where the Gate is. Professori Laila and her team are either in the bay beyond this door, working on the last airlock, or they've managed to breach it and gain the ruins, which could be bad. Very bad."

" 'Bad'?" said Nuka. " 'Very bad'?"

"Depends," said Pipaluk, hoping against hope that her quarry was still fiddling with the last airlock and not beyond it. "Even with the feeble half-lives they were capable of producing, back when this was all built, the fail-safes in the ruins should still be operational. So, in a best-case scenario, the fail-safe will have arrested the Professori's advance. Worst-case scenario, Laila will have somehow gained the Gate."

"Fail-safes?" Nuka whimpered. "*Issi.*"

"Act like you've got a quad," Ane snorted, petting the slimy muzzle of her microwave spitter as she sidled up to Pipaluk. The weapon purred at the subgineer's touch and Pipaluk made a mental note to invite Ane over for a soak in her breeding bath when they were safely home—the Ingeniøri's whiskers needed a serious stroking and she had a feeling this was just the *Voormi* to give it to her. This wasn't really the time for such concerns, admittedly, but stress always made Pipaluk's glands overproduce.

"Remember," Pipaluk said, as her fingers danced over the airlock's panel, "we need to stop Laila at all costs. Alive to stand trial is preferable but by no means necessary. The main thing will be avoiding the fail-safes, if those idiots have opened the airlock, and the Professori's formless spawn if they haven't. We may already be too late, so from here on out, we move faster than fast, got it? Now, let's get this heretic."

"Oh *yeah*," said Ane, and her weapon shivered in anticipation.

Nuka whinnied and made the sign of Saint Toad.

Pipaluk opened the airlock. A rush of cooling, semi-congealed blood poured out over their feet.

III

The bay between the second and third airlock doors glowed a faint turquoise from a K'n-yan luminance system, and before the Voormis' bio-helms could tint out the blinding, pale light a fail-safe leapt on Ane and bit off her head. The thing's gears screamed and spat puffs of rust as it thrashed atop the decapitated subgineer, a blur of slick, amphibious tails and bluish metal pincers. Nuka panicked, his high-pitched howl nearly blowing out Pipaluk's com-membrane, and the Ingeniøri had to force herself not to attack the subgineer before taking out the fail-safe. She spat out the immolation code for Ane's suit, even as she leapt out of the way of the imminent blast. Even through her own salamander armor, she felt the wave of heat buffet her like a solar flare.

The fail-safe was still alive, but its metallic components had melted to the point of incapacitating the thing. Nuka had managed to avoid the worst of the blast, but was still crying like a Gnophkeh, sitting in the tacky, smoking blood that had flooded the bay. The bio-helm filtered out everything but the smell, the bouquet of burnt hair and engine oil making Pipaluk's eyes water. She didn't look down at the fused mass of mewling fail-safe and gorgeous, dead subgineer. Instead, she yanked Nuka to his feet and fired a cold-shower code down his channel—the result was instantaneous, the coward straightening up and shuddering as his suit doused him in a psychoactive chemical spray.

"Subgineer Nuka," Pipaluk barked in his face while he was ripe for imprinting. "Ready your weapon and follow me. Those *hymirbjarg*-brained academics have obviously breached the last airlock. Hurry!"

The subgineer saluted and snapped his olid-pistol off his belt. It was no microwave spitter, but it was better than the ceremonial *gladius* that Pipaluk had brought—had she known Laila wouldn't be in her lab, ready for arrest, she obviously would have brought something more substantial. At least there weren't any more fail-safes between them and the final airlock. Probably.

They cautiously entered the final bay, splashing in puddles as they moved through the cobalt twilight. Judging from the oily whorls of colour in the blood, the team of grad students, servitors, and spawn had taken out a fail-safe, as well, but there was no sign of the fallen guardian, nor, for that matter, any of Laila's crew, beyond the blood. That was . . . odd. Holding her hand up to the last panel, Pipaluk saw her talons were shaking. She gritted her fangs, willing herself to enter the code, when Nuka nickered excitedly behind her. She lowered the volume on his channel before turning to see what was bothering him now.

A pillar of blood had flowed straight up into the air behind them. Pipaluk went into a roll, just as the formless spawn crashed down. Of course that was why there were no bodies—this must be one of Laila's, injured in battle with the fail-safe and left behind to heal itself on the corpses of the fallen. It probably couldn't have hid from the fail-safe for long, trapped alone with it in this bay, which meant they might be just behind the blasphemous Professori . . . unless she had died in this place, too. Well, no sense being optimistic just yet, Pipaluk reasoned, as her reflexes carried her backward, up, down, sideways, flipping away from the relentless, deadly ooze.

"Stink it!" Pipaluk panted, as she lured the pursuing wave back toward Nuka, who sat with his back to the final airlock. "Stink the thing, already!"

Nothing came over the subgineer's channel and, cartwheeling up to his splayed body, she saw he was not simply lying down on the job; he had quit it altogether: His neck had been twisted almost completely off when the spawn had hit him, only the suit keeping it attached. Gross. The pistol in his hand seemed intact, however, and all she had to do was—

—Go spinning across the bay as the formless spawn caught her foot and hurled her away from her prize. It was on her before she stopped sliding over the slick basalt, but a low heatburst from her suit drove it back, the thing hissing as it smoldered. Before it could throw itself atop her again, she was on all fours and dashing back to Nuka's corpse. It tried to put itself between her and the gun, but another suit-pulse let her slip past it, then the bony handle of the stinker was in hand. The spawn tried to hide in the pools on the ground, but her bio-helm filters picked up the creature immediately and she blasted it into oblivion with the foul little weapon.

"For Ane," she caught herself saying, as she depressed the trigger a second, superfluous time, which surprised her—she was not one for redundancy or sentimentality, as a rule. If anyone found out she was going soft, they might make a move for her position, try to hit her with the old bump-and-shuffle. But there was no time for politics, not now. Giving the bay another scan, just to make sure she hadn't missed any of the spawn in her haste, she turned and opened the final airlock, praying she wasn't too late.

IV

The ruins of Eibon's tower retained their pentagonal design but little else, at least that Pipaluk could recall from the blueprints. There certainly hadn't been any mention of mineral cacti, molten streams of metal crisscrossing the floor, or a perpetual ashy cloud in the toxic air. A yellow moss coating the walls and fallen blocks confused her, for it was surely a close relation to the squamous fungus that grew only in the most hallowed temples of Tsathoggua, and yet she could not imagine a place less-favoured by the god than this foyer to his uncle's realm.

The moss also carpeted the floor wherever the mercurial creeks did not, but was trampled down so thoroughly that she could make no estimate of who had passed this way, or when. Everywhere she looked were wet scraps of Voormis, oily hunks of fail-safes, and puddles of deconstructed formless spawn, but nothing seemed alive in the ruins. The grotto was cramped, dark, and malodorous; it immediately put her at ease.

Pipaluk crossed the bizarre chamber, ducking beneath acid-dripping stalactites that whispered to her in a foreign tongue as she methodically searched the area. She paid them no mind, for she made out the name 'Hziulquoigmnzhah' amidst their stony gibberings and knew them to be heretical deposits. Then, at last, she saw a florescent reddish panel set in a spit of black gneiss that rose from a pool of the liquid metal—the small plate had a crack at its base, and from this fissure issued the iridescent fluid that dribbled down the ebon rock to feed stream and puddle alike. There was no sign of Laila, any member of her team, or even an active fail-safe. Pipaluk had failed.

"Pipaluk!" Provost Ole blared in her ear, the Quorum channel forcejacked back on. He sounded upset. "We've been monitoring everything. You've failed."

"Impossible," she sneered, too tired and disappointed for diplomacy. "You're bluffing; you can't—"

"Subgineer Refn here sneakpatched us into your bio-helm before you even reached the second airlock," said Ole. "He's also filled us in rather *thoroughly* regarding the *numerous* infractions you have committed in the course of your tenure. Effective immediately, you are to return to the first bay, where *politibetjents* are waiting to relieve you of your government equipment. Thereupon, you will stand trial for putting your subgineers in harm's way instead of using spawn, *as is basic protocol*. And *then* there is the matter of your refusal to obey my direct order to return to the Quorum for further instruction, and—"

Pipaluk couldn't deactivate the channel anymore, but she found she could still mute it. Subgineer Refn, eh? She hadn't seen that coming—she'd taken him back to her warrens a few months ago, but hadn't found him particularly enjoyable or even memorable. Now she wondered if he had been researching her, probing for weaknesses, rather than probing for—well, no matter, the damage was done. She had to admit he'd made a decent play of it, going directly to the Quorum, but it was hard to admire an action that would most likely result in her being painfully sacrificed to the inscrutable god she had spent her entire life trying to serve.

Of course, there was a second option. Depriving Ole, Refn, and their cronies of the political points her public trial would bring was a proposition too tempting to pass up, interdimensional, reality-shattering horror be damned. Pipaluk smiled to herself, shaking her head, and stepped into the shallow pool of shimmering metal. Just as she put her hand on the portal, however, a cry came from just behind her. Spinning around with the olid-pistol primed, she saw Professori Laila rising from behind a softly-chanting stalagmite, the camouflage of her suit falling away as she willingly revealed herself.

"Wait!" Laila repeated. "Don't!"

"Fancy seeing you here," said Pipaluk, dialing the gun down to Reek. She wanted Laila alive and sane enough to stand trial, after all. Pipaluk might be going down, but it wouldn't be alone. Then she remembered the portal just behind her, her potentially suicidal resolution of moments before, and she cocked her head curiously. "What *are* you doing here? I thought the whole point was to go through the Gate, not get your team killed just to skulk about some ruins."

"The point was to determine *if* the Gate could be safely used," said Laila, crossing her arms. "Just as I always said. You were the one who insisted I was trying to enter the damn thing."

"Right," said Pipaluk. "Sure. So, you're telling me you didn't have any of your team go through?"

Laila winced. "Most of them didn't make it this far. Those fail-safes were—"

"Most. But you made it. And so did . . . ?"

"A couple of grad students." Laila shivered. "Their names aren't important now. They'll come up at the trial, I'm sure, and—"

"What happened to them!" Pipaluk barked. "You crazy *kanaak*, what happened to them?!"

"They went through." Laila looked down at the blurred shadow of her reflection in the metal pool. "Dorthe went first. She was supposed to return immediately, if she could. When she didn't, after a day, Nivi went and—"

"A day," Pipaluk groaned. "Those toe-dragging fools on the Quorum."

"More like two," Laila said sheepishly. "No sign of either of them. Which, well, isn't surprising—the portal is older than we could date. Even if it still leads to Cykranosh, there's no telling what might be on the other end by now. Maybe the Gate projects you into solid rock, the bottom of an ocean. Maybe the planet's shifted so much it just dumps you into space." The Professori shuddered. "None of the probes we sent through came back, observation cables were severed as soon as they crossed over, remotes failed, blah blah blah, and so those two volunteered. And now we know—it's not safe, anymore. If it ever was."

"Maybe," said Pipaluk thoughtfully. "Maybe not. Surprised you didn't take your chances with it when you saw me coming. Surprised you warned me off it."

"Despite your slanderous campaign of character assassination, I'm a devout Klarkashian," said Laila, straightening her shoulders. "I would never allow a fellow servant of the Sleeper of N'Kai to unwittingly fall into that devil Hziulquoigmnzhah's realm without a sure means of escape. I told you and I told the Quorum time and again, I'm not a heretic. I'm just—"

"Hush!" said Pipaluk, her com-membrane rippling. The second airlock had just been activated. The *politibetjents* were coming to arrest them. "They're coming. For both of us—I violated orders by pursuing you and got a few subgineers killed in the process. That puts us in the same bath, so let's make a break for it. I'll take a possible death of my own making over a certain one of theirs."

"Pipaluk, Pipaluk, Pipaluk," Laila chided. "Where is your faith? There is nowhere to run. We have committed crimes, you and I, and must be taken to the Eiglophian Plains for punishment. It is written that they who err in the service of the slothful ebon god shall be forgiven, so long as they are purified by a sacrificial death. I go willingly to my justice and suggest you—blargh!"

Laila doubled over in agony, retching into her bio-helm. A faint wisp of stench danced at the end of Pipaluk's pistol as she tucked the hot weapon into her belt and went to the incapacitated Professori. The final airlock was beginning to open as Pipaluk hoisted her former adversary and shoved her headlong through the Eibon Gate, the back of the hinged metal panel banging softly against its gneiss setting as the Voormi disappeared into the misty haze that obscured whatever lay on the far side. Without a backward glance at her pursuers, Pipaluk hoisted herself up and squirmed after, through the door to Saturn.

V

The team of *politibetjents* and formless spawn sent to capture Pipaluk waited for days in the mossy ruins, neither wishing to follow the Ingeniøri through the mysterious portal, nor daring to leave in disobedience of Provost Ole's orders. At length, they were recalled, but the result of the whole affair was highly regrettable from the standpoint of the Quorum. It was universally believed, due to a leaked bio-helm file here and an uploaded simcreation there, that Professori Laila and Ingeniøri Pipaluk had not only escaped, by virtue of the luminous science they had learned from Hziulquoigmnzhah, but had made away with a dozen formless spawn commandos and fail-safe behemoths in the bargain. As a consequence of this belief, the public's trust in the Quorum declined and there was a widespread revival of the dark worship of Tsathoggua's paternal uncle throughout Mhu Thulan in the last century before the onset of the great Solar Firestorms.

THE DEEP ONES

Bryan Thao Worra

Bryan Thao Worra is an award-winning Lao American author whose work has appeared in *Illumen*, *The Book of Dark Wisdom*, *Tales of the Unanticipated*, *Mad Poets of Terra*, *Historical Lovecraft*, *Innsmouth Free Press*, and *G-Fan*. His books include *On the Other Side of the Eye*, *BARROW*, *Winter Ink*, and the *Tuk-Tuk Diaries: My Dinner with Cluster Bombs*. You can visit him online at: thaoworra. blogspot.com.

From the sea we come,
From the sea we come,
Our mouths, the inns of the world

The salt of the earth unwelcome
At the tables and charts of
Explorers who expect:

Commodity and pliant territory.
Kingdoms, not wisdom.
Blood, not heavens children.

We grow with uncertain immortality
At the edge not made for man,

Bending, curving, humming cosmic
Awake and alien,

Our mass a dark and foaming mask,
A bed of enigma to certain eyes.

One with the moon,
One with the stars,
One with the ash that whispers history

In the same breath as myth and gods
Whose great backs yawn before us,

As we change with a growing tongue
Growling amid the dreamlands.

We built one blade, one leaf, one golden wall at a time.

THE LABYRINTH OF SLEEP

Orrin Grey

Orrin Grey was born on the night before Halloween, and he's been in love with monsters and the macabre ever since. *Never Bet the Devil & Other Warnings*, his first collection of supernatural stories, is coming soon from Evileye Books. You can find him online at: www.orringrey.com.

Beyond the wall, the first moon has already risen. Kendrick stands still for awhile, getting used to the changes to air, to gravity. He can taste the last bitter dregs of the cigarette he stubbed out just before hooking up to the machine, can still smell the antiseptic tinge of the room he's left behind, as a breeze perfumed by distant and unnamed glades carries it away.

Down below him, at the bottom of the hill, is a forest of tall, white trees and, beyond that, the beginning of the Labyrinth. He's been here before, maybe not *right* here, but near enough. He's seen this moon before, stood under its light. He's been in that forest, even if maybe some other part of it. He's seen the split-headed giants that live there, the doors that they build in the ground, the men with cloven hooves and the heads of dogs, the black shapes that occasionally flit in front of the moon. All of this is familiar to him, but something about the night, *this* night, feels different. A smell in the air, like the ozone smell before a storm. Something.

Maybe it's because this trip *is* different. Not some hapless dreamer he's riding in, this time, but another rider, another professional. McCabe, lying in a drugged coma in his hotel room. McCabe, a few milligrams of noxitol short of dead, lying there on his bed, hooked up to monitors and IVs and to the machine. McCabe, waiting somewhere in the Labyrinth for Kendrick to come in and find him, to learn why he'd gone to the needle instead of his oldest friend.

The company is paying for the hotel room now, for the monitors, and paying Kendrick double his usual rate, but this one he'd do for free. He has to know what happened, what changed. Or, the worse answer, if nothing has, if this was always what waited at the end of McCabe's street and he's just been blind to it until now.

One way or the other, he has to know, and so, he starts down the hill, toward the Labyrinth.

ⴽⵏⴹ

It probably started with the drugs, the new kinds of sleep aids to help a world full of light and motion find the time to dream. But it was the machine that ultimately did the job, that brought the wall of sleep crashing down. And what we found on the other side wasn't what we had expected, not at all. Not a changing jungle of Freudian symbols, not personal, not subjective. An actual place: the Labyrinth and the lands that surrounded it.

It took the machine to find it. The dreamers themselves never remembered, somehow, that they all went to the same place. On their trips back to consciousness, the details of the dream world were lost, their minds replacing them with the minutiae of their memories and their own imaginations, the things that they remembered as their dreams. Always keyed to events in the Labyrinth but never identical to it.

The machine was the silver key. With it, another person, a rider, could piggyback in on the dreamer's trip to that secret world. Not asleep, not really, and therefore, not subject to the forgetfulness that true dreaming entailed.

It became a fad, a drug, an industry. In the waking world, there were dream parlours in every mall, where you could hook into someone's sleeping mind and take a ride to the Labyrinth. But most people were nothing more than tourists in the dreamlands, children stumbling along the turns of the Labyrinth. Kendrik and McCabe, they were professionals.

Or they had been, before McCabe tried to make himself sleep forever.

ꝺﻉ

The walls of the Labyrinth are always black. Basalt, or something that can pass for it; the dreamland equivalent. They always rise up too high to scale, too high to jump. Once you're in the Labyrinth, you're in it, submerged, blind to anything except the next corner, and then the next.

Countless efforts have been made to map it. Kendrick has never known a professional who didn't have at least one in-progress map tacked up somewhere. But no one has ever managed. You can't see the Labyrinth from anywhere except the top of the hill, near the wall, and from there, it all looks the same and once you're in it, well . . . .

There are landmarks. Some have been seen by more than one person. He and McCabe had compared their lists late one night. They'd both seen the fountain choked with moss. They'd both seen the doorway in the middle of the courtyard, the ground on the other side of it darker than on this side, but neither of them had been brave or stupid enough to step through. Kendrick had once seen a river, miles down, that cut a roaring chasm through the midst of the Labyrinth. McCabe claimed to have found a building that looked like an abandoned mosque, with no one inside, but an altar set in the back, with some kind of mummy in an alcove behind it, one he couldn't quite make out without getting closer than he suddenly found himself wanting to.

Some people say that the Labyrinth changes and, certainly, Kendrick has never known two pros whose maps ever really lined up. Most people have an opinion on the subject, once they've put a few beers in themselves at the end of the day, but Kendrick never really thought about it before. To him, the Labyrinth was what it was. It was always there, on the other side of the wall, and it was always the same, really. Even if the paths changed, its nature never did and that was enough for him.

ꝺﻉ

He stands at one of the gates to the Labyrinth. All the gates he's ever seen looked identical. No horn or ivory, just unadorned clefts in the sides of the Labyrinth. Others have tried to mark them, he knows, but the markings were always gone when they came back. Either that, or no one has ever gone to the same gate twice.

It should be impossible, what he's doing. Going into a place that can't be mapped to find someone who's been lost there, already. It should be, but it never is. Something's different about the dreamers, maybe, or about the pros. Something in how they approach the Labyrinth, or in how it approaches them, but he's never gone in after a dreamer, never once, and not found them.

It isn't by any conscious art that he does it, though, at the same time, he knows it's not something everyone can do. He walks the Labyrinth as blind as if he were a dreamer, himself. No one really knows how the professionals do it, the dreamhounds, the *oneiroi*, as some in the industry have tried to dub them, though the name never stuck. Kendrick has this theories; all the pros do. To him, it's all in the thinking. Dreamers don't think while they're in the Labyrinth, not really. They can't. They're caught up in the black, forgetful rivers of sleep. But the riders, those who follow them in, *can* think and, by thinking, by keeping their minds on their quarry, they can track them down, whether that's by changing the turnings of the Labyrinth itself, or simply by knowing which way to turn their own steps, Kendrick doesn't know and has never bothered to care.

Though time has no meaning here, still he knows that this is the longest he's ever been under. Out of the corners of his eyes, he sees what might be landmarks down curving paths, but already, his feet are carrying him in another direction. He wonders how much time has passed out there in the waking world. It could be hours, minutes, days. They were prepared before he went under. IVs to feed and hydrate him, so that he could stay down, no matter how long it took.

How long will they let him stay? How long before they pull the plug, before they decide that this errand is costing more than it's worth? He wills himself to hurry.

There are things that live in the Labyrinth. He's always known it. Not the giants nor the dog-headed men nor any of the other things that live outside. These are different, he knows, even though he's never seen them. He hears them, sometimes, their hopping, shuffling gait just on the other side of a wall, just a few turns away. Sometimes, in the waking world, he tries to picture them, to imagine them as he goes about his day. He always sees them as pale, eyeless things, adapted to a life lived deep underground, though, of course, the Labyrinth is always open to the perpetual twilight of the dreamlands' sky.

When he's here, in the Labyrinth, he tries not to think of them at all, because he believes that thinking here has power. Even now, as he hears them behind him, he tries to think only of putting the next foot in front of him, then the next. Of going faster, not of why. Even when they sound like they are right behind him, just around the next turn, not even that far. That if he turned his head, he would see them, see them at last as they are and not as he imagines. Even then, he keeps his eyes forward, keeps his thoughts only on McCabe, McCabe, McCabe.

And then he turns a corner and he's somewhere he's never been before. Normally, in the Labyrinth, he can't say that, not with certainty. Most of it looks the same, excepting the occasional landmarks. But this is something else entirely. More than a landmark. This is *the* landmark. He knows it without even having to look around, knows even before his mind has processed what he's seen, knows with the faultless logic that is sometimes the province of the dreamlands, that this is the center of the Labyrinth.

The things behind him are forgotten and, as if they are driven back by some invisible barrier, or as if it really has been his attention, however indirect, that held them here, the sounds of their pursuit cease. Or was it ever really pursuit? Were they herding him here?

What would he call the structure that he sees before him, this extruded building of green stone, with its soaring towers and many gaping windows, if he saw it in the waking world? A castle, a tower, a house?

There have been countless attempts to map the Labyrinth and even more to explain it. Is it the first step of an afterlife, a tiny taste of death that we get each night when we close our eyes? Is it a representation of something from the collective unconscious, an enormous symbol housed in all our psyches? Is it literally just the maze of our own neurons? These were things Kendrick never thought about, not outside the Labyrinth and certainly not within it, but he thinks about them now.

What does it mean, this structure? No map of the Labyrinth has ever found its center. No rider, no dream hound has ever come this far and returned, at least, not that he's ever heard of. In the mind of every sleeping man and woman, a maze, and in the centre of the maze, this place. And inside this building, he knows with that same faultless logic, McCabe.

Without hesitating any further, he goes through the front door.

Inside, the house is *like* a castle, though strangely sparse and unfurnished. There are no guttering torches in sconces on the wall, but it isn't dark, either. The green stone seems to provide its own illumination.

When he passes windows and looks outside, what he sees isn't the Labyrinth and that doesn't surprise him. Out one window, massive storm clouds gather into an anvil-shaped thunderhead, crackling with multihued lightning. Out another, he looks down upon a misty valley, where golden statues nestled in peaks watch some kind of gladiatorial game on the distant floor below.

He walks here as he walked in the Labyrinth, one foot in front of the other, keeping his mind focused always on McCabe. This house isn't separate from the Labyrinth, he knows. It's part of it, maybe the greatest part, and here, more than ever, he must be very careful.

He tries to clear his mind of expectations, and so, he is surprised when he suddenly stops walking. He's standing in the doorway to a room. At first glance, it's not different than any of the other rooms he's passed, but then it is. It's furnished, with a fireplace and a single, high-backed chair, and the window in the far wall is covered with a thick, velvet curtain. Kendrick stands in the doorway for a long moment, holding his breath, and then he steps inside.

"McCabe," he says, because he knows that McCabe is sitting in the chair, turned away from him, facing the window. He knows in the same way he's known all along which way to turn his feet to find this place.

There's no answer, not right away. Instead, the figure in the chair stands slowly and turns to face him.

In the waking world, Kendrick isn't a handsome man. He was, once, when he was young, but a poorly-healed job of plastic surgery done to repair a face mangled by a broken bottle left him much the worse for wear. In the dreamland, though, he has greater control over his features and he always looks as he did when he was a young man, the way he still sometimes sees himself in his own dreams.

Kendrick has never seen McCabe in the Labyrinth, before, and he had never thought to ask what the other man looked like here. He's surprised to see his friend looking old, worn, tired beyond his years. His hair, which is still black in the waking world, is grey, here, and wrinkles of worry mar his eyes. He looks, Kendrick thinks without being able to stop himself, like a man who might welcome death.

"I had hoped they wouldn't send you," McCabe finally says, when they're facing each other across the suddenly-small room. "Though I knew they would. And, to be honest, once I failed the job, myself, I needed them to, because I knew there was no one else I could trust."

Kendrick hasn't rehearsed the lines he'll say now. He's kept them out of his mind, just as he keeps everything out when he's inside the Labyrinth, everything except the thought of his quarry. "Why?" he asks and he's surprised, himself, by the notes he hears in his voice, the betrayal, the hurt.

"I'm sorry," McCabe says. He doesn't step forward; he stays standing by the chair and Kendrick can see the effort it takes him not to turn his eyes back toward the curtains. "I suppose I should have come to you, first, but I wanted to spare you. I see now that I couldn't, that, no matter what I did, you'd have found your way here, sooner or later. I wish I could have, though, that there'd been a way. Now, more than ever. Now that I know what you would do for me, how far you'd go."

Kendrick feels like he should be confused by what McCabe is saying, but it makes a strange kind of sense. McCabe learned something. Of course he did. Something that he wanted to keep secret. But men like he and Kendrick were in the business of finding secrets, of running them to the ground, even in places like this, places *made* of secrets. So, he tried to hide in the one place he knew that no one, not even dreamhounds, could track him: death.

"You should have told me," Kendrick says, taking a step forward. "I could have helped. I could've protected you."

McCabe shakes his head, takes a step back to match the one that Kendrick has taken forward, which makes him freeze. He's made a mistake, he realises. He's misunderstood something.

"I'm not protecting the secret, Kendrick," McCabe says sadly and Kendrick can see that there are tears in his eyes, this man whom he's seen shot, who he's seen kill, and never seen shed a tear. "I was protecting you. But I can't, not anymore. You're here, now, and even if I could make you leave without explaining, without showing you, you'd come back. Again and again, until you found out. Wouldn't you? Even if I asked you to leave it alone? Even if I asked you to walk away?"

"I'd try," Kendrick says, softly.

"But you'd fail, yes?"

A nod.

"I know. I would, too, if our places were reversed. I'd come here, eventually, to see what it was that had taken you from me. So, I'll show you, I will, but you have to promise me something first."

Kendrick nods again, knowing already that he's lost, somehow. Lost a friend and more than that. "Anything," Kendrick says, and McCabe tells him the secret, and then he pulls down the curtains and shows him.

꒡⫟⛨

The men guarding the two bodies are bored. It's been three hours since Kendrick plugged into the machine and dropped away from the waking world, and since then, they've had nothing to do but stand and wait. There's nothing here to guard, not really, but their jobs depend on them staying, so they stay. The technician who monitors the readouts on the dozens of screens connected to McCabe and Kendrick is asleep in a chair. One of the guards stares out the big picture window; the other plays solitaire on his phone. Neither is prepared when Kendrick suddenly wakes up.

Normally, riders coming back from the Labyrinth are sluggish, half-drunk from the things they've seen, their senses still attuned to the dreamland. But Kendrick is a professional, one of the best, and he's gotten accustomed to acclimating quickly. He's on his feet before the machines can give their warning beep and he's crossed the room before the guard has even looked up from his phone. Before the technician has come awake, Kendrick has the first guard's gun out of his shoulder holster and is using it to kill the second guard, whose phone drops to the floor and shatters. The first guard tries to elbow him, but Kendrick steps back, faster than he looks, and shoots the guard twice, once in the back and once in the side.

If the technician hadn't been asleep, he might have had time to run. Might have made it as far as the door of the hotel room. But as it is, by the time he's gathered his wits enough to be afraid, Kendrick is already standing over him, his finger already squeezing the trigger. Then he walks over to McCabe and begins unplugging machines. McCabe will die on his own, given time, without the machines to keep him alive, but there will already be more men coming and neither of them has that much time. Kendrick touches his friend's cheek, puts the gun under his chin, and pulls the trigger.

The door of the hotel room is already locked, but he pushes a chair under the handle to slow the men who'll be coming to break it down. Then he walks over to the window and looks out and down, down all those many stories to the street below. He could do for himself the same way he did for McCabe and he will, if he has to, but he wants a few more minutes, first. He can hear the men out in the hallway, already, hear their muffled shouts and the banging on the door. It won't be long until they're inside. He looks down at the gun in his hand.

Three shots are enough to shatter the window and then he steps out. For a moment, he's flying, flying as he sometimes does in his own dreams, and then he stops dreaming for good.

ᗡﻪᕽ

"We're so goddamned arrogant," McCabe had said in that room, in the heart of the Labyrinth. "We think we're the masters of this place, the makers of it, that it sits out here for our entertainment, our enlightenment, our edification. But we're fools and we're wrong. That's the secret, Kendrick, just that.

"Look at this place. Look around. It doesn't seem familiar, does it? This isn't something we made with our thoughts, our wishes, our prayers. This place is a dream, of course it is; what else could it be? But it's not *our* dream." And here, he had pulled down the curtain, torn it from the wall, and Kendrick had felt himself carried to the window to look out across a vast expanse, like an alien planet, with hillocks that darted at the movement of the eyes beneath, and vistas that rose and fell with gigantic breath. He had seen the great, dreaming, cyclopean thing and he had finally understood.

ﻪᕽﻪᕽᘏ

DEEP BLUE DREAMS

Sean Craven

Sean Craven regards H.P. Lovecraft and Alfred Jarry as the two literary figures with whom he most strongly identifies. The accuracy of this self-assessment is a stark and shocking testimony to the loving nature, powerful will, and extremely poor short-term memory of his beloved spouse, Karen. Sean's creative output includes paleontological illustration; editorial illustration; bass, vocals, and songwriting for The Dizzy Toilet Devils; assistant-editing, designing, and illustrating *Swill Magazine*; scripting for old-school internet cartoons like *Thugs On Film*, *Absolute Zero*, and *The God And Devil Show*; and gallery art in the form of surrealistic landscape montages made out of macrophotographs. Try and make a resume out of that.

All the jellyheads are going to the beach. Emily and me, all our friends. It's like the water drawing back before the big wave washes everything away. I cared at first, but the world is too big. Now, all I care about is Emily. I don't get to be her lover, anymore, but I'm still something.

When I started this, it was going to be a book or an article or something. The jellyhead story, the real story. Now I don't know who I'm writing for, but I can't lie down and sleep the way she can, and I can't just sit here. I'll start screaming or jump through the glass doors or something. I don't know what. I don't know how to have a breakdown and I don't want to find out.

Before Emily lay down, we covered the bed with sheet plastic. She looks so small, curled in the middle, naked, gleaming, the organisms seeping from her body, pooled inches deep around her, ropes of clear jelly clustered in mounds, each snotty, knobbly tendril writhing, burrowing into the mass, away from the air. Just like Brad in jail, in the hospital. Jason in the tank.

Emily, you're six feet away from me, and we're going to be together forever, and I still miss you.

That's why I'm going down to the sea with Emily, instead of checking into the hospital to die. It's the difference between something and nothing.

Maybe I'm not writing this for anyone. Maybe I'm writing it for Emily. I won't let her see it, though.

 כתב

Jelly is not a specific chemical; it is an animal venom. The primary active components are tryptamines, including DMT and bufotenine, but these are potentiated by a variety of psychoactive chemicals, including oxytocin and tetrodotoxin. It cannot be stored. It cannot be eaten. The dose must be delivered by a living source. Jelly.

They talk about the way meth and crack faded away in favour of jelly as a shift in national character, successful drug education, or some other ripe bullshit. Oh, no. The collapse of the shipping economy did it.

When the RIAA gained the rights to aggressively mine government records of Internet activity, they provided solid evidential chains enabling tax boards to monitor Internet sales. And local boards tend to tax out-of-state goods at a higher rate.

Internet shopping had changed the nature of warehousing; in a greenhouse world, fleets of trucks had become the equivalent of warehouses on wheels. All because it was cheaper to buy online. When they added out-of-state sales tax to your Amazon spree? The wheels stopped rolling.

Jelly was something you could grow in cold saltwater, something hard to kill that just needed some mice or something every once in a while. Something that took you away to a place so blue it was black, so cold it snuggled you down, someplace you weren't alone. And when you came back, you never felt alone again. You'd see someone who'd been there and you'd know.

Brad was lucky. His tank was meant for lobsters and crabs, had a filter and aerator and everything, and it only cost him two hundred bucks and a quarter-pound of seedy ditch weed. In all the shitty little towns and fucked-over industrial centers, all the side-tracked cities and worn-out projects, people were having the same kind of luck. It spread fast. By the time people started pointing at the freaks in Hoboken and Innsmouth, the Omaha scene had been going on for more than a year. Long enough to start feeling permanent, like we'd found our way of life.

Lying there in the dark, all day and all night in piles, listening to slowbeat, hands linked. People who say slowbeat is bad music are missing the point; it's there to synchronize heartbeats. Emily would lie in my arms for hours, letting me pet her as she pushed against me, moving with the same, slow insistency as the animals in the tank. It was living in a dream, a dream we had on purpose.

And every time we'd touch a strand of jelly to the underside of our tongues (They said Sylvia would hit up in her vagina and we believed it), the tiny little stingers that got us high would break off and swim into us, and make themselves at home.

�❂ᶠ

The motel we're staying in, we have the living room in the front and a bedroom in the back. At night, when there isn't any traffic, you can hear the sea. Everyone I know is in the hospital, or they've left for the coast.

Emily could still talk when we got here, so when the news hit, she was able to call me from the other room. I came in, and she shushed me and pointed at the screen. "They keep showing it over and over." Her voice was choked and it was all I could do not to put my arm around her.

The image on the screen was Brad's big, refrigerated tank, one end bubbling furiously from the aerator. Through the one glass wall, you could see a thick, brown mat growing on top, thinning to threads of clear jelly underneath. Animals float in the chill water, imbedded, threads of jelly bursting from their heads and hindquarters. They are not dead; they shift constantly but very, very slowly. Primitive motion. Mice and dogs and cats and one nude human body, pale, thin, clothed in jelly.

"Shit," I said. "That's our house. That's Jason."

Brad, microphones in his face, orange jumpsuit, looks awful; he's crying.

"I swear, I didn't know this . . . I didn't know what to do. He crawled in there and he was still alive, and he's dead now, right? When they took him out, they killed him. I was the one who took care of Jason—"

The way they cut him off, he must have started swearing.

Now we knew we weren't going home. It was settled.

ƆƻƐ

When Emily seemed asleep, before her jelly came out, I cupped her breast. The nipple pushed into the palm of my hand and made me think of a kitten nosing for a caress. I drew my hand away, filled with shame at my act and resentment that Emily's body still remembered me, even if Emily had forgotten. I don't understand why she won't let me go, but I understand why I'm staying. Hope is a bitch.

ƆƻƐ

There's a booklet, a 'zine I made the spring Emily and I got together. I called it "*Deep Blue*" and Xeroxed it onto light blue paper, and embarrassed goosebumps just lifted the hair on my arms. Every time a friend asked for a copy, I gave them a handful and they made their way around. Sometimes, I'd find a copy in someone's bathroom and get a chance to wave it around and say, "I did this." I talk about the specimen they found in the Smithsonian from an old Antarctic expedition, claim it was a jelly-infected penguin. It could have been. And there's something I found from a website for fishermen, talking about ghost nets.

Drift nets get loose from time to time, walls of plastic mesh moving on their own through the ocean, harvesting for nothing but rot. They call them "ghost nets". So, when the strange things started showing up on sonar, unmoving schools of fish with dolphins floating among them, orcas and seals in an unmoving mass in the dark of the ocean, they figured they were ghost nets.

And when some boats that reported those strange things disappeared, the fishermen figured ghost nets were bad luck. Then they found out some ghost nets had been overgrown with something strange. Jelly. Turns out a polluted, overfished ocean turns into a slime farm—jellyfish, medusas, salps, and so on and so forth are opportunists that thrive in the areas man cleared out and poisoned. That's what they think is happening. Jellyheads have other ideas.

I printed the story over a faint photograph of Emily on jelly. I called it "Oneirovore." That's what I think the jelly needs from the animals it infects. I think it eats our dreams. And isn't it just too perfect the way jelly uses the mammalian diving reflex? Of course, I'm a fucking jellyhead and that's the kind of thing we say.

The jelly organisms are colonial mesozoans, parasitic relatives of jellyfish and the other slimes. They aren't a single animal; they're a self-contained ecosystem. The stingers, the nematocysts, can't penetrate human skin. You need to touch them to a mucus membrane.

At first, jelly was like jenkum, another fake drug the news gets panicked about. If you were actually doing it, the first news stories were hilarious. Then they found the way it entrained people's brains. The mirror cells, the areas of the brain that allow us to understand other people by mimicking their hypothetical behavior, enlarged and became more active. There was talk of using jelly as therapy for sociopaths.

Jelly was too cheap and easy to cultivate to interest the investment class of criminals. And nobody ever got mugged by a jellyhead. After crack and meth and heroin, it was such a fucking relief.

It took a couple of years for the infections to advance to a stage where people started noticing anything was wrong. And let's be serious. Not everyone was as honest with their doctors as they could have been.

ɔﾉﾆ

Now I'll be honest. I talk about jellyhead love, but Jason wasn't my friend. He was just an asshole I had to put up with because I wanted to be around Brad and Brad's jelly. Getting high and crawling into the tank is exactly the kind of thing that creepy little moron would do, and it's different than what Emily and I are doing.

I can hear the noises, the slicks and bubbles as Emily's jelly draws back in. I don't like to look. In a few minutes, Emily is going to stand up. Then she'll get her sun dress off the back of the chair, put on her flip-flops with the daisies on the toe-strap, and we'll walk down to the beach, walk toward the lighthouse until we're alone.

Then we'll wade out into the water. And I know Emily. When the waves hit her, she'll be scared. She'll reach for my hand and, when I take it, she'll hold onto me for protection, and I'll help her under the waves until we get out far enough to swim. We will dive into the dark, a soft place where noises are all muffled by distance, take our place in the ghost net, and I will go to sleep and never be lonely again.

BIG BRO

Arlene J. Yandug

Arlene J. Yandug was born in Bukidnon, a region in the southern part of the Philippines. She teaches literature at Xavier University; paints blooms, clouds and stardust. Like her paintings, many of her poems reflect local colour and landscapes. While generally cheery, she sometimes dabbles in surreal writing, especially after reading grim or gothic books, or when she is terribly, terribly upset.

His darkest thoughts
Grow wings and tails,
And roost
In the middle of our mind's
Eye
Watching the dust
of our names
in the wake of our own thoughts,
crawling out
through the cracks of cubicles.
Lest they leave footprints on the floor,
they march tiptoeing
on the ceiling
huddling around, distended
like the bellies of question marks.

The keys jingle in his pockets
As he slithers across the room,
His filmy eyes behind
thick glasses
trace for shadows of doubts,
uncertainties,
The littlest disarray of thoughts.

As he sloughs his skin
Once more, renewing
His potent poison, testing the limit
Of his strength,
We are on the point
Of breaking
Into a million shards of silence.

ﻻﺨﻫﺨﻻ

COPYRIGHT ACKNOWLEDGMENTS